35

BACKLASH

BACKLASH

Nick Oldham

Severn House Large Print
London & New York

This first large print edition published in Great Britain 2005 by
SEVERN HOUSE LARGE PRINT BOOKS LTD of
9-15 High Street, Sutton, Surrey, SM1 1DF.
First world regular print edition published 2001 by
Severn House Publishers, London and New York.
This first large print edition published in the USA 2005 by
SEVERN HOUSE PUBLISHERS INC., of
595 Madison Avenue, New York, NY 10022.

British Library Cataloguing in Publication Data

Oldham, Nick, 1956 -
    Backlash. - Large print ed.
    1. Christie, Henry (Fictitious character) - Fiction
    2. Police - England - Blackpool - Fiction
    3. Detective and mystery stories
    4. Large type books
    I. Title
    823.9'14 [F]

ISBN-10: 0-7278-7444-6

Printed and bound in Great Britain by
MPG Books Ltd, Bodmin, Cornwall.

To Sarah and Philip

Prologue

Wilmslow, Cheshire, England

It was time to kill again.

David Gill placed the newspaper down across his lap and took a deep breath to steady his excitement and anticipation. He could feel the tension building up to bursting point in his body; like an enraged beast, it tore through his veins. Uncontrollable, but wonderful. Demanding to be released.

With tingling fingers he folded the newspaper neatly, slotting the sections back inside each other as though it had only just dropped through the front door. He put the heavy broadsheet down on the coffee table, aligning it carefully with the edge of the piece of furniture.

He flexed his fingers and eased a pair of disposable gloves onto his hands, pulling them up his wrists and over his cuffs. After this he adjusted the elasticated shower cap on his head, fitting it halfway over his ears, totally covering his short cropped hair. He wriggled his toes in the disposable paper shoes he wore over his feet and shook his

7

head, uttering a snort of a laugh and grinning sardonically as he thought, 'Bloody forensics ... the trouble you have to go to...' He had a light feeling in his chest and, as he stood up, he shook himself and shrugged his shoulders inside his neat blue overalls. He was ready to perform.

Gill went out of the living room, walked down the short hallway, crept upstairs to the landing and slid quietly to the closed bathroom door. The only sound he could hear was that of his own blood pounding through his head, driven by a heart working in overdrive. He stood stock still by the door, head cocked, brow furrowed, as if listening for something. Then he knocked lightly. Politely even.

There was no response – even though he knew there was someone inside.

He knew because he had put them there.

'Hello. It's me. Mind if I come in?' he called brightly through the door, awaiting a reply which did not come. Not that he truly expected to hear one. The person in the bathroom was in no position to make one. Gill was just playing a silly old game. His idea of a little joke. Designed to lighten and brighten up a heavy – very heavy – situation. 'Well,' he announced, 'here I come anyway – ready or not, whether you're decent or you're not.'

Gill gripped the door handle and, for effect, pushed it down with excruciating slowness, just to pile on the agony. He also cackled maniacally, like a pantomime witch. He was really beginning to enjoy himself now.

The woman in the bathroom could not have responded in any way to Gill's original question even if she had wanted to. Her whole head had been encased in parcel tape, with the exception of a slit for her eyes and a gap underneath her nose to allow her to breathe. The tape covered her mouth and had been looped under her chin and back round the top of her head so that it was impossible for her to move her jaw at all. She was quite a small woman and had been laid full length in the bath, naked. Her hands had been bound behind her by the same type of tape, which had also been wrapped round her legs from her thighs to her ankles. She was quivering with fear, her whole body shaking.

Her name was Lucinda Graveson. She was a lawyer.

The bathroom door creaked open, inch by inch. Gill curled his fingers round the edge of it, cackled again, and then showed his face and stepped fully into the room. 'How are you doing?' he asked her gently, a smile of sadness playing on his lips. 'Oops, sorry ... can't speak, can we? All trussed up and nowhere to go. How inconvenient for you. Still ... it's for the best ... now, what shall we do here?'

Lucinda Graveson began to squirm in a valiant, but ultimately useless attempt to free herself. Muted, terrified noises emanated from somewhere deep inside her throat. She was exhausted from trying and the effort subsided until she once more lay quivering and whimpering. Gill gazed at her indulgently, shaking his head.

'I wouldn't bother,' he advised her.

Gill had previously arranged his tools in a line along a folded towel on top of the toilet cistern. He turned away from Graveson and made a show of inspecting the shiny instruments: he counted them, touched them, picked them up and held them up to the light, assessed them, hummed and hawed, muttered a few words such as, 'Nice ... lovely piece ... wow!' and replaced them in their neat row. He twiddled his fingers with mock indecision and then made a selection.

A scalpel. Long. Sparkling. The blade honed to perfection. Sharper than a razor.

He spun back to Graveson and showed her the scalpel. A gurgle of despair churned inside the lawyer's guts as, at last and inevitably, she lost bowel control.

Gill's shoulders sagged impatiently. 'Bloody hell, Lucinda – why did you have to go and do that? You've gone and shit yourself. Ah well, never mind, let's get you all cleaned up, shall we? You see, the problem is that blood and shit don't really mix well.'

He replaced the scalpel on the towel and reached over the bath for the shower head fitted above the taps. It was a power shower and he went to work, whistling as he sprayed away the runny faeces down the plughole, constantly adjusting the temperature control so it was just right. Not too hot, not too cold.

'There we are, done and dusted,' he

declared eventually. He slotted the shower head into its wall fitting and turned it off. 'Now,' he said, wagging a finger, 'you're not going to do anything like that again, are you, Lucinda?'

She shook her head.

'Good, that's good.'

Gill reached for the scalpel again, chatting brightly. 'I've just been reading the *Sunday Times* downstairs. God, it's a weight, you know? I wonder what the paper boys think about Sunday papers, they're so heavy now ... and Saturday's too ... I mean, *The Times* on Saturday is almost as bulky as the Sunday one!' He spun round with a flourish, scalpel in hand, making Graveson cringe and cower. He leaned over her and she tried to contort herself away. 'Don't bother struggling – you'll only make things worse for yourself ... and anyway, what do you think I'm going to do with this little thing?' He held the scalpel up right in front of his face and drew it towards his nose, making his eyes cross. 'D'you think I'm going to kill you with it? Don't be an arse. Now relax, Lucinda ... let things progress.'

Gill's hand hovered a few inches over Graveson's face, the scalpel pointing downwards. He placed the tip of the blade into the parcel tape wrapped over her mouth, then he drew the scalpel along the tape, cutting a two-inch slit in it which allowed Lucinda a tiny fraction of movement of the lips. 'There – see – didn't hurt a bit, did it?' Gill squatted down onto his haunches by the side of the bath and patted her on the head. He stood up and crossed to the toilet, positioning the scalpel carefully back into its allotted place on the towel.

A murmur came from the slit in the tape that was now Lucinda Graveson's mouth.

'Sorry – what? Didn't quite catch that one.' Once more Gill leaned over her, his ear a couple of inches above the slit. 'Say it again.'

'Why?' Graveson was able to hiss. 'Why?'

Gill laughed. He had known this would be the question, had been anticipating it. It was the one they all asked. Why me? Why fucking me? Of all the unfortunate people in the world, why does it have to be me? Gill scratched his head. 'You mean you don't know? Hmm? Let me think now. I'd say it's because you are one of the causes of the problem, Lucinda Graveson, LLB, and whatever other stupid, petty, meaningless qualifications you possess. The problem being society and the way tradition has been stepped on and crushed and brushed under the carpet as though it's dirt.' His voice began to rise as he spoke, becoming an hysterical whine. 'The way the ordained order of things has been turned upside down. The tail wagging the dog, that's what!' He slammed an angry fist hard into the bathroom door, hurting himself. 'That's why,' he said, shaking his hand, 'that's the fucking reason why! I'm just doing my bit – my little, inconsequential bit – to try and rectify all this injustice.'

He stopped suddenly, his face red and

12

swollen with anger.

Graveson was sobbing underneath the parcel tape.

Gill got a grip on himself, calmed down and shook his head with a little chuckle, pleased that he could laugh at himself. Able to keep a sense of humour and perspective while around him the whole world had gone completely mad. 'Sorry, sorry about that,' he said, apologising profusely, even blushing a little. 'High horse galloping merrily away. Not good to lose it ... so, what was the question. Oh, yes, why? That's why. What you are and what you do and what you represent, Lucinda. And your colour doesn't help much, admittedly. Happy now?' He placed the palm of his right hand over his heart. 'Heck: beating like an express train. Better calm down. Don't want to lose my sense of reason, do I?'

He took a few deep, steadying breaths.

'That's better ... now, back to you, Lucinda Graveson. What am I going to do here? What will the police think when they find you? What blind alley should I send them whizzing down, incompetent bunch of bastards? Slaughtered by a jealous lover? You know the kind of thing – tits hacked off, something stuffed up inside you; make 'em think you're really a lesbian. That would send everyone into a real tizz, wouldn't it? – for you to be revealed as a lesbo, even though I know you're as straight as a die. Or how about battered to death in a frenzied attack after discovering a burglar in your house? How

13

should I make this look? Ho-hum, decisions, decisions.'

Gill turned to the assortment of tools on the towel. He selected a ball hammer, testing it for weight and effectiveness by smacking it gently into the palm of his left hand. He stopped and looked at the woman in the bath. He sniffed. 'Actually I quite fancy giving you a "Yorkshire Ripper".'

He said it as though he was about to give Lucinda Graveson a cut and blow dry.

Over the last six months, Gill had studied Lucinda Graveson's habits quite closely. He knew enough to switch off all her house lights at 11.30 p.m. This chore done, Gill sat behind drawn curtains in the darkened house for another forty-five minutes, looking out through a narrow gap at the street outside.

He used the time for some deep reflection about the future. Making plans, deciding the way forwards.

At 12.15 a.m. he went into the kitchen and stepped carefully over the body of Lucinda Graveson's husband before letting himself out of the back door. He edged to the front corner of the house and stayed there for a while.

Nothing moved. Few lights shone in the surrounding properties. It was one of those neighbourhoods – weren't most? Gill pondered depressingly – in which everyone kept themselves to themselves, kept their noses out of other people's business and curled up in their alarm-protected houses. It was the sort of community that, directly and indirectly, people like Lucinda Graveson contributed to, Gill firmly and obsessively believed.

Five minutes more he waited. Still no movement. When he was certain there was nothing to worry about, he flicked the hood of his coat over his head and trotted confidently down the drive, past Lucinda's natty little MGF and her husband's BMW.

Gill walked down the avenue and criss-crossed his way through a large good-class housing estate until he reached a main road. In a few more minutes he was at his motorcycle, which he had left secreted between two units on a crappy industrial estate. Over his shoulder he carried the black plastic bin liner which contained the protective clothing he had worn and the tools he had used while committing his crimes, including the electric-shock baton with which he had subdued the Gravesons before killing them. As he stuffed the bag into one of the panniers he reminded himself to check the baton because he'd had to give Mr Graveson a second blast with it when the first one hadn't worked. Maybe there was a loose connection in it somewhere, he thought. From the back box he removed his full-face helmet and pulled it on over his head and mounted the big bike.

He was aware of the possibility of getting pulled up by the police on his journey, but the chances of it happening were remote and even if it did happen there was little chance of

the panniers being searched. Gill acknowledged the risk, but was prepared to take it
because he knew that the hundred per cent
safe disposal of the clothing was guaranteed
at home. In this game, the gauntlet sometimes had to be run.

The machine fired up first time, its engine
ticked over smoothly.

Within minutes he was on the motorway,
accelerating easily up to his cruising speed of
eighty. Just about right to make good progress but not too fast to attract any unwelcome attention. Less than an hour later his
bike was parked up in a secure garage and
Gill was walking into his flat.

He chilled out, wound down for a while,
wrote things up and glanced over some old
articles. He bathed in a little self glory and
patted himself on the back, wondering how
his latest exploit would hit the news. While
relaxing he lifted a few weights, did fifty
press-ups, a hundred sit-ups and 5,000
metres on his rower, just to keep himself
buzzing.

Just before 4 a.m., he left the flat to make
his way home.

The urge to kill again was already permeat-
ing through his soul.

Miami, Florida, US

The bomber – his name was unknown – had
planted nineteen bombs and spent six years

16

making the world's most prestigious law-enforcement agency look stupid.

The first bomb had been a low-key affair – as bombs go. It had been placed in any bomber's favourite location, a bar. This one was in San Francisco and was frequented by the gay community. An easy target on a steamy Friday evening in June when the place was heaving with vest-clad, muscle-bound bodies. The surprise was that it only ripped the guts out of three people, those unfortunate ones seated on the bench under which the innocuous looking sports bag containing the bomb had been placed. Four others were maimed, another dozen injured.

The bomb had been a try-out. It had worked.

Each subsequent bomb was better, more powerful, more deadly and sophisticated than its predecessor. The death toll could easily have passed one hundred, but twenty-four it was, with two more in comas from which they would be unlikely to surface, eight wheelchair bound and another forty with lost limbs.

The FBI had reacted predictably, throwing the bulk of their resources at the numerous right-wing terrorist groups which were sprouting up across America like cancerous tumours. They did their best to infiltrate this movement – fast becoming very clever and more security-conscious where law enforcement tactics were concerned; a movement that had studied, liaised with and learned valuable lessons from other terrorist groups, particularly the successful European ones, such as the Provisional IRA, and had begun to operate in self-contained units, making it virtually impossible for an outsider such as an undercover officer to penetrate successfully.

And so the Feds had tried and tried and, humiliatingly, discovered nothing. No hints. No whispers. No names. Not a thing. The bomber remained nameless, faceless, untouchable, able to conduct a campaign of terror with impunity across the country, wreaking havoc, misery, mayhem and death, inducing fear into his targets.

The FBI began to suspect the bomber was a loner. He (although the actual gender of the individual was not a certainty to them, it was unlikely to be a female, according to the behavioural psychologists) was, they deduced, either not affiliated to any particular group or was operating independently on the periphery of several. He was classified as a New Offender Model Terrorist, acting out his deadly rages and frustrations in total anonymity ... and outwitting the FBI at the same time.

The twentieth bomb exploded in Miami. Another gay bar. The eighth such target chosen by the bomber.

It was a huge, devastating explosion, completely and utterly destroying the inside of the bar in the Coral Gables area of the city. It blasted out the massive plate-glass window at the front of the premises, sending horrific shards of glass scything out across the sidewalk drinking area. Five people were blown to smithereens, many more injured, including numerous passers-by who were both white, male and heterosexual.

An FBI team from the Miami Field Office were at the scene within ten minutes, under the supervision of the Special Agent in Charge. They took control of the carnage, usurping, bawling out and chivvying the local cops and, as per textbook procedure, establishing a suitable rendezvous point (RVP) through which all approaches to the scene had to be channelled.

The SAC had made an excellent choice for the RVP – a small parking lot about a quarter of a mile distant from the scene of the bombing, some six blocks away and out of sight of it. The SAC brought in a mobile-communications truck, staffed with highly trained operatives who looked after all the phones, radios and agent deployments. The SAC seated himself in the cramped office at one end of the unit and directed operations from there. He had visited the scene briefly, but had come away quickly so as not to get involved, leaving his assistant in charge, while retaining overall strategic command and control from the truck, well removed from the hysteria and emotion. The chain of command had therefore been set up.

This was the first time the Feds had been able to react so swiftly with a full team and a well thought out approach. There had to be

19

the chance of a good result because of it.

Unfortunately, people who bomb other people are unpredictable, usually smart, always devious and, of course, very dangerous. The bomber had decided to up stakes with this bombing and the FBI, despite their preparations, were not ready for the change in modus operandi. The bomber knew what procedures the FBI would adopt at the scene, in particular that an RVP would be established some way away. After reconnoitring the whole neighbourhood several times over a period of days before he planted the device in the bar, the bomber had concluded that the only place the RVP could realistically be set up was in the parking lot. It had the necessary elements needed: space and control of the main routes to and from the scene.

The secondary device was much larger and more powerful than the one he had used in the bar. It had been placed and taped to the underside of a storm-drain cover in the parking lot and – beautifully and coincidentally – the mobile communication truck was parked slap-bang over it. The bomber waited several hours before detonating the bomb, at a time when the RVP was at its most hectic with milling FBI personnel.

He was positioned on the high roof of an apartment building with an excellent view down to and across the lot. He had been there since the first bomb exploded, waiting patiently and happily, watching the emergency services hurtling by. He had observed, with a wry smile playing on his lips, the FBI commandeering the parking lot, as predicted, and driving the state of the art communications truck onto it and setting up shop. He remained cool and relaxed, holding back for the exact moment that would produce maximum impact.

He picked up the remote control, his hands covered by thin latex gloves, pointed and thumbed the button.

A classic.

The blast almost blew him across the roof. He held on tight to the railings, keeping his eyes wide open, unwilling to miss one fraction of a second of the devastation he had caused.

He had destroyed the communications truck, killed three agents and severely injured a dozen more. But, through one of those inexplicable freaks of fate, the SAC, who had been sitting in his temporary office in the truck, only a matter of feet from the epicentre of the blast, emerged shaken and shocked, his clothing having been torn from his body, but otherwise unscathed.

It wasn't long before a pair of keen agents were on the apartment rooftop looking down at the scene of tangled metal from which smoke still rose languidly in the hot night and from which two of the dead had yet to be cut free. They immediately radioed control that they believed they had found the point where

21

the bomber had been sitting. They could not believe their good fortune. This was the closest anyone had ever knowingly been to the bomber. They were literally hot on his trail.

Professionals that they were, the two agents approached the eyrie with extreme caution from the roof door. Their senses tingled with excitement and they took nothing for granted. Their weapons were drawn at the ready. They slid slowly across the flat roof, eyes never still, checking for booby-traps and trip wires, until they reached the edge of the roof. Here they found a folding stool of the sort used by anglers, a pair of binoculars on it and what looked like a TV remote-control unit discarded on the ground.

The agents eyed each other.

'Don't touch anything,' Colin Brewster whispered hoarsely and unnecessarily. Booker nodded and tried to hide a disgruntled 'Tch' with a short cough; though he had far less experience than Brewster, he knew his job and resented the older man telling him what to do. Booker had a very tight feeling in his chest. This could be the breakthrough. This could be it – the bomber's first mistake. Even if there were no fingerprints to be found here, the amount of information that could be gleaned from the three items they had found was phenomenal. There could be numerous lines of enquiry here. He squatted down onto his haunches, his knees cracking loudly, and squinted at the evidence.

Brewster moved to the low wall with railings at the edge of the roof. He gazed pensively down on the scene of the bombing below. He had lost one very good friend down there. Arc lights illuminated the whole area as the time moved on towards midnight. Brewster's forehead creased. He knew this was a terrific breakthrough, yet something was nagging – gnawing – at him.

Booker said, 'This could tell us a lot, pal.'

'U-huh,' agreed Brewster laconically.

Both agents had their backs to the roof door.

'The bastard'll regret this,' Booker growled, 'leaving this gear.'

The roof door opened a fraction.

Brewster did not answer. His mind was still unsettled as he worked through this scenario. This bomber did not make mistakes, he thought. He does not leave clues or evidence. So why now?

The roof door opened a little wider. The old rusted iron hinges did not squeak or groan as they should have done. They had been well oiled, lubricated and tested. They moved smoothly. Noiseless.

'This is just fantastic,' Booker gushed. He wasn't really thinking straight.

Brewster remained silent, brooding, not keying in to his partner's enthusiasm. He folded a piece of gum into his mouth and chewed.

'Somethin' ain't right,' he said.

Booker regarded him, puzzled.

23

Now the door behind them opened wide enough to allow the barrel of a silenced pistol to peek through. The agents were fifteen feet away, muttering to each other. For someone as good as the bomber, the distance was no problem, even though it was some time since he had used a gun in anger. He was supremely confident in his abilities. But this was not the right moment to kill them. He wanted the agent who was standing by the edge of the roof – Brewster – to step back a few feet. He didn't want the guy toppling over the edge and splatting down on the sidewalk.

Their radios squawked.

Booker, still bouncing on his haunches, answered and had a short conversation, confirming some detail or other. Brewster stayed by the edge of the roof.

The bomber pushed the door open and stepped out behind the special agents. Brewster sensing something, turned quickly. Booker stood up and followed his colleague's gaze.

Then Booker smiled and Brewster's shoulders relaxed.

'Guys.' The bomber nodded.

'Hey.' Booker beamed. 'What the hell y' doin' here?'

Then Brewster became rigid again and the smile dropped from his face as the bomber revealed his gun.

'Shit!' Booker cried, raising his own weapon.

He and Brewster were too slow. The

24

bomber double-tapped both men with deadly efficiency, the untraceable slugs drilling their chests. He walked across and straddled each man in turn, putting another bullet into each of their heads, just to be on the safe side. Then, calmly, coolly, he picked up his three items – the remote control, the folding stool and the binoculars – and put them into a plastic carrier bag.

Before leaving the scene he allowed himself one last look. The smile of satisfaction which came to his lips was pure evil. Now the time was right to offer his skills to the world.

MONDAY

One

It was a tarantula, Henry was sure of it. Its long legs were creeping down his neck, over his Adam's apple, across his chest, pausing at his right nipple to paw it, sending a shiver right through him. He hardly dared swallow, hardly dared breathe even ... then the huge, but incredibly light, arachnid began to move slowly down his ribcage as though descending a ladder, down onto his stomach which he could not prevent from fluttering ... surely it must bite, sink its fangs into his soft flesh, shoot its deadly poison into him. No. It moved towards his groin, across his pubic hair and suddenly, without warning, pounced, wrapping all its legs round his penis and squeezing tightly.

'Jesus!' Henry Christie crashed like a ram-raider out of his vivid dream into wakefulness. His sweat-encased body leapt as though an electric shock had passed through it. His eyes flipped open. He looked sideways at the woman who had sneaked into his bedroom, undressed silently while he was asleep, then slid into bed alongside him and playfully grabbed his cock.

She smiled wickedly at him.

29

'You scared the hell out of me,' Henry admitted. He flopped back, relieved he wasn't going to be bitten by a ... what was it? Even now, only seconds after waking, the dream was virtually gone into the mist, impossible to recall.

Unlike the other dream.

'Good,' she said.

'What time is it?'

'Nearly five o'clock.'

'Bloody hell, I need to get going.' Henry made to rise, but the woman held him back firmly.

'No way ... you've got time ... we've got time ... if we make it quick.'

'You said that at seven o'clock this morning ... ahhh,' he groaned throatily, unable to continue with his remonstration. Her skilful fingers had started to arouse him, drawing back his foreskin, making him catch his breath, squeezing the end of his damp, hardening penis.

Henry lay back, submitting to the inevitable, happy to be dominated, relaxing into an almost comatose state, allowing her to do whatever she wanted, going along with it in spite of the time constraint.

Afterwards, they lay entwined, savouring the ebb tide of a magnificent bout of sex.

'Damn. Now I have to go,' she murmured petulantly. Unwillingly she eased him out of her with a soft 'plop', draining the last ounce of pleasure from the encounter with her internal muscles. She rolled off him. 'I open up in ten minutes and Monday's usually busy – and I am well and truly exhausted.' She planted a wet kiss on his cheek.

Through droopy eyelids, Henry watched her scoot round and collect her clothes from the floor. She dashed out of the bedroom, pausing briefly by the door to blow him a kiss and wiggle her backside provocatively. The bathroom door slammed, then the sound of taps running and water pipes clanking resounded round the big flat.

The digital clock said 5:14. Blink. Blink. Henry could not believe it was that time already. He yawned long and wide and almost left his skin behind when the alarm sounded unexpectedly. His groggy mind half remembered some upbeat, positive colleague of his referring to it as an 'opportunity clock'. Henry thought, 'My arse.' To him it was purely and simply an alarm clock. A cold-blooded device designed by evil people to bring you into the real world as rudely as possible. The future held no opportunity for Henry, certainly not immediately, and the way he was feeling, not distantly either.

He rubbed his eyes, making them squelch. He was sorely tempted to pull the quilt back over himself and say, 'Fuck it, fuck 'em all.' But he'd said those words too often in the recent past and was beginning to realise their futility.

Henry rocked up into a sitting position, glancing round the darkened bedroom, spluttering derisively as he thought of his current situation. Here he was, for the second time in his life, living in the chilly, cavernous, rented flat on the first floor over a veterinary practice near the centre of Blackpool. As ever the constant whiff of animal scent and disinfectant wafted up from the ground floor. The difference was that there were a couple of changes that had not been part of the original equation when he had lived here before. Firstly, he was not just separated from his wife, he was lawfully, legally and painfully divorced from her. Secondly, he was sleeping with the lady vet who owned the practice.

Henry marvelled at her stamina. The previous evening they had been out night-clubbing, then gone to a 'bit of a gathering' at her snotty friend's house where the Bang and Olufsen hi-fi oozed cool jazz and the conversation dribbled bullshit – to Henry's working-class ears, anyway. Then he and his veterinary ladyfriend – her name was Fiona – had taken a pre-dawn stroll before ending up in bed at the flat at seven that morning where they had made energetic love for another half-hour ... animal sex, he had christened it ... and after less than a couple of hours' sleep she had opened the surgery at ten, worked through the day, operating on a series of unfortunate beasts, and had now indulged in further sex before reopening the surgery at 5.30 p.m. She had been on the go for twenty-four hours. Henry wondered if she was pumping any drugs into herself which should perhaps have gone into animals ... but it wasn't a serious thought.

While she had been working all day, Henry had had the best part of ten hours solid, dreamless slumber – with the exception of the spidery dream which had wakened him. It had been the first time he had slept without having the recurring nightmare that haunted him.

Maybe he had finally recovered.

And now here he was, after almost two months of stress-related sick leave, about to return to work. This would be his first day back. The prospect filled him with abject terror: not only was he returning to work, he was starting a new role, one unfamiliar to him. This combination of factors was doing nothing for his brittle self-confidence, which was lurking somewhere below rock-bottom. He shivered, swore inwardly to exorcise the demons and went into the bathroom now vacated by Fiona.

It was 5.25 p.m. He had to be at work by 5.45, ready for a twelve-hour night shift.

Just to try and see himself as others might, Henry dressed in front of a full-length mirror. He started from scratch, looking at his stark, thin, unhealthy-looking body which had lost weight so quickly over the past months. Fortunately he was just beginning to regain some poundage. His ideal fighting weight, so he believed, was thirteen and a half stone, a weight he felt comfortable at. Not twelve, which, for the size of his broad frame, made him look and feel ridiculous. Meat pies were on the menu for a few weeks.

After stepping into his Y-fronts – comfortable but not fashionable – he pulled his black, cotton-rich socks on. He batted his eyelids stupidly at his reflection and flexed his biceps a few times like a circus muscle-man – without the muscles. He reached for his trousers which were on a wire coat hanger. He eased his legs into them, gritting his teeth as the cheap, rough, sandpaper-like material scraped his skin. They were too generous round the waist, too short in the leg and sagged underneath the groin. He adjusted his privates in his underwear, but still felt very uncomfortable. He fed the black leather belt through the trouser loops and fastened it loosely.

His white shirt was still in its packaging. He ripped it out of the plastic wrapper, carefully extracted the pins, eased out the cardboard collar stiffener and held the shirt up. It was criss-crossed with creases and should have been washed and ironed before today. His lips curled with annoyance at himself for not getting things ready earlier – a character trait which seemed to have crept up on him during his sickness. Procrastination was a way of life with him at the moment. There was no time to do anything about the shirt now, though. He was running late. He put the shirt on, forcing his hands through the cuffs without bothering to unfasten them. He tucked it into the waistband and yanked his belt tight.

On the floor in front of him were his plain black shoes (as per regulations). As the exception to prove the rule, these were ready, cleaned and polished – bulled, actually, to mirror-like perfection. The act of spit-polishing them had become an obsession for him over the last week. He found the task relaxed him for some reason, gave him pleasure. He knew the shoes would be comfortable to wear. He put them on, tied the laces, and gazed proudly down at them.

'God help any bugger that steps on these,' he muttered out loud.

He stood upright, fastened his top shirt button and clipped on his black tie. The first time he had worn such a thing for over a decade.

Lastly, he affixed his epaulettes to his shoulders, the two shiny pips on each side reflecting the light.

He gulped, closed his eyes, then opened them to take stock of the finished article: Henry Christie, uniformed police inspector, Blackpool Section, about to go on duty and perform the reactive cover function, dealing with the 'here and now' of policing ... in the unwritten uniformed inspector hierarchy, the job usually given to newly promoted officers or those long in the tooth with no ambition or career advancement prospects.

Henry Christie was not newly promoted.

He could not believe the way he looked: how transformed he was and how unlike a uniformed inspector he felt. The whole idea was completely alien to him. His usual dress code was a pretty slick suit, a decent shirt and tie, good quality shoes and an air of superiority over all other mortals.

There was no way on earth he was a uniformed cop any more. He was a fucking detective, for God's sake. A detective inspector, actually. And a bloody good one at that. At least he had been good. Once. Not very long ago. And now here he was, wearing a uniform, looking like an Italian waiter, and having to work long, unsocial shifts.

With a snap salute to the mirror, which morphed into a sloppy 'V' sign at himself, he collected his brown nappa leather blouson from the wardrobe and slunk out of the bedroom wondering how the hell he was going to deal with it all.

With almost half his monthly salary going in maintenance payments, Henry could no longer afford a car. He therefore walked to work, using the opportunity to clear his head and get his brain into gear.

The early evening was dark with a distinct nip in the air. Hunched deep into his jacket, he found the chill to his nose, ears and cheeks pleasant and invigorating. He breathed deeply, expelling stale air from his lungs, feeling new, cold, fresh air circulating round his chest, lungs and heart.

It was a ten-minute journey on foot, giving him ample opportunity to reflect upon his predicament and how he was going to face people at work. The problem was that most

36

people would see the move to uniform as a demotion, although it was not: busted from CID, they would think. Not many people willingly made the transition out of civvies into blues unless it was a specific career move. Usually it was for reasons of bad discipline or poor performance and was perceived as punishment, whatever the circumstances.

At the busy junction of Hornby Road and Coronation Street he stopped and got his first glimpse of Blackpool police station. Every window in every one of its eight floors was illuminated. It was the first time he had seen the building in two months, having avoided looking at it on his infrequent forays into town, hoping that it would go away.

He winced. His insides churned nervously.

It had not moved. It was still there, large and forbidding.

The tips of his fingers twitched. He bunched both hands into fists to stop them shaking – and succeeded. But even repeated swallowing did not eliminate the taste of apprehension at the back of his throat.

He dithered by the kerb edge and almost lost it there and then, almost spun round on his heels and turned back to seek refuge and solace from his friendly and accommodating veterinary surgeon. He knew he could have conned his tame GP to sign him off for a further four weeks. Easy. Another month of grace, avoiding the issue, hidden away from the prying eyes of the world, screwing himself silly.

The green man at the pedestrian crossing began to make his 'pipping' noise.

Henry stepped onto the road, his feet feeling as though they were trudging through treacle.

No going back now, he told himself firmly. You have crossed the river and the waters have filled in behind you.

A minute later he was approaching the back door of the police station, puzzled by the sight of two uniformed cops standing there, obviously on security duty. He did not recognise either. He edged past them towards the door.

'Excuse me, sir,' one said, preventing Henry from passing, firstly with a hand, then the bulk of his body. 'Can I see your pass, please?'

Henry regarded him with incomprehension. 'My pass...?' he started to say.

The officer clicked on a small, but powerful Maglite torch and shone the beam up into Henry's face. Henry squinted, drew his head back slightly.

'Yes, sir, your pass,' the PC insisted firmly. 'You need a pass to enter the police station this week ... party conference?'

'Oh, right,' Henry said as it dawned on him. While ensconced in the cosseted world of sickness he had moved out of sync with the real world and its goings-on. He had fed himself a diet of mind-numbing daytime TV and satellite sports channels, occasionally dipping into the *Daily Telegraph* to keep abreast of crime and rugby, but little else.

Certainly not politics – a subject which bored him rigid even when in good health. He had completely forgotten about the annual party conference taking place in town that week.

'I don't have a pass yet.' He nodded towards the nick. 'This is my ... er ... first day back for a while ... here, here...' He rooted through his pockets and produced his warrant card from his wallet, flashing it to the officer. 'DI Christie,' he said unthinkingly, then lamely corrected himself. 'Inspector Christie ... I'm the night cover inspector this week.'

The PC scrutinised the laminated card – a document which invested an individual with incredible power – comparing the photograph on it with the reality of the bearer. Satisfied, he nodded at Henry, stepped to one side and said, 'There's somebody dealing with emergency accreditation inside ... you'll need to get yourself a pass.'

'Yeah, right.' Henry found his swipe card and went towards the pedestrian entrance next to the shuttered garage door. He did not have to use it because the garage door itself clattered upwards and open. As it rose on its rollers it revealed two CID Ford Mondeos, waiting to leave, two detectives in each motor, engines revving dramatically.

The first car accelerated past him, followed by the second. Henry caught fleeting glimpses of the detectives in both cars, but it was one person in particular in the second car who caused him to draw breath; the one in the front passenger seat. It was the officer

39

who was now doing the job of the detective inspector, Henry's old role. The officer did not look up, or acknowledge Henry in any way, just stared dead ahead. The second car tailgated the first, as they tear-arsed down to the end of the street.

They were in a hurry. On their way to a job.

A pang of bright-green envy hit Henry in the solar plexus, making him wince.

He ducked under the already descending door, and walked through the dimly lit garage to the rear entrance of the police station. As he entered, the custody office was to his left. He glanced quickly through the bars and, with relief, saw that the place looked reasonably quiet. A major part of the job of the reactive inspector was responsibility under the Police and Criminal Evidence Act for what went on in the custody office. It was a duty he had never performed before, having been promoted directly into the DI's job from detective sergeant. He knew that he would have to swim rather than sink and by the end of this first night, he intended to be doing the butterfly. The custody office had to be got right straight away if he was to survive with any degree of credibility in his new role.

Shaking his head at the prospect, he walked to the lift and took it up to the level where the CID office was situated. He needed to get a few things from his locker before taking over.

Henry slid his key into the padlock and twisted. The lock did not snap open. He tried again. Nothing. He peered at the key, wondering if he was using the correct one. Yes – the only one of its type on the fob. He put it back into the lock. Again it failed to open. Only at that moment did he notice that his name was not on the locker as it always had been. It had been scrubbed and replaced by the name of the new DI who had superseded him. The next thing he saw was the bulging black bin liner on the floor next to the locker with his name on a tag. He bent down and opened the bag, an acerbic expression on his face. All his gear had been taken out of the locker and dropped into the bag. Now, like a cuckoo, the new incumbent ruled the roost.

The message could not have been more obvious: Henry Christie's days as a detective were over.

The illusion that the day-shift inspector, who had been on duty for twelve hours, would be pleased to see him was shattered as soon as Henry walked through the door of the inspectors' office.

Burt Norman gave him one nasty glance, looked pointedly at the clock on the wall, then returned to the report he was reading on the desk in front of him, giving Henry a view of the top of his balding head. Before Henry could say anything, Norman muttered gruffly, 'What fucking time do you call this? We don't keep CID hours down here, y'know; we arrive early so everything can be passed over properly and give the one who's finishing – me, on this occasion – the chance

41

of an early dart.'

Norman turned a page of the report, still not having looked up, though, plainly, he was not really reading it.

Henry sensed there was more to come. He leaned against the door jamb, his lips twisted cynically, and waited for the bollocking to continue. He was not wrong.

'That happens day in, day out, without fail, whether you want to be here or not. Unwritten rule. Get my drift?' Norman sniffed superciliously and raised his eyes, inviting Henry to challenge him.

The ex-DI shrugged. 'Sure.'

Norman was long in the tooth, bitter, twisted, an acknowledged dinosaur. He had never been able to pass a promotion board to chief inspector, having had six unsuccessful attempts in consecutive years which nearly destroyed him and his marriage. But he was an extremely efficient reactive inspector, dealing well with the nuts and bolts of day-to-day policing. He ran a tight custody office and knew his job in terms of the 'here and now' intimately. These days, though, that was not enough when so much was expected of someone who earned over thirty-five grand a year. The force wanted strategic thinkers and leaders who could do so much more than be 'gung-ho' with the troops. Norman, who did lead from the front, was extremely popular with the officers under him, but that was not what was wanted by the service. So he had been sidelined.

'Good.' Burt Norman gave a curt nod, closed the file with deliberation and tossed it into a tray. 'Anyway, having said all that, good to have you with us, Henry. Just a pity you're here because you've been shafted by the powers that be ... bunch o' twats ... I know what it's like. Still, never mind, it's a good job and at the end of a shift you go home knowing–' and here Norman counted using his fingers – 'one: you've earned your crust and two: you can put the job out of your mind until you're next on duty. In other words, you can forget this shit-hole ... now then, what do I need to hand over to you?'

There was not much. Four prisoners were currently in custody, but Norman had taken care of their reviews, which Henry was thankful for. It gave him some time to play with at the start of the shift to get his feet under the table. As Norman pulled on his leather biking jacket to leave, he said, 'Obviously there is the conference going on, as you know – but steer clear of it. Not your job to get involved in any aspect of it.'

Henry nodded. It was his responsibility to police the streets of Blackpool. There were enough cops drafted into the town from all over the county specifically for the conference.

Norman scooped up his helmet and gave a quick wave.

'Bye,' said Henry, slowly taking off his coat, hanging it behind the door and looking dejectedly round the office. He sighed deeply.

'Oh – I knew there was something.' Norman stuck his head back round the door. 'Forgot to mention it. There's an ID parade being held at 7.30. You're running it. Some Asian done over good style by one of the scummy Costains last night. Still alive, but well whacked. Could pop his clogs, I believe. One of the Khan family, I think. Anyway, the suspect is coming back in on part four bail tonight. There's one witness I think ... see ya.' He disappeared like a shot, clearly and absolutely aware of what he had just dropped on Henry's toes on his first tour of duty as a uniformed inspector.

A certain queasiness overcame him. He sat down slowly at the desk, cursing. An ID parade was the bane of a uniformed inspector's life. Difficult to manage and co-ordinate; so much could go wrong and often so much depended on their success. They had never bothered Henry before because as a detective he just smugly handed them over to uniform and waited for the result. Now he was on the other side of the fence and the grass was not very green. He blew out his cheeks and wondered where the best place to hide would be.

Before Henry could slide under his desk, curl up into a foetal ball and start sucking on his thumb, his senses were invaded by a shrieking, piercing, screaming noise which erupted all round him, stunning him. For the briefest of moments he thought it was the onset of a major panic attack. Then realised

44

the noise was external.

It was the personal attack alarm from the custody office.

Without further thought or hesitation, Henry hurled himself out of his chair, grabbed the personal radio on the desk and bolted through the door towards the origin of the sound, one floor below. Even as he ran he was grateful that his cop conditioning had kicked in so quickly. One of his recurrent fears over the last few days was that he might have lost his edge.

The prisoner had struck without warning, although the custody sergeant had been wary of the guy from the moment he had been presented to him by the arresting officer, PC Rod Phillips.

He had started off placid and compliant, happy to stand where he had been told, a stupid lop-sided grin on his chops, while the PC outlined the circumstances of the lock-up, which was for an assault: whacking a beer glass over somebody's head and then gouging the broken end into the guy's face. The heavily blood-stained prisoner intimated he understood the reason for his arrest, and offered his name – Kit Nevison – address and date of birth quite willingly. He seemed to be acting rationally, did not smell too strongly of booze, and kept that inane smile on his face. The custody sergeant did notice he had glassy eyes with dilated pupils and he wondered if the prisoner was on speed. When

45

asked, Nevison emptied his pockets and dropped the contents onto the desk.

As the sergeant listed the property on the custody record, a female duty solicitor was shown into the office. The sergeant glanced past Nevison and smiled at her. 'Come to see Grant?' he asked, referring to another prisoner. The solicitor nodded. 'Be right with you – soon as this chap's been booked in.' The solicitor moved to the back wall of the room and leaned patiently against it.

Nevison turned slightly so he could watch her unobtrusively.

'Just stand back a bit and extend your arms out to the side, Kit,' PC Phillips instructed him.

The prisoner obeyed and the body search began. But as the arresting officer moved in and invaded his personal space, he reacted – or, in police terminology, 'kicked off'.

Somehow, from somewhere – probably from down a sleeve – a triple-bladed Stanley knife appeared in the man's right hand; triple bladed in that three blades had been super-glued together side by side, thus ensuring that the injuries it would cause would be three times more difficult to stitch together.

With a manic scream, Nevison slashed the knife down across PC Phillips' face, first one way, then back the opposite way, literally slicing the cheeks open wide. The officer reeled away, emitting a yowl of agony, his hands coming up to cover his face.

The custody sergeant immediately pressed

46

the panic-alarm button underneath the desk and reached for his side-handled baton.

Things then went from bad to worse. Nevison spun round and grabbed the female duty solicitor.

It took Henry less than thirty seconds to reach the custody office.

'Inspector to Blackpool,' he said into his radio, 'buzz me through to the cells.'

He leaned on the barred gate, his eyes surveying the scene as the communications operator several floors above released the catch. He stepped into the danger zone. The high-pitched alarm still sounded.

PC Phillips was doubled over on the floor by the custody desk, holding his damaged face, blood dribbling through the gaps in his fingers. He was making a noise which was a cross between a gurgle and a moan of pain. Henry could see the wide-open gashes across his face.

Beyond the wounded PC was the custody sergeant, baton extended, standing there hesitantly. When he glanced back over his shoulder and saw Henry, the relief on his face was visible. Beyond him was the cause of the problem: Kit Nevison holding a woman hostage, the triple-bladed Stanley knife stuck into her neck, a line of blood trickling down from the cut, disappearing behind the high collar of her blouse and then blossoming out into a crimson stain.

Henry recognised Nevison immediately.

Local trouble maker and hard man. Convictions well into double figures for petty dishonesty offences and a string of assaults which were becoming progressively more serious. He was a man on the verge of being a psychopath, a man who, one day, would definitely kill someone, enjoy it and then probably kill again – unless he got caught. He was a heroin addict and the combination of an unbalanced mind and dangerous chemicals made him very unstable and volatile. Henry had dealt with him several times over the years and had tried to have him sectioned into mental institutions, but had never succeeded beyond the short term.

Henry allowed himself an inner smile. He had been back on duty less than ten minutes and was already faced with a bit of a challenge. The good thing was that he was relishing it.

'Fuckin' come any closer and I'll cut the bitch's head off,' Nevison warned. 'Especially you.' He pointed at Henry with the blade. 'Especially you,' he reiterated more strongly, 'because you are a CUNT!' he screamed.

Henry and the custody sergeant were perhaps eight feet away from Nevison.

'OK, Kit, we're moving back,' Henry said placatingly. He laid a steady hand on the sergeant's arm and intimated a slight withdrawal, just a couple of steps. 'Who's the woman?' Henry rasped under his breath.

'Beth Young, duty solicitor,' the sergeant hissed through the side of his mouth.

'Is there an ambulance coming?'

'Not that I know of.'

Henry looked over his shoulder. A gaggle of onlookers had gathered at the barred door, gawping in. 'Someone call an ambulance – now,' he instructed. He turned back and kept his eyes on Nevison who was jigging agitatedly, the knife dangerously close to the woman's throat. 'You see to Rod,' he said to the sergeant, gesturing at the injured PC. 'Get him out of here and away.'

'What about you?'

'I'll be fine – and get that alarm switched off.'

The sergeant nodded and bent to deal with the slashed PC.

Henry placed his radio upright on the custody desk, leaned nonchalantly against the desk itself and regarded Nevison and the hostage through calculating eyes, the glimmer of a smile not far away from his lips.

Nevison looked Henry in the eye and sneered down the bridge of his large bent nose at him.

Standoff.

The din of the alarm subsided, leaving a nagging echo battering round the walls.

'OK, Kit, what's all this about?' Henry asked evenly. His eyes did not acknowledge the woman even though he was agonisingly aware she was staring pleadingly at him. He did not engage her eyes because he did not want to give her any false hope in a reassuring look. Not very long ago he had faced a similar

49

situation and the woman had died. He had learned his lesson the hardest way possible, and was focused exclusively on Nevison.

'It's about life and death,' Nevison responded with a growl. He grinned stupidly. Henry tried not to blink as he realised Nevison had completely lost it. 'I want to slit this cunt's throat and saw her fucking head off ... because I want to and you are not going to stop me and if you try I'll cut you to fucking pieces.'

Ah well, that's cleared that up nicely, Henry thought. Nevison wants to kill someone. His life had reached the point of no return – as Henry had suspected it would one day – and unless he could be talked down, this little scenario was probably going to end with more blood spilled on the custody office floor than usual.

'Now, come on, Kit, you know that's not the way to talk,' Henry said smoothly. 'There's no profit in that, not for anyone – you, me, her – everyone'll suffer and it doesn't have to be that way.'

'Really, pig bastard?' Nevison twisted the point of the blade into the woman's neck. She gasped and squealed. Nevison's large dirty hand clamped over her nose and mouth, stifling the noise, almost suffocating her. She was on the point of collapse.

Henry quickly raised his hands, palms out. 'Whoa. Hold on, Kit,' he said, probably too quickly, betraying his anxiety. 'Let's take a step back from this ... Think what you're

50

doing, Kit.' Henry's mind galloped, because he wasn't a hundred per cent sure what he was doing either: the words just babbled out as he played for some time and a possible advantage. 'Come on, man, come on ... cool it ... ease off.' He was working out the distance between himself and Nevison, estimating whether he could reach the woman before she got carved and her jugular sliced open. Henry had a dreadful image of himself and Nevison fighting, slopping and sliding around in her blood. If he moved, it would have to be fast, hard and decisive.

Over Nevison's right shoulder, Henry caught a movement in the periphery of his vision at the door which led down to the cells. He did not allow his eyes to flicker or register anything to alert Nevison. He concentrated on him.

A uniformed sergeant – whom Henry did not know – appeared from the cell corridor. He had a small aerosol-like canister in his right hand: CS spray. Generally, but wrongly known as CS gas. It wasn't a gas at all.

Henry forced himself to relax.

'OK, Kit. You want to kill someone – fine. But you've hurt someone here–' he pointed to the woman solicitor – 'who's done you no harm whatsoever. If you need to kill someone, why don't you make it somebody who's wronged you? Hmm? I suggest you let her go...' he carried on speaking as the sergeant crept into the custody office from the cell corridor, 'and take me instead. I've done you damage, haven't I? I'll bet I've arrested you at least four times in the past, if not more...' Behind Nevison, the sergeant slithered silently forwards, CS at the ready. Henry continued to talk, desperately trying to keep Nevison's attention. 'I'll bet I've sent you to prison at least three times ... and I know I've had to thump you before now ... this is your opportunity to get one back on some bastard who really deserves it.' Henry opened his hands dramatically. 'Me.'

On Henry's final word, the sergeant screamed, 'Kit!' from behind.

Nevison's head spun round and the sergeant aimed the CS canister at Nevison's face, pressed his thumb down on the discharge button and the CS solution sprayed out full into the centre of Nevison's face. Nevison screamed as the CS took instantaneous effect as he inhaled and the sensory receptors in his skin, eyes and lining membranes of his nose, mouth, upper respiratory and gastrointestinal tracks burned fiercely as if in contact with acid.

Henry moved in from the front, ducking to avoid any excess CS, and grabbed Nevison's knife hand – the right – forcing it away from the woman. She staggered out of Nevison's grasp and crashed down onto her knees on the hard, tiled floor. Henry stepped over her, taking hold of Nevison's right forearm with both hands and driving all his body weight into the prisoner's chest, bowling him over. He landed on top of Nevison, forcing his arm upwards, squeezing his wrist with all his strength in an effort to get him to release the knife, whacking the back of Nevison's hand repeatedly against the floor.

All the while Nevison writhed in agony and anger. The pain of the CS had deranged him more rather than subduing him. With an animal-like roar and a surge of strength he heaved Henry off him – though Henry managed to keep hold of his knife hand, refusing to let that go. Even though Nevison could not possibly breathe or see properly, he punched and kicked Henry, who held on as grimly as a pit bull terrier.

There was a 'crack': the sound of a side-handled baton being extended, then a 'swish' like a whip as the sergeant smashed his baton down across Nevison's head, narrowly missing Henry. There was no time for niceties, such as aiming for muscle, or the areas of the body less likely to suffer severe damage. He deliberately went for Nevison's head because the man had to be stopped – and stopped good.

And stopped he was.

The blow had the desired effect: it knocked Nevison senseless. He went limp and ceased to struggle. The fingers of his knife hand curled open and Henry scooped it up and got to his feet. He caught his breath from the brief but intense exertion, standing doubled over, hands on hips. Raising his eyebrows, he looked up at the sergeant and gave a short nod. 'Well done,' he acknowledged. 'Don't think we've had the pleasure ... Henry Christie.' Henry reached across the prostrate body of Kit Nevison and shook hands with the sergeant.

'Dermot Byrne,' the sergeant introduced himself. 'Me and my shift are on nights with you this week. Welcome back.'

'Thanks,' Henry said dubiously.

Simultaneously they looked down at the subdued prisoner. Blood pumped through a gaping split in his temple by the hair line. He moaned, his eyes flickered showing yellowy, bloodshot whites. He was alive, if not quite kicking.

'Nice to be back,' Henry mused dully. 'Better get him trussed up and taken to casualty.' He turned to the woman solicitor, now up on her knees, still groggy and disorientated by her ordeal. Henry assisted her. 'You OK?'

Plainly she was not. 'Thanks ... thanks...' she mumbled a little incoherently, holding her neck. Blood trickled from the cut.

'We'll get you to hospital too.'

'Thanks ... thanks,' she continued to say.

Henry checked his watch. 6.15 p.m. Only fifteen short minutes into the twelve-hour shift. He just hoped the rest of the night wasn't going to be quite so fraught.

Two

Once the shakes had stopped and after his jangled nerves had settled, Henry made his way to the CID office. For many years it had been a sanctuary, his comfort zone. Now, as he passed through the door, in uniform, he felt strange and unsettled. Like an intruder.

The office, with one exception, was devoid of personnel. Desks were unmanned and had been left untidy: papers and files were stacked up or scattered about as though the 'big one' had come in and everyone, with that one exception, had rushed to it.

Maybe they had.

Henry cast his mind back to the detectives he had seen earlier tearing out of the garage.

The one detective remaining in the office had his back to the door and was hunched busily over something at his desk. Henry walked towards him and tapped him on the shoulder. Anyone else would perhaps have been startled, but not the slightly slow-witted Dave Seymour. He turned ponderously at the touch, giving Henry a view of what Seymour was working on. It was, unsurprisingly, a donner kebab, everything on – chilli sauce, lemon juice, salad – and lots falling off.

'Fuckin' hell, Henry,' Seymour said, munching a mouthful of the dubious meat, chilli sauce trickling down his cheek. He finished the mouthful and wiped his lips clean, using a piece of the toilet roll on his desk. Seymour, a man of not inconsequential bulk, was one of the longest-serving detective constables in the division, now only three pay cheques away from retirement. It would probably be not one of the most significant losses to the service when he started to draw his pension, but despite his myriad faults – sloth, greed, envy, arrogance among them – Henry had a bit of a soft spot for Seymour, but rarely allowed it to show.

Seymour positioned the kebab carefully on his desk jotter and drew his head back slightly to allow his eyes to take in the sight of his ex-boss in uniform. Henry let him gawk. People were accustomed to seeing him in plain clothes. The spectacle of him in uniform was something they would need time to adjust to.

Seymour's eyes narrowed. 'Suits you,' he said diplomatically.

'Cheers.'

'Actually, I tell a lie – you look bloody weird.' Seymour shook his head. 'Anyhow – at least you're back at work, albeit...' He struggled to find the words to express his thoughts.

'In uniform?' Henry suggested.

'Mmm,' Seymour murmured doubtfully. He took a long swig from the can of cola on his desk.

'Anyway,' Henry said briskly, deciding to get into gear, 'one of my first jobs is to run an ID parade. I wanted a bit of background. Burt Norman said something about the Khans and the Costains. Can you fill me in?' Henry shrugged and opened his arms, inviting Seymour to speak.

'Yeah ... the Khans and the Costains.' He lifted one cheek of his backside off his chair, screwed his face painfully, and expelled a slow fart. 'Been at each other's throats all bloody weekend.'

There had been a series of skirmishes throughout the weekend between the two factions, Seymour explained to Henry. The culmination was a violent confrontation just after midnight on Sunday on a piece of waste ground near to a poorly run nightclub not far away from the main bus station in Blackpool centre.

More often than not such inter-gang conflicts do not involve the police. But things take on a very serious complexion when someone ends up in hospital with a fractured skull, broken cheekbones, a cracked jaw, a face mashed to a gory unrecognisable mush, broken arms, broken ribs, a collapsed lung and testicles the colour, size and consistency of peeled plum tomatoes, being kept barely alive by a machine and with brain scans that did not bode well. In cases like that, the law cannot help but become involved. At the very least it was attempted murder.

That was the basic scenario as sketched out

by Seymour.

'Who's in hospital?'

'Mo Khan.'

Henry raised his eyebrows and gave a short whistle. Khan was the head of a tightly knit Asian family and had a range of businesses operating in Lancashire, such as grocery shops, newsagents and taxi firms. Henry knew Khan well. He was a dangerous, violent individual who had a nefarious underbelly to his legitimacy: drugs, prostitution and importing illegal aliens from the Indian subcontinent, the latter line having become the most profitable of them all.

Khan was supported by four sons, their ages ranging from late teens to early thirties. Henry knew Khan had a daughter too but, like her mother, she rarely saw the light of day.

It was pretty unusual for Mo Khan to be caught out on the streets.

'What was it all about?' Henry asked.

'Dunno.' Seymour shrugged, a little agitated now because his kebab was starting to go cold. 'Same old crap, I expect,' he explained, and picked up his delicacy. 'Drugs, turf ... love, even.'

Henry also knew the Costain family very well. Blackpool toe rags born and bred, though they proclaimed themselves – rightly – to be descended from Romany gypsies. Generations of them had lived on the same council estate for years, which they terrorised constantly. They made their living from

58

drawing the maximum amount of state benefits, coupled with burglary, theft, deceptions, low-level drug dealing and protection by intimidation. The big problem they faced was that when the Khan family took over the general store on the estate, they had refused to be intimidated by the Costains. This resulted in numerous incidents over the last two years, usually between Khan's sons and the younger end of the Costain tribe.

Though racism did play a part in the scheme of things, the main reason for their conflict was that in the eyes of the Costains, the Khan family were not showing them due respect. Often the Khans outmanoeuvred and belittled the Costains – who were not very large in the brain department – and these humiliations only served to fuel a bitter hatred.

It had been an escalating situation observed carefully by the police – and now, apparently, it had got out of hand.

Henry did not relish dealing with either family. They both despised the police.

'Drugs, turf and love?' Henry repeated. 'What do you mean, love?'

'There is some suggestion,' Seymour said through his munchings, 'that Khan's daughter has been screwing around with Joey Costain and old man Khan had tried to put an end to the liaison.' He emptied more cola into his mouth. 'Real sorta Romeo and Juliet stuff.' He snorted. 'Anyway ... Joey Costain got locked up for the assault on Mo and then

59

said bugger all in the interview ... it's unlikely there'll be any forensic, no weapon has been found, so he's been bailed and it's ID parade time and it's over to you uniforms.'

Seymour smirked. Henry smirked back.

'Who's the witness?'

'Ah well, that's part of the problem ... it's Mo Khan's daughter, Naseema ... not a bad-looking bird for a Paki, actually.'

Henry flinched and stifled an uncomfortable cough. He looked round quickly to see if anyone had overheard Seymour's offensive remark. The coast was clear. Henry's unease was because the use of derogatory terms such as 'Paki' were a definite no-no in the police these days. It was considered to be an outright racist term and managers were expected to put staff right about such things at the very least. But Henry could not be bothered to tackle it at the moment. He had far too much on his plate and the thought of getting to grips with such a touchy subject on his first day back, his first hour back at that, and probably alienating Seymour at the same time, did not have any appeal. Maybe it was cowardice, but an ally like Seymour in the CID might prove useful – and just at that moment, Henry thought he needed all the friends he could get.

Seymour, unaware of his gaff and Henry's inner dilemma, checked his watch. 'She's due in at seven.'

'Right, thanks.'

'And Joey Costain is due to answer his bail

at quarter past ... no doubt with tame brief in tow.'

'Shit – that was a bit of good planning,' Henry said sarcastically. 'Suppose they bump into each other on their way in? If they do, you can kiss the parade bye bye – and the job, too.'

'Yeah, that's true.' Seymour did not seem overly concerned.

'Who's the officer in charge?'

'DI Roscoe.'

Henry blew out a lungful of exasperated breath. 'Better go and sort it out.' He turned to leave the office but was stopped in his tracks as the new DI, accompanied by a DS called Mark Evans and two detective constables, bustled purposely in through the door. The DS and the DCs acknowledged Henry with muted embarrassment, their eyes running up and down his uniform. Henry caught Roscoe's eye, gave a nod and edged quickly out of the office, feeling very uncomfortable.

As he trotted down the stairs, he realised why he felt like that. It was because of the eyes and expressions of those three jacks, all members of his team not long ago. They all seemed to be looking and sneering at him as though he'd been demoted and was no longer one of them. An outsider. A uniform. Even though he had expected this, it hurt him. Deeply. But what wounded his fragile ego even more was that his place on the branch had been taken by someone like DI Roscoe.

'Everything's sorted.'

'What do you mean?'

'The witness and her brother are waiting in your office – accompanied by a policewoman – all the stooges are in the ID suite being looked after by a couple of lads and I'll do the scribing for you. The video cameras have all been set up and everything else that you need to know is on this ... idiot's guide, if you'll pardon the expression.' Sergeant Dermot Byrne handed Henry a laminated A4-size sheet of paper with a blow-by-blow explanation of how to run an identification parade.

'No, you're right, Dermot – idiot's guide.'

The sergeant smiled sympathetically. 'I don't think so really, but I did think you might need a chuck-up, this being your first tour of duty and all that.'

'You are dead right. Thanks, I appreciate it.' Henry genuinely meant it.

'All we need now is for Joey Costain to answer his bail, but he's got a few minutes yet.'

'Brilliant,' said Henry. He cast his eyes down the idiot's guide. 'I think I'll have a quick word with the witness.'

'I'll keep an eye out at the front desk for Joey and let you know when he lands.'

Byrne walked away towards the front desk and Henry thanked God for watching over him and providing a sergeant the calibre of Byrne who was worth his weight in gold.

★ ★ ★

Saeed Khan, scowling sullenly and lounging indolently against a filing cabinet, did not move when Henry walked into the inspectors' office. Henry gave him a quick once over, then ignored him and directed his attention to Naseema who was seated. Behind her, arms folded, looking very stern and intimidating, was a policewoman.

Henry had often had dealings with the Khan family, but had only ever caught glimpses of the daughter. She never seemed to be involved in any of the business, legit or otherwise, and Henry had never really given her much thought. Except for now – he had to agree that Dave Seymour's grudging accolade of her looks was spot on.

Naseema was an exceptionally beautiful young woman, exotically so, with dusky mysterious eyes, a wonderfully smooth complexion the colour of milk chocolate, and a small mouth shaped like a heart. She was dressed in a stunning red Indian trouser suit. Her slim legs were crossed, displaying finely boned ankles and petite feet in sandals. Henry knew she was twenty-three and unmarried. He did not know enough about her culture or religion to be certain as to whether this was an unusual state of affairs.

He introduced himself and offered her his hand which she shook with such delicate fingers that he could easily have crushed them. 'I'll be running the identification parade, so there's just a few things I need to go through with you beforehand, OK?'

She nodded and looked past Henry towards her brother. Her face clouded over with annoyance as Saeed pushed himself away from the filing cabinet and said, 'No, not OK. You'll talk to her through me – is that understood?'

Henry bristled. He pursed his lips and slowly reappraised Saeed, a young man he had arrested twice previously for quite serious assaults. He had a quick temper and was always ready with a fist or a knife to ram home his point of view.

'It's our custom,' Saeed stated.

'And it's a necessity for me to talk directly to witnesses – unless they don't speak English, in which case I'll use an official interpreter. And I know that your sister speaks English, so while I respect your customs, I have a job to do here and not much time to do it in – so we'll achieve more, quickly, if you let me get on without interruption, OK?' He spoke to Naseema, 'If that's OK with you?'

Throughout the exchange Henry had noticed that she had been glowering stonily at Saeed. Henry knew, therefore, he was on to a winner. She smiled radiantly, if falsely, at Henry. 'That will be just fine, Inspector,' she said with a hint of triumph.

Henry shot Saeed a quick warning glance and he backed down with an angry snarl of his lips, eyes blazing at his sister.

Henry wondered what the undercurrent of tension was all about; maybe Dave Seymour had hit the nail on the head with the

Shakespearean scenario. It was obvious there was a sparking friction between the two siblings and Henry began to suspect that maybe the family had lost control of Naseema. Was she a wild child? Was she seeing one of the Costains? If so, this whole job could be a tricky one to handle. For the most transient of moments Henry was glad that his only involvement was the ID parade ... but it was only a passing shiver of thought: secretly he would have given his back teeth to be the Officer in Charge.

'Good,' said Henry. 'You've already made a statement, I believe.'

'Yes, she has,' Saeed interrupted rudely, 'which says that Joey Costain assaulted our father in her presence in an unprovoked racist attack. This parade will just confirm that.'

'Saeed!' Naseema clucked with hostility. 'Let me speak, please.'

'And don't give me the pleasure of showing you out of the police station. Just let her answer – OK?' Henry had had enough of Saeed now.

Saeed's nostrils flared wide.

Henry turned slowly back to Naseema. 'Did you actually see Joey Costain assaulting your father?'

She thought hard for a few seconds. 'They had a push and shove while I was there, but nothing much. I saw them walk away together towards the bus station. I knew they were going to fight. Next time I saw my father he was being put in an ambulance.'

Henry nodded. He was about to say something when suddenly the office door burst open, no knock. A huffing and puffing Dave Seymour stood there, his bulk filling the doorway, tie askew, shirt stretched over his expanding gut. But for the hair – Seymour's was short, neatly trimmed – he reminded Henry of Kojak's sidekick, Stavros. The journey from the CID office, with his insides recently filled with kebab and cola, had exhausted him. 'Henry ... can I have a quick word?' His eyes took in the Khan brother and sister, then returned to Henry. 'In private ... urgent.'

'I'll be back in a moment.' Henry smiled at Naseema, stared coldly at Saeed, then followed Seymour outside. As he closed the door, Saeed launched a verbal assault on his sister in Urdu.

'What is it, Dave?'

'Bit of bad news, actually.' Seymour flinched. 'Mo Khan clocked out about half an hour ago. We've now got a murder investigation on our hands.'

'Fuck,' said Henry eloquently.

66

Three

'How would you feel,' Henry demanded, 'if I knew your father was dead and I didn't tell you?' He raised his eyebrows, daring a response. 'If we don't tell them, they'll have good grounds for a complaint and we will look completely and utterly stupid and insensitive. We have no justification for it at all.'

Detective Inspector Roscoe swallowed and stared coldly at Henry. Roscoe had been the one who had decided that Naseema and Saeed Khan should not be informed about their father's death before the ID parade took place.

'Despite that,' Roscoe said stubbornly, 'I still don't think we should tell them. That way no pressure is put on the girl – at least no more pressure than she's already under. If we drag a hysterical, sobbing female down a line of stooges, it's more than likely she will not perform.'

'Perform to our standards, you mean, by picking Joey Costain out of the line-up?'

Henry saw he had momentarily hit a nerve before the DI spoke again. 'What I mean is that she needs to be able to think straight, keep her head together and pick the little shit out.'

'If she wants to pick him out,' Henry observed.

'Yeah, well, there is that to it,' Roscoe conceded. 'Rumour has it they're shagging each other.'

There was a beat of silence between the two officers. They were discussing this delicate matter in a corridor – a location often used to conduct police business – both trying not to raise their voices. The atmosphere between them was fragile to start with, but when Dave Seymour had told Henry that Roscoe did not want the relatives informed of Mo Khan's death until after the ID parade, it had smacked Henry's 'ethical' button. He had immediately stormed up to the CID office and confronted Roscoe. There was a degree of devilment involved too, because he knew that if he had been in Roscoe's position, he would probably have pushed for the same thing: a nice, clean parade at which the suspect was identified – then arrested for murder.

But he wasn't in Roscoe's position and the last thing Henry needed was to be the subject of a complaint, which if attached to the 'race card' could be very uncomfortable. As much as anything, he was watching his own back. He had enough complications in his life without taking on any further grief.

'No easy answer,' Roscoe admitted. She looked thoughtfully down at her wedding ring, twisting it around her finger, while making a clicking noise with her tongue. 'I could really do with a quick result and, to be honest, I know that if we did tell them about Mo's death, Joey Costain would probably have to be re-bailed and I'd've lost the element of surprise. I intended to drop it on his toes tonight, because he won't know Mo Khan has died.' She was pensive. Henry watched her face carefully. 'And that estate they live on is buzzing with tension. If Joey Costain was out of the picture, the place would be a lot calmer. He's a real shit stirrer. A riot up there – and that's not an exaggeration – is the last thing the town needs this week with the conference starting tomorrow.'

Henry let her ramble on, while he remained tight-lipped. His problem was the here and now: how to deal properly and sympathetically with the brother and sister. Yet he could appreciate where Roscoe was coming from, even though she had not expressed it in so many words. She was new to the job. This was her first big case here in Blackpool and there was a good chance Roscoe and her crew could bottom it without help from the headquarters SIO team. And if they did, her credibility rating would soar with her team of detectives, predominantly made up of white males lying in wait for women officers to trip up and show their fannies.

'So what are you going to do? I know you probably don't like me very much because I've got your job, even though we hardly know each other. I can understand if you don't feel inclined to help me, but the end might justify the means in this case ... for the greater good.' She obviously had more to say, but shut up there and let the words hang around, knowingly playing on Henry's instincts as a jack ... former jack, that is.

He rubbed his face, jaded already. Not much more than an hour into the shift and he was having to look to his morals now ... morals he had often hung out to dry when he had been a detective, just to get that result.

'Right, this is how it stands, Jane: we haven't had this conversation; I don't know that Mo Khan is dead; you haven't told me a thing, OK? But the minute this ID parade is over, I want to know. Get me?'

'Thanks, Henry.' Roscoe sighed with relief. Henry was pleased to hear her words were not tinged with triumph. However, he was highly annoyed with himself for being swayed from what he knew was the right course of action.

'By the way,' Roscoe said. 'I didn't ask for this posting, I was given it.'

Henry spun quickly away without responding and headed towards the identification suite, hoping that his decision would not be one which would come back like a crocodile and bite his arse. It was 7.15 p.m.

'How much longer are we going to give him?' The question from Sergeant Dermot Byrne was directed at Henry Christie.

70

It was three minutes before eight and Joey Costain had not yet answered his bail. He was almost three-quarters of an hour late. Restlessness was beginning to creep in. The pool of ten stooges – the volunteers rounded up to make up the numbers on the parade and paid the paltry sum of £10 for all their hanging around – were becoming bored. The novelty value of the experience was wearing dangerously thin.

Saeed Khan was becoming increasingly obnoxious, muttering and ranting about ill treatment and racism.

Joey Costain's solicitor, one of Blackpool's best-known defenders of criminals, much despised by police officers, was also agitated. He had arrived at ten past seven, having arranged to meet his client in the public foyer of the police station.

Henry turned to the solicitor, a man by the name of Keith Dasher. He knew Dasher well and had developed a tolerably good working relationship with the guy over the years. Henry sighed. 'He definitely said he was coming, yeah?'

'Yes.'

'When did you last speak to him?'

'Earlier this afternoon, by phone. He was going to come, definitely.'

Henry raised his eyebrows and wondered why solicitors believed their clients.

'I could've told you he wouldn't turn up,' Dermot Byrne said. Henry's eyes moved to him quizzically. 'Because people like him

71

don't,' Byrne said, responding to Henry's expression. 'I don't know why we give people like him the chance,' he added, looking challengingly at Dasher, anticipating a reaction but getting none.

Dasher looked extremely indignant about the whole situation. It was evident that Joey Costain's non-appearance was irritating him immensely. Even Dasher had better things to do in the evening than wait around in a cop shop. His problem was that the Costain family paid him good money, well over and above the normal rate, to represent them, so keeping them sweet was a necessity.

'Perhaps you could give him a ring now and see where he is,' suggested Henry. 'If he's not here by 8.15, he'll be circulated as wanted.'

Dasher opened his briefcase and pulled out his mobile phone. He left the ID suite, punching a number into it.

Byrne said, 'I find it hard to be civil to people like him. Really annoys the life out of me.'

'It's just business, isn't it? He's got a job to do and so have we. The catalyst is our prisoners.'

'Suppose you're right,' Byrne said grudgingly. He did not look terribly convinced by Henry's liberal viewpoint. In his turn, Henry was not too surprised by Byrne's attitude. A lot of cops thought in very clearly defined terms of right and wrong, them and us, and often lost sight of the overall picture – a tableau which Henry knew was very murky indeed with no fine lines and lots of ambiguity. He had long since stopped trying to make any sense of it.

Dasher came back into the room, a forlorn expression on his face. 'No reply.'

Henry nodded. It was close enough to 8.15 to call it a day.

'Give them their money and send them on their way with our thanks,' he instructed Byrne cheerfully. More seriously he added, 'And I'll go and see Mrs Roscoe.'

As he put on each piece of equipment, his shoulders became a little more rounded, sagging a fraction more as the weight pulled them down.

First the heavy stab vest went on over his shirt, then the black Gore-tex blouson, followed by the Batman-like thick black leather belt round his waist onto which he hung his side-handled baton, personal radio, CS canister, rigid handcuffs and mobile phone. He felt like he was going to topple over. He put on his inspector's flat cap – more comfortable and better padded than a mere sergeant's or PC's cap. More befitting such a high rank, Henry thought. It seemed the only perk going, a soft cap.

He had a look at himself in the mirror, aware that critical self-appraisal seemed to be the order of the day. He hoped he wasn't getting to be vain. He thought he resembled a New York street cop rather than a Lancashire

73

bobby and it hit him quite hard that the traditional days of policing were long gone.

There was a sharp knock on the office door. Henry pulled his cap off quickly and tried to move away from the mirror, but was not fast enough. The door opened and Dermot Byrne came in. He just knew what Henry had been doing.

'You'll get used to it,' he reassured Henry. 'By the end of the night you'll hardly remember being a detective ... it'll be a vague, distant memory.'

'Won't be if I have my way,' Henry stated firmly. 'Right,' he announced, businesslike, unconsciously coming to attention, drawing his heels together with a click. 'As there's nothing of great importance for me in the custody office at the moment, I quite fancy a chauffeured ride out ... see what's happening at the conference, then maybe we could have a look up on Shoreside and see what's bubbling. After that we'll nip up to casualty and see how things are panning out up there with our injured parties.'

'Sounds good,' Byrne said.

'And you can fill me in as to who's on duty, what's been going on around here and what's going to happen this week. I am so out of touch, it's unbelievable. I'm going to be relying on you for a few days, Dermot – and I don't mind admitting it.'

'Yeah – no worries, boss.'

Henry was quickly getting to like Byrne. He seemed cool, capable and very much in control: the kind of sergeant who could be depended on. Byrne pointed to a black canvas duffel bag in the corner of the room. 'Is that your public-order gear?' Henry nodded. 'Best put it in the boot with mine, just in case.' Byrne picked it up and slung it over his shoulder.

'Let's go then and see what the streets of Blackpool have to offer.'

Feeling very self-conscious in all his gear, Henry walked alongside Byrne through the police station. They passed the report-writing room on the way in which a lone PC sat scribbling away at a statement.

'Just a second, boss,' Byrne said. He swung into the room and the PC looked up. Henry continued to shuffle himself inside his uniform, taking little heed of the conversation. 'John,' said Byrne, 'sorry I didn't get a chance to welcome you back properly at parade.'

'That's OK,' the PC said.

'Good to have you back, anyway.'

'Good to be back – a month of searching the Garden has sent me scatty,' he said.

'At least you'll know the place well,' Byrne said.

'Like the back of my hand.'

'Anyway – see you later,' Byrne waved. He and Henry continued on their journey. 'He's just done a month of pre-conference searching at the Winter Gardens,' Byrne felt the need to explain to his inspector.

'Oh, right,' said Henry.

★ ★ ★

75

The conference security operation was very obvious and very high profile because this year it was the party in government holding its annual bash in town.

As Byrne drove north along the promenade, through what had become an extremely blustery, cold, wet night, Henry's sympathies were with the numerous uniformed officers drafted in from all over the county who were very much in evidence along the route. When they reached the Imperial Hotel on North Shore, the police presence was even more high profile, the hotel virtually surrounded by sodden, miserable-looking cops, all wearing high-visibility jackets.

The planning for the policing operation had actually been underway since the beginning of the year, but it was only since the previous Friday night that a ring of steel had been wrapped round the Imperial – the main hotel where government ministers, including the prime minister, were staying during the conference (which took place from Tuesday to Friday). The routes likely to be taken by VIPs from the hotel to the conference venue, and the venue itself – the massive Winter Gardens complex in the centre of Blackpool – had also been subject to the most rigorous security checks and searches.

'It's a big one this year,' Henry commented. Over the last few years security had actually been scaled down, but this year had been one of those controversial ones which seemed to come to every government, when they seemed to upset everybody. The consequent threat level from many sources had therefore risen dramatically.

'Yeah, tense on a lot of fronts this year,' Byrne said. 'Irish peace talks fucked up as usual and the IRA have already hit a couple of targets on the mainland; the animal liberationists are up in arms about testing chemicals on hamsters, or something ridiculous ... er...' Byrne was thinking '... the right wing has had a big resurgence recently – could be a big demo from them later in the week – the anti-capitalists have threatened some sort of action, too – all sorts of things happening. Could be an interesting week.'

Henry sat hunched, listening to his sergeant bringing him up to date with topics he should have really known more about. Although the policing of Blackpool was his main responsibility, as Burt Norman had made plain, he decided to make himself au fait with the strategic and tactical written orders issued for the conference. He was not naive enough to believe that the conference had nothing whatsoever to do with him. If something did happen it was more than likely that he and his shift would be called in to assist.

Byrne drove past the Imperial and up to the Gynn Square roundabout where they passed an armed response vehicle or ARV, whose occupants had stopped a suspect van. The firearms the officers were carrying were overt and very frightening.

'Serious stuff,' Henry commented.

'Yeah – four ARVs on the road twenty-four hours a day from now until Friday afternoon, instructed to be high profile and very proactive.'

Byrne negotiated the roundabout and doubled back along Dickson Road which ran directly behind the Imperial.

'How many have we got out on nights this week?' Henry asked.

'Four double-crewed cars and two pairs on foot in the town – which is pretty good going. Usually lucky to get five out, but all leave has been cancelled this week. It's Scale D, by the way,' he added, referring to the shift which was on duty.

Henry's eyebrows shot up. Scale D, hm? They had a reputation, well deserved, as a team of hard nuts who went in tough and asked questions later. They generated complaints by the bucket load. 'Lucky me,' Henry mumbled. 'Scale D. D for Death.'

'The very ones ... they're my shift now, for my sins.'

Henry peered at Byrne in the half-light, aware he and his sergeant hadn't been properly introduced to each other yet. Henry knew very little about Byrne's background, other than that he had transferred into Blackpool while Henry had been off sick. He was about to ask what Byrne's sins were when he looked out of the car and spotted someone he knew. 'Hey – pull in next to that guy, will you?'

It was a constable, standing on a street

78

corner, looking ultra-wretched, obviously glued to the point to which he had been assigned. Byrne slewed in and stopped alongside him. Henry wound down his window.

'Dave – all right?' he called.

The officer peered suspiciously through the sheets of rain, seeing only the pips on Henry's shoulder and wondering what he was going to get a bollocking for this time. As he approached the police car his look of wariness turned to one of pleasure when he recognised Henry.

'Bloody hell! What the fuck are you wearing?'

'Pantomime gear. How the hell are you, mate?' Henry had joined the police at the same time as this guy back in the seventies when times had seemed so much simpler and more clear cut, when cops could get away with most things unpunished and juries believed them. They had been good mates for a short while back then, but had since maintained only irregular contact because their respective postings, shift patterns, job progressions and private lives had made anything more substantial an impossibility.

In reply to Henry's question, Dave lifted the palms of his leather-gloved hands to the downpour, 'Other than this shite, I'm OK ... but I'll tell you one thing–' He sidled up to Henry's window, leaned in and spoke with a conspiratorial air. 'This must be the most important fucking point in the whole shagging operation.' He pointed down to the concrete pavement underneath his size eleven Doc Marten boots.

'Why's that?' Henry had a smile on his lips, ready for the punchline.

'Why the hell else would they put their best fuckin' officer on it and tell him to stay there, get wet through and not move on pain of death and discipline – and stay positive?'

Henry's smile became a chuckle. 'You're obviously happy with your work.'

'Normally – yes. But this? Fuckin' politicians! Why can't we just let the bastards get blown up? And it's all right for those twats, too – just look at 'em.' He nodded towards the rear gate of the Imperial Hotel car park where a sleek BMW saloon was pulling out onto Dickson Road. Henry narrowed his eyes. 'They never get fucking wet, do they?'

As the BMW drove off towards Blackpool centre, Henry made out the figure of Assistant Chief Constable Robert Fanshaw-Bayley at the wheel. He was the Gold Commander of the whole operation for policing the conference – which meant he had overall responsibility and accountability. He had a front-seat passenger and there was a dark figure in the back of the car. Henry caught a profile of the front passenger and, with a jolt of surprise, recognised him.

'Fanshaw-Bayley, the ignorant, arrogant twat,' Dave bleated. It was another remark Henry should have challenged. He didn't this time because he agreed with the sentiment expressed.

The constable's personal radio blared loudly, operating on a channel dedicated exclusively for the conference, separate from the normal radio channel used by Blackpool section patrols, the one to which Henry's set was tuned. The officer listened then acknowledged the message. He stepped back to Henry and pointed up to a CCTV camera high on a lamp post nearby. It was trained directly on them. 'That message was for you. They say that even though this is a police car, you're not allowed to stop here and I'm not supposed to be chatting to you, so I've had a rollocking too. If you don't move, they'll get the bomb squad in to blow you up.'

'Fair enough,' Henry said, understanding. Any unauthorised vehicle parking near to the hotel would be seen as a potential bomb this week. 'See you, Dave.' He gave his old mate a quick wave. To Byrne he said, 'Let's follow Fanshaw-Bayley and see if he's on his way into the nick. I recognised one of his passengers and I'd like to have a word.' He wound his window up gratefully – his arm and leg had got quite wet.

As the car drew away, their personal radios screamed to life.

'All patrols, please be making to Shoreside Estate. Officers requesting assistance. Repeat, officers requesting assistance, Shoreside Estate. Large disturbance in progress, officers under fire. Repeat large disturbance officers under fire. Patrols to acknowledge.'

Four

Following her conversation with Henry Christie about Mo Khan's death, DI Jane Roscoe had not been looking forward to her next encounter with Henry with any degree of anticipation. In fact she was dreading it. She was sharply aware that their embryonic relationship had got off to a very rocky start right from the moment she had first seen him when the garage door had opened, and her driver, DS Mark Evans, had said through the side of his mouth, 'That's Henry Christie, boss,' and she had not even dared look at him as she was driven past. Then there had been the frosty, wordless encounter in the CID office when Henry's gaze had settled on her oh so fleetingly with an expression that seemed to scream at her, 'I'd like to tear your heart out with my fingernails.' And lastly, the blatantly unethical request she had made to him, which Henry, much to her surprise and shock, had agreed to. Because of all these things and more, Roscoe knew that their association would be edgy at best, most probably doomed.

Although she was certain Henry would not have believed it she had not gone out deliberately to poach his job. It had been offered to her out of the blue by ACC (Operations) Fanshaw-Bayley. Apparently he had decided on a whim that she was the right person for the job, though it was never explicitly articulated to her why she was that person, but such was the way the Constabulary worked: mysteriously.

As anyone else would, she had grabbed the opportunity with both hands. Not knowing Henry Christie personally, though having heard of him by reputation, and being unaware of any of the background to the situation, how could she have refused the offer?

At the time she had been a uniformed inspector at Chorley, to the south of the county, living in Fulwood, near Preston. Travelling to Blackpool, in the opposite direction, therefore, presented her with no real problems. In fact it was an easier journey – motorway all the way. She had been working long, tiring shifts which were causing serious ructions within her married life, and saw little of her solicitor husband. She knew the DI's job would also mean long hours and would not solve any problems at home, but at least she would be happier at work because having spent much of her time in the CID, both as a DC and a DS, she had always wanted to progress to detective inspector.

Her feelings for the job itself did not change when she got to Blackpool, but she soon discovered that her appointment was not a popular one, particularly within the CID office. And it was all down to one man: Henry Christie, even though he wasn't even there in the flesh. Everyone regarded him as some sort of icon. But to Roscoe, his reputation hung around like a bad smell.

He was worshipped by the DCs and could do no wrong in their eyes. Within hours of starting the job Roscoe knew she was on a hiding to nothing and that everything she said and did would be judged by the benchmark of Henry Christie. The man whose job, she overheard one detective remark, Roscoe had 'fucking nicked'.

She had rehearsed numerous times for the inevitable meeting with Henry. She had practised nonchalant facial expressions and devil-may-care body language and one or two sharp-tongued phrases which would put him slap-bang in his place. But all her good intentions had deserted her when the moment finally came. She'd become like an overawed dithering schoolgirl unable to think of the words to finish her little speech about the Khans. Then she had been so completely taken aback by Henry's unexpected reaction she had made that stupid, inane closing comment. Where the hell had that come from? 'I didn't ask for this posting, I was given it.' Jesus. She might as well have rolled over on her back like a submissive puppy and given in there and then. She had been furious with herself, mentally kicking her own arse down the corridor after the meeting and gritting her teeth to stop snarling, because, without trying, Henry had firmly taken the psychological upper hand. And, whether it was true or not, she perceived herself to be in his debt. She owed him one. It was a hole she had unthinkingly dug for herself, fallen into and didn't know how to climb out of.

As she waited for Henry to come to her office to give her the result of the ID parade, she fidgeted, wondering how to play it to get back on top, how she should manipulate Henry, what the strategy should be.

She reached for the Khan/Costain file which contained all the statements taken so far and opened it, plugged in her little travel kettle and made a mug of tea, no sugar, skimmed milk. She switched on her laptop on the desk and slotted an audio CD into the drive, volume low.

This was how it would be when Christie showed his face: she would be concentrating deeply, reading the evidence, brew in hand, Handel's 'Water Music' just audible, drifting softly out of the tiny speakers. She would be halfway down a page, glance up at him as he entered, show slight annoyance and say, in a friendly way, 'Just give me a second, will you?' She would point to a chair and pretend to continue to get to the end of whatever it was she was reading. Then she would close the file, look up at him, having kept him waiting – albeit for a very short time – and allow him to speak. It was a good plan, she thought wickedly.

But it never came to fruition. Firstly because the waiting was intolerable. She began clock-watching. And a watched clock never damn well moves, does it?

She finished her tea and re-read the file twice. Then she needed to pee. The urgency to do so increased slowly but inexorably.

Forty-five minutes. Just what the fuck was going on down there? Her bladder seemed to be bloating to the size and weight of a medicine ball.

Almost an hour. No sign. Shit.

She tossed the file back into her in-tray with an angry flick of the wrist. It missed, skittered across the desk, and fell on the floor fanning the contents out across the carpet. She surveyed her handiwork, her right leg shaking rhythmically.

'He's getting to you again,' she told herself. 'Don't let him ... don't...'

There was just a cold dribble of tea remaining in her cup. She sucked it out with a vulgar slurp, banged the mug back down and stood up abruptly. Suddenly there was an incredible itch on her rib cage underneath her left boob. It screamed out to be scratched. She went for it. Flipped open a button on her blouse and inserted a hand, her fingernails easing the irritation, only to experience another itch, this time at the top of her right leg below the cheek of her backside. Sod's law, Roscoe thought. No doubt Henry Christie would walk in through the door to find me scratching away like mad, contorted like a bloody baboon.

He did not arrive.

Over an hour gone now.

Roscoe made her way around the desk and began to pick up the scattered papers from the file – and it was then Henry came into the room as, on her hands and knees, Roscoe was at full cat-like stretch underneath her desk, reaching for that last sheet of paper beyond her fingertips.

She heard the office door open behind her. She closed her eyes momentarily, an expletive formed silently on her lips. Unsaid but definitely there. She could sense Henry Christie standing behind her, gazing down at her slightly overweight rear end which was stuck up in the air like an offering to the gods. She waited a beat. Waited for the smart-aleck remark which would surely come. She could guess what it was going to be.

But there was nothing. Silence.

Roscoe withdrew from under the desk, pushed herself to her feet and brushed herself down. 'Sorry about that.' She could feel the prickle of redness in her cheeks.

'That's OK,' Henry said. 'Costain didn't show up for the ID parade, so I've sent everyone packing. The Khans are waiting for you in the front foyer. I haven't let on about Mo. Thought I'd leave it for you.'

'Right, thanks Henry.'

He gave a short nod and paused briefly before spinning on his heels and leaving.

Roscoe stood there, lips parted.

For the second time that evening, Henry Christie had confounded her expectations. Now he really was beginning to irritate her.

Ten minutes later she was being driven by Dave Seymour to the Shoreside Estate. In the back of the car were Saeed and Naseema Khan. Roscoe was taking them home.

Immediately after Henry had gone, Roscoe had spoken to the brother and sister in a quiet waiting room and broken the tragic news to them about their father. Saeed had taken it like a stomach punch – badly. Naseema's grief, if there was any at all, had been more controlled and dignified.

Roscoe, who had been thinking about her bum sticking up in the air, shook the picture out of her mind and looked over her shoulder at the Khans in the back seat of the CID car. Saeed was doubled over, face in hands, head between his knees, rocking back and forth, uttering guttural howls of anguish. Naseema was sitting staidly next to him, a cool hand resting on his back, patting him.

Roscoe gave Naseema a wan smile, which she ignored. Roscoe settled down into her seat as Seymour turned the car into Shoreside. She was wondering how the family would take the news of Mo's death. Unless they already knew, of course. That was a distinct possibility. Her eyes scanned the wet pavements which glistened under the halogen lighting of the few street lamps which were still intact and working. She peered down dark alleyways into the black shadows between houses, but she was not really concentrating on what she was looking at – her mind still stuck on Henry Christie – until she spotted the first unusual movement.

'Stop, Dave,' she said quickly, using a chopping motion of the hand to reinforce the order. Seymour pulled in.

'Back up a few feet. I want to get a look up that alley we just passed. Thought I saw something.'

Saeed raised his head, his cheeks were smeared with tears. 'What's happening?'

'Don't know yet. We won't be a second, then we'll get you home.'

Seymour coaxed the unwilling gear lever into reverse and backed up to the entrance to the alley, one of numerous rat-runs which criss-crossed the estate. They were often used by kids to rob other kids of their Reeboks, or grannies of their purses, and to then evade the cops when pursued. Roscoe's eyes probed through the rain, shaded by her hands cupped over her brow.

There was a quick flash of torchlight. Some movement. Several people were up there. Doing what?

Then they were gone.

'Kids.' Seymour spat – just another spectrum of society he despised.

'Mm,' Roscoe agreed without certainty, a funny feeling in her bones. 'C'mon, let's get these people home.'

A couple of minutes later the car drew up

outside the general store. It was a large, low-roofed, purpose-built shop, with living accommodation at the rear. It was part of a row of other smaller shop units, one of which was a fish and chip shop, the others were boarded up. Mo Khan's shop had once been part of the Spar chain until he took it over to join the growing number of his shops scattered throughout Lancashire. They all opened from six until midnight. Tonight, even though there was a family crisis, the shop was open and trading.

Roscoe got out of the car and opened Naseema's door, scanning the area. Opposite the shop was a small grassed area with a children's playground. The swings had all been dismantled and only the frames remained, rather like the skeletons of dinosaurs. Beyond that was a curve of houses, quasi-semis, all council owned. A few were occupied, most were boarded up, others just burnt-out shells. Shoreside was not an estate people clamoured to live on; it was one of the poorest and most deprived in the region, if not the country. Unemployment was sky high, crime rife.

Roscoe felt uneasy. She knew the place was tense because of the Khan/Costain confrontation. Standing outside the shop she could almost taste the atmosphere. It was quiet – too quiet. She didn't like it, her instincts nagged at her.

Naseema got out followed by Saeed. Seymour opened his door, but Roscoe held the

90

top of it, preventing him from moving. 'Stay with the car, Dave, I won't be long.'

'Why?'

'Humour me, OK? There's something buzzing round here and I don't want to come back to a damaged motor. And don't fall asleep.'

Seymour looked round, puzzled, wondering what he had missed, but saw nothing. He resettled his broad posterior on the driver's seat, actually relieved he did not have to go into the Khans' home. He hated being surrounded by coloured people. He prayed he would not be given the job of family liaison officer.

Roscoe followed Naseema and Saeed inside the shop.

The family already knew and Roscoe found herself at the centre of a bereaved family at its most emotionally charged.

Mo Khan's widow was sobbing and wailing hysterically on the sofa, wringing her hands and beating her fists into cushions. Naseema immediately went to comfort her, while maintaining her own cool, cold, facade. Two of her sons were incandescent with rage. They paced the living room like Bengal tigers, muttering angrily, punching the air. A third son, the eldest, sat quietly on an armchair, watching the others while smoking a pungent cigarette. Then there was Saeed, the youngest, thrown into this vortex, a live wire, bursting with tension, vowing revenge.

91

All in all, a volatile mixture.

Much of what Roscoe heard was in Urdu. Some English was spoken obviously for her benefit. The talk was of retribution. Justice. Racism. Bloodshed. Death.

Roscoe knew she had to exercise some authority but it was difficult to know where to begin. She had to lay down the law, tell them to keep it cool, keep a lid on it, let the police do their job, make promises, reassure them ... for what good it would do. She picked on the brother seated in the armchair. He was the oldest and appeared to be most in control of himself.

The rain had stopped, but the car was still misted up on the inside. Bloody crappy police cars, Seymour thought and turned the fan heater up a couple of notches. The windscreen started to clear very slowly.

He leaned back. His right hand dropped to the side of the seat and fumbled with the recline knob. He turned it and the seat angled back a few degrees. Might as well be as comfortable as possible, he thought shuffling his bulk. He switched on the car radio and found a nice, jazzy station, pumping up the volume so he could hear it over the clatter of the de-mister.

He was pretty whacked. The long day and the recently devoured kebab was having a somnolent effect on him. His eyelids drooped heavily. He drifted into a light sleep and his chin sagged heavily onto his chest. A loud snore jarred him awake for a brief moment before his eyes clicked shut again. This time his chin fell gently. He was gone. A grunting sound came from somewhere in his nose as his breathing became heavy.

So he did not see them coming. He had no chance.

Mo Khan's eldest son was called Rafiq, almost thirty, now the head of the family and its various businesses. Roscoe managed to manoeuvre him away from his relatives, into the back of the shop behind the counter where she could speak to him alone.

The shop was quiet, only a couple of customers browsing. A young Asian girl was working the till and reading a magazine.

'I know what you're going to say,' Rafiq said before Jane Roscoe had a chance to begin. 'Don't take the law into your own hands. Let the police sort it out. I know, I know.' He dismissed her with a contemptuous wave. 'I also know that you are institutionally racist and do not care one bit about us.'

'That's not true,' Roscoe said defensively. 'I care and I will do my very best for you. I won't labour the point about the other things you said. You know full well there is a suspect for your father's murder. We're going to arrest him. So leave the justice to us, Rafiq. It's our job, not yours or your family's.'

'I hear what you say, Mrs Copper, but I don't know if I can hold my brothers back – or even if I want to. They are very angry. The

Costains have been at our throats ever since we came here and you have done nothing to protect us – and now this has happened. You cannot be too critical if we do take the law into our own hands, can you, lady?'

From the research Roscoe had done very recently into the Khan/Costain situation, Rafiq's version of the conflict between the two families was not entirely accurate. However, she didn't want to argue the toss now.

'We would be critical of anyone who takes the law into their own hands, under whatever circumstance, under whatever provocation. I'm asking you to give us enough time to sort this matter out. I don't want to have to come and arrest you or any of your family at a time of grief. Understand?'

Rafiq looked her up and down.

'I will do what I can for the moment,' he promised her lamely. She knew it was as good as she was going to get.

'Thank you. I will personally keep you informed of all our progress, once a day at the minimum.'

'Don't take too long about things,' Rafiq began, 'because if you do, this estate will burn—'

There was a series of small explosions outside the shop. Pop-pop-pop. Roscoe knew exactly what had caused them. Petrol bombs. It was a sound embedded into her psyche, a sound she had heard for the first time in 1981 when, as a probationer PC, she had been part of one of the many police support units sent to assist Merseyside police when the Toxteth area of Liverpool blew up into a major riot. She had heard the noise in anger several times since.

A wall of flame blew up against the shop front, followed by a buffeting surge of hot air.

Rafiq growled, 'It's already started.' To the girl on the till he shouted, 'In the back, now,' and jerked his thumb to emphasise the order.

He started toward the front door of the shop but halted after one stride when the door was kicked open and two youths with balaclavas pulled down over their faces burst in. Each carried a petrol bomb – a milk bottle half filled with fuel, oily burning rag stuffed down the neck. They only seemed to be bits of kids, Roscoe thought quickly. Couldn't be more than twelve or thirteen. But they looked evil, all in black. Terrifying. She could not help but draw a breath.

They raised the bottles. One screamed, 'Have these, you black twats.'

'Get down!' Roscoe shouted. She threw herself at Rafiq and dragged him to the floor behind the counter. As she moved she saw the petrol bombs arc through the air, spinning slowly, almost in slow motion, flames whipping round like a Catherine wheel.

The bombers scarpered, screaming glee-fully.

The bottles landed virtually simultaneously on the hard floor in front of the counter. Petrol and flames sprayed everywhere. Roscoe and Rafiq huddled down behind the counter. For a few moments the heat above them was intense. Tongues of orange flames licked across the counter top, then died back.

Roscoe could not stay down for long. Christ, she thought, what's happened to Dave?

Another explosion, this time a massive one, boomed outside.

Dave Seymour's eyes jumped open as the first three petrol bombs hit the wide paved area between where he sat in the car and the Khan's shop front. All three ignited with a powerful whoosh. He saw two youths kick the shop door open and enter, each holding a lighted petrol bomb.

Before he could open the car door, the front windscreen was smashed by someone wielding an iron bar. The side window was broken by another person, sending pieces of glass into his face and his clothing. Then the rear window went. There must have been a dozen of them surrounding the car, all brandishing iron bars, bats or chunks of wood, all wearing black hoods or masks.

Seymour's insides contracted and he knew he was in deep trouble.

One of them hurled a petrol bomb into the car through the hole in the windscreen. Seymour saw it coming and cowered away, but there was nowhere he could go, nothing he could do, it landed on his lap but did not smash.

Seymour had a moment of relief. Just a moment.

As he picked up the flaming bottle the lighted wick dropped out of the neck. Petrol gushed out over Seymour's thighs and groin. It ignited.

'Cop bastard! Cop bastard,' the people surrounding his car chanted mercilessly. There was laughter and triumph in their voices. 'Burn you bastard, burn!'

Seymour screamed horribly. He managed to open the door and fell out of the car onto his knees, desperately trying to bat out the flames with his bare hands. Where one flame went out, another came to life. Bigger. Hotter. Taking a better hold on his clothing, licking up his shirt front towards his face. 'Help me, help me,' he screamed.

No one did.

Somehow he got to his feet and staggered towards the shop.

'Cop bastard, cop bastard,' rang in his ears. 'Burn! Burn! Burn!'

Behind him more bombs smashed around the CID car. It went up in flames.

Roscoe had had enough petrol bombs thrown at her during the days when she did riot training to know not to be afraid of them. 'Petrol reception' the classes had been mis-called. But unlike the majority of the training she had done in the police, the lessons learned about petrol bombs had stuck with her – because they had been about self-preservation. They had taught her that if you kept your eyes on the bombs as they came towards you and made sure they didn't hit you on the head, they did not present too great a personal threat. They looked effective, frightened the living daylights out of people, made for good TV but, if treated with respect, they were not something to worry about too much.

Having walked through pools of blazing petrol during those training sessions – albeit kitted up with stout steel toe-capped boots, flame retardant overalls, protective masks and headgear – she knew it was quite feasible to walk through flames unscathed – if you were quick enough and didn't admire the country-side along the way. Although not exactly dressed for the part, she knew she had some-how to get through the flames and see what was happening to Dave Seymour.

'Call the fire brigade,' she instructed Rafiq before turning towards the flames and smoke on the other side of the counter. Thick black smoke was hanging just below the ceiling, beginning to fill the shop with its deadly vapours. She put a hand over her nose and mouth, protected her eyes with the other, took a deep breath of clean air and ran.

The fire tried to catch her as she leapt through it. She could feel incredible heat beneath the soles of her shoes and the flames shooting up her legs, underneath her skirt. It was only momentary. In a split second she was through the flames, emerging from them

98

like a phoenix. Unscathed.

Which could not be said for Dave Seymour as he hit the shop door, bursting it open and tumbling through, twisting and writhing. He was ablaze.

Seymour could not see anything that made any sense to him. His vision was a blur, an out-of-focus lens disorientating him. Neither could he hear anything. The chants behind him turned into an all-encompassing, rushing and booming noise, surrounding him completely, like being deep underwater. He could feel the fire. Burning him, frying him – from his belly to the underside of his chin.

He knew he was screaming, knew he was being burned alive.

Roscoe reacted without a second's thought or moment's hesitation. A surge of grade-A adrenaline sluiced into her system. She dived for Seymour instinctively thinking: Get him down, get him on the floor, smother the flames.

She grabbed one of his arms, but in his own blind panic he wrenched it away from her, lost his balance and crashed into a wire magazine display. He stayed on his feet and staggered down the main aisle of the shop, fresh produce on one side, tinned goods and hardware on the other. Still screaming, writhing, twisting.

'Dave!' Roscoe bellowed – to no effect. She lunged for him again and leapt onto his back, riding him, trying to over-balance him and take him down, put him to the floor. 'Get the fuck down!' she hissed through clenched teeth.

At the end of the aisle, he crashed into the chilled food display. Seymour fell over, but backwards, onto Roscoe who suddenly found herself trapped under his bulk.

The fire blazed up him. He screamed again.

Rafiq appeared from behind the counter, moving quickly through the last of the flames from the petrol bombs. He was holding a fire extinguisher which he directed at Seymour. Within seconds Seymour had been put out. Rafiq then turned what was left in the extinguisher onto the petrol bomb flames.

Roscoe heaved Seymour to one side and got shakily to her knees, looking down at the huge detective who lay there, semi-comatose, with severe burns all the way up his front. Her mouth sagged open with shock. The adrenaline left her system as quickly as it had entered. She felt sick, weak and dithery, needing a sugar boost.

Her hand went for her radio to call in for assistance. Before she could speak, every window in the shop was smashed, bricks, half-bricks, rocks, stones, flying through, sending glass showering everywhere. She instinctively ducked down and tried to cover the vulnerable Seymour as the missiles landed all around like meteors crashing in from outer space.

Five

The thrill had never gone for Henry Christie. Even approaching the twenty-five-year mark in his career had failed to diminish the excitement, the rush, the exhilaration of sitting in a cop car, all lights blazing, two-tones shrieking, driving with considered recklessness through traffic, shooting red lights, going the wrong direction up one-way streets, heading to some emergency or other. The emergency in this case being other cops needing assistance.

Henry had a slightly fixed, wonky grin slapped across his face as Dermot Byrne pushed the under-powered Vauxhall Astra at crazy breakneck speeds through the crowded streets of Blackpool. Henry's right foot instinctively pushed down on an imaginary brake pedal. His left hand clutched the broken arm rest on the door, steadying himself as the car lurched round corners, apparently on two wheels, and skidded out of the turn, the back end twitching on the wet roads. But Byrne handled the car with great expertise and experience, taking it all the way to its limits where possible, holding back when necessary. All the while he concentrated totally on the function of driving. Henry, while tense, was never in fear.

Henry handled the communications side of things.

Normally the radio channel was not on 'talk-through'. This meant that transmissions from patrols could only be heard by communications room and selected other receivers, such as the radio console in the inspectors' office, and not by other patrols. This enabled communications to keep tight control over radio traffic, which sometimes had a tendency to deteriorate when patrols could chat to one another without discipline. There were occasions when it was appropriate to override this and put talk-through on. This, Henry deemed, was one of those times, because he wanted to hear directly from the officers in trouble and not have to wait for their messages to be relayed by communications staff, efficient though they were.

'Tell patrols to maintain strict radio discipline,' he said into his personal radio, 'then put us on talk-through,' he instructed communications.

'Roger.' Communications transmitted the command and flicked the button.

The first voice they heard belonged to Jane Roscoe. For some unaccountable reason, Henry's heart tightened at the sound.

'...pinned down in Khan's shop. Must be well over thirty of them outside ... very well organised ... petrol bombs and bricks still coming. We need the fire brigade and an ambulance – Dave Seymour's been badly injured. Someone's going to die if we don't get out of here soon...'

Henry turned to Byrne. 'Can you make this thing go faster?' he demanded.

Byrne – focused on the driving – nodded. 'Yeah.' And miraculously, from somewhere deep down, the car speeded up.

Henry cut into Roscoe's radio transmission. 'Inspector Christie to DI Roscoe – keep your head down. We'll be with you very soon.'

'Thanks,' she breathed. Henry could feel the tension in her voice, and the relief, yet she still sounded very cool. Henry was impressed.

'Communications?' he said. 'Did you get that about the fire brigade and ambulance?'

'Onto them now.'

'Inspector Christie – be careful when you approach—' Her voice stopped abruptly. Henry heard a bang, some rustling and a heavy breath being expelled. Then a crash. 'Another petrol bomb,' Roscoe's voice came back. 'Yeah, Henry, watch yourself. This is a well-organised job, so do it right. I want to get out of here in one piece. Wouldn't be surprised if ambushes have been laid – scanners'll be in use too.'

'Thanks for that,' Henry acknowledged. She really was cool, telling him not to get into a position where he too would be trapped. 'Inspector to Blackpool,' Henry barked, getting well into the inspector mode now. He was aware that for the first time in months he was thinking clearly, buzzing and, perversely, enjoying himself. This was fun of the highest, gut-wrenching order.

'Inspector – go ahead.'

'If you haven't already got a log running for this – get one. Also inform the superintendent on cover if she doesn't already know, and deploy all patrols to an RV point on Preston New Road, junction Kentmere Drive. Ask them to meet me and PS Byrne there for further instructions, and tell them to be getting into their public-order gear just in case. No one is to drive onto Shoreside without my express permission – understood? If anyone is already there, tell them to withdraw to the RV point now! Pass the location of the RV point to the fire brigade and ambulance. Advise them not to go onto the estate without speaking to me first. Got all that?' Henry knew he had been speaking quickly, speaking as the thoughts tumbled through his mind. 'And also turn out the helicopter, please.'

'Roger,' the very in-control communications operator responded, taking charge of Henry's requests in the sort of smooth, un-hurried manner Henry could only dream of. 'And by the way,' the operator added, 'treble-nines coming in thick and fast from Shore-side residents now.'

'Received,' said Henry. 'Have I missed anything?' he asked Byrne quickly.

'Don't think so,' said Byrne. 'I take it we're not just going to pile onto the estate?'

'No, I have a plan.' Henry tapped his nose.

104

'Not a very cunning one, but a plan nonetheless.'

A section van, one armoured personnel carrier and two patrol cars were already at the RV point when Henry arrived with Byrne. The occupants were putting on their riot overalls.

Throughout the journey Henry had been glued to Roscoe's commentary of events unfolding in and around Khan's shop. The confidence in her voice began to waver as the situation grew worse. Fear crept into her words. Henry did not blame her for being afraid. In the same circumstances he would have been terrified.

Roscoe, the badly injured and now unconscious Seymour, and the Khan family were effectively pinned down in the shop and its living accommodation. To flee was not an option. The whole building was surrounded and leaving would have meant running straight into the mouth of the lion. To stay put and wait for help was only marginally the lesser of two evils. So far they had been lucky. The petrol bombs hadn't taken hold of the building properly, the sprinkler system in the shop was now working after a false start, but it was only a matter of time before fire beat water. She needed help – fast.

It was tempting for Henry and his troops to wade in, but he knew this could be a bad idea, making a crap situation worse because of lack of thought.

105

He was out of the car before the wheels stopped turning, gesturing for the officers – eight of them, including Constable Taylor, whom he had seen writing reports earlier – to gather quickly round him. They were eager to do something. Crack some heads. Save some lives.

The force helicopter, two minutes after he had asked for it, radioed to say it was en route from its base in nearby Warton. Henry gave them instructions, then concentrated on what he was going to say to Scale D for Death.

'You all know the situation: two of our colleagues are trapped by a mob in Mo Khan's shop. The Khan family are trapped in there too. It sounds like a very organised, big, nasty, orchestrated situation. That is why we're not just going to plough in without a plan and get the shite kicked out of us. We need to work as a unit: go in, effect a rescue, then get the hell out and take as little flak as possible. Nothing fancy. No confrontations. These people are dangerous and there's a good chance they'll be expecting us – so we need to be wary.' Henry drew breath.

Over the radio Jane Roscoe announced the arrival of yet another petrol bomb in the shop.

'Better get a move on, boss,' one of the PCs said agitatedly.

Henry nodded. 'You're not wrong. Now listen up – this is how it's going to be. I don't want any deviations, don't want any heroes. Now, what equipment do we have?'

106

The armoured personnel carrier crept onto the estate. Henry's guts tightened. His mouth went dry and popped open. 'Fuck,' he whispered to no one but himself. Every street light had now been smashed. Apart from house lights, the place was shrouded in absolute darkness. Most houses had their curtains drawn but in some windows, Henry could see terrified faces.

Anarchy had taken over the streets. It was his job to restore law and order.

The only time Henry had known anything remotely similar had been during the miners' strike of 1984. He had vivid memories of driving through mining villages at the dead of night, always in fear of being attacked.

He glanced at Byrne, driving the carrier; then over his shoulder at the eight constables, all in their public-order gear: helmets on, visors down, all grim-faced and serious. No banter. At the rear of the van, the six-foot-high riot shields were stacked up like dominoes, ready for rapid deployment. In the footwell in front of him, Henry had a short shield ready.

Henry, too, was now in his public-order gear, having hopped and pulled himself into it after briefing his officers.

The heavy overalls were making him sweat. The flame-retardant material was as thick as cardboard and the garment, pulled on over his normal uniform, was not designed for comfort. Beads of sweat trundled one after the other down his forehead and dripped into his eyes, making him blink.

'You'll need to keep your wits about you,' Henry shouted back to the officers. 'It'll be loud and disorientating – so be ready and keep your cool.'

He was about to say more as Byrne turned a corner to find the road immediately ahead of them blocked by two cars which had been rolled onto their sides. Behind the cars was a bunch of youths, all wearing ski-masks or balaclavas. Henry quickly estimated there were a dozen of them. All youngsters, some as young as ten years old.

'Back out of here now,' he said quickly to Byrne, who was already ahead of him – but could not seem to be able to ram the gear lever into reverse.

'Shit, shit, shit,' said the sergeant, with each word trying to hit the gear.

'Come on,' Henry encouraged him. Then he shouted: 'Missiles!'

A wave of lighted petrol bombs flashed over from the line of youths and smashed on and around the carrier.

Henry ducked instinctively when one of the milk bottles burst against the metal grille pulled down over the windscreen petrol erupted in flames. The intense heat was immediate and breathtaking.

'Get us out of here!' Henry growled to Byrne.

The sergeant's face was grim as he tried repeatedly to get reverse.

'Try using the clutch,' one of the PCs in the back quipped. This brought nervous laughter.

'Thanks for that,' Byrne said. With an ear-crunching grating of metal on metal, the syncromesh yielded and the gear went in.

A cheer went up from the rear.

Using only his side mirrors as a guide, Byrne gunned the carrier backwards, unconcerned that anyone could be behind. If they were, it was tough. They wouldn't be innocent bystanders. The big bus slewed from side to side as a hail of stones, bricks, bottles and lumps of wood and metal followed the petrol bombs, clattering on the bonnet and roof like debris from a twister. Inside the carrier, the sound reverberated, amplified a hundred times.

Shouts of fear and excitement came from the officers. Henry remained silent, gripping the dashboard to steady himself.

Byrne reversed expertly around the corner, out of the line of fire, trying desperately to keep control of the vehicle which pitched and swayed alarmingly at speed in reverse. The lighted petrol on the windscreen burned out quickly.

Byrne whipped the steering wheel down and executed a one-eighty-degree turn, completely about-facing the carrier, crashing up onto the kerb as he did so, miraculously keeping the engine going, revving it to screaming point. He accelerated away from the ambush site. In his rear-view mirror he saw the small gang of rioters spill out, throwing anything they could get their grubby hands on at the retreating police van.

'Well done,' Henry said. He asked everyone if they were all right. No one said they weren't. 'Right – fuck this for a game of soldiers. I think we've pissed about long enough,' he said so everyone could hear. 'We need to get to that shop now, otherwise it'll be too late – everyone agree?'

The response was emphatic – if muted by the visors in front of everybody's faces. Yes, they agreed.

'OK, Dermot – swing this beast round and let's cut through Osmond Avenue. No caution this time. Blue lights just as we get there, sirens too.'

'Right,' Byrne said through his tightly clenched jaw.

Henry put his radio near his mouth. 'Oscar November 21 receiving? Inspector to Oscar November 21, are you in position?'

It would have to be done very quickly. No messing. No delays. Because if it went wrong there would be hell to pay, maybe lives lost.

Henry deleted all negative thoughts from his mind. This was going to work. He would make damned sure it would.

The carrier veered into sight of Khan's shop.

Henry took in the crowd surrounding the place. There seemed to be hundreds there at first glance – maybe not at second, but still a lot. A car burned brightly outside the shop. It was the CID car.

'Oscar November 21 – go now,' Henry said, his voice cool and controlled reflecting his inner self. He had moved on from fear and from excitement. He was tense, of that there was no doubt, the adrenaline was rushing into his system like fuel injection into a sports car – just the right amount for perfect performance. But what he felt now was cold controlled anger.

'Oscar November 21 – we're there now,' came the response from the force helicopter.

Henry received the message. He flicked the switch for the blue lights and the two-tones.

Above them, from out of the black night sky, like some massive avenging insect, the helicopter swooped down, deceptively low and ear-shatteringly loud. It did an impressive fly past just feet above the heads of the rioters, spiralled spectacularly through a tight circle and came back to hover over Khan's shop. The powerful night-sun searchlight slung underneath the helicopter came on, swathing the scene below with incredible brightness.

'Foot down,' Henry commanded Byrne. The carrier hurtled towards the backs of the rioters, horns blaring and Henry shouting through the public-address system, volume turned up high, deliberately distorted, adding to the clatter of the helicopter. 'Clear the streets,' he hollered. 'This is the police. You are requested to clear the streets. Anyone remaining will be arrested. I repeat, if you do

111

not disperse, you will be arrested.'

He was going for the psychological upper hand which he knew, if successful, would only be short lived. He was hoping this assault on the senses of the rioters would give him the window of opportunity he needed to achieve his goal.

It worked.

Overawed and disorientated by the helicopter above, threatened by the reckless approach of the personnel carrier at ground level, the rioters ran like rats down a sewer. They scrambled away from the lights, shocked and surprised, maybe frightened, by the approach. Suddenly there was a way through for the carrier to the shop front. Byrne, gripping the steering wheel tightly, concentrating hard, powered the heavy machine through the clearing. He mounted the pavement with a back-jarring, head-thumping thud, and skidded to a halt at an angle across the shop entrance.

'Out now,' Henry roared. 'Move it, move it.' He slammed down his visor.

The side door of the van sprang open. The first officer leapt out. He was handed one of the riot shields which he hooked onto his left forearm. He ran to the back of the van and took up his position. He was immediately joined by three more of his colleagues who slammed their shields down – smack-smack-smack – next to his, all edge to edge. The idea was to provide some protection to the officers who had been detailed to enter the shop.

112

Henry was using his short shield which was designed to give more manoeuvrability in his supervisory role. He ensured the long-shield party were deployed to best advantage – shouting muffled orders at them through his visor and checking to ensure they all understood their role. Making himself heard was extremely difficult with the helicopter directly above. He knew this was one of the drawbacks to his plan. When satisfied, he turned to the four others left in the van and beckoned them to follow him into the shop.

Inside was a blackened, smoky mess, but no flames were burning seriously. Thick smoke clung to the ceiling like a thunder cloud and all the officers had to keep their heads low in order to see anything. Even then it was difficult because all the lighting in the shop had blown. Two of the officers were equipped with dragon lights – big, powerful torches. The beams criss-crossed each other like Second World War searchlights in the night sky.

'Jane? Where are you? It's me, Henry.'

'Here – over here,' she called out.

Henry moved towards the origin of the sound and with his merry band of four ran down the aisle to her. They found her kneeling with Dave Seymour's head resting in her lap, her hands gently holding him. The dragon lights shone briefly into her face, making her squint.

Henry dropped onto one knee beside Seymour. He pushed his visor up. Seymour did

113

not look good.

'He needs a hospital – now,' Roscoe said urgently.

'There's an ambulance waiting on the edge of the estate,' Henry told her. His eyes surveyed her face. It was smoke-blackened. 'But we've got to get him there first. Are you OK?' he asked quickly.

'Smoke damaged, otherwise saleable.' She managed a grin.

He nodded. 'Right,' he addressed his troops, 'you two without torches help me lift Dave into the carrier. Jane – you'll have to give us a hand too,' he said apologetically. 'He's not exactly a featherweight.'

'No problem.'

'Once he's in the carrier we're going to have to get the Khans out to safety as well.' Henry's voice was bleak. 'And we're gonna have to move like shit off a shovel – 'cos they'll be back for more very soon and we're a nice new target.' Henry laid his shield down and wondered which bit of Dave Seymour he was going to have to lift.

Following behind the two torch-bearing cops, Henry, Roscoe and the other two lifted and half-dragged Seymour through the shop. The process wasn't doing him much good, but under the circumstances it was the best they could do. He was immensely heavy: twenty stones if he was a pound, Henry guessed, twenty stones of virtually, but not quite, dead weight.

At the shop door they eased him down and

114

paused to take a breath.

Henry checked outside. Byrne was still at the wheel of the carrier. He gave Henry a thumbs-up. The four shields were still in position, the helicopter hovering nearby. It seemed to be flushing out some miscreants hiding behind some wheelie-bins. A tinge of annoyance pricked Henry. He had previously told the crew that he wanted them to stay right over the shop, not go away doing their own thing. Still, he shrugged mentally, no harm done and there was no time to remonstrate. With a 'One, two, three – lift', they heaved Seymour fairly smoothly from the shop and deposited him in the back of the carrier, laying him out between the seats. His breathing was laboured.

'Hold on there, pal,' Henry told him before jumping out of the van and leading his officers back into the shop to liberate the Khan family from their burnt-out shop and home.

This went smoothly and without argument until only Rafiq was left. He stopped at the shop doorway. 'I need to lock up,' he insisted. He turned to Henry. 'And I expect you to keep it protected.'

Henry did not respond but could not keep an expression of annoyance off his face and he and Rafiq locked eyes for a few tense moments as they had often done at past encounters.

Rafiq turned to the door and inserted the key.

'Boss!' one of the PCs shouted at Henry from the shield line. 'They're coming out of the woodwork.'

Henry went up onto his toes and peered over the shields. He could see indistinct shapes moving in the darkness. It was like a camp surrounded by a pack of lions. 'OK, we'll be out of this in a minute.'

Rafiq finished locking the door. He dived into the carrier.

Henry yelled at the shield party. 'Back in the van – now!'

With relief they lifted their shields, peeled back from their line and began to load themselves into the carrier, handing their shields in ahead of themselves until there was just one officer and Henry to climb in. Henry was not going to board until the last man was safe.

Then – wham! Something fell from above and the last officer went down with a scream as a microwave oven slammed down onto his shoulder.

'Jesus!' Henry cowered down, raising his short shield over himself and the fallen man. Up on the edge of the roof of the shop he could see figures moving about. While the helicopter had been distracted away from the shop, other rioters had sneaked around the back of the shop and climbed onto the low roof armed with various missiles and got into a position over the front door from where they could bombard the police below.

Several empty plastic crates were hurled

down. Henry fended them off, surprised at how heavy they were. 'November 21,' he bellowed into his radio, 'get back over the shop. Get the roof cleared. We're under attack.'

He saw a beer barrel being raised. Empty or not, this was going to hurt – or kill.

'Christ – my fucking shoulder,' the injured officer moaned.

Henry braced himself for the impact, his left arm holding the shield above him and the prostrate man. He knew it offered little real protection.

The helicopter swung back and lit up the whole area, swooping down over the roof. The rioters dropped the barrel over the edge and it bounced harmlessly two feet away from Henry. Moments later he and the injured officer had been grabbed and yanked into the carrier. Byrne gunned the vehicle away before the side door was closed properly.

Henry got his breath, steadying himself. He eased his helmet off and ran his sleeve over his dirty, sweat-streaked forehead, blowing out his cheeks. He looked round at everyone crammed in there: eight constables who had worked together superbly; the Khan family, no doubt ungrateful but safe; Dave Seymour and Jane Roscoe.

He wanted to have a little victorious smile, but events ensured he was not allowed to savour the moment.

'I think he's stopped breathing,' Roscoe said.

'You do the heart,' he said to Roscoe and, bravely, 'I'll do the lungs.'

He held out his helmet for someone to take, then stepped over Seymour and squeezed down between some seats so that he was at right angles to the man's head. He glanced at Roscoe. She was almost directly opposite him, but had skewed her body so that she was in a position to start pumping Seymour's chest. Both of them were in very tight, restricted positions with little or no room to move.

Henry felt for a pulse in Seymour's chubby neck. God, it was hard to tell in the circumstances. His fingers pressed to the side of the windpipe did not detect anything.

'No pulse.' He shook his head at Roscoe.

The carrier rolled sideways wildly as Byrne took it round a sharp corner and crunched the gears again. Henry lost his balance and fell forwards, the crown of his head clashing with Roscoe's cheek.

'Shit!' he yelled in Byrne's direction, a sore head now compounding the situation.

'Soreee,' Byrne apologised.

Henry rubbed his head, Roscoe rubbed her cheek.

'OK – go for it,' he told her.

Henry watched her move into action, counting herself in. Immediately she began heart massage, one hand on top of the other. 'One ... two ... three...' she intoned, leaning heavily into the task, putting her whole weight behind it. She stopped. 'Now you.'

118

To be honest, Henry was not looking forward to this moment: mouth to mouth with Dave Seymour was not a prospect to be savoured at the best of times, although he did remember once snogging him at a CID party years ago. He bent his head over the detective's face and tilted the big man's head right back to open up the air passage. He closed the finger and thumb of his right hand over Seymour's nostrils, clipping them tight shut and held open Seymour's mouth with the other hand. Henry opened his own mouth, inhaled, and clamped it over Dave Seymour's, while fighting back the urge to retch; ensuring there was an airtight seal, he blew into his mouth.

From his position, hidden away from the prying eyes of the world, secreted in a way in which no one would ever be able to discover him, David Gill had watched the proceedings take place in and around Mo Khan's shop. In fact he had been so close to the action that he could have made things happen. But he held back. That wasn't his role. Others had been tasked to do the donkey-work. Gill did not need to get involved.

All the while it was happening there had been that smug look of superiority on his face as he watched the cops running round like headless chickens, then their fancy idea of using the helicopter to scare the shit out of the rioters.

In fact Gill quite admired that touch. It had

119

given them an advantage they would not have had otherwise and they had used it well. It had given them the chance to rescue the Asian family, which wasn't what Gill had wanted at all. He had planned for them to be slain, burned to death in their shop which they had bought from under the noses of white men. Their deaths would have been true justice, but maybe that had been a little too ambitious and maybe it was to his advantage that they stayed alive. It kept the embers of unrest aglow. It gave a focus. Yes, Gill thought. Embers which in the very near future would have more petrol thrown on them.

All in all, a good start to the campaign.

David Gill was pleased.

TUESDAY

Six

Henry Christie checked his watch under the dim glow provided by the interior light above the rear-view mirror. He yawned widely at the same time and realised he had not actually taken cognisance of the time, so he did a double-take and exclaimed, 'Bloody hell!'

It was ten past midnight. Already. 'Doesn't time fly when you're enjoying yourself?' he asked no one in particular.

Dermot Byrne nodded agreement and yawned himself, set off by Henry. 'Must be catching.' He shook his head and rubbed his eyes.

They were still in the armoured personnel carrier, Henry and Byrne up front, two constables in the back, pretty much flaked out from the chasing around they had been doing for the last few hours. They were parked on the outskirts of the Shoreside estate.

As best he could in the cramped conditions, Henry stretched his aching muscles and limbs. Suddenly he too was very weary. He needed a shot of something. He was very aware that he had had enough of wearing his cumbersome riot gear, wanted to get out of it, shower and get into a nice clean uniform.

'I'm fucked,' he admitted. 'Need my bed ... any bed, actually.'

'First night's always the hardest,' Byrne said.

'Yeah, I vaguely remember that being so.' He stifled the next yawn with some difficulty. 'Let's take a sweep round the estate, Dermot,' he said, 'and let's start pulling patrols in for refreshments. Things seem to have quietened down somewhat.'

The engine had been ticking over so Byrne sat up and crawled onto the estate while relaying terse instructions via his radio to the patrols, allowing some to stand down for breaks while ensuring a very visible presence remained on the estate. The latter point was purposely laboured because it had been obvious from the shenanigans of the past few hours that the disturbances on Shoreside were being skilfully co-ordinated by people equipped with scanners tuned to the police frequency. Byrne wanted the unwanted listeners to know the police would not be withdrawing.

Henry's blood pressure rose slightly as the carrier entered the areas which had earlier been hotspots. Now they were peaceful. Nothing had gone down for at least half an hour.

The streets were full of prowling police vehicles, mainly reinforcements drawn in from neighbouring divisions. Henry would soon have to decide whether or not to release them but he did not want to act in haste.

Probably keep them there another hour or so and if it all stayed cool, pull them out, say thanks and bye.

The estate was scarred by a night of rioting.

Four cars, including Dave Seymour's, had been burnt out, leaving shells of blackened and twisted metal, two of them overturned. The street lights were all out having been systematically smashed. Debris, consisting of bricks, stones, rocks from garden rockeries and broken bottles, was scattered all over the roads. A youth club made of Portakabins had been razed to the ground, but little damage had actually been caused to domestic properties. This made Henry think that the leaders of the riot had briefed their foot soldiers well and that the show had been well orchestrated. Something about the whole thing made him feel uncomfortable, but he kept his thoughts to himself for the time being.

And the police had had no real success. True they had been taken by surprise, but Henry had managed to bring in assistance pretty quickly and after a tough couple of hours of face-to-face confrontations, guerrilla-like skirmishes and running around like idiots, order had been restored. Or so it appeared. However, only two people had been locked up, both stupid juveniles out for the crack.

At least Mo Khan's shop was still standing, even though the destruction caused to the interior was considerable from smoke and fire damage. Four cops in a carrier were guarding the premises until a decision was made about the way forward. The Khan family had been taken safely to Blackburn where they owned a large house.

Byrne drove past the shop, stopping briefly to exchange a quick word with the officers detailed to protect it. They had seen nothing; it was peaceful, they reported. Byrne gave a quick wave and set off again, past Dave Seymour's burnt-out car which would soon have to be recovered and brought in for forensic examination.

'Seems to have died a death,' Byrne commented on the rioting.

'Yeah – let's go in.' Henry decided on this for purely selfish reasons. Since starting his shift he had not eaten or drunk anything and his body ached for sustenance. He looked over his shoulder and asked the two officers if they wanted to stop anywhere on the way to the station to pick anything up. Both blurted out the name of a well-known kebab shop which served the best in town and offered a police discount.

'Sounds good,' Henry said. Byrne turned away from the Khan shop and headed towards the main road. As he rounded a sharp right-hand bend they saw two people in the middle of the street, caught like rabbits in the glare of the powerful headlights, carrying a milk crate between them. The men stopped dead and Byrne slammed on the brakes.

These were not two milkmen on an early

morning delivery round. The ski masks covering their faces helped to establish this fact. Their black clothing and gloves were also a bit of a give-away for any bright cop, and the rags tucked into the necks of the bottles in the crate completed the picture.

They were two very guilty people carrying a stash of petrol bombs – about twenty-four of them.

Even before the carrier had lurched to a halt, Henry was opening his door, a shout of 'Stop – Police!' on his lips. The constables in the back were only a nano-second behind him.

The hypnotic effect of the headlights didn't last long and the two men dropped the crate with a crash and sprinted away in opposite directions. Very fast.

Henry knew this was an important one. Capturing at least one of these guys could lead to further information about who was behind the troubles and maybe to the persons responsible for attacking Dave Seymour.

As soon as he had seen them, Henry had locked onto the person nearest to him – and he was determined not to let the bastard get away. He hit the ground running, but his adversary was fast and lithe. Henry powered after the figure, driving himself hard despite his heavy clothing, lack of energy and general lack of fitness.

In his prime, many moons ago, Henry had been a passable rugby player and had possessed a sprint which could, on occasion, leave others standing. Back then he had been un-encumbered by heavy clothing and life-long excess and encroaching middle-age, but he wasn't going to let something like a two-ton pair of overalls and a predilection for lager stop him now. He imagined himself going for that great try in the sky, envisaged himself in rugby boots, shorts and shirt. Told himself he was tough, mean and very quick ... and that if he hadn't caught this villain within a hundred metres, he would call it quits. His arms pumped like pistons. His legs pushed and drove him.

The figure in front of him was moving like the wind. He dodged into one of the many alleys connecting one part of the estate to another by means of a double dog-legged passageway, one of those ideas which looked so good on an architect's jotter, but in reality was a superb place for drug dealers and muggers to loiter in.

Henry's ears pounded. As his heavy boots crashed to the ground, jarring his bones, his whole body rattled. Christ, this was hard work.

The figure ahead of him twisted round the first right-angled corner and disappeared from view.

He cursed under his breath. That was bad, losing sight of the toerag. As he ran, Henry's mind fast-forwarded to the trial, he could hear the sneer of the defence solicitor. 'Ahh, officer, so you lost sight of the person you were chasing? In that case how can you be a hundred per cent certain my client is actually the person you were pursuing?' Pause. 'You can't, can you?'

Henry had given identification evidence in so many trials that he knew the words off by heart.

He increased his pace and skidded round the same sharp bend, just in time to see his quarry disappear round the next corner. Out of sight – again.

Now his heart felt as though it was on the verge of bursting out of his chest like something from a horror movie; his lungs were stretched to their absolute limit, ready to pop. But he wasn't going to give this one up. He made one last surge as he came flying out of that second corner.

The man was barely ten feet ahead.

'Got you!' Henry shouted. He hadn't, but that didn't matter. He was going to collar the guy. 'Cunt!' he added for good measure. He was in the bag. Henry could feel it. A prisoner coming up.

Without warning the man stopped dead in his tracks, spun on his heels, a thick stick of some sort in his right hand. Henry could not tell for sure what it was exactly – except that it was swinging towards his head and he was running right into the blow. Henry's left forearm shot up in defence. The stick crashed down against his forearm. Like a matador, the felon pirouetted out of Henry's way as Henry stumbled past, driven on by his own propulsion.

The blow hurt his arm, but he had managed to glance off most of the force of it.

He was still on that imaginary rugby pitch. Wrong footed by an opponent, but recovering instantly. He veered round sharply and launched himself, low and hard, head tucked into his chest, anticipating and ducking in under the second intended blow which swished harmlessly less than an inch above his head. He slammed himself into the man's lower abdomen with all the power and violence he could muster, colliding hard with the masked figure.

Henry had expected to come into contact with something firmer, more resilient, more muscled. Instead he was amazed to find out how easy it was to bowl the figure over; there seemed to be very little weight in the body mass. Even so, Henry was remorseless, driving the man to the ground, forcing all the wind out of his diaphragm, while reaching out for the hand which held the stick, grabbing it, cutting his fingernails into the narrow wrist and whacking the hand onto the ground, ensuring the weapon was released.

Even as Henry grappled with the masked figure something did not seem right. The realisation dawned on him that he was fighting a woman. Her free hand went for his face and tried to gouge lines down his cheek with her fingernails.

Henry caught the hand and pinned it down.

She wriggled, twisted and bucked underneath him. Henry took his time. His weight

130

moved over her, straddling her chest, never letting go or losing concentration, a smile of triumph on his face, which was probably lost to her in the darkness.

Then his colleagues burst round the corner onto the scene. The chase was over.

Though manhandled by three burly cops and in handcuffs, this did not prevent the woman from fighting and struggling all the way back to the personnel carrier. The gestures were futile but she obviously believed they had to be made. Allegations were already being screamed about police brutality and violation of human rights.

Once inside the carrier the struggle against the oppressive regime continued. Eventually, his patience running low, Henry ordered his men to lay her out on the floor and sit on her. He flicked on the interior lights illuminating the inside of the vehicle brightly.

He reached for the top of her ski mask and with a flourish – 'Da-daah!' – something he later regretted because it was unprofessional, he yanked the mask off and revealed her face to the world.

The fight went out of her as though the mask somehow gave her courage. Now exposed, she was weak and vulnerable. She glared defiantly at Henry. A wild cat cornered.

Rings were in her nostrils, eyebrows, lips; studs were in her ears. Her hair was bright red with a green diagonal flash across it. The expression on her face reminded Henry of one of Mel Gibson's *Lethal Weapon* looks. Mad and bad.

Before Henry could utter a word, all the personal radios blared out in unison. 'Inspector Christie receiving?'

Henry turned away and said, 'Go ahead.' There was a certain amount of trepidation in his voice, having recognised the less than sweet tones of the person calling him.

'ACC Fanshaw-Bayley here,' came the clipped, no-nonsense tone. 'Come in and see me immediately, Inspector.'

No 'please', no politeness. Just arrogance of rank. Henry hated him.

'Roger,' he responded pleasantly, wondering what the bastard wanted.

On the way back to the station Henry found himself chewing his thumbnail, biting little pieces off and spitting them off the tip of his tongue. When he realised he was doing this he ceased immediately and sat upright rather sheepishly. He knew exactly why he was doing it: it was the thought of coming face to face with Robert Fanshaw-Bayley, ACC (Operations), referred to widely as FB by most people. He was a small, bull-like man who had spent his entire career with Lancashire Constabulary which was quite exceptional in modern times when officers of that rank usually flitted about like butterflies from force to force. No other force would bloody well have him, Henry thought. Who would wish to take on someone who combined the management styles of Hitler and Genghis Khan with a hint of Stalin?

The relationship between Henry and FB went back a long way. It had never been a smooth association because of the ruthless way in which FB had often used Henry's skills in situations which had almost cost Henry his life. Henry had always come up trumps for FB in terms of results but with hardly ever a word of gratitude from the higher-ranking officer.

Yeah ... Henry had always done the business and this was how he had been repaid: booted off CID, dumped into uniform. Instinctively Henry glanced down at the public-order gear he was wearing and took stock of how he was feeling physically. In his steel toe-capped boots his feet were swollen and the boots were now tight and chafing. Somewhere down beneath his right big toe a lovely blister had blossomed. His legs were jittery and weak and he was experiencing a great deal of pain from the two physical confrontations he'd had that evening. Muscles not used in many a month had been brought speedily out of semi-retirement to do things alien to them. A dullish throb pounded remorselessly in his head over the bridge of his nose. In all, he felt like shit.

So thanks a bunch, FB. Thanks a bundle for transferring me from the refined, laid-back, super-cool calm of the role of detective inspector and putting me head first into this God-forsaken mother of a job. Two fights, one riot, arson, an officer critically injured, another slashed open with a Stanley knife. Henry was more used to picking up the pieces, not being there when things were being smashed.

Instead of biting his nails, he ground his teeth, ensuring his headache went up a few more notches on the Richter scale.

The transfer to uniform duties had come out of the blue.

Henry had been off sick for the best part of two months, stressed up to the eyeballs, trying to sort his head out and get his life into some sort of order after almost a year of false starts. He'd been to see his tame GP in the middle of the previous week. With reservations, Henry had said he was feeling better, needed to get back to work, needed something to occupy his time. Yes, I am thinking straight, he'd answered the doctor's question. Sleep was OK-ish. Still can't shake off the nightmare, but it was getting less frequent. I don't snap at everybody all the time now, I'm even coming to terms with being divorced, he'd told him. (That, Henry admitted, had been a very difficult thing to say out loud: 'My ex-wife.' It was the first time he had ever actually voiced the phrase. It had felt very uncomfortable coming off his tongue. My ex-wife! Christ!) Blood pressure's down. Had a few counselling sessions. Haven't drunk a drop for ... well, three days. Yep, I'm as right as rain.

The doctor had looked at Henry in disbelief. Eventually he had sighed and relented. 'I'll sign you back to start next Monday.'

Oh my God, Henry had thought desperately on leaving the health centre, clutching the doctor's note. What have I done?

With a great deal of trepidation he had phoned his detective chief inspector to announce his imminent return to work. He should have suspected something was not quite right when he became aware of the hesitation in his supervisor's voice. He had not seemed comfortable talking to Henry, had been evasive, extremely vague and noncommittal when it came to answering questions, and it had only been when he had told Henry that Fanshaw-Bayley wanted to see him that the alarm bells had clanged in Henry's brain.

FB? Why the hell would Fanshaw-Bayley want to talk to him?

'Dunno.' The chief inspector had responded sheepishly to the question.

'OK – see you Monday then,' Henry had said cheerfully.

'Yeah.' The relief at having the conversation over had been apparent even in that short, single syllable.

Henry had hung up thoughtfully. Something just not right.

After a few deep breaths he had phoned headquarters and asked to be put through to FB. He had not expected to be connected, because people at that level are secretary-protected, so it was no surprise when Lucy,

135

FB's newish secretary, had come on the line. What was of greater astonishment was that she had immediately put him through to FB who spoke in a particularly fawning, falsely caring tone.

'Henry? How are you? It's so good of you to call. You must be feeling better – coming back Monday. That's fantastic. Really sorry I haven't had any chance to speak to you while you were off ... busy, y'know. Anyway, I do need to have a word with you. I'd love to pop over and have a chat, but I'm tied up all day in meetings with just one window. How about three p.m. for fifteen minutes? Can you make it? Splendid. Look forward to seeing you.' Clunk. Conversation concluded.

Henry had been left holding a dead phone which had given off bad vibes.

He had made it to headquarters with ten minutes to spare, driving Fiona's car in through the gates and parking in one of the visitors' bays outside the front doors of the building. He looked across the rugby pitch and even now, the grass was still charred where the helicopter had exploded.

Lucy let him wait in her office and covertly Henry watched her working. She was pretty and seemed very efficient.

A few people whom Henry knew either by sight or personally trailed in and out of FB's inner sanctum, often referred to as the burial chamber. A couple of times he caught the dulcet tones of FB's raised voice coming through the panelled door. Each time the

136

person who had gone in to see FB had come out shortly after, tail between legs, very pale-looking, eyes fixed firmly downwards. FB was known as the constabulary hatchet man with good reason. Today seemed to be one of his 'people days'.

Lucy had looked up from her work and smiled reassuringly. 'He's running a little late, I'm afraid,' she said pointlessly. It was 3.30 p.m.

At four o'clock FB stuck his chubby face round his office door, nodded at Henry and apologised for his lateness.

Like a black widow spider to her unsuspecting husband, FB beckoned him in with a crooked finger and directed him through the office to a chair by means of digital gestures.

The ACC sat down slowly behind his expansive and very neat desk which had a large clean blotter on it – no spilled blood, Henry noticed – and an in-tray and an out-tray, both empty. This seating arrangement retained the psychological advantage for FB, who was physically much smaller than Henry. The ACC sat back, steepled his fingers and rested his chin on the spire, critically appraising the lower-ranking officer.

'You wanted to see me, sir,' Henry said, uncomfortable under the scrutiny.

'Yess,' FB said, drawing out the word. 'How are you feeling? You've really been through the ringer, haven't you?'

Henry acknowledged this with a slight tilt of the head and a raised eyebrow.

137

'And now you're coming back.'

Henry was not sure whether this was a question or not. To compromise he nodded. He found himself increasingly puzzled: FB didn't seem quite sure where to begin or what to say. Even so, Henry didn't liked being here: something bad was going to happen.

'On Monday,' FB said.

'Yes, sir. Back Monday. Can't wait to get stuck in again.' He almost punched the air with forced enthusiasm. 'Too much idle time, too much doing nothing – my head's cabbaged.'

FB's fingertips were still supporting his chin, his lips pursed. He took in a huge deep breath through flared nostrils and laid his hands flat on the desk, announcing via body language that things were about to be declared. Henry prepared himself.

'Right,' he said with the finality of decision, 'I've pussy-footed around too long already. Can't stand all this touchy-feely stuff. You know and I know I'm a man who likes to come to the point and I think we've known each other long enough to be able to say things straight to each other. You wouldn't want it any other way, would you?' Giving Henry no chance to respond he steamrollered on. 'I've looked very closely at what's happened to you over the last few months, then even further back over the last four or five years. You've had to deal with some very high-profile stuff, some dangerous and messy stuff too. And this came to a head for you after

138

Danny Furness died – and the result was that you had a nervous breakdown – a good and proper one.'

Henry stiffened. His mouth dried up and his poor heart began to pound. This felt like the overture to an ill-health pension. The bastard was going to get rid of him. Henry tried to speak but nothing came out.

'Between Danny getting killed and you going off sick, your work suffered dramatically, I'm sure you'd agree. To be honest, Henry, your performance was a shambles. The whole of Blackpool CID suffered because of you.'

Henry rolled back in his chair, stunned. This was the first time anyone had ever said that to him – that he could recall. So, FB, just say what you mean, don't mince your words.

'Detections plummeted, discipline was non-existent, there was no management to speak of—'

'I was going through a bit of a rough patch,' Henry interrupted. He emphasised the word 'bit' and hoped he sounded reasonable, but was aware of a slightly hysterical edge to his voice.

FB instantly held up a hand to shut him up. 'Let me finish, and let me be brutally honest, Henry, something this force has been a little short of recently, honesty. The good running of the CID is my responsibility, as you know. The shit stops here, in other words.' He placed a hand on the left-hand side of his chest where he believed his heart to be. 'And

139

I'm not afraid to make hard decisions to keep the department running smoothly. I believe very firmly that, at the present time, you do not have the capability or the capacity within yourself to go straight back into your former role and operate a hundred per cent effectively, which is what I need – especially in Blackpool. Fourteen murders this year. Fourteen of the fuckers! I need people who are with it.' He clicked his fingers a few times while speaking. 'On the ball.' Click. 'Operating slick and fast.' Click. 'And at the moment you don't fit the bill. So I've had to make a tough decision – even tougher because I know you and like you.'

Henry kept his mouth closed.

'I've decided to transfer you to another job and maybe in a few months' time we'll review the situation. Your replacement has already been in post for a few weeks.'

'Transfer to what?' For a moment Henry thought he might get something decent out of this. Major Crime Unit would be nice. The look on FB's face informed him otherwise.

'Uniform Inspector, Blackpool Central. As of Monday. 6 p.m. to 6 a.m. Reactive cover.'

The words sank slowly into Henry's skull.

'It'll give you time to settle in, find your feet again,' FB smarmed management bull.

Henry could not find a response. He almost went for the cliché, the line so beloved of the second-rate movie where the hero gets busted (usually for gung-ho antics as opposed to a stress-related sickness), the line, which in an

140

army flick, might be something like, 'It's the SAS or nothing, sah!'

However, Henry's reality was that he was a real person, a cop, a small cog in a big, lumbering organisation which rumbled on from day to day, decade to decade, oblivious to the movement of its staff. Even if it was 'CID or nothing', the police force would not bat an eyelid if he chose the 'nothing' option. It would get along just fine and dandy without him, as it had done for the last couple of months. He was, he realised, very dispensable.

'I haven't got any uniform that fits me any more,' he whined weakly.

'I thought of that,' FB said paternally. 'Clothing stores will be expecting you.'

FB glanced at his wall clock and gave Henry a look which said, meeting over. And that was it. Dirty deed done.

Henry had left the office immediately.

Henry could have delegated one of the PCs to present the woman prisoner to the custody officer. Just to be awkward and keep FB waiting, he chose to do the job himself.

The girl walked meekly from the carrier into custody reception, standing with head bowed in front of the desk, not looking directly at anyone, but muttering under her breath. Henry outlined the circumstances of the arrest and the amount of force he had used in effecting it. The custody sergeant dutifully recorded everything. When it came

141

to the girl's name, she refused to give it.

A female PC was brought in to search her and found nothing. Henry suggested that a strip search should be carried out because she could well have articles concealed on her which might be used to injure herself or others. After all, the stick she had whacked him with had been hidden somewhere, so there could be more secreted inside her clothing.

'You'd love to strip search me, wouldn't you, you bastard,' the girl said, sneering at Henry. For the first time she lifted her face to the light and Henry got a proper look at her. She had a harsh, white face, with an embittered expression which looked incapable of cracking into a smile.

'No, I don't think so.'

'What about you, then, lesbian bitch?' She nodded her head at the female officer.

'I'd rather search a decomposed body, luv,' the officer responded.

'Liar!'

The custody officer summoned another female officer to help out and they steered her away to an interview room.

Henry took the opportunity to ring communications and got them to tell FB that he would be delayed slightly because of the prisoner.

The strip search was carried out quickly and efficiently and the policewomen emerged with victorious smiles. They had found a packet of white powder secreted between the

cheeks of her bottom and a flick knife sello-
taped uncomfortably in her bra, underneath
her left breast. Her clothing was bundled up
for forensic examination and the girl, dressed
in a white paper suit was led away to the cells.

As Henry walked out of the custody office
towards the lift, Dermot Byrne was walking
out of the building.

'Good arrest that,' he said to Henry. 'You
ran like a whippet, boss.'

'Thanks.' Henry beamed, thinking: Whippet? More like a cheetah, actually.

Seven

The pleasure was short lived. It lasted all of
the four strides it took Henry to walk out of
the custody office and turn left into the dingy
corridor leading to the stairs and lift. It lasted
until he came face to face with ACC Fanshaw-Bayley who was storming down in the
opposite direction.

Henry came to an abrupt standstill. FB
scowled angrily at him, his mouth a tight line,
his eyes ablaze. The silence was short and
sour. Just long enough for Henry's Adam's
apple to rise and fall.

FB's voice, initially, was measured and
precise in its tone. 'When I ask a lower-ranking officer to come in and see me, I expect

143

him to drop everything and come in straight away.' Then he erupted, having kept his cool for long enough: 'I do not expect to be kept waiting for almost three-quarters of an hour! Do you understand, Inspector?'

The hairs on the back of Henry's neck crawled like a mass of insects on his skin. He could feel redness creeping up under his collar. His nostrils dilated. He was aware that Dermot Byrne was now standing in the corridor behind him, witnessing this very public dressing down. He managed to keep his voice controlled. 'I understand.' However, he could not manage to add a respectful 'sir'.

'I am not fucking accustomed–' FB continued with the tirade, seeming not to have heard Henry – 'to having lower-ranking officers taking the piss out of me. I've a bloody good mind to put you on paper for insubordination.'

'Could we possibly do this elsewhere?' Henry asked mildly. To say the least, it was very poor management practice to bollock people in front of others.

'I'll decide where and when I speak to you,' FB raged at this insolent suggestion. His face was crimson. He was trembling. In passing, Henry half-prayed that FB's heart would explode, but realised it was unlikely, and he had no desire to give the man the kiss of life.

Henry shook his head. 'I'll be in my office,' he said stiffly, 'and you can speak to me there if you wish – but I will not be spoken to by anyone like this in a corridor with other

144

people watching. It's embarrassing – and not just for them.' He brushed roughly past the smaller, rounder, man before another word could be uttered, and bounded up the stairs three at a time. He was on the ground floor before FB could formulate a response.

He virtually booted open the inspectors' office door. It crashed back on its hinges, smashing against the cabinets behind it. Henry stormed in and slammed the door shut behind him.

'I do not have to put up with this kinda crap,' he said through his teeth and threw his heavy leather public-order gloves across the room.

Slumping into his chair, he began to unfasten his boots, drawing out the long laces, muttering angrily at the same time. 'I do not have to do this, for Christ's sake. I don't have to put up with the likes of him.' He yanked the boot off and threw it against a locker. It stuck for a moment, then thudded to the floor like an injured crow. He started to untie his other boot and by the time it was unfastened, much of his annoyance had dissipated. He removed the boot slowly and lobbed it gently across the room where it fell against its companion.

Henry stood up and began to peel off his outer layer of clothing: the public-order overalls which he rolled up and placed on the desk. The uniform underneath was now even more creased than when he had initially put it on. The white shirt was grubby and sweat streaked around the collar and cuffs.

'Shit,' he said, sitting down and putting his elbows on the desk. He dropped his head into his hands, intending to spend some quality time feeling sorry for himself.

The office door inched open. Henry looked up, wiping his grimy face, expecting the row with FB to continue. But it was Dermot Byrne bearing a mug of steaming tea and Henry's now very scuffed uniform shoes which had been left in the carrier.

'Thought you might like these.'

'Thanks, Dermot.' He took a sip. Hot and life saving, it tasted superb.

Byrne placed the shoes neatly on the floor and stood on the opposite side of the desk, nervously realigning the correspondence trays so they were edge to edge with the desk as he spoke. 'If it's any consolation, I thought he was bang out of order ... if you don't mind me saying so. He had no right to speak to you like that.'

'He does and says what he wants and everybody's expected to roll with it. That's FB. It's just that I'm too long in the tooth now to be taking crap like that. There's nothing he can really do to me, so he can get stuffed.'

'He's an ungrateful bastard,' Byrne said with feeling.

'What do you mean?'

'Oh, nothing,' he said back-tracking sharply. 'Nothing. Anyway, you must be finding it hard, Henry, coming back to this – thrown in

146

at the deep end – and your job given to some-one else ... and a woman at that.'

A big sigh escaped Henry and he said, 'At least she seems capable.'

'Still a woman, though, doing a man's job.'

Henry shrugged. 'That's life – especially these days.'

Byrne shook his head, saddened by the state of affairs. 'I'm surprised FB gave your job to a woman, actually, after all the shit he's been through recently.' He was alluding to the Employment Tribunal FB had faced recently, accused of sexual harassment which had never been proved.

'Maybe that's exactly why he did it, to show he still believed in fairness and equality.'

Byrne opened his mouth to say something but the office door opened revealing FB. With a flick of the thumb he gestured for Byrne to get lost and leave the room. He came in, closed the door softly behind him, leaned against it, hooded eyes on Henry.

'You and me need to talk,' he said. 'I take your point about the corridor being an un-suitable place for a bollocking, but I still stick to what I said, even though I could have phrased it more ... eloquently. I am a very busy man this week and I don't have the time to be waiting around for anybody, let alone a bloody inspector.'

'And this inspector is also very busy – in case you hadn't noticed.' Henry was deter-mined to stand his ground. 'A whole bloody council estate has been hit by a riot, an officer

147

is lying critically injured in hospital and I've just arrested someone who was carrying petrol bombs who may, or may not, be the one who burned Dave Seymour. I've got one bloody big problem out there and it needs policing – sir.' Henry had decided he'd spent too many years bending over backwards and being used by FB and he'd had enough of it. 'And if you think that by bunging me back into uniform that life's a gas, then think again, boss. This is the sharp end and it hurts. CID is a piece of piss compared to this.'

FB had been pacing the office as Henry spoke. He stopped right in front of him and rocked on the balls of his feet while considering his response. He clicked his tongue. 'I'll let it go this once, but that's it. I'm bearing in mind your little "problems"–' he tweaked the first and second fingers of both hands to parenthesise the word – 'and that this is your first day back and you're struggling a bit. But that's it. Now there's no quarter. I've let you blow off steam and have a go and if you speak to me like that again in any forum, I'll cut you off at the knees. Understand?'

Henry said nothing.

'Good – what you've also got to realise is that I want everyone on the ball and responding because I'm under severe pressure this week – pressure that would just pop you – and I don't need anything else on top of it, like insubordinate subordinates. Get me? This is where it starts.'

148

This time Henry gave a curt nod.

'Good.' FB inhaled, suddenly aware he'd been holding his breath. 'Now come with me. I didn't ask you to come in to see me on a whim. There's people I need you to meet.'

He led Henry wordlessly through the corridors and into the lift. On the seventh floor Henry followed him into what had once been the officers' mess and was now a lounge for everyone to use, even the riff-raff. Except this week it had been commandeered by FB for use as his gold command post.

There were two men and a woman inside the room, sitting, talking quietly, drinking coffee. They looked up when FB and Henry came in.

'You already know Karl Donaldson,' FB said, waving dismissively towards the nearest and biggest of the three.

Donaldson got to his feet, smiling his big, toothy, Yank smile. His big paw of a hand shot out towards Henry, who was also beaming with surprise. They shook hands warmly. Henry felt a surge of pleasure as his eyes took in the vision of his buddy.

'Karl – good to see you.'

'And great t'see you, H.'

Donaldson was assigned to the FBI office in London where he was a legal attaché. He was no longer a field agent as such; his job was to act as liaison between US law enforcement and British and European police forces. Most of his work was taken up with the Metropolitan Police. He and Henry had met several

149

years earlier when they had been investigating links with American mob activity in the north of England. Since then their working relationship had continued sporadically, but their friendship had blossomed. Donaldson had even married a Lancashire policewoman now working in the Met. Henry and Donaldson had not actually seen or spoken to each other for some time due to the former retreating into a hermit-like shell during his bout of sickness.

It was Donaldson Henry had seen earlier that evening in FB's car as it had pulled away from the Imperial Hotel. He had intended to catch up with him then but the riot had slightly diverted him.

'What are you doing up here?' Henry asked him. Their warm handshake continued as the question was posed.

'That's what we're coming to,' FB interrupted brusquely, bringing the friendly greeting to a stony close. FB did not have a great deal of time for Donaldson who, for several reasons, tended to rub him up the wrong way. Henry and Donaldson completed their handshake. The American gave a sly wink. The feeling between the American and FB was mutual – he couldn't stand the prick.

The other man and woman in the room got to their feet.

FB indicated the woman with a pleasant, open-handed gesture, totally opposite to the crooked finger he had pointed at Donaldson. In fact his whole manner had changed as he

150

introduced her. He became slick and smooth, almost reptilian and very attentive. It was screamingly obvious he would have liked the opportunity to get into her panties.

'This,' he said sweetly, 'is Detective Super-intendent Andrea Makin, Met Special Branch. Andrea, this is Henry Christie, the night inspector.' As FB's eyes left her, they changed from languid pools of passion back to hard chunks of ice.

Makin smiled and proffered her hand, which Henry shook. He nodded pleasantly and gave her the once over – discreetly – but did not feel too sexist by his actions because she did exactly the same to him. Henry had only the most fleeting chance to take her in before returning to business, but he liked what he saw. A tall, rangy woman, with a lovely face – wide nose, full lips – and a body which he knew instinctively would be in tip-top shape under the practical, well-tailored suit she wore. He put her in her late thirties – the minimum she would have to be, realistically, to have achieved her rank, unless she was a high flier.

'Pleased to meet you.'

'Same here ma'am,' he responded formally, almost clicking his heels and kissing the back of her hand.

'And this,' FB said – a slight trace of annoy-ance in his voice because he had picked up the exchanged glances between Henry and Makin, 'is Basil Kramer, MP, who I'm sure you'll have heard of.'

Henry turned his attention to Kramer: early thirties, cool, suave, plausible and impeccably dressed. Henry had heard of him, as had most of the population of England and Wales. At least those who possessed a TV set.

Kramer was extremely rich, having inherited the family business in his late teens following the death of his father and then doubling its already massive profits within five years, making it a leading global clothing manufacturer. Then, bored with business, he turned with equally spectacular success to the murkier world of politics. He was a bachelor, reputed to have dated and bedded several high-profile, but legally available females. Even in Henry Christie's self-woven cocoon, he had heard of Basil Kramer. The man with the potential to go all the way. The young flier who, having been given the chance to fight a by-election three years earlier in a constituency which was blatantly anti-government had, by dint of his charm and endeavour, turned round a massive loss into a tiny majority and become an MP at the first attempt and in so doing he had become the prime minister's blue-eyed boy and chief spin-doctor into the bargain.

He had all the necessary attributes to go far: boyish good looks, charisma, credibility, a fine brain and, unusual in a politician, the ability to actually answer direct questions with apparently direct answers. If the press wanted a soundbite on any subject, Basil Kramer obliged. If the government needed spin, he provided it. And if Jeremy Paxman wanted a TV lashing, Kramer was the man to crack the whip.

He had become the PM's right-hand man. It was rumoured in hushed tones that it was Kramer, not the PM, who ran the country.

They shook hands. Kramer flashed Henry a winning, professional smile. 'Very pleased to meet you, Inspector. I know you've been extremely busy for the last few hours ... even just arrested someone, I hear?'

'That's right.'

'Good to know the streets of Blackpool are in such capable hands – at least this week, anyway.'

'Thanks.' Little did Kramer know that Henry's hands felt about as safe as a sieve.

'Very unfortunate about your colleague, Mr Seymour,' Kramer said, adopting the correctly sympathetic tone of voice.

Henry's heart crashed to his stomach. He spun to FB, his face betraying his anxiety.

FB held up two hands, palms out, in a calming gesture. 'No need to worry – he's still alive,' the ACC said quickly. 'Grab a coffee, Henry. Then take a seat.'

He did as bid, then sat in one of the low, comfortable leather chairs – remnants of the good life of the officers' mess – and sniffed the aroma of the coffee. It was real, filtered, very strong. He took a sip. The caffeine hit the spot immediately.

Henry looked expectantly at the four faces, waiting for one of them to begin.

'I think you should kick this off, Andrea,' FB said to Makin.

She cleared her throat. 'OK.' She sat down opposite Henry and leaned towards him. 'One of my specific responsibilities is to keep a check on the activities of extreme right-wing organisations and their members. It's pretty much my main job, actually, because they are increasingly active, mainly on the back of the Nazi movement in Germany which is very powerful at the moment. Their British counterparts do tend, on the whole, to be less inclined to violent action, even though they promote and support it through their literature and rallies. That said, they are a very organised and nasty bunch of individuals driven by a warped philosophy aimed primarily against black and Asian people, lesbians, gays, Jews – the last group probably inherited from the Germans.'

'Who are we talking about here?' Henry asked

'The Right Wingers, the National Socialist Party, the One True Race and Combat 18 among others – but those are the main players.'

Henry had heard of them all. Thoughts and images of them made the corners of his mouth twist down in distaste. It made him sad and angry that such groups could exist and thrive in Britain, but they did. They prospered.

'All thoroughly bad, but why are you telling me this?'

FB uttered a short 'Tch!' intimating that Henry should have automatically made the connection already. Actually he did have an idea where it was leading, but wanted someone else to say it. He kept his eyes firmly on Makin and pretended not to have heard FB.

'Conference week,' she said patiently.

Henry nodded.

'I've had an undercover cop working in some of these groups for the last three years – a pretty hairy job, as you can imagine,' Makin said. Henry could imagine. He had been undercover several times. It was not glorious or pleasant. It was an awful job which wrecked nerves and marriages. 'Two years ago there were big ructions in the top level of the Right Wingers. Their leaders fell out big style. The issue was that some of them believed the Wingers had become soft. Not enough direct action going on. All the right words being spouted, all the right-wing posturing being done, but the only thing that was happening in a co-ordinated manner was football violence, and even that was pretty poor. Some people in the Wingers wanted more – much more.'

'Such as?' Henry asked.

Makin cleared her throat and shifted uncomfortably. 'Forgive the use of the language, this is their terminology: they wanted Paki bashing; they wanted queer bashing; they wanted racial hatred and tension stirred up endlessly; they wanted Jews harassed – and the Wingers were not delivering. In essence, a

155

lot of the people wanted to provoke a race war.'

'So there was a split?' Henry suggested.

'Spot on.' Makin clicked her forefinger at Henry. 'And then for a short, intense period there was violence on the streets – but it was between themselves. Power struggles. Beatings, counter-beatings. The Right Wingers were in disarray.'

'It was in the newspapers,' FB chipped in.

Henry remembered reading it. Such a long time ago – two years.

He glanced at FB and then at Basil Kramer. The latter had not spoken or tried to say anything while Makin was speaking. Henry admired him very slightly for that – but only slightly, because he did not like politicians. However, he knew that most would have tried to hog the limelight, whatever the forum. His eyes returned to Makin who was massaging her face and yawning.

'Yeah, it hit the papers,' she said. 'Bit of a nine-day wonder as far as the media was concerned, but it threw up lots of useful intelligence for us because people were arrested left, right and centre for assault. Then it all went quiet. The Right Wingers regrouped and a splinter group began to get their own act together. They consisted of the more militant-minded ex-Wingers. They got their strategy together and from that came their plan and from the plan came action. They are well organised. Tight little cells all on a need-to-know basis. I put an undercover cop in, but it's been difficult to get much information.' She stopped.

Henry blinked dumbly, waiting for her to continue.

'So the information that's come to us is very late and caught us on the hop because things have already started to happen on the streets.'

'The disturbances you've been quelling tonight,' Kramer said.

'Yes.' FB grunted. 'They've already kicked off on our patch.'

Makin said, 'The information we have received is that this new splinter group has decided to use conference week to bring their cause to the streets and in their words – "Blackpool is gonna burn this week".'

Makin wrapped her fingers around her left knee and smiled at Henry.

Occasionally he had a flash of clarity, usually accompanied by extreme anger. Like for instance, just then, just for a moment. Everything up to that point had been a meaningless jumble. A whirl of multi-layered, slow-moving images, colours and pain. Nothing seemed to make any sense. Even his own voice had sounded strange to him: deep and inhuman as it responded to the distorted sounds coming from other people's mouths. It had been awful.

Suddenly it cleared. Like a gate opening. Like the beam of a searchlight in the night sky. Almost like the light of God.

And here he was, knowing exactly what had

happened over the last few hours, where he was, why he was here and how long he had been waiting for treatment, flanked by two burly uniformed cops in the A&E department of Blackpool Victoria Hospital.

'Hours!' he blurted unexpectedly, making both cops jump. He twisted round and tried to get to his feet. 'I've been waiting friggin' hours – yet that bastard cop got treated right away. All patched up and nice, the twat! Not me. Nooo! A second-class citizen, me. Kit Nevison – cunt and troublemaker. You don't care about me, do you? A junkie. Out of work. Out of fuckin' money!'

The two cops hauled him back down to his seat.

'Siddown y'tosser!'

Kit Nevison thudded back into the chair, feeling weak and ineffective. He knew he needed more dope, more booze ... a fag, even. Something to tide him over. He spoke pleadingly to one of the cops. 'True, though, innit? He got treated an' I didn't. Me? Nowt – fuckall except for this.' He indicated a temporary bandage on his head by means of his two hands which were bound by a rigid pair of handcuffs. 'I need stitches puttin' in.'

'You need a humane killer, Kit,' one officer said.

'Well fuck you,' Nevison hissed, feeling it all welling up again. He hacked up and spat into the officer's face. He stood up again, screaming, 'I want treatment, I want my fuckin' head doin' now! You set of twats...'

158

Everything became blurred again. Blood seemed to pump into his head, clouding his vision, thumping, thumping – he was aware of movement, aware of a tumbling sensation, heavy weights on him, some sort of slow-motion struggle, all clarity gone.

Basil Kramer adjusted his tie and got into his stride as soon as Makin finished.

'As you know, Inspector Christie,' he said, 'this government is one hundred per cent committed to the maintenance of law and order and ensuring equality for all, regardless of race, creed, religion, whatever. We have pumped literally millions into the police service and thousands of new recruits are due to come off the production line soon, so to speak. Lancashire has had a generous allocation of both money and bodies, so it would be extremely ironic if, during our conference, when all policing in Blackpool is of a high profile, the streets were taken over by petrol-bombing yobbos – wouldn't you agree? The press would have a field day.'

Henry waited for the punch line.

'This is where you come in,' FB cut in. Henry's face remained immobile. His eyes slid sideways to take in the ACC. 'You have to keep a lid on it all. Tighter than a duck's arse.'

Kramer recoiled visibly at the poetic turn of phrase. Makin allowed herself a minor smile. Donaldson shook his head sadly.

'My instructions are that you will police the streets hard.' FB slammed a fist into a palm.

'You will police high profile and you will take no shit from anyone. You will nip all trouble in the bud and crush it.' He tightened his fist.

'From all viewpoints,' Kramer said, 'if the streets are not seen to be peaceful during a week when the PM will be making one of his strongest pro-law speeches, we will all lose credibility.'

'What about the likelihood of public-order situations developing around the Winter Gardens, the conference venue? Surely that'll be the flashpoint?'

'Not your problem,' FB answered. 'The Police Support Units drafted in will deal with any disturbances during the day. You are the night shift and that's what we're interested in here. Keeping Blackpool quiet.'

'Are you expecting trouble like we had tonight all week?' Henry wanted to know.

'That's what the information suggests,' Makin said.

'Obviously I'll do what I can—' Henry began.

'No!' FB stopped him. 'You will do as instructed. This is not a half-hearted instruction, Henry. I want you to make some plans, go out there and do a job – OK?'

Henry tensed up. Could this be stress surfacing, he asked himself. What would the bastard do if I just got up from here and walked out, went back to my doctor and got signed off again? Just get some other poor sod to do it, most probably.

He stayed put, nodded tightly, cleared his
160

throat and said, 'I won't be able to do what you say with the staff I have. How many more officers are you going to give me?' He expected zero for an answer and was slightly wrong-footed when FB said, 'I've arranged for one full PSU to assist you from Blackburn until Friday morning, but you can't have any more. The budgets have all dried up. They'll be here from eight p.m. to four a.m. each night.'

Bloody hell – one PSU, Henry thought jubilantly, that was astounding. One inspector, three sergeants and eighteen constables, plus van drivers and the vans themselves. Better than a kick in the guts. He accepted with good grace.

'There is one thing nagging at the back of my mind, though,' he said slowly. The others waited for him to continue. 'And that's the trouble between the Khans and the Costains. I was led to believe it was a dispute between two families. How is it linked to what you've told me?' He looked at Makin for a response.

'Call me Andrea,' she said in a friendly but businesslike way. 'We think the whole thing was pre-planned.' She sighed and said, 'Joey Costain is a member of this new splinter group.'

Henry tried to keep a straight face but ended up guffawing.

'What's the joke?' FB demanded.

'Well, it's pretty rich, isn't it? I wouldn't mind so much if Joey could claim pure Anglo-Saxon heritage, but he's a gypsy

161

through and through. Even got the curly black hair to prove it – like a character from D. H. Lawrence.'

'It's a good point,' Makin conceded. 'The kind of group we're talking about hates anyone who doesn't fit in with their white-male criteria. Joey isn't a great thinker. My guess is that he's been used by the group as an in to the streets of Blackpool. Once they've used him, he could well be dumped.'

Henry nodded. 'Interesting. If you're right, then someone must know about the problems between the Khans and the Costains and the fact that there was trouble waiting to happen...' Henry's musings brought silence to the room. He glanced round at the four of them. 'There's the distinct possibility of loads more trouble. The Khans won't let things lie and the Costains are likely to keep pushing the white kids on the estate to keep rioting ... could be a bloody hectic week.' And suddenly twenty-one extra cops did not seem very many. Added to the few he had, who also had the rest of Blackpool to look after, it was an inadequate number.

He swore under his breath, uttered a short laugh and smiled in Karl Donaldson's direction. The American had said nothing for some time. 'But what makes me even more worried,' Henry admitted, 'is what you're doing here, Karl. I presume you have more to tell me?'

Donaldson licked his lips and nodded. He glanced at FB and raised his eyebrows. FB

162

gave him the nod to continue. 'Unfortunately, yes, and it could be even more of a nightmare than street rioting.'

The woman prisoner Henry had arrested sat numbly in the small cell, crying.

The flap in the cell door crashed open and an officer's face filled the rectangular space. He did not say anything, just looked in. The prisoner wiped her eyes and stared defiantly at him.

'I just wanted to know what you looked like,' the officer said. 'Just wanted to know what the person who half fried one of my colleagues looked like.'

The young woman's shoulders slumped.

'The one who nearly killed a cop ... or who might have killed a cop, because he might die yet.'

The flap slid back up and the catches banged into place. The officer – whoever it was – had gone. The prisoner flew to the door, smacking her hands and feet against it, screaming words which were lost behind the heavy metal panelled door and which could not be heard down in the custody reception area because it was too far away, down too many steps, around too many corners ... and no one would have really cared anyway.

'There's been a spate of bombings across the States over the last six years,' Donaldson said, 'aimed at minority groups – gays, blacks ... you name it. Twenty-one bombs and over

163

thirty people have been killed.'

FB stifled a cough. All eyes turned to him for a moment, then went back to Donaldson who visibly bristled but tried to ignore the interruption. He knew FB held the world's premier law enforcement agency in very low esteem.

'As happens with these things, it took a while for connections to be made. It was only by the time the third bomb exploded that we realised we had a serial killer on our hands, but his infrequency of attacks and the fact that they have been all over America have made it virtually impossible for us to apprehend him. The bombs get better and better and more people get killed and injured each time.'

'Presumably you must have some ideas about him,' Henry said.

'Yeah. Hazy, cloudy ones, but yeah.'

'Such as?'

'We went all the usual routes: undercover operations into right-wing organisations, covert operations, overt operations, busts left, right and centre – mainly right, of course,' he slid in and got a titter of laughter. 'But we got nothing. No hints, no whispers, no names, not a damn thing ... so we think he's a lone wolf, classified as the new offender model terrorist.'

'Making it virtually impossible to catch him,' Henry said, knowing about the model referred to.

'And making you look like nob-heads into

the bargain,' FB contributed destructively.

This time no one looked his way. There was a beat of embarrassed silence.

Donaldson reached for the briefcase by his side. He took out a series of grainy, indistinct black and white photographs, handed them round the room. 'These are from CCTV cameras in three locations: Miami, San Francisco and LA. We think they're of the same man. Our facial analysts are seventy per cent sure it is the same guy. Caught on camera just minutes before bombs exploded in these cities.'

'It's a bit slim – and they are very poor photos,' Henry said as objectively as he could.

'Agree,' Donaldson said. 'But it's all we have. Three images of an unidentified person at the scene of three out of nineteen bombings, who could be the same person. If it is...'

'The odds of one person being at three out of nineteen attacks are pretty remote,' Henry said. 'Unless...'

'Exactly – unless it's the bomber – so I'm willing to go with it. Gut feeling and all that.'

'Gut feeling isn't evidence,' FB said.

'Very true, sir,' Donaldson said. He fished out more photos. 'Charles de Gaulle Airport two weeks ago.' He handed them round. They were still grainy, but slightly more defined. They showed a male, maybe mid-thirties, medium height, casually dressed, the peak of a baseball cap pulled down covering his face. Henry held one of the new photos up

165

alongside one of the first batch and compared them. He shook his head unsurely.

'Could be,' he said, doubtfully.

'Facial analysts give it a seventy-five per cent nod,' the FBI man said. 'Which as far as I'm concerned means the guy is in Europe. Two days later there was a bomb in Paris, one person killed, thirty injured. Jews. Coincidence? Not a chance.' He looked round the room for someone to defy him. No one did.

'Anything from flight records, the passenger lists?' Henry asked.

'Nothing conclusive. Some things still being followed up.'

'OK ... say it's the same guy – where is this leading, Karl?'

'Maybe nowhere, Henry. Just a warning. Paris isn't a million miles away. With all this upsurge of right-wing activity, it's possible this guy might be operating around here. It's a health warning.'

Henry thought about the large gay community in Blackpool who would be easy targets for a fanatic. 'OK, I'll bear it in mind. Can we circulate these photographs around the clubs?'

'No problem with me – sounds a good idea.'

'I'll sort it – get some posters done and sent out to the gay bars for tonight with a warning to be on their guard.'

'Yeah – do it,' FB snapped.

'Is there anything else you can tell me about this guy, Karl? Do the bombs get left in the

166

same sort of packaging? Sports bags, carrier bags?'

'All different.'

Henry nodded acceptance. He checked his watch. 'Too late to do anything now because everywhere should be closed.'

'OK, that's it for the moment, Henry,' FB said with finality. 'Unless anyone has anything more?' He glanced round the room.

'Oh, I do, actually,' Henry said brightly.

FB wilted.

'Just one thing – this new splinter group. I forgot to ask – do they have a name?' He aimed the question at Andrea Makin.

'Yes they do. They call themselves Hellfire Dawn.'

Eight

'It's the way their twisted minds work.' Andrea Makin was walking alongside Henry Christie as he descended the steps towards the basement of Blackpool Central Police Station. She matched him step by step. 'Do you know the rationale behind the name Combat 18, for example?'

Henry had to admit that he did not.

'It's a number-letter combination, related to their good leader, Adolf Hitler.'

167

Henry thought about that. 'You got me there.'

'The number one relates to the first letter of the alphabet – A; the number eight refers to the eighth letter.'

'Which is?'

'H.'

Henry stopped suddenly on one of the landings. Makin too.

'A-H?' he questioned.

She smiled. 'Come on, get a grip, Henry,' she said lightly. 'A is for Adolf and H is for Hitler – hence 18. They are devoted followers of Adolf Hitler and all his fine works and deeds.'

'It's a good job he wasn't called Xavier Zakynthos, then, otherwise it'd be Combat 24-26.'

Makin smiled and ignored him. 'They just haven't got round to genocide yet – but on Allport's Scale they've got well off the bottom rung.'

Henry's simple mind was getting confused now. He knew he should have known something about Allport's Scale, but in what context he could not remember.

'What's Allport's Scale?' he asked stupidly.

'Gordon Allport wrote a book in the fifties about the nature of prejudice. He devised a scale about prejudice which runs from simple avoidance to extermination in extreme cases. Like Hitler and the Jews.'

'Oh. So, anyway, what does Hellfire Dawn relate to?' he asked, trying to mask his

168

ignorance with a half-passable question. He waited with bated breath.

'H is for Hitler – obviously.'

'Goes without saying.'

'D is for Disciples: Hitler's Disciples.'

'Sad bastards.' He shook his head. 'Still, it's a pastime, though.'

'Yeah – a dangerous one, don't forget that. One which doesn't keep them off the streets.'

'And Allport's Scale – where do Hellfire Dawn figure on that?' He hoped that sounded a reasonably intelligent question too.

'They believe in extermination, but they're pretty much round the level of physical attack. In other words they beat people up.'

'Just what I thought,' he said knowledgeably, continuing downstairs. 'Do they have a leader, other than the late, lamented Adolf?'

'Guy by the name of Vince Bellamy leads the main political group, but we also believe he is the leader of the paramilitary wing, although he denies their actual existence. Very clever individual. Former university professor. Very political animal and has the ear of several right-wing MPs, we believe.'

'How are they financed?'

'Don't know. Sympathetic businessmen, probably. But anyway, Bellamy is a real stirrer. Very motivational in a dark way.'

'Sounds like Hopper out of a *Bug's Life*,' Henry chuckled. They had reached the basement.

'Looks like him too – and he's got a bunch of grasshoppers around him who'll do

169

whatever he wants them to do. He's also a bit like Fagin too, and apparently he does a great Hitler impersonation.'

'Or maybe he's more like FB,' Henry mused, mainly to himself as they approached the custody office.

'You don't like him very much, do you?'

'Is it that obvious? I must be slipping.'

They stopped at the barred door leading to the complex. He turned and looked at Makin. 'He and I have a pretty sordid history, shall we say?' Makin's mouth opened to respond, but before she could ask, Henry was talking into his radio, 'Inspector to Blackpool – custody door please.' He leaned on the door as, accompanied by a loud buzz, it was released.

He intended to hold a short interview with the nameless female prisoner he had arrested, just to see if he had some of the old magic left, see if he could get anything out of her before handing the job over to CID. Makin had volunteered to have a look at the woman to see if she could identify her through her extensive knowledge of right-wing activists.

As Henry pushed the door open there was the sound of van doors slamming from the car park and of voices and two constables appeared steering Kit Nevison between them, just back from hospital. He was stitched up and very subdued, like a sleepy baby, compliant and easy to handle. Henry held the door open and allowed the trio in ahead of himself and Makin. Nevison did not even look at him.

Inside the custody office there was a delay caused by a backlog of prisoners. Henry drew Makin to the back of the room.

'Where does this Bellamy guy hang out?'

'South London, usually, but not this week. This week he's right on your doorstep, one of your residents. Set up in a hotel in central Blackpool fairly near the Winter Gardens, so no doubt he'll want to be made to feel safe, involved and reassured.' Makin smirked as she quoted the words from Lancashire Constabulary's mission statement.

'If I've got anything to do with it,' Henry growled, 'he'll be unsafe, uninvolved and totally unassured – if there is such a word.'

In interview room 2 they sat awaiting the arrival of the nameless prisoner who was, at that moment, consulting with the duty solicitor. Henry had a sealed double pack of tapes in front of him, together with the necessary paperwork he was obliged to hand over to the prisoner at the end of the interview which explained her legal rights.

There was silence, but not uneasy, between him and Makin. He gave her a pallid smile, which she returned.

'How long will you be up here?' he asked, making conversation.

'How long is a piece of string? As long as your ACC wants me to stay, as long as I have something to offer.'

'Where are you staying?'

171

'At the conference hotel.'

'The Imperial?' Henry said, surprised.

'Basil fixed a room up for me.'

Ahh, Basil, Henry thought. 'Nice,' he said.

Makin turned in her chair to look squarely at Henry. 'I'm fascinated by your relationship with FB. It's as though you can say almost anything to him and get away with it. It's unheard of.' She sounded amazed, impressed, almost.

'Not true. I can't say anything to him and get away with it. After all, he's an ACC and I'm only an Inspector. But our joint past does give me certain rights, I suppose. What it boils down to is that I hate him and he despises me, it's a very balanced thing.'

Makin's lips pursed thoughtfully. Her eyes roamed his face.

'You married?' she asked out of the blue.

'No – What?' he spluttered, suddenly very hot under the collar. 'Why?'

'Just wanted to know.' She smiled.

The interview-room door swung open and the female prisoner sauntered in cockily, followed by the duty solicitor. Henry exhaled with some relief. He shot Makin a quick, troubled glance and turned his attention to the job in hand. Something he felt more equipped to deal with than Makin's highly personal questions.

The tapes were running. For their benefit Henry had introduced himself, as had Andrea Makin and the duty solicitor. The only person not speaking was the prisoner. Henry shrugged when she refused to talk and cautioned her to the letter. He asked if she understood the caution. She blinked blandly at him, made no movement and betrayed no body language, other than indifference. Henry almost smiled. He loved the 'no response' interview to bits, especially these days when it had been made explicit that a person's defence could be harmed if they did not say something during an interview which they later relied on in court. In the past, too many defendants had used the 'ambush' defence and got away with things unfairly. Now the defence was obliged to reveal all before any proceedings, just like the prosecution had always had to do.

It amused Henry that people still thought they could get away with saying nothing. Still, it was their prerogative. She could stay dumb for as long as she wanted because Henry would just throw the allegations at her. If she chose not to respond, it was her hard luck and bad judgement.

'My client has decided to remain silent during the interview,' the solicitor said. He looked annoyed at her decision. Henry guessed he had told her to speak and give her side of the story. She obviously had not taken this advice.

'Fine,' Henry said. He went into his opening gambit. 'So far you have declined to reveal your name, address and date of birth. I hope you realise the fairly immediate implica-

173

tions of this for yourself. You have been arrested for several serious offences – possession of petrol bombs, as well as on suspicion of causing damage by fire, which is arson, serious public-order offences and the attempted murder of a police officer. If you do not reveal your personal details, your fingerprints will be taken, by force if necessary, and, should you be charged with these offences, don't even begin to think that bail will be considered. It won't.'

'I think you're getting a little ahead of yourself here, Inspector. The question of bail is not a matter for you, but for the custody officer,' observed the solicitor.

'I am simply letting your client know the harsh realities of the course of action she seems intent on taking.'

'That is very kind of you, Inspector, but she is already fully aware of the implications. I have already outlined them.' The solicitor scribbled down some notes.

Before Henry could continue, Makin said, 'Could I just say something?'

Henry sat back. 'Fire away.'

Makin addressed the solicitor. 'I think it would be wrong of me not to appraise your client of the situation in terms of her identity before we proceed. I know her name.'

The girl, who had been sitting fiddling with her fingertips, raised her face sharply. Her eyes darted between Henry and Makin. The colour drained from her face to match that of the white zoot suit she was wearing.

'You are Geri Peters, aren't you?'

Her face cracked into a flood of tears.

As quickly as it had begun, the interview ended. The girl was clearly in no fit state to continue. The tears grew into a crescendo of racked, desperate sobbing, which developed in intensity until it morphed up a gear into hysteria and there was no way she could continue.

The duty solicitor requested a break. Henry agreed, saying that he thought he had done enough for the moment and perhaps the best course of action would be to let her get some sleep and continue the interview process in the morning when the CID took over. The solicitor, who should not have been on duty that night anyway – he was covering for the woman who had been attacked by Kit Nevison – readily agreed.

The gaoler led the girl away.

Henry and Makin watched her go.

'Sorry about that,' Makin said. 'Her name came to me in a flash – you know what it's like. She's on the periphery of Hellfire Dawn. She's been seen in the company of Vince Bellamy a few times.'

'That's OK. I think she'll be a different proposition in the morning when they get to her – all soft and pliable.'

'Rather like me,' Makin suggested, then stifled a yawn and laid a hand on Henry's chest. 'Excuse me.' She shook her head and slid her hand slowly down his shirt, her eyes fixed on his. She checked the time – nearly 2

175

a.m. 'Time I got to bed. What time do you finish?'

'Six.'

'Another four hours! I'll be all tucked up and warm.'

'I'm sure you will.'

DI Jane Roscoe stood just inside the door to the custody office, out of the eyeline of both Henry and Makin. She was watching their verbal and non-verbal exchange, but was unable to hear any of the words passing between them. Henry seemed stiff and stilted. Nervous. Worried, maybe.

Roscoe could see why. The woman was all over him.

It was so bloody obvious, Roscoe thought angrily, that the woman, whoever the hell she was, was coming onto Henry in a big way with the preening gestures: touching the hair; smoothing her clothing down; a hand on her hips which were pointed towards him; that clumsy hand on Henry's chest, which Roscoe had seen with delight, had made Henry jump as though stung by a wasp; her increasing attempts at eye contact. Henry was not responding, but Roscoe could see it was only a matter of time before the woman dragged him into her web.

For some inexplicable reason, she found herself fuming as she walked towards the couple as nonchalantly as she could, confused over why she should be feeling this way. After all, she did not even like Henry very much.

'I'm sure you will,' she overheard Henry say to the woman.

'Henry – have you got a moment?' Roscoe interrupted breezily.

As they both turned towards her, Roscoe was pleased to see a shimmer of annoyance cross the woman's face.

'Hello, Jane,' Henry said. 'Have you met Detective Superintendent Andrea Makin? Metropolitan Special Branch.'

'No.' The single syllable sounded curt, rude and unprofessional.

'Call me Andrea,' Makin said coldly. She did not offer a hand, merely a faint smile.

'This is DI Jane Roscoe,' Henry said, completing the formalities. 'She's investigating Mo Khan's murder.'

'Ahh – so I've heard.' Makin regarded Roscoe with a smirk. Suddenly Roscoe felt she wanted to crawl away and hide under a stone somewhere because she realised what a God-awful state she was in. Although she had washed and freshened up since the riot, her make-up was long gone and she probably reeked like an old settee and her rat's tail hair was a disgrace. The complete opposite to Makin, who was damned near perfection, the bitch. Makin looked up at Henry with soppy eyes. 'Anyway, Henry, no doubt you'll be able to fill her in on the details she may need about Joey Costain. Goodnight.' She shot Roscoe a false smile and swayed off with a last glimpse over her shoulder at Henry, who completely missed it.

Roscoe dropped her shoulders in relief and opened her hands.

'What?' Henry said, perplexed.

'I'm surprised she didn't shag you here and now.'

'Who? Andrea? What do you mean?'

'Are you a complete numbty?' Roscoe hissed. She would have said more, allowed her mouth to run away with her, but held back because she was not yet sure where she was coming from with this. She shook her head sadly and almost said, 'Men!'

The gaoler returned from the female cell area.

'Said she wants to speak to you, boss,' the PC said to Henry. 'Off the record.'

'Right, thanks. Coming?' he asked Roscoe.

'I've just got back from the hospital,' Roscoe said to Henry's back as they walked to the cell. 'I've come in to let you know how Dave is getting on.'

Henry continued to walk and waited for the news, guts churning.

'It's touch and go,' Roscoe said. 'He's critical, in intensive care. Badly burned upper chest, neck and face. He's breathed in smoke and fire which has caused major injuries to his mouth, throat and respiratory system. He's in a very bad way. The doctors say we did well to keep him alive.'

'More by luck than judgement on my part,' Henry said.

'No it wasn't,' Roscoe stated firmly. 'It was

178

professional life saving. You did a great job. Don't do yourself down.'

'And so did you,' he responded genuinely. 'But enough of this mutual congratulation and back slapping. Let's just hope he pulls through. Are his family aware?' he asked over his shoulder.

'Hmph,' Roscoe snorted. 'Two ex-wives, neither interested. A daughter of twenty-six who hasn't spoken to him for three years and doesn't want to start now, and a son some-where in Europe on his year out, or whatever they call it, between school and university.'

'Parents?'

'Both dead.'

'Jeez, that's a shame,' said Henry. He blink-ed a tear away at the thought of Seymour's lonely predicament, only because it made him realise he could so easily end up in a similar position. The prospect of becoming a sad, old, lonesome bastard hit him with the force of an express train. He could end up on the verge of retirement with no one to care for, or to care about him. He swallowed dryly and thought: What the hell have I done with my life? Just cocked up time after time after time. That was the stark reality of adultery.

At Geri Peters' cell door Henry dropped the loosely fitting inspection hatch and looked in. In her white, oversized zoot suit, the prisoner reminded Henry of the Michelin man. She was sitting on the edge of the low bed, head in hands, desperately alone. She

179

looked up through her fingers. A little girl lost.

'You wanted to see me.'

'Yeah, yeah,' she snuffled, wiped her eyes on a paper sleeve. She crossed the cell, stood by the door. The crying had abated. 'What'll happen to me?'

Henry shrugged. 'Put it this way – don't bank on seeing next Christmas, or the one after that,' he said cruelly. 'And if we make everything stick, you'll be eating cold turkey Christmas dinner a lot longer than that, even.'

She closed her eyes despairingly, then raised them to the ceiling, rocking unsteadily on her feet. Henry thought she was going to fall over.

'I'm frightened. Frightened of being here alone. Frightened of what might happen to me.'

'You should be.'

'I didn't bomb that police officer.'

'You're the only suspect we have at the moment, dear, so I'm sure we'll do a pretty good job of placing you at the scene and the petrol bombs we found in your possession are pretty good supporting evidence – unless you want to tell us who actually did it, and the name of the person you were with.'

She leaned her back against the door, arms folded.

'If you didn't do it, who did?' Henry probed, picking up on the vibes emanating from her. She wanted to save her own skin, he

180

could tell. 'Or do you want to take the rap for committing murder – that detective could well die.'

'Shit, shit, shit,' she said, banging the back of her head on the cell door in time with each word. She whacked it hard, making Henry wince with vicarious pain. 'I don't know what to do,' she whined pitifully. 'I'm afraid to tell you the truth.'

'It's your decision. I can't influence it, other than by laying the cards on the table.' Henry was cooing now, knowing full well he was seriously influencing her thought process. 'What's the point going down for someone else?'

She did not respond and shuffled back across the cell, and sat heavily on the bed, looking down, blanking Henry out.

Slowly he closed the inspection flap.

He winked at Roscoe and gave her a thumbs up. 'She'll crack,' he said positively.

They turned away from the cell door and were slightly surprised to see Dermot Byrne, Henry's patrol sergeant, standing behind them. Neither had heard his approach.

'Boss,' Byrne said. 'Ma'am,' he acknowledged Roscoe with a bluff nod of the head. 'I'm turning out to have a look round Shoreside. It all seems to be quiet, but I thought I'd give it the once over and if it is, we could start standing patrols down.'

'Good idea. I'll come with you if you can hang on for twenty minutes so I can make sure I'm up to date with the custody office.

181

And then I've got a few things I need to brief you about, very pertinent to this week. We need to have a heads-together to sort something out.'

Byrne looked intrigued. 'Right. I'll catch up with you shortly.' He walked on, ahead of Henry and Roscoe.

'He seems pretty good,' Henry said to her.

'Mmm,' she sounded doubtful. 'He gives me the creeps.'

'Oh, right. So, what are you going to do now, Jane?'

'If I can keep awake, I'm going after Joey Costain. The sooner he's off the streets, the better. I could do with a chuck-up, though, maybe borrow a few bods? I'd like to spin a few drums simultaneously.'

'Sure. I'll see who I can spare.'

'And you have some information for me, I believe,' Roscoe said. 'That ... that Met superintendent seemed to suggest you had something to tell me.' Roscoe hoped she had kept the dislike she felt for Andrea Makin out of her voice, but she doubted it. Then, without warning, it struck her why she had reacted so strangely to Makin's obvious come-on to Henry.

She was jealous.

Apart from wanting to clear the decks in the custody office, which he managed to do in about ten minutes, Henry also wanted to try and catch Karl Donaldson before he left the building.

182

After concluding his custody reviews, he hurried out of the office and saw Fanshaw-Bayley returning from the underground car park adjoining the police station.

'Is Karl Donaldson still here?' he asked FB.

'No – gone. He's staying at the Jarvis, which I presume is the answer to your next question.'

'Thanks.' Henry tried to edge past FB in the narrow corridor. FB's hand shot out across Henry's chest, stopping him.

'A word.' FB applied some pressure, then lifted his hand off Henry's chest and pointed towards the car park. 'Out here.' He brushed past Henry, who followed.

FB walked a few metres down the car park, stopped, glanced round edgily. No one was nearby. He beckoned Henry closer.

'I'll let you into a little secret, just between me and you.' On 'me' he pointed at himself; on 'you' he pointed sharply at Henry. His voice was no louder than a whisper. Henry had to cock an ear. 'Just so you know where you stand – OK?'

Henry wondered what the hell was coming this time.

'It's imperative I make a good impression this week,' FB said flatly. His eyelids were half-closed, nose tilted upwards slightly, looking down at Henry and reminding him of Kenneth Williams. 'A very good, lasting impression. That is because very good things could happen for me if everything goes well –

which is where you come in. You have to do your job, I mean, really pull out your tripe this week, and keep Blackpool well under control. You do not allow a bunch of yobs to take over – understand?'

Henry's eyebrows knitted together.

FB huffed in frustration at Henry's apparent lack of comprehension. 'Because if you think that being a uniformed inspector in Blackpool is bad enough, how would you like to be one in Barnoldswick, or Bacup for God's sake? Out in the sticks with members of the public who resemble the cast of *Deliverance*? Or maybe Skelmersdale, full of fucking scousers? Because I'll tell you now, Henry Christie, if you don't keep a lid on it, you'll end up in some Godforsaken hole where the only pastime is whittling and making people squeal like pigs – and I'll do it in such a way that everyone'll think you're an incompetent cunt.'

Henry's jaw cracked. 'Why?' he croaked.

'Because Basil Kramer is my ticket out of here, my passport to promotion. He has the home secretary's ear and if this week goes well, under my leadership, I'll have the choice of plum jobs at the HMIC or NCIS.' FB delayed a second for effect, letting his words sink in. 'Now do you get my drift? He is my meal ticket. And you never know – if you do well this week, maybe you'll get a CID job back sooner than you thought. You scratch my back...' He arched his eyebrows, but then his face became very dark. 'If you cock up,

184

you'll suffer big style. Get me now?'

'I think so,' Henry said.

'Good.'

Without a further word, FB patted Henry patronisingly on the shoulder and left him standing in the chill of the car park.

'It's been a very good night,' David Gill said. 'The movement has started.'

'Yes, you've done well,' Vince Bellamy said down the phone. 'We've all done well but I have a little problem that has cropped up which needs sorting out. David, I know it's asking a lot, but I want you to oblige.'

'Tell me,' Gill said.

After Bellamy had explained the situation, Gill paused in thought for a long time. 'That's tough,' he said. 'It could really backfire on me if I'm not a hundred per cent careful.'

'David, you are always a hundred per cent careful. I want you to try. Do your best – it's all I ever ask of you.'

Nine

In the new scheme of things, being a manager of resources as opposed to an old fashioned jack, it wasn't actually Jane Roscoe's job to go round kicking doors down anymore. Which was a shame. It was something she enjoyed doing: bursting uninvited, sometimes even lawfully, into people's property at unexpected times of day, backed up by a bunch of hairy-arsed bobbies – it was one of the last perks of being a cop these days. Not many things could touch the buzz of seeing a door leaving its hinges in the middle of the night.

The modern DI was expected to be distanced from such front-line activity, to deploy, delegate and plan. But fortunately in the early hours of that particular Tuesday morning there weren't enough other officers on duty for Jane Roscoe to do that sort of management crap. They were badly under-staffed and it would have been criminal for her not to make up the numbers. Nor, she thought selfishly, would it do any harm for her credibility rating in the eyes of her sub-ordinates. This was how she justified leading an arrest squad to hit one of Joey Costain's

186

known addresses, while a detective sergeant led the other.

She changed out of the suit she had been wearing earlier, which had been damaged during the petrol bombings at Khan's shop, into the scruffy black jeans and T-shirt she always kept in her locker (formerly Henry Christie's) for such situations as this: when a skirt and blouse would be totally useless for climbing through half-beaten-down doors or smashed windows. It felt great to get out of the clothes she had been wearing for almost eighteen hours since the previous morning.

Mark Evans, the detective sergeant leading the second team, accompanied her as she strode confidently to the ground-floor parade room where officers had gathered for the briefing. She could sense there was something on his mind and had a good idea what it was.

'Spit it out, Mark,' she ordered him.

'The lads are on pins. They feel they should be getting into that petrol bomber, the one who did Dave. They're not bothered about Joey Costain at the moment. After all, all he did was whack a Paki.'

Roscoe came to a sudden halt.

'I understand your sentiments, Mark. It's only natural you want to get whoever burned Dave, but that's going to be properly organised in the morning as it happens. There's nothing more we can do evidentially at the moment, that'll be for the morning people. Our job is to get Joey Costain – and if I ever hear you using a racist term like "Paki" again, your job will be on the line – OK?'

'Ugh!' The DS gasped as though sucker-punched.

'Now come on, let's get this job sorted.' She walked on to the parade room.

The number of officers surprised her pleasantly. Six uniforms rustled up by Henry, plus her three detectives, the DS and herself. Pretty bloody good, she thought. The only trouble was that Henry Christie himself was sitting at the front of the room, chatting intently to one of the detectives. Probably one of his old mates, one of the lads. Sod him, damn him, Roscoe thought. She took a breath, put her head down and decided to get on with things.

The briefing was short and succinct and Roscoe thought it went well enough. No major hiccups, no drying up. The officers had been divided up randomly into the two arrest squads. The team of six – Alpha Sierra 1 – was headed up by Roscoe. They were going to take the Costain family home. The second squad of five were allocated the flat Joey was known to rent in South Shore.

Ten minutes later, Roscoe and her team were parked in two unmarked cars round the corner from the target premises which was situated pretty much in the dead centre of the Shoreside Estate. The area was quiet now, nothing stirring in the night other than cops on the prowl. The debris on the streets, left over from the disturbances, was the only indication of what had been going on earlier.

The other team – Alpha Sierra 2 – was a spit and a stride away from Costain's flat.

Henry Christie – having had the foresight, or luck, not to stand down the PSUs which had come to assist earlier – was sitting in the passenger seat of a personnel carrier on the outer edge of Shoreside. Six officers in full riot kit were in the back. Another carrier full of more sweaty cops was parked on the far side of the estate. They were here because the raid on the Costain home could easily be the trigger for further trouble on the streets. As soon as Roscoe gave the go-ahead to hit the house, Henry and his little army would become a very visible presence.

'Alpha Sierra 2 to Alpha Sierra 1 ... in position,' DS Evans radioed in.

'Received – likewise,' Roscoe acknowledged. 'Sierra 1 to Inspector.'

'Also in position,' Henry said.

'OK,' said Roscoe. A tinge of excitement crept into her voice as she said, 'Let's do it!'

'Sierra 2 responding.' In the background of the transmission there was the scream of an engine being revved.

Thirty seconds later, Roscoe and her team were outside the Costain house, disgorging from their transport, running up the path. Two of them made straight for the back door to prevent escape. Ten seconds after that the front door was battered open, cops streamed through and were on the premises and Roscoe's heart was in her mouth.

The first sign of opposition was Joey Costain's elder brother, Troy, who had been sleeping on the settee in the living room. He had woken up feeling mean and ready to fight.

'Alpha Sierra 2 to Alpha Sierra 1.'

'Go 'head,' said Roscoe. Maybe they had got him.

'No joy,' DS Evans said over the radio. 'The flat's empty.'

'Has everything been thoroughly turned over?'

'Affirmative.'

'Roger. In that case, stand down and make your way back in.'

'How are you doing?' Evans asked.

'Still searching,' she said. She was standing on the landing at the top of the stairs, looking up into the square black hole that was the loft entrance. A pair of legs appeared and a detective eased himself out and dropped lightly onto the landing floor. He brushed himself down. 'He ain't up there.'

Roscoe hissed with frustration. A blank. 'Thanks.'

In the lounge, several generations of Costains had assembled, roused from their various sleeping arrangements. There were more people than Roscoe could have imagined the house was able to accommodate. Rather like an extended Asian family under one roof, though they would have been furious at the comparison. They had actually been quite compliant with the exception of Troy who had been smothered and subdued before he became a problem. He had come very close to being locked up.

The living room smelled awful: stale, boozy breath, body odour and flatulence combined to make a foetid aroma.

Roscoe walked in and, without exception, they glared at her. Including, she was certain, the babe in arms being cuddled to the bare, floppy breast of one of the women-folk.

The room betrayed their gypsy origins. It was all very clean and well cared for, but the leather furniture, ornate horse brasses and outrageous fittings gave the game away. Everything was larger than life and twice as tacky – even down to the massive TV and video set in the corner of the room with speakers that would not have looked out of place behind a rock 'n' roll band.

'OK, we're done,' she announced. 'The only damage caused was to your front door and I've got a before and after photo of it. A joiner will be round later to fix it at our expense.' She smiled. 'Would anyone like to tell me where I can find Joey? It would be in everyone's interests. That way we won't have to keep coming back and hassling you.'

'You must be fuckin' joking,' came a reply from somewhere. Roscoe could not pinpoint the mouth. For a moment she thought the babe in arms had uttered the immortal phrase. No doubt they would be the first words the little dear would speak.

'Thought as much,' said Roscoe. 'Thanks for your co-operation. The necessary paperwork's on the mantelpiece – underneath that lovely candlestick. Bye.'

She gave them a royal wave and left.

Once in the car, en route to the station, she called Henry on the radio. 'Negative, both addresses.'

'Thanks for that. I'll stand our helpers down now. Everything seems to be QT.'

'Roger,' Roscoe said. She sat back, head against the headrest, feeling the energy draining out of her. Time to go home and get some sleep. The arrest of Joey Costain could wait until she could think clearly again.

The personnel carrier dropped Henry off at the front of the police station. He went up the steps, strode across the concourse which separated the station from the Magistrates Court and let himself in through the front door at ground level. He had to trot down a flight of stairs to the basement level to get to the custody office, a location he was heartily sick of already. Once he had finished his business there he promised himself a twenty-minute break during which he would savour a wonderful cup of tea and put his swollen feet up.

Coming in the opposite direction, out of the garage, dragging her feet, was a jaded Jane Roscoe. She was less than ecstatic to see him.

'Thanks for all your help tonight, Henry,' she said, trying not to sound too begrudging.

'Cheers. I'm just sorry you didn't get a result – but I'm sure you'll pick Joey up sooner rather than later. He doesn't exactly keep a low profile.'

'Yeah – if I ever wake up, that is.' She yawned widely. 'I'm going to phone the hospital before I go to see how Dave's getting on, then I'm going home to sleep – unless I nod off in the car on the motorway, in which case you'll find me in a ditch.'

Henry was standing in front of her in the narrow passage, impeding her progress. There was a hesitant pause between them.

'Could I just...?' Roscoe intimated she wished to proceed.

'Sorry, sorry,' Henry babbled, realising he was stopping her. He twisted sideways and they passed within an inch of each other, not touching. When the manoeuvre was complete, Henry said, 'By the way, Jane – I was probably out of order earlier. I know it's not your fault you got my job. If it means anything, I think you're a bloody good DI on tonight's performance.' He shrugged with a hint of embarrassment and pouted.

Roscoe regarded him. Her expression betrayed nothing. She nodded, turned and was on her way. Only then did her face crack into a big smile.

Henry, on the other hand, having extended the olive branch of peace was gobsmacked by her non-reaction. 'Ignorant cow,' he muttered, then put her out of his mind, veered right into the custody office.

193

It had become fairly busy. A normal, early hours Tuesday morning in the Blackpool cells. Full of drunks, thieves, wife-beaters – although husband-beaters were in the ascendancy these days. It was just run-of-the-mill horrendous.

The Blackpool Central Police Station Prisoner Sausage Machine. The baddie-processing industry at its most efficient. Twelve thousand or more bodies pushed and prodded through every year with no let-up for the police, the courts, the duty solicitors. The wheels of justice grinding inexorably on and on: churning out files, charge forms, bail forms, fingerprint forms, descriptive forms to infinity, decimating South American rain forests by the acre. One of the busiest custody offices in the country. A well-oiled, finely tuned mangle of humanity. Each detained person bringing in his or her own story, sometimes tragedy. Most were from backgrounds where the descent into crime was inevitable.

Henry pushed his way through the prisoners and their escorts and picked up the 'live' custody binder, which held the records of all the prisoners currently in cells. He found a quiet space – as if – and settled himself down to read every record, ensuring they were as up to date and accurate as they could be. Too many officers had fallen foul of wily solicitors by not ensuring the forms were filled in correctly. Henry had almost lost his job once for adopting a cavalier attitude to filling in custody records. It had been a salutary lesson.

As satisfied as he could be that everything was OK, he decided on a walk round the cell complex to visit all the inmates. Fifteen people were locked up. Most were fast asleep. One drunk was constantly kicking his cell door, bawling obscenities. Henry paused for a few extra seconds to peer through the spyhole into Kit Nevison's cell. The big man was soundly sleeping, snoring loudly.

Once the male side had been done, Henry moved through the reception area, across to the female block. Only the one female was in custody, the one he had arrested.

As soon as Henry stepped into the corridor, he knew something was amiss. His sixth sense kicked in. He stiffened. The air did not smell right or feel right. The hairs on the back of his neck crawled like tiny insects. Then his eyes zoomed onto the bootlace protruding under the sliding door hatch of the girl's cell. It was looped down and pulled up tight over the hatch-locking mechanism, basically a spring-loaded latch, which gave it the necessary purchase, then back up through the gap between the hatch and the cell door, a gap which, in an ideal world, should have been non-existent, but which had appeared over the years as the door had aged and the steel had buckled slightly from constant use. It was a gap which many prisoners in many other similar situations, intent on taking their own lives, had used to good advantage to achieve their aim.

195

Henry knew immediately that by fastening the bootlace on the inspection hatch, the girl was now hanging by the neck on the other side of the door.

'Oh God,' he muttered, dashing to the cell door. He attempted to open the hatch, but the girl's dead weight on the other side made it impossible for him to move the latch. He cursed again and put his eye to the spyhole. By standing on tiptoe and looking down he could just see the dark shape of a pair of legs splayed out on the other side of the door.

He had to act fast to save her – if she wasn't already dead – and until he knew otherwise he had to assume life was still there. He kept his voice calm but urgent as he spoke into his radio.

'Inspector, get the custody officer to come to the female cells immediately with his keys and the ligature scissors, and call an ambulance please. There's an attempt suicide in here – a hanging.'

'Received.'

Henry assessed what he might be able to do in the intervening seconds before help arrived.

He had seen this before.

The bootlace somehow smuggled into the cell, long enough to be wrapped around any suitable object and then around the neck. They did not hang themselves in the true sense of the word, just put the makeshift noose around their necks and leaned into it, letting the whole body go limp and heavy, cutting the blood supply to the brain, stopping breathing. Dying quickly. Very quickly. He knew that if a prisoner was desperate enough, they would succeed in their morbid endeavour. He also knew from research done into the subject of deaths in police custody, a point nine inches above ground was sufficiently high to achieve the objective.

But how had she managed to sneak the lace into her cell? Henry was already preparing to ask tough questions. She'd been strip searched. Henry knew she had. She was wearing a paper suit. Who the fuck hadn't done their job properly?

Henry could not even manage to slide his fingers between the bootlace and the door. He banged the wall and hopped with frustration.

'Where the fuck are you?' he yelled out loud.

There was the sound of running footsteps, keys jangling, shouts. The custody officer came racing in, the gaoler at his heels. Henry stood back and allowed him to get straight to the door. No explanations were necessary. Henry was considering the ramifications of a death in custody and all the things that might result from it: the protracted investigation; the awkward questions; the Police Complaints Authority; inquests; discipline, possibly criminal proceedings; maybe demotions or job losses. Shit, he thought. The implications were terrifying. Not on my first night as a uniformed inspector, he prayed, do not be dead, you bitch.

The big key went in, turned and the heavy brass lock opened. The sergeant heaved the door outwards with difficulty, the girl's weight on the other side of it making it hard to open.

There she was, legs akimbo. The weight of her body being held by the bootlace which was cutting deep into the soft flesh of her neck. Bootlace, Henry thought again. Where did that come from? Her head lolled forwards, her chin almost on her chest, purple tongue lolling out obscenely. Spittle bubbled out of the corners of her mouth, snot hung from her nose. The eyes bulged out of their sockets. Her skin was tinged blue.

She looked dead.

The custody sergeant inserted the flat-edge ligature scissors, specially designed to slide between skin and ligature, underneath the bootlace. The gaoler went on one knee and took the girl's weight. The scissors snipped. She sagged and fell loosely against the gaoler's hands. He eased her gently to the floor.

The severed bootlace hung from the door hatch, swinging from side to side.

'Leave it where it is for now,' Henry instructed the sergeant, thinking about preservation of evidence. If the girl was dead, which seemed pretty likely looking at her, Henry would start from the premise that he was dealing with a murder, which was standard practice at all sudden or unusual deaths, even though this had happened in a police establishment and it was a highly unlikely scenario. When murder was ruled out, only then would he move onto suicide. Murder first, other causes second. It was his golden rule.

The gaoler was kneeling over her, breathing heavily from the exertion of running. His first and second fingers prodded her neck for signs of a pulse.

'Can't find a thing,' he said.

'Fuck, fuck,' growled the custody sergeant. He too could see the bleakness of the future. After all, this was his custody office. He would have a lot of difficult questions to answer.

'Right,' Henry said. 'Try to resuscitate.'

The gaoler looked up at him as if he was barmy. 'She's dead, boss.'

'Not until a quack says so,' Henry insisted. 'Let's get on with it.' He tapped the sergeant on the shoulder. 'You do the heart, I'll do the lungs. We keep at it until the paramedics arrive.'

For the second time that night, Henry dragged his first-aid training knowledge and skills out of the deep recesses of his mind. He knelt down at her head, tilted it back and blew. The only difference with this casualty was that he did not think there was a hope in hell of success this time round. He and the sergeant worked on her for ten minutes. Constantly. It was exhausting work. Henry sweated, drops of perspiration blobbing down onto the girl's lifeless face. He glanced up once during the procedure, his vision reeling, head full of air, temples thumping. A group of onlookers had gathered, cops drawn to the spectacle like moths to a flame. In among them was Jane Roscoe, an expression of grave concern on her face. Their eyes met for a brief instant, then Henry resumed his task. It was like being in a different world, as if it was happening to someone else. It was a world of slow-moving disorientation where nothing was real except the fight for life.

He opened his lips and re-formed the airtight seal around the girl's lips. Suddenly she convulsed and coughed upwards into his mouth. Disgusted, retching, Henry spun away, spitting and coughing, emptying his mouth of whatever it was she had coughed up. It tasted like slimy gravel. But looking back at her, the disgust left him. She was wracked in a fit of choking and alive.

He wiped his mouth with his shirtsleeve and nodded triumphantly at the sergeant who had kept going with him. They had done it. They had brought a seemingly dead person back to life. Persistence had paid off. The sergeant held out a hand. Henry shook it. A few watchers clapped and shouted 'Well done!'

The paramedics arrived just as they turned the girl on her side into the recovery position.

So sucked in by the emotional drama of it all was he that Henry found himself accompanying the girl as she was stretchered away through the narrow twisting cell corridors to the ambulance waiting in the police garage. He held her hand all the way, squeezing, patting, leaning over her and clucking soft, reassuring words of comfort.

Her eyes rolled like a pair of doll's eyes, fluttered open showing bloodshot whites. They never seemed to focus on him or anything until they reached the ambulance. Then she became more lucid and tried to sit up. Henry gently pushed her back down. 'It's OK ... don't move ... you'll be fine.'

Underneath the transparent oxygen mask, her swollen, cracked lips moved, trying to say something. Henry could not hear the words. He bent over her.

'Shouldn't,' she said, her voice just a whisper.

'What?' He did not understand and shook his head. Her lips moved again. He put his ear an inch above the mask.

'Afraid ... afraid...' she said. Tears streamed out of the corner of her eyes. 'One of yours.' The effort of speaking drained her, but at least Henry thought he had made some sense of her words, though not all of them. He recalled the fear she had expressed when he had talked to her in the cell: the fear of retribution – that if she said what she knew, something terrible would happen. Was this enough for her to try and take her own life? To do such a thing, she must have been terrified ... so what did she know?

He had no further time to think about it as the paramedics slid her into the ambulance. One went to the front of the vehicle to drive, the other stepped in beside her. 'You sendin' anyone up with her?' he asked Henry.

'Christ – yes.' He clicked his fingers, thinking fast. She needed protection and, technically, as she was still in police custody, someone had to stay with her.

Everyone had slithered back into the station, all onlookers gone now that the drama had ended, except for the constable who had been in the report-writing room earlier. Henry turned to him decisively before he too could skulk away. 'John, you're in the wrong place at the wrong time. Hop in and go with this lass to the Blackpool Victoria Hospital and look after her while I decide what needs doing, OK?'

PC Taylor looked decidedly unenthusiastic. His shoulders sagged at the prospect of a nannying job. 'I've just been told to walk the town centre,' he bleated.

'And now I'm telling you to get in the ambulance, OK?' Henry cocked a slightly annoyed thumb at the open door. 'Now,' he said firmly.

The officer removed his helmet and climbed in wearily. The paramedic gave Henry a thumbs-up and closed the door. The vehicle moved off.

Henry watched it go, hands thrust deep into his pockets. When it was out of sight a huge lion-like yawn crept up on him from somewhere. Very long, very wide. It went on forever. He shook his head when it had finished and turned – straight into Jane Roscoe. She had been standing behind him.

'Just how I feel.' She smiled.

'What are you still doing here?'

'Love the place so much, can't bear to leave it.'

'Me too.' He smirked.

She considered the lie for a moment. 'Beats Barbados, hands down.'

'Better than the Maldives, I'd say.'

'And the town. Blackpool has the allure of the Left Bank in Paris, all the pavement cafes. It's somewhere you just want to chill out in and watch the chic world go past.'

'I think the allure is more akin to a pair of a Blackburn hooker's panties.'

'Oh, Henry,' Roscoe gasped, 'you say the most wonderful, evocative things.'

'It's a gift,' he said modestly.

'But you did spoil my dreams a little.' She punched him lightly on the arm and at that moment both realised there was something between them. Undefined as yet, but definitely there. A split second of silence passed.

'Well done – again – by the way,' Roscoe said. 'The old mouth to mouth. Bit of an expert now. You and your lips.'

'Another of my many talents ... Superman, eat your heart out, Inspector Christie's on the prowl.'

'More Inspector Gadget, I'd say,' Roscoe said cheekily.

203

'Now you've spoiled my moment.'

'Doesn't do to get too far removed from reality.'

'Not much chance in this place ... how's Dave Seymour?'

'Very poorly.'

'Likely to improve?'

'Well,' Roscoe folded her arms, 'if we are talking reality Dave is overweight, drinks like a fish, eats like an elephant, y'know, twenty hours a day grazing, smokes like a factory – and not one of those things helps his cause. Even if he was the fittest guy in the world, it'd be touch and go.' Her voice trailed off miserably. She sighed and admitted, 'I want to cry ... but I'll get home first.' She walked past him and touched his arm. 'By the way, thanks for getting us out of that shop.'

'Superman.' He winked.

'Yeah, you could be right. Bye.'

He watched her walk away. He had wanted to dislike her but had found out that she was OK. Nothing ever seems to work out as planned, he thought. What he disliked was the way in which the job itself had put them both into a position where they had wanted to dislike each other.

PC Taylor stayed with Geri Peters from her reception at A&E, all through her treatment at the hands of skilled casualty doctors and nurses, and then remained with her in a tiny curtained cubicle while efforts were made to admit her to a ward. They wanted to keep her in for observations. Taylor was bored rigid with the deployment. He had watched disinterestedly as the staff had poked and prodded her but had actually done very little because there wasn't much they could do. What was wrong with Geri Peters was more in her head than anywhere else.

It was hardly a riveting episode of *ER*. Come to that, Taylor thought, it was hardly an episode of *Casualty* either. The doctors, nurses, porters and paramedics were exceptionally polite to each other, and no one seemed to be having an affair. It was all very dull.

In the cubicle, Taylor became restless. The thought of a cup of coffee from the machine down the corridor was a good one. He checked the prisoner: sleeping now, drugged up to the eyeballs with a hell of a concoction. She was going nowhere fast. He placed his helmet on the bedside cabinet and pushed his way out through the curtains.

Almost as soon as he had gone, the curtains swung open again. A man entered the cubicle. David Gill. He approached the girl on tiptoe, gently removing a pillow from underneath her head without disturbing her. He fluffed it up and smiled.

It was time to kill again.

Ten

Peace at last. Henry strolled slowly through the corridors of the station, unable to inject any speed or purpose into his step as he came down from the high of his recent experience. He made it to the inspectors' office and plugged in the kettle. Next to it were several mugs, all obviously personally owned by other inspectors, a box of teabags, some powdered coffee, sugar in a stainless-steel bowl (appropriated from the canteen, probably) and a couple of jars of Teamate. No doubt he would be required to join the inspectors' tea fund. As he helped himself to a teabag, a spoonful of Teamate and dropped both into someone else's mug, he hazarded a guess that the wonderful Inspector Burt Norman would be the tea-fund administrator. It seemed the type of thing he would relish taking on and running with a rod of iron. He would savour telling Henry about the unwritten rules concerning payment of monies, the use, or otherwise, of other people's crockery (not permitted, Henry assumed) and the penalties levied for late payment of dues.

Henry smirked as he thought back to the

welcome Norman had extended to him at the start of the tour. It seemed days, not hours ago, so much had happened since. All in all a pretty usual sort of night for the reactive inspector in Blackpool, Henry guessed. Reactive inspectors had to be the jacks and masters of all trades; it was something Henry had not realised before. God, get me back onto CID, he prayed.

No, the meeting with Burt Norman hadn't just been hours ago. It had been a lifetime ago.

The kettle boiled and clicked off. Henry made his tea and because of his distinct lack of energy, heaped a large spoonful of sugar into it. False, short-lived energy, maybe, but energy nevertheless. He sat slowly down, easing his aching back and other joints into the chair. He lifted both feet onto the desk. They were throbbing continually in his boots, a persistent thud, thud, thud. He unclipped his tie, tore open his shirt collar and looked forward to his proposed oasis of calm.

Only when he had chilled out, drunk his tea and enjoyed its effects, would he get his mind round the things he had to do. First, the hospital. He had to decide what protection, if any, the girl needed and more importantly, perhaps, whether or not the police had the resources to keep a constant watch on her. Then there was her attempted suicide. Some searching questions had to be asked soon.

The first sip of the hot brown tea was a wonderful experience. He sighed and his mind drifted to the subject of Jane Roscoe. He had wanted to hate her with a vengeance, but had found he quite liked her. Liked her a lot, to be truthful. Firstly because she seemed very capable and no nonsense. She was a good DI, of that there was no question. Secondly because he actually quite fancied her. He liked her manner, her appearance, voice, hair, face – whoa, Henry! Put on the brakes. He stopped this line of thought with a sardonic grin: do not even think about it; do not let what lurks behind your Y-fronts rule your mind. That had happened far too often and, anyway, he was in a 'relationship' now with the vet lady.

His face creased at the thought of a situation he was not a hundred per cent comfortable with. Fiona did not seem to be on the same intellectual plane as him: she was several places higher and the only common ground seemed to be bed and sex. And even Henry knew that was no basis for a lasting relationship. How he hated that word. It meant nothing these days. He took a second sip of the tea. He never got the third sip.

PC Taylor thundered down the hospital corridor, heaving a nurse to one side. A second nurse took shelter in the doorway of a side ward and almost ducked as he flew past. The constable screamed, 'Stop him! Stop him!' He was hampered by the weight of his uniform and the cumbersome equipment belt around his waist. Police appointments were not designed with speed in mind. Nevertheless, Taylor ran hard and fast after the dark figure, his strong physique enabling him to move pretty quickly.

His right hand fumbled for the radio transmit button on the mike attached to his shoulder. He shouted his collar number and then screamed, 'Assistance! Assistance needed at the Blackpool Victoria Hospital. Chasing suspect down corridor away from A&E. Murder suspect – killed a prisoner – ASSISTANCE!'

Henry shot out of his seat. There was a special radio set in the inspectors' office which gave the inspectors the facility to listen to both sides of radio conversations. He had heard Taylor's desperate transmission and could hear the breathlessness, the pounding of the feet, the rustle of clothing and the fear in the voice. Something bad had happened.

'Inspector to PC Taylor, what's the job, John?'

'Ahhh – chasing–' pound, pound, pound of boots – 'Chasing suspect – GET OUT OF THE WAY! Girl in custody – dead, I think—'

The radio went dead.

Then: 'Jesus – fucking move, will you!'

Henry was not absolutely sure what was going on.

'Inspector to all available patrols, make for BVH. Urgent request for assistance – officer chasing a suspect,' he instructed over the air. 'Inspector to Blackpool – put talk-through on and get a grip of this job, please.'

'Roger. Talk-thru on.'

'Inspector to PS Byrne. Are you in a position to pick me up?'

'No. I'm thirty seconds away from BVH.'

'Roger. Forget it.'

Henry grabbed his hat and a set of car keys from the hook on the wall and ran out of the office, giving one longing look at his tea. He tore down the steps eight or ten at a time, down into the basement car park.

All the while, the radio transmissions continued.

Byrne shouted, 'PC Taylor. Exact position within BVH?'

'Not sure, not sure – heading from A&E towards X-ray. He's gone in that direction.'

'Got that,' responded another patrol. 'I'll drive round to that side of the building.'

'Me, too,' a dog handler cut in.

'PC Taylor – any description?'

The winded officer was doing his best to respond, but was getting more out of breath all the time. 'Big guy – dark clothing – dark hair–'

Meanwhile, Henry Christie was standing in the covered car park with a set of car keys dangling between his fingers, feeling very stupid and frustrated because he did not know which car they fitted. There was no number on the fob – it must have fallen off and never been replaced – and there were four cars parked around the garage. It didn't help that they were all Astras and the keys in his hands were Vauxhall keys. No process of manufacture elimination to go through there. Just straightforward trial and error.

He dashed to each car like he was on some sort of game show: how long will it take you to find the car which the keys fit? Do it in less than thirty seconds and the car's yours! He could almost hear Bruce Forsyth wittering in his ear.

Sod's law kicked in. It was the last of the four cars he tried. Valuable time wasted doing a completely idiotic thing. He got in, the seat wobbling precariously and started up the reluctant engine, revving it hard, blowing out a mushroom of blue smoke with a serious sounding backfire. He saw immediately that the petrol gauge did not budge. He swore and prayed there would be enough fumes in the car to get him as far as the hospital. He drove the much-abused car out of the car park and accelerated away, re-tuning his ears to the radio transmissions.

'Lost him, lost him,' PC Taylor was gasping agonisingly, 'somewhere down near the X-ray department–' he took a long, shuddering breath – 'he can't be far – must've gone to ground in here.'

'Me an' me dog's on t'outside of the X-ray department,' the dog handler said and just to prove he had a dog, it barked. 'I'll stay in the vicinity till further notice.'

'Roger,' the communications operator said.

'I'm in A&E now,' Dermot Byrne called in. 'Meet me somewhere, John. You name the

211

location.'

'Er ... X-ray reception, Sarge,' said the less than certain Taylor. 'He must be here somewhere, must be.' He sounded harassed.

'Inspector to PS Byrne.'

'Go ahead.'

'Situation report, re the female prisoner, please.'

'Standby.'

Henry pushed the underpowered car through its gears, taking it to the limit at each change. He ran red lights, depending rashly on the protection afforded him by the meagre flashing blue light on the car roof. It was a false sense of security, he knew. Other cops had relied on the same in the past with fatal consequences. But at that time in the morning on the almost deserted streets, he felt reasonably confident of not wiping anybody out.

'PS to Inspector.'

'Yo!' said Henry in the middle of a sharp bend, one hand on the wheel, tyres squealing, the other hand on his transmit button.

'Bad news – she's dead, sir.'

Henry had real problems controlling the car coming out of the bend, it was swerving all over the place. He narrowly missed a milk float trundling innocently down the street, the milkman's terrified face was a sight to behold.

'I'll get you next time,' Henry growled.

Because it was now a fully fledged crime

scene, the young girl still lay in the bed and would remain there until all the necessary scenes-of-crime and forensic work had been carried out. It was a very inconvenient arrangement for A&E, but Henry Christie was resolute. They would have to work round it until he was satisfied the police had done their job, so nothing was going to change. He came close to a very nasty head to head with the charge nurse – a woman of formidable stature – but the determination on Henry's face and in his body language made her back down submissively. When he was on a roll, he could be irresistible.

He allowed himself just one extended look at the dead girl through the curtains. He was not going to be drawn in by morbid fascination. And, anyway, his presence would only contaminate the scene. However, his experience of murder scenes told him all he needed to know for the time being. Geri Peters was dead. From the way in which the pillow was laid across her upper chest and underneath her chin, there was a better than average chance that she had been suffocated.

Henry was angry with himself that he had not been switched on enough to see the danger she had been in.

Ducking under the police crime scene tape which now criss-crossed the A&E ward like a huge spider's web, he made his way to the staff rest room.

PC Taylor was there, doubled over, head in hands, rocking slightly. Dermot Byrne sat next to the well-built officer, a hand on his shoulder.

When Henry entered the room, feeling stern and unforgiving, Taylor looked up through his fingers, then rose unsteadily to his feet, ready for the broadside. His arms dropped open by his side, hands palm outwards in a sort of acceptance of blame. He had been crying. Henry felt great sympathy for him but he did not let it show. He had no plans to let Taylor off the hook. Yet.

The officers from the night shift who could be spared had spent the best part of the last hour carrying out as methodical a search of the building as their few numbers allowed, which was not easy in a hospital as huge and sprawling as the Blackpool Victoria. Henry had them carry out a room-by-room, corridor-by-corridor search from beyond the point at which PC Taylor said he last saw the killer. The officers went up and through the X-ray department, right to the end of that particular leg of the hospital. To do more would have been impossible. Henry had even won the battle with the staff nurse to bring in an unhygienic and slavering dog to assist the search. The pooch had found nothing either. The guy had disappeared into the ether. Now Henry had several cops roaming the corridors and outside he had a few officers positioned at strategic points in the grounds with orders to 'turn over' anyone found wandering. Now Henry wanted some hard information.

Byrne, seeing the grim expression on Henry's face, stepped in between the inspector and PC Taylor.

'Don't be hard on him, boss,' Byrne said protectively.

Henry regarded his sergeant stonily. Byrne stood aside and Henry transferred the hard-edged gaze to Taylor, who wilted visibly. The PC sat down and stared glumly at the floor.

'Tell me what happened – again.'

'Well, as I said, I came to the hospital with her like you instructed—'

'Like I instructed,' Henry cut in patronisingly, unable to stop himself. 'Yes, like I instructed – and what did I instruct, PC Taylor?'

'To look after her,' he said lamely.

'Exactly,' growled Henry through clenched teeth, his face a sneer.

'Y-yes,' Taylor muttered feebly, sounding frightened.

'Right – what went wrong?'

'Er, she got treated and they put her in the bed – where she is now – down at the far end of the department and I went to sit with her – next to her.'

'Go on,' Henry urged him on as he seemed to come to a full stop.

'It'd been such a long night, what with the trouble up on Shoreside, that I was tired out. I couldn't keep my eyes open and I thought that if I had a coffee, maybe it would keep me awake.' Taylor paused. 'So I went for one.'

This time Henry did not prompt.

215

'I was away for what? God, less than two minutes and as I came back through the curtain with my coffee I just saw the back end of someone going out the other side – it was so quick. I looked at her, saw the pillow, saw her face and I just went into autopilot and went after him. I realised I had to get him, whether she was dead or not. I legged it. I went like hell for leather down the corridor.' Taylor's head wobbled in disbelief at the vivid recollection in his mind. 'I couldn't get near him. He was bloody fast, like a shadow – and as I came round the next dog-leg in the corridor I was running down he was gone!'

'Description?' Henry said coldly.

Taylor hesitated, marshalling his thoughts. 'I didn't get a good look, really,' he admitted. 'Like I said, he was like a shadow. I just saw his back.'

'His back? Are you certain it was a man?'

'Yeah, yeah, hundred per cent. Ran like a man. About my height and build – say around six feet. Wearing dark clothing and something pulled over his head – balaclava, I reckon.' Henry was expecting more but Taylor had apparently finished his description.

'Is that it?' Henry's brittle voice held utter disbelief.

Taylor nodded worriedly.

'Not very much to go on,' Henry commented dryly.

'I know, I know,' Taylor bleated forlornly. 'But that's all I saw. I'm wracking my brains to dig more out, but it's just not there. I'm really, really sorry.'

'So you bloody well should be – sorry for that girl.' Henry's voice started to rise, but he got a grip and sighed down his nose, flaring his nostrils.

'Oh God, I feel ill.' Taylor got to his feet abruptly and swallowed. His face was the colour of best-quality typing paper. 'I wanna spew.' He swallowed again.

'Well, don't fucking well do it here,' Henry shouted, 'go and find a bog.'

'Urrggh!' Taylor pitched himself out of the office, holding his guts with one hand, the other clamped over his mouth.

'Poor sod,' Byrne said.

'You're too bleedin' soft,' Henry muttered. He plonked himself down next to Byrne on the sofa, clasped his hands behind his head and crossed his legs. He cogitated awhile, arranging his thoughts.

'We can't afford to wait for the circus to turn out. I want to get a start on names and addresses of everyone in A&E at the time of the murder and I want statements to start being taken. Staff, patients – anyone. I want you to get going with that, Dermot. I know we haven't many spare bods, but let's start the ball rolling, get a tick in the book.'

'Sure, boss.'

'And get PC Bloody Taylor to do his statement immediately – I want it to be as detailed as possible from the moment I gave him the instruction until you arrived on the scene, OK?' Henry paused. 'What do you

217

think of him?'

'PC Taylor?' Byrne shrugged. 'He's OK. I don't really know him all that well. Bit long in the tooth and needs motivating, but still gets stuck in now and again. He's just had a good job up at court, a date-rape, which the CPS binned on a technicality, much to his annoyance. He'd done a lot of work on it, so I think that's pissed him off quite a bit.'

'I read about it,' Henry said, now bored with the subject of PC Taylor. He changed the subject. 'You managed to get here pretty quickly,' Henry observed innocently.

Byron reacted to the comment by stiffening slightly and pulling at his collar. 'Happened to be driving past – purely by accident.'

'Yeah, whatever...' Henry's ponderings had drifted on to the crime scene. Being in a clean and hygienic hospital made it unlike most of the murder scenes he'd had the pleasure of visiting over the years. Henry was aware he would have no further part in the subsequent investigation which had already been allocated to the on-call senior investigating officer from headquarters who was already on his way, but it did not stop him from slipping back into CID mode for a few precious moments.

Detailed analysis of the crime scene was crucial to any murder investigation. At every crime scene the offender leaves messages about him- or herself, indicating what the motivation and drive is behind the crime. As a seasoned investigator, Henry consciously

218

tried to reconstruct what had happened to try and find the links between the location, the victim and the offender and the other things he could not even guess at yet, such as what the forensic and post-mortem investigations would reveal.

Already, this murder troubled him deeply.

He started putting together some hypotheses: firstly that the victim could have been a source of potential danger to the offender; that the crime had links with the dead girl's knowledge of activist right-wing groups; that she had known too much and was a danger – these would all be areas for detailed investigation. However, Henry realised that to be rail-roaded by such a narrow band of thought could skew the investigation into a direction which could be totally misguided. It could be that this was simply an opportunistic crime: some passing loony who, feeling murderous, might have seen a chance and gone for it. It sounded a faintly ridiculous premise to Henry, but he knew it could not be overlooked. Which brought him back full circle to his initial conjectures. And the one big question which needed to be answered if the girl's death was connected to the dangerous knowledge she might have possessed about right-wing groups.

'How the hell did whoever killed her know she was here, at the hospital?' Henry asked and quickly explained his background reasoning to the question.

Byrne shrugged. 'Radio transmissions?' he

suggested. 'Could well have been listening in. We thought they'd been scanning us earlier on Shoreside.'

'Possibility.' Henry chewed the inside of his mouth, making a squelching noise. 'And if that is true, then they also stalked the A&E department until Taylor – God bless his socks – went for his fatal coffee break.' Henry thought about what he had just said. Something clicked in his brain, then went. Probably nothing.

'It's a busy department,' Byrne said. 'People come and go all the time. It wouldn't be difficult to blend in and hang around.'

'My head hurts,' Henry said prophetically – because just then he was hit by a stinking headache which came from nowhere and lurked nastily behind his eyelids.

David Gill grinned happily to himself. He loved it when a plan came together – and this one was coming together easier than a children's jigsaw: slot, slot, slot, all the pieces fitting snugly together – fucking wonderful.

First Mohammed Khan's death – better late than never – then the riots where the detective got torched – a bonus – and now the extra problem solved, the one that could have been a difficulty – the girl. It was unfortunate that she had been arrested in the first place, but because of the liability aspect, she had had to be dealt with.

He was not proud of the way in which he had killed her, though. Because it was

220

something that had had to be done quickly, it had lacked finesse. A pillow over the face, for Christ's sake. Where was the panache with that one? Just a means to an end, a functional tool. No flair. No fun. He loved to talk to people first. Loved to explain things to them, to outline the reasons for that ultimate question they all asked: Why? Why me?

Because you have to get killed, that's why. Because you are a cog in the machine and the machine needs to be destroyed. And this week powerful moves were going to be made to destroy the machine and show the country that a sea-change is about to take place. The balance of power was about to shift and return to where it belonged. The old order is going to be restored and revamped for the people.

So he regretted not having had the chance to tell the girl why she had to die. He also regretted that she had been drugged up to the eyeballs because that meant she could not struggle – although there had been the faintest blip of self-preservation when her body found the air had been cut off, but it had been nothing really, just a twitch, a reaction.

Still, David Gill took some solace from the fact that Joey Costain had known full well why he had to be murdered. Gill had talked to Joey for quite a while.

Gill picked up the telephone.

Time to alert the police. What a shame. They were so busy.

'Here.'

Henry's eyes opened. He had allowed himself to wallow in his headache and had sat back on the sofa in the staff rest room, closed his eyes and drifted. He hadn't heard the door open. The next thing he knew was that Dermot Byrne was standing over him, PC Taylor just behind him. Two paracetamols were in the palm of Byrne's outstretched right hand, offering them to Henry, a glass of water in the other.

'Thanks.' He took the tablets and threw them down the back of his throat, swallowing them with the water, which was very cold. 'Right, let's get things up and running.'

'I've told John he can go back to the station and get his statement written,' Byrne said, 'if that's all right.' He looked at Taylor, then back at Henry. 'I don't think he'll mind me saying, but it might be the best use of his time at the moment.'

Henry stared at the constable who looked dreadful.

'I think you're probably right,' Henry said. 'Best place for him.'

'Blackpool to inspector,' the personal radios shouted in unison.

'Receiving.' Henry almost tutted. He was beginning to detest having to carry a radio around with him all the time. There was no hiding from it. Not like when he had been a DI, back in those balmy, rose-tinted days, when Henry had only used the radio when it suited him. Being at everyone's beck and call

222

did not sit easily with him.

'Can you give me a landline number where I can contact you, please? Or can you phone in?' the radio operator requested. 'It's urgent and not something I want to put out over the air in case of scanners. Don't want to call your mobile for the same reason.'

'Give me a minute,' Henry said. 'Wonder what it is now?' he said to his officers. He hurried out of the rest room to the charge nurse's desk where the charge nurse regarded his approach with some hostility.

'What d'you want now?' she asked. 'Should I close the hospital while you dust it down for fingerprints?'

Henry smiled ingratiatingly. 'If I was a bit assertive before, I apologise.'

'Aggressive, not assertive,' the nurse corrected him.

'Sorry.'

'And now you want something else, don't you?'

Henry gave her his best boyish grin. 'Just a little thing.'

'A little thing, dearie,' she said flirtatiously, showing Henry a surprising trait to her personality, 'is all I've got. What d'you want?'

'Borrow your phone?'

She actually looked disappointed. 'Be my guest.' She slid the phone across her desk. 'Nine for an outside line.' She resumed browsing through the patient notes.

'Appreciate this.' He perched one cheek of his backside on the desk and stabbed the direct dial number in for Blackpool Communications. 'Inspector Christie here.'

'Thanks for calling in so quickly, sir.' He had managed to get straight through to the radio operator who had talked to him on the radio. 'We've just received an anonymous call from a male person, untraceable, to say we can find Joey Costain at an address in Withnell Road, South Shore.' He gave Henry the house and flat number of the property. It was not far away from the address which they had searched earlier without success. 'The caller said we should get there now because Joey's in a bit of a mess.'

'Joey's in a bit of a mess? What does that mean?'

'Don't know, sir. Those were his exact words.'

'And he didn't say what was meant?'

'No, sir.'

'When did you get the call?'

'Exactly six minutes ago.'

'Any details from the caller at all? I take it you spoke to him?'

'Yes, sir, me.'

'Stop calling me sir,' Henry said with a tone of annoyance.

'Sorry sir – oops!'

'Caller details?' Henry reminded him.

'None. All refused. Sounded like an Asian or someone pretending to be one.'

'Was it a treble nine?'

'No – direct dial. Tried to trace it, but the caller must have used 141 before calling. Not recorded, either.'

Only 999 calls were recorded as a matter of course.

'And, "Joey's a bit of a mess". Those were the exact words?'

'Affirmative.'

Henry went quiet. In the distance a casualty nurse called out a patient's name. Henry was thinking it would be very nice to have Costain ready and waiting in a cell for Jane Roscoe in the morning. Not only because arresting Joey was one of life's great pleasures, but because it would be one over on Roscoe, and no matter how much he had begun to like her, he could not resist the temptation to come up smelling of roses.

'OK, give me a few minutes to sort things out up here, then I'll let you know what we're going to do about it, if anything. And well done for not broadcasting this over the air.' He hung up.

Byrne and Taylor were behind him, having listened to his end of the conversation. Byrne looked eager, Taylor like death warmed up.

'Got an address for Joey Costain,' he told them, 'from an anonymous source.'

Acting on anonymous information, not backed up by other intelligence, was fraught with the danger of going shit-shaped, as so many police operations had shown in the past. There was always the possibility the information was simply being misleading or malicious, often the result of someone getting back at someone else for purely personal

225

reasons. There was also the chance of booting down the wrong door and giving some innocent old granny heart failure, or shooting a kid. It was a position very difficult to defend in the arena of a Coroner's Court. And it was always newsworthy.

'I don't think we need to go in with all guns blazing,' Henry conjectured, biting his top lip while his mind ticked over. 'Right,' he said abruptly, coming to a decision. 'You carry on up here, Dermot, and make sure everything's ready for the senior investigating officer, and I'll take John, here–' he cocked his thumb at Taylor – 'back to the station, but we'll go via South Shore and check out this address softly, softly. If Joey is there, all well and good. I'm sure we can handle the little shit between us. If he's not, we'll make profuse apologies and leave and at least we haven't gone OTT. Come on then,' he said to Taylor, who for the second time looked less than enamoured by another of his inspector's instructions. 'Let's hope that car of mine has enough juice in it to get us back. You be OK here?' he asked Byrne.

'Absolutely.' Byrne indicated something beyond Henry's shoulder: the on-call SOCO team arriving at the hospital.

The circus was rolling into town.

South Shore, known nationally and inter-nationally as the location of the Blackpool Pleasure Beach and the roller-coaster ride, 'The Big One', was interlaced with thorough-

226

fares such as Withnell Road. They all looked very similar, with long, multi-storeyed terraces of houses, most of which were either bona-fide guest houses, or had been divided up into tiny flats to house 'doalies' – unemployed people drawing state benefits.

Generally, South Shore was the fairly seedy backdrop to the colour and brashness of the promenade. Car crime, burglary, muggings were rife, all symptomatic of an out-of-control drug culture which pervaded the whole resort, not just the south.

Henry cut the engine and the lights and coasted in to what he hoped would be a silent stop at the end of the street. He cringed, but was not at all surprised, when the brakes grated and squealed. He climbed out with a 'Come on,' for PC Taylor. 'Leave your helmet in the car. Let's go and have a shuftie.' He closed the door quietly. Taylor did likewise.

Several street lights had been smashed or were simply not working which ensured there were many shadows for the two cops to flit between as they edged their way to Joey Costain's alleged address. It was quiet. Four thirty in the morning, the most peaceful time of day in Blackpool. The sky was showing the faintest grey-grittiness of the sluggish approach of dawn. A chill was in the air. Less than 200 metres away, Henry could hear and smell the sea as it lapped against the sea wall.

The officers paused outside the address given by the unknown caller. The information said Costain would be in flat number 3 on the first floor. The whole building was in darkness. Nothing stirred on any of the three floors; however, number 3 could easily be at the back. Concrete steps led up to the front door.

Henry led Taylor up, treading carefully but still failing to spot a broken syringe which Henry's boot crushed.

'Shit,' he whispered, looking down.

'Fucking junkies,' Taylor added, startling Henry with his language.

On the wall next to the front door was an array of doorbells, each connected to a flat inside. Henry counted them: twelve. The flats must be minute, he thought. Some of the bells had the names of the occupants next to them, most did not. Anonymity was easy to attain and retain in South Shore. Henry flicked on his pen-like Maglite torch and read them. Number 3 was a blank. Number 8 seemed quite interesting, Henry thought in passing: Maria. French Lessons. *'Merci beaucoup,'* he said under his breath.

He tried the door knob, which did not turn, but amazingly the door opened when he gave it a firm shove, opening to reveal a dark, unlit vestibule. On the left was a narrow, steep set of stairs leading to the first floor. Straight ahead was a high-ceilinged hallway with three closed doors off it.

Henry had been in many such dives. In his time as a cop he had probably been in thousands and hoisted out hundreds of criminals from them. Inevitably all these premises were much of a muchness: similar layouts, similar facilities, similar smells and similar occupants. The truth was that the same social template could be laid over most of the people he'd had dealings with over the years in these properties: mostly mid-teens to late twenties; they all drew their giros, never paid into bank accounts because bank accounts were for rich people; all smoked and drank, although they never had two ha'pennies to rub together; they were drug abusers, thieves; often with lives that were overshadowed by their own violence or abuse against themselves; they were usually from broken homes – and yet, despite these common characteristics, each was an individual. Henry had even quite liked some of them and had some sympathy for their predicaments, but it stopped short when their deprived backgrounds and shortcomings meant other people suffered.

His thin torch beam shone at the first door he came to in the hall. Number 1. Next was number 2 and the one at the far end of the hall was 2A. Taylor had crept down the hall behind him. When Henry turned after checking the number on the last door, he bumped into Taylor. Both nearly fell into a tangled heap of manhood on the sticky carpet.

'Hell fire!' exclaimed Henry, only just keeping his voice down.

'Sorry.'

Shaking his head angrily and muttering, Henry brushed past the constable to the foot of the stairs. He peered up into the darkness, beckoned Taylor to follow – not too close this time – and went up, using his torch intermittently until both of them were on the first-floor landing.

Henry stood still, his heart pulsating with excitement. He was enjoying himself, having forgotten how much fun policing could be. He put a finger to his lips and added a 'Shh' just in case Taylor didn't understand the gesture. Too late: both their radios blared out a distorted message with plenty of static. They turned them off immediately and waited for the inhabitants to start coming out of the woodwork like forest animals in the night.

No one came.

The officers listened. Someone, somewhere, was snoring loudly. Music was coming from one of the flats. Henry cocked his ear to it, concentrated – it was barely audible, but he recognised the riff with a flush of pleasure: The Rolling Stones, 'Midnight Rambler'. From the floor above he heard footsteps and another unmistakable sound, a couple having sex. Henry adjusted his hearing to listen, a quirky smile at Taylor who grinned back with embarrassment. Henry quickly realised the couple consisted of two men.

'All human life is here,' he whispered.

But, all in all, nothing untoward was happening. Henry was as certain as he could be that their entry to the building had not been clocked.

The nearest door was number 5. Down the corridor to 4, then 3, the one they were interested in. Both officers made silent progress even though the carpet was worn through to the boards in places.

Outside number 3 Henry realised this was where the music was coming from, which was good – being such a dyed-in-the-wool fan of the Stones himself would give him some common ground with Joey Costain, something to talk about, to break the ice, unless Henry had to break Joey's head first. 'Midnight Rambler' climaxed and ended with Jagger threatening to ram a knife down someone's throat. If the track was on the *Let It Bleed* album, Henry expected to hear 'You Got the Silver' next, instead, 'Midnight Rambler' began again, the haunting Keith Richards' riff filtering out through the door.

Without knocking, Henry tried the door handle. It opened. He turned to Taylor, winked, and pushed the door open slightly. No lights on inside the flat. Henry paused on the threshold. His senses were now razor sharp. Expect the worst: an attack; an escape – or for this not to be Joey Costain's flat.

The music was louder with the door open. It was an insistent, urgent riff. Henry knocked gently on the door, almost making no sound with his knuckles, his mind concocting a fabricated story in case Joey wasn't here and someone else was.

'Hello,' he whispered into the flat, not loud enough for anyone to hear. He twitched his head to Taylor who had a look of abject horror on his face.

'Can you do this, sir?' he gasped. 'What about the Police and Criminal Evidence Act?'

'Didn't you know – we're in the police. We can do anything.' The smile he gave Taylor was mischievous in the extreme. 'We're entering premises under section one of the Ways and Means Act. Stick with me. We'll be OK.'

Taylor remained unconvinced.

The front door opened into a short hallway with two doors off it. One on the right, the other directly in front. No signs of lights under either door. Henry opened the one on the right and put his head and torch round. It was a poky, smelly, toilet and bathroom. He flicked the torch beam round to confirm it was empty, populated only by the putrid smell of urine and shit. Not nice.

He closed the door and walked down the hall. His right hand withdrew his side-handled baton.

Behind him, Taylor followed suit.

Henry extended his baton with a crack as did Taylor, although it took him two tries to extend his because he was shaking so much.

Henry was positive this door would lead into the living room, kitchen and bedroom all rolled into one. Something the upper class would call a pied-à-terre and would cost a quarter of a million in London, but because it was in Blackpool, it was what Henry would call a shit-hole.

The music played on relentlessly. Mick Jagger sang with a sinister malevolence never achieved since. Henry's guts churned at the words of the song which had been inspired by the antics of the Boston Strangler.

Henry went for the direct approach, knocked loudly on the door, pushed it open and announced, 'This is the police. We're looking for Joey Costain.' The door swung open to reveal another room in blackness. Curtains closed. No light from outside filtering through at all.

A strange smell grappled with Henry's nasal passage, making him wince. He recognised it immediately. Death. Sweet and sickly.

Without stepping into the room, Henry leaned forward and located the light switch by the door. He touched it with his baton tip and knocked it down.

The light produced by the single, swinging, unshaded bulb, hanging limply from a wire in the centre of the ceiling was not dramatic, but curiously restrained. It did not have to be bright; in fact, a powerful light would probably have reduced the impact of what it revealed. The low wattage produced a dull, grainy light which cast grey-to-black shadows across the tableau – and the effect was terrifying.

Henry whistled, then covered his nose and mouth with his hand. 'At least we now know why Joey didn't answer his bail.'

Behind him, PC Taylor stood on tiptoes, eager to get a glimpse of the room, then wished he had not bothered. As soon as he realised what his eyes were seeing, his legs turned jelly-weak and folded underneath him. He keeled over as the blood left his brain and he hit the floor. Hard.

Henry did not move, even with Taylor wrapped around his ankles, groaning as he came round.

'Feel sick,' Taylor said, retching.

'Again? Well don't do it on my shoes, do it in the hall.'

Taylor got onto all fours and crawled down the hall where he vomited what was left of his stomach contents – a surprising amount since he had already thrown up not long before at the hospital.

Henry gulped. Joey Costain lay dead in the flat. Butchered. Mutilated. Torn to shreds. Ripped open from his pubes to his neck, his insides turned outside, intestines wrapped around his neck like a garland. His hands were bound together by parcel tape, as were his ankles and lower legs. He was lying on the floor, on a rug, in the centre of the room. Dark gobs of blood were everywhere, like puddles of tar on the carpet. The walls were splashed and smeared with the stuff.

Henry tore his eyes away from the body, scanning the room, letting them take in everything they could. He would not be setting foot any further into the room for fear of destroying evidence. He dreaded to think how much he might already have spoiled by actually coming into the flat. His gaze moved across the walls. Something registered. He realised there were words there, written on the wall in blood. He squinted and shone his torch on them. They read: 'Gypsy scum.'

He switched the torch off. Mick Jagger on the Boston Strangler: 'He don't give a hoot or a warning.'

Eleven

Tuesday morning was when the party conference really kicked into gear, good style. It was the day Blackpool was deluged by thousands of politicians, would-be politicians, spin-doctors, hangers-on and everyone and anyone else who thought they had any remote connection with the political bandwagon. The prime minister was expected to arrive in the resort today with his controversial wife; they would show their faces at conference, then disappear until Wednesday afternoon and then stay until the conference ended on Friday after what the prime minister hoped would be a rousing, motivational speech, the quality of which would be measured by the length of the ovation.

Tuesday was also the day when anti-government, anti-anything protesters, campaigners and demonstrators landed en masse in Blackpool. Some were harmless slightly potty cranks, who reappeared year after year peddling their skewed points of view to anyone who would listen, regardless of who was in power. Others were seriously dangerous people, dedicated to their, often, warped causes and their right to inflict their message on the world by whatever means necessary.

The media also came into town on Tuesday. TV broadcasters had been in the resort setting up their outside broadcast equipment all weekend, both at the conference venue and at the conference hotel. Tuesday was the day they plugged in and started transmitting in earnest from breakfast to bedtime. They were joined on this day by their brethren from all other branches of the media.

Tuesday was therefore the day on which the massive police operation moved into top gear. Hundreds of officers were flooding into town from the surrounding countryside, rather like descending hordes of vandals intent on rape and pillage. They would work fourteen-hour shifts, day and night, and very few of them would enjoy the experience of the four very long, usually monotonous, tours of duty. The only good thing was the overtime – which came in useful in their December pay packets – and the free food and drink provided.

At 8 a.m. on that morning, now into his fifteenth hour of the first proper night shift he had worked in almost fifteen years, Henry Christie found himself in an emergency planning meeting in FB's commandeered officers' mess. FB was describing the get-together as a 'strategy and resources' meeting. Henry thought of it more as a 'shit's hit the fan, don't panic' sort of meeting.

Henry was with such luminaries as the local divisional commander and the head of the conference operation for that day, both chief superintendents. A detective superintendent senior investigating officer was there, together with Jane Roscoe, another DI called Corner and the Met superintendent Andrea Makin. Karl Donaldson, the FBI representative, stood at the back of the room, chewing, coolly taking it all in.

To Henry's surprise, Basil Kramer was also there, or perhaps he wasn't so surprised following FB's word in the shell-like a few hours before. FB was obviously out to impress by being an all-dancing, all-singing, all-round entertainer and Assistant Chief Constable.

Henry struggled to concentrate on the meeting but his mind felt like mush because he was so exhausted. However, when he did manage to focus he rather enjoyed the way in which FB fawned in one direction to Basil Kramer and preened in the other to Andrea Makin as he spoke. It was plain to see that FB was seriously stressed out: he'd had little sleep and now his police force had let him down by allowing two murders to happen right under its nose.

'We find ourselves in a very grave situation,' he was saying, 'and I don't need to tell you what effect these murders will have on the streets as well as on our image – particularly as this week we are right under the spotlight.'

'So what are you going to do about it?' Basil Kramer asked, applying pressure which Henry thought was out of order. 'The PM will be extremely eager to hear, particularly as tomorrow he will be making his keynote speech on law and order and the home secretary will be making one on how he proposes to relax immigration laws. The PM will be pledging millions of pounds of extra cash to the police service and Lancashire will get a sizeable chunk of this cash. It would be ironic to see the forces of law and order collapsing around his ears as he spoke – wouldn't it?' Kramer's voice held a hint of threat: perform, or you don't get the dough.

FB blanched. Beads of sweat tumbled down his forehead, his jaw muscles tensed visibly. His eyes criss-crossed the room, landing on Henry Christie whom he blamed totally for the current predicament. 'Henry,' he said, 'maybe you'd like to brief us all about last night's events.'

Henry had expected this to be dumped on him. FB was a past master at buck passing. 'Yes, sir, no problem.' He cleared his throat and began to recount the happenings of the busy night to his attentive audience. He had spoken in such forums before and was unfazed by it. He knew all the Lancashire detectives in the room well, having worked extensively with them all, bar Jane Roscoe. He concluded by recapping his thoughts on

238

the two murders, because as an ex-detective, he believed he had the right to do so and as FB had given him the floor, he was going to take advantage. He kept it pithy and to the point, though. He didn't want to bore or alienate his audience with too many details.

'Geri Peters had already intimated she knew something about the right-wing extremist group, Hellfire Dawn, but that she was afraid to tell us. I think she would have said something to us eventually and whoever killed her believed this too. I know that an impulse killing will have to be a consideration, but I believe the answer to her death lies with the knowledge she possessed. So what was that knowledge?' Henry stopped, allowing the question to hang in there. He went on, 'Joey Costain was linked to Hellfire Dawn, too. He was an activist, although his own ethnic background doesn't quite sit with their ideals of white purity – he's from a gypsy background,' he explained to the one or two puzzled expressions in the room. 'So how come he was doing their dirty work for them? Having said that he was the main suspect for Mo Khan's death, so things point to the Khan family taking retribution, right down to the slogan written in blood on the wall. So, yeah, the Khan brothers have to be pulled in for questioning, but the way he was butchered doesn't sit easy with that line of thought, not to my mind anyway. The Khans are very handy with knives and guns and I think they would quite happily have slit Joey's throat and let him bleed to death. They wouldn't have carried out the post-mortem.' Henry's face screwed up. 'The Khans don't feel right for it – that's it,' Henry ended.

'Right, thanks for that ... er ... insight,' FB said insincerely. 'You can go home now,' he continued, dismissing him. 'Now, gents – and lady – we need to make some decisions about how we are going to divide up our meagre resources for these murders.' His eyes roved the room and landed back on Henry, who had not moved. 'You still here, Henry? I thought I'd told you, you can go home to bed now.'

A titter of laughter rippled round the room: Henry Christie was being publicly shown his place in the new order of things. Reactive inspectors were very low on the food chain, somewhere just above plankton.

'And by the way,' FB rubbed it in, 'be back here for five o'clock. I want to know your plans for keeping the peace tonight – because they weren't very good last night, were they?'

Patronising twat, Henry thought as he rose, red-faced, not making eye contact with anyone. He slunk out of the room thinking, Stuff you!

FB continued, 'We might well be overrun with bobbies, but each and every one of them is tied up with the conference, so you can forget them. The next few days are going to be very tight manpower-wise so you can forget full murder teams until the weekend. As I see it, we need to get two investigations

240

up and running side by side, but linked by the same senior investigating officer – anybody disagree?'

No one did.

'Detective Superintendent Thomas – Dave, you're in overall charge, OK?' FB indicated the man, who nodded. 'DI Corner, you can have Geri Peters, and DI Roscoe, you can have Joey Costain because his death seems like a follow-on from the job you were already running.'

By the time he was putting his arms into his leather jacket Henry had calmed down somewhat and was glad to be going home. Maybe some of the dubious words of wisdom from the great Burt Norman from last night were not far off the mark: do your tour, go home, forget about the job. There had spoken a man who felt he had been shafted by the organisation and now Henry was on the verge of agreeing with him because had Henry not also been shafted? The problem with Henry was that he loved the job. He had loved being a detective. And, if the truth were known, if FB had offered him an office cleaning job on a murder team he would have grasped it with both hands and kissed his feet in gratitude.

You sad bastard, he told himself.

Burt Norman, who had arrived for work at 5.40 a.m. that Tuesday morning, was out of the office, making his presence known over the radio, constantly giving orders to the troops. Sometimes Henry wished he was a bit more like that, with an assertive, almost aggressive management style. The truth was he felt uncomfortable dishing out instructions like a bloody general, leading from the front all the time. When it was necessary, yes. But overall he preferred a more laid-back approach, leaving the shouting and bawling to people who revelled in it. Like FB.

He put the man out of his mind.

The walk back to the flat on his tired, aching legs did not have great appeal. He squinted out of a window at the sky. The day was bright and clear, which lifted his spirits a little.

In his head he planned the next half-hour in fine detail: Stroll home via the newsagent's, pick up a copy of the *Daily Telegraph*. Back to the flat, avoiding Fiona if at all possible. He craved silence. Into the shower to soap and shampoo off the night and get that fresh overall feeling. Into the kitchen wrapped in his dressing gown. Tea and toast. Skim the headlines. Two Nurofen, then approach the bed. Slide in between the cool sheets by nine and then go for seven uninterrupted hours sleep and pray that Fiona would be too busy neutering dogs and spaying cats to have time to pay any attention to her overactive libido.

Henry knew he could not have responded, even if the flesh had been willing. For the first time in his life he did not want sex, he wanted sleep. The realisation startled him.

His plans were unfolding as he walked through the station and out through the back doors of the huge covered garage and he suddenly remembered that he had not yet got a conference pass. Must do that tonight, he thought.

The place was buzzing with cops and their vehicles, all for the conference.

Henry's butterfly-like musings – the product of a tired mind – turned briefly to his ex-wife Kate and his two daughters, Jenny and Leanne. He longed to be going back to the marital home, with a doting wife who would once have done anything for him, gone anywhere with him, and the chaos of the two girls who adored him and would not give him a minute's peace, demanded cash with menaces, drove him up the wall and gave him the most wonderful cuddles...

Stop! Cease those unproductive thoughts. Live with the fact you have fucked up your life good and proper. There was no going back now. No restarts, either, he thought. Kate was all cried out of second chances and the business with Danielle Furness had effectively ensured that.

Which spun his thoughts to Danny – but all he could see was the last moments of her life, the twist of her head as her neck had broken and she had died with his unborn child inside her.

Stop! he told himself again. Move on! He put his hands over his ears and screamed silently. Stop this fucking nonsense.

'Boss – can I give you a lift?'

At first the words did not register with

243

Henry. He was still in that Tenerife bedroom watching Danny's attacker, one arm around her neck, the other smothering her face. The man had broken her neck expertly in one flowing motion. He had probably done it a hundred times before, practising on prisoners held in Soviet prisons. One loud crack. Instant death. Danny was the last person that man ever killed. Henry had seen to that as he fired a bullet into the man's throat. But it had not been a sweet revenge, just revenge. No consolation for the loss of the woman he had grown to love.

'Henry?'

He stopped, snapped out of his depressing reverie and pulled his hands away from his temples. He shook his head and looked at the car crawling along by his side. The driver's window was down, and Dermot Byrne's face looked out. 'Are you all right?' There was real concern in his voice.

'Yeah, course, just lost in thought.'

'Want a lift?'

He didn't really, but it would have felt churlish to refuse. He climbed into the back because PC John Taylor was in the front passenger seat, still looking very shaken and stirred.

'Are you two only just finishing?' Henry asked, realising he would have known the answer to that if he had been a better manager.

'Just helped John to finish off his statement and stayed with him while a couple of detec-

244

tives had a chat to him,' Byrne said.

Now that was a good manager speaking, Henry thought. Byrne was a caring sergeant who would probably go far.

'John's going off sick, by the way,' Byrne informed Henry over his shoulder.

The constable was hunched down in his seat, head bowed, hands clasped between his thighs as though he was freezing cold, utterly dejected and miserable.

'It's been a bit too much for you, hasn't it, John?' Byrne said sympathetically. The officer nodded.

Been too bloody much for us all, Henry said to himself, but kept his mouth tight shut. 'Enough for anybody,' Henry agreed, though the tone of his voice didn't. He wondered why, other than the tiredness which permeated his body and soul, he did not feel especially affected by the events of the night. He had been dreading the return to work but despite the ups and downs of the tour he had found he had loved it like mad. The hurly-burly. The here and now. The immediacy of it all. The responding. All in all it had been a great experience, even if at the time it had been very tough. On reflection it had been fun. Not as much fun as being a detective, maybe. Henry hoped his appetite for the job had come back with a vengeance and that innate mechanism most cops had for distancing their emotions from the horrors they witnessed was back with him. On the other hand, Danny's death still haunted him day

245

and night, but that had been personal. What he had been through last night was not really personal, so yeah, he could cut himself off from it.

PC John Taylor apparently could not. Despite his length of service, it was getting to him. Sometimes that happened. No doubt he was experiencing great difficulty coming to terms with the death of the girl at the hospital, perhaps blaming himself for it.

'Maybe it's as well you have some time off,' Henry said. 'Get things back into perspective.' He leaned forward and patted Taylor on the shoulder.

Taylor jumped at the touch, nearly leaping out of his clothes.

'Yeah, thanks, sir,' he said meekly.

'Dermot, could you possibly be in for five tonight?'

'Sure, why?'

'I have to see FB to appraise him of our public-order plans.'

'What public-order plans?'

'Exactly,' Henry said. 'What public-order plans? We need to get something together, plus there's some intelligence about the possibility of bomb attacks on some targets. We might have to do some warnings to licensed premises.'

'Bomb attacks?' Byrne exclaimed. Taylor lifted his head to listen. 'Where's that come from?'

Henry said, 'I can't say much about the source, but I'll brief everyone properly

246

tonight.'

'Fine,' Byrne said.

'Drop me off here, will you? I'm going for a newspaper. Thanks for the lift.'

Henry watched them drive away and bobbed into the shop.

Because virtually all the CID resources had been channelled into the murder investigations, the file on Kit Nevison had been passed down the line like a hot potato, landing squarely in the lap of a probationer constable called Standring who, it was decided, was the only person with any time to deal with it. Fortunately he was approaching the end of his two-year probation and had the makings of a sound bobby. He bounced his few doubts and queries off his sergeant, got told to get on with it and went down to the custody office. The cell keys were tossed in his direction, the custody sergeant pointed to a tray bearing all the prisoners' breakfasts and told Standring to dish them out before dealing with Nevison. Such were the pleasures of being at the bottom of the pile.

Standring shrugged philosophically and got to his task with a smile.

Ten minutes later all the prisoners, with the exception of Nevison, were eating a lukewarm breakfast of sausage, beans and toast. PC Standring returned to Nevison's cell with a breakfast and let himself in. The smell of Nevison was almost overpowering. Sweaty feet, putrid armpits, bad breath and blood-soaked hair all combined to turn up the officer's nose in disgust.

Nevison was deep asleep. It took several minutes of shaking and slapping to rouse him. Eventually he sat up, coughing horribly, holding his sore head in his hands, moaning. His skull apparently hurt like hell.

'Want some breakfast?' Standring asked, offering the plastic plate which had an unappetising display of food on it.

Nevison glanced at it and retched. 'No thanks. I'll have a brew though – shit, I feel fuckin' awful.'

'Bad news, Kit, you look awful too.'

'Thanks.' Nevison touched his bandaged head and winced, then took the plastic mug from the officer containing weak, but very sweet tea. He sipped it gratefully.

'Come on,' Standring coaxed him. 'We'll get you some aspirin, then you can have a shower and a shave. You'll feel much better. After that I'm going to interview you.'

'Eh?' Nevison looked stunned. 'What have I done?'

'You don't remember?'

'Can't say I do.'

'You don't remember whacking somebody in a pub with a beer glass, then slashing a cop with a Stanley knife and holding a woman hostage?'

Nevison pouted as he thought about this. He truly did not recall any of these things.

'Hence the bash on the head,' Standring added.

'Oh, that's what it was.' He rose unsteadily to his full height, towering above the constable who was no short-ass. Standring backed out of the cell, praying Nevison did not have a rush of angry blood.

The big man stretched, yawned and farted. As he relaxed he seemed to contract into himself, become hunched up and round shouldered, and very old-looking for his age. The years of excessive drink, drug and nicotine abuse had certainly taken their toll on him.

'Shower's down here,' Standring pointed.

Nevison emerged from his cell and walked in front of Standring, who stayed and supervised the shower and shave, ensuring the safety razor was returned to the locked cabinet.

'I need a fix now,' Nevison said, towelling himself dry. 'And I need to see the doctor and I want a fag.'

Henry's meticulous timetable went to plan. At 9.02 a.m. he slid between the sheets in his darkened bedroom and closed his eyes. Sleep came quickly.

Jane Roscoe had been stunned when FB announced she was to lead the investigation into Joey Costain's murder. She had been expecting to be sidelined and ousted by the big boys.

At first she flushed with pleasure, but when she began to piece together the implications of the situation, she was swamped by them. If only by virtue of the way in which Joey had been slaughtered, media attention would be intense, certainly in the early days. If the possible racial element came out, always a hot spud for any police investigation these days, it would mean that Roscoe had drawn the shit end of the short straw – and maybe that was why she had got the job. Conspiracy by the rednecks!, she thought.

Another issue which concerned her, but in which she had little say, was the way in which the few precious resources had been carved up. After Henry Christie had skulked out of the meeting, daggers were drawn and a messy fight had ensued which she had felt unprepared for. She'd said her piece, made her requests and then awaited the outcome which, when it came, had not been good from her point of view.

The problem was that everyone was making big assumptions about the direction the inquiry into Joey's death would go. It was obvious that the first port of call would be the Khan brothers. Bring 'em in and get 'em charged had been FB's simplistic approach. It would be that easy, he had reassured her. 'Mmm,' Roscoe had murmured to herself, unimpressed. And for that reason, FB had gone on to explain, she would not be getting half the resources available. Not even a quarter. She had ended up with four detectives. At least the administrative and IT side of the investigation would be shared between the two inquiries. Some consolation.

The meeting had dispersed about an hour later.

Roscoe stayed seated while everyone else left the room, deep in thought, wondering how she would kick-start the job. It was difficult to believe that the person whom she had been expecting to arrest for a murder that morning was now a victim himself, so topsy-turvy was the whole scenario.

Having had little sleep – she had only just got into bed before she had been called out again – and a fleeting but bitter argument with her husband about her apparent lack of commitment to home and marriage (again!), her grey matter was struggling to get going. She was only partly conscious of someone sitting down in the chair beside her. Only when an outstretched hand cut into her line of sight, did she react by jumping out of her skin.

'Allow me to introduce myself.'

Roscoe did not have a clue in hell who this person was. She had seen him earlier, standing at the back of the room – you could not fail to notice him. Tall, square-jawed, good-looking – drop-dead gorgeous, actually – in a Clark Kent sort of way, broad shouldered, athletic-looking physique, with his blond hair trimmed into a crew cut. He had a bright twinkle in his eye and looked so fit and healthy he made her feel like a slob.

She gripped his big warm hand, feeling herself go slightly giddy.

'Name's Donaldson, Karl Donaldson.'

'Pleased to meet you.' Her eyes quickly dropped to his left hand. She saw the wedding band on the appropriate finger. It was just a check for interest's sake, she told herself. 'I'm Jane Roscoe, detective inspector.'

'Yes, I know,' he drawled in his very pleasing American accent.

'Er ... I was wondering – what's your role in all this?'

'Just liaison with the Metropolitan police. I'm a legal attaché for the FBI. I work from the American Embassy.'

'Oh wow – a spy.'

'Hardly.'

'Anyway – lovely to meet you,' Roscoe said with finality, but he made no move to go.

'I hope you don't think I'm being forward, ma'am, but would you indulge me for one moment?'

When you call me 'ma'am' like that, she thought wickedly, you could indulge me for a good hour. 'Sure,' she said.

'Could I be so bold as to offer you some advice? One law enforcement officer to another?'

Roscoe sat back. 'I'd be rude not to listen.'

'Thanks,' Donaldson said with a smile that must have sent a thousand women's hearts a-flutter, as well as their erogenous zones. She was wondering what the words of wisdom were going to be. She had a horrible feeling, nice and sexy as the guy was, she might be in for some down-home, good ole Yankee yee-hah balderdash here.

'Having noticed you've been given a pretty tough assignment and seen your reaction to it—'

'My reaction! What d'you mean?' she demanded.

'Your non-verbals screamed discomfort.'

'I don't think they did.' Roscoe fidgeted haughtily, offended, her body language betraying her again.

Donaldson held up a hand to calm her down. The hairs on the back of her neck seemed to be burning with the hot redness which flushed her. She gritted her teeth. Donaldson could see he had to get his say in quick.

'On and off for the past five years, I've worked with Henry Christie. He's also a good friend.'

'Well woppy-doo, I'm so pleased to hear it.' Her face was drawn as tight as though she'd had plastic surgery gone wrong. Livid was the term which sprang to her mind.

'What I'm saying is that despite his faults – I mean, he's always close to the edge – he is one of the best detectives I've ever known and I've known some of the best detectives in the world, believe me. He has a remarkable instinct about people, things, situations, so I truly think you should take heed of what he said before he was belittled out of the room by Fanshaw-Bayley, who I also know well and find to be a first-class asshole and I've known the best assholes, too.'

'Well thanks for taking the time to offer me that advice,' Roscoe retorted primly. 'But, y'know, I think you probably misinterpreted my body language and I know exactly what I'm going to do in respect of this inquiry.'

Donaldson flicked a mock-salute. 'In that case, accept my apologies, ma'am, but to quote, "Many people receive advice, only the wise profit from it." '

'Eh?'

'Pubilius Syrus – first-century Roman writer – bye y'all.' Donaldson was gone.

Roscoe sat speechless for a few beats, then gasped. 'First-class asshole, my arse.'

PC Standring inserted the timed interview tapes, switched on the recorder and robotically went through the pre-interview spiel with Kit Nevison and the duty solicitor now representing him.

Nevison, now clean shaven, showered and smelling of soap, had a large plastic mug of sweet tea (six sugars) on the table in front of him. He said he understood what PC Standring had said and the interview commenced after he had been cautioned.

'So, Kit, do you know why you've been arrested?'

'Other than what you've told me – no.'

'What recollections do you have of last night's events?'

Nevison thought about the question for a moment. 'None.'

'Why is that?'

'Drugs 'n' booze, I expect. I was very drunk and I took loadsa different shite.' He shook his head at the recollection. 'Everything's just a blank after about the ninth pint. My mind was clouded,' he said proudly, 'and so was my judgement I expect.'

Standring sighed. This was going to be a pretty short, one-sided interview.

Back at his flat David Gill exercised to the limits of his physical capabilities: sit-ups, press-ups, ten thousand metres on the rowing machine, and then progressed onto cocaine which he was refining on the surface of a shaving mirror using a razor blade.

'Chop, chop, chop, chop,' he intoned breathlessly to himself with each downward stroke of the blade. 'Chop and separate, chop and separate, make some nice lines, just like soldiers marching along, one, two, three, four, left, right, left. But I'm not going to dip these soldiers into my boiled egg.'

With extreme care he perfected the lines of the white powder so they were all the same length and width. He had an eye for such things. Very precise.

'I deserve this,' he said.

He used a shortened straw to inhale, following the lines quickly, sniffing deeply, tossing his head back as though swallowing a pill. Then he licked the mirror clean and waited for the rush. He gasped as the drug entered his system.

It had been a hell of a night. Much achieved, much more yet to do and he was not remotely tired. The coke had cleared his head. The physical exertions, far from exhausting him, seemed to have given him more energy, more desire. There was no way he could sleep.

He jumped up and paced the small living room, tensing his muscles, bouncing on his feet, growling like a leopard – which was often how he saw himself. A leopard, but one which could change its spots, could adapt, but could remain camouflaged in the undergrowth, waiting to strike and destroy. He needed to feel the rip of flesh again. He wanted to get his fingers around someone's hot heart.

'No,' he said firmly. 'No.' He tried to get a grip.

He forced himself to sit down, but he needed to be on the move, on the hunt.

Twelve

After the short conversation with Karl Donaldson, Jane Roscoe had wandered through the corridors of Blackpool police station, going round and round, worrying about the enormity of the task that lay ahead of her. Despite the brave face for Donaldson, it made her feel quite ill because she did not know how she was going to tackle the murder inquiry.

In the canteen, now transformed into a rather plush dining room following the privatisation of the catering side of things, she found an empty table near a window overlooking the rear of Sea World on the promenade. She devoured three slices of hot buttered white toast and had a cappuccino (unheard of pre-privatisation).

Her thoughts turned to the American. Despite his glaringly obvious physical attributes, he had managed to irritate her by offering advice. And that quotation of his by who? Some bloody first-century writer no one on God's earth had ever heard of fuelled her annoyance. Supercilious git, she thought, what does he know? An FBI legal attaché – in other words some pen-pushing diplomat's lackey. Not even a field agent. What really riled her was that he had been able to read her body language as easily as a book of ABC. If he had been able to, so had others.

The other thing that made her seethe was that the words of advice he had offered actually sounded like common sense: speak to Henry Christie, listen to what he has to say. Something she had failed to do when Henry had said his piece before leaving the pre-breakfast meeting with his tail between his legs. Foolishly, the only thing she had been thinking about then was the fierce confrontation she had left behind with her husband. It had been going round and round in her head and, for the first time, had contained the word 'separation'. It had unsettled her more than she cared to admit. Hence she had missed Henry's little speech and to be truthful, the only time she had started concentrating was when FB had singled her out and said, 'You can have Joey Costain.'

Yikes! He had chosen her as a DI and now he expected her to get results.

So an approach to Henry would be a sensible thing. After all, he had been the first officer on the scene along with PC Taylor. For very practical reasons, an in-depth chat was a must. Yet she did not want him to perceive it as a cry for help. She would have to be a bit clever in the way in which she tackled him. The last thing she wanted was to make him feel superior again.

It was 10 a.m. At eleven she had the first

scheduled briefing for her murder team – if four detectives could be classed as a team. She needed something constructive to say to them. She unfolded a paper napkin and began to jot some ideas down.

Four Jacks. One DS, three DCs.

Roscoe smiled at her team. She knew the sergeant, Mark Evans, but not one of the DCs who had all been drafted in from other stations around the county. They all looked eager to get going. She unfolded the napkin and announced, 'This is the plan of action.' It raised a titter and a few smiles which died bit by bit as they all realised that Roscoe was telling them the truth: it really was the plan of action.

'Bail refused.'

Kit Nevison did not bat an eyelid. He had been expecting this. The duty solicitor representing him did not even open his mouth to make any representation. To remain in custody had a certain inevitability about it.

Lugubriously the old sweat of a custody sergeant wrote the details of why bail had been refused on Nevison's custody record, read them out and asked him if he understood.

'Aye,' said the big man.

'Sign here.' The custody sergeant pointed out the relevant spaces in the charge sheets where Nevison signed his name with a big black cross. The sergeant handed him a copy

259

and the solicitor snatched it out of his client's hands.

'I'll have that, thanks.' He folded it, slid it into his briefcase. 'I presume Mr Nevison will be taken to the next available court – i.e. this afternoon?'

The sergeant turned to PC Standring, the lucky officer who had been given the job of dealing with Nevison, and raised his eyebrows.

'Depends on how quickly I can get the file done,' he said truthfully.

The solicitor peered at him haughtily. 'Today would be nice.'

'We'll do us best,' the custody sergeant said, coming to the young PC's rescue. 'Don't make no promises, though.'

'Fine,' the solicitor conceded, adding again, 'But today would be nice.'

Standring nodded. A remand file was actually quite a straightforward piece of paperwork. He knew he could have it done within an hour if pressed.

'I'll see what I can do.' He smiled at the solicitor, who frowned back.

'Take Mr Nevison down to the cells,' the sergeant said to Standring. 'I'll order lunch for him.'

'I still want the doctor,' Nevison demanded weakly. 'I'll cold turkey if I don't get a fix soon.'

'I'll give him a ring,' the custody sergeant promised, 'but don't get your hopes up. The days of prescribing methadone willy-nilly

260

have long gone.'

Nevison gave the sergeant a dagger of a look. 'Just remember what I did last night,' he warned.

'That was under the influence of drink and drugs,' the sergeant pointed out, unruffled by the veiled threat. He'd seen much worse than Nevison in his time. 'I'll ring the doctor, see what he says.' He flicked his thumb in the direction of the cell corridor. 'Trap number four.'

The ringing seemed distant at first. It came nearer, became louder, encroaching on the pitch blackness in which Henry Christie had been sleeping since his head hit the pillow. His eyes opened grittily. He was deep in the warm bed, the quilt drawn over his head, sleeping in the recovery position with one knee brought up. He slurped back the dribble from his cheek.

The ringing continued. Not the phone. The door bell. He closed his eyes, ignoring it. It persisted. Constantly. Continually.

Angrily he threw the covers off and sat up on the edge of the bed. 12.05 p.m. A grand three hours and three minutes of sleep.

He swallowed, almost choked and grabbed his dressing gown which he wrapped tightly around him. Scratching, yawning, rubbing his face and hair, he walked slothfully down the back steps to the flat door at the rear of the premises. The veterinary surgery was closed. Fiona was out making home visits.

261

'Sorry to bother you,' Roscoe said as soon as he opened the door and before he could say anything. He dropped his hands to his side in a gesture of submission and edged back a step. 'Come in.' Already he had realised it would have been too much to hope that after such an eventful night he would be allowed to get an uninterrupted run of sleep. Roscoe stepped past him and went ahead up the narrow steps. He followed and showed her into the spacious and high-ceilinged lounge and offered her coffee.

'If it's no trouble. I'll try not to keep you long.'

'Not a problem,' he lied. 'I'll put some clothes on.'

'Not on my account,' Roscoe was tempted to say, but held back. She had decided this needed to be a pretty focused, professional meeting and flirting was not on the agenda.

Henry shuffled into the bedroom, dragged on a pair of jeans and a T-shirt, slid his feet into his granddad slippers and trotted into the kitchen to brew up.

'Thanks,' Roscoe said, taking the coffee. She was standing by the large bay window which had a view over one of Blackpool's quieter, mainly residential side streets. She dropped down into an armchair, holding the mug tightly as though desperate for warmth. She glanced around the room.

'Nice pad,' she commented.

'Rent's cheap and it's better than nothing.' He sounded sad. 'Anyway, if you don't mind me saying, you look dead beat.' It was not said unkindly.

'Shattered. Three hours sleep is no good for anyone.'

'Tell me about it.'

'Yeah, sorry.' She laughed. 'I need to speak to you about Joey Costain.'

Henry gave a light shrug. 'Fire away.'

'I'm heading the investigation into his murder.'

The news jolted Henry like a whip-crack. 'Oh,' he said coldly, shocked, then tried to cover up the way he was feeling with a bright, 'Good luck.'

Fleetingly she was tempted to soften the blow to his fragile pride by going belly up, telling him how exposed and vulnerable she felt at being given the job, and pleading for any help and direction he could offer. No bloody chance. 'With you having been first at the scene and knowing the background about the Costains and the Khans, it seemed appropriate for me to have a chat with you.'

'Me? A mere uniformed inspector,' he said bitterly. 'How touching.'

'Henry, you and I both know you shouldn't be a uniformed inspector. You are a detective and this is merely a blip. You'll soon be back in civvies because they can't afford for you to be otherwise. Being a detective is what you're good at – one of the best, according to Karl Donaldson.'

Henry guffawed. 'What's he been saying? I wouldn't believe a word of it.'

263

'To say he sang your praises is an understatement.' Roscoe saw Henry actually blush. She wondered how far to take all this buttering up, but it was evident he needed it. He was in the pits professionally speaking and, looking round this flat, probably personally as well. Yet she did not want to go over the top and allow it to become patronising. 'If it makes you feel better, I'll make an admission, OK? I'm out of my depth here. I need someone to help me out, a mentor, whatever.'

'No, you're right,' Henry maintained with frost, 'it doesn't make me feel better, so why don't you just open your *Murder Investigation Manual*? That should tell you all you need to know.'

'Whoa, hold on there, Henry. Talk about cutting off your nose to spite your face. Just because you've had a bad time of things, are you going to withdraw into your shell and waste all that knowledge and experience you have?' Roscoe was getting impatient. 'I've come here to ask for your help. OK, I didn't want it to seem like I needed it, but I do and that's a hard thing for me to say to you, Mr Perfect, the CID god who all the stupid, macho male detectives look up to like some sort of role model. Well, you might be a good detective, but that doesn't stop you being an arsehole in the bargain.' She banged her cup down on the coffee table, angered by the turn of the conversation. He had touched a raw nerve. 'If you don't want to help me, fine, I'll handle it. Wallow in your self-pity. The only person who is going to suffer is you.' On the last word she pointed accusingly at him.

'I feel very resentful about the way in which I've been treated.' His voice was like that of a spoiled child.

'And I don't blame you, but don't blame me, either. We're both in a situation neither of us made. Blame that ultra-tosser Fanshaw-Bayley – then show the bastard he's made a great mistake. Being awkward will just confirm to him he did the right thing – don't you see?'

'Yeah, sure. Easier said than done.' He stood up and stormed across to the bay window where he sulked. Roscoe sat back and exhaled with frustration. She gave him a few seconds.

'Can we start again, Henry. Pretty please? I've got a job to do and I want you to help me. I've had a bad start to the day, including a barney with my bloke, so stop being a prima donna and start being the professional cop you're supposed to be? Eh?'

Henry groaned in embarrassment. This was not his style and Roscoe was perfectly right. It had all just welled up in him when she had told him she was heading the Joey Costain job. 'I'm being a prick, aren't I?' He came back to the settee and slumped down next to her.

'A fully erect one.' She smiled.

By the time the police surgeon got to him, Kit Nevison was in a mess. He was sweating

265

profusely, shivering and shaking, pulling at his clothes and had started seeing serpents coming out of the cell walls, spitting fire and venom at him. He was pleading like a beggar for help. It was an easy option the surgeon should not really have taken, but the look in Nevison's eyes said, 'Danger,' so she prescribed methadone, the heroin substitute in a linctus form, which PC Standring obtained from a local chemist.

Nevison eagerly drank two measured capfuls of the green liquid, gulped it down and desperately licked out the inside of the cap to get the last trace of it. The warmth from it was immediate and wonderful and serene. He then took a swig from the cup of tea thoughtfully provided by Standring. A hot drink, as the officer knew, speeded up the dissemination of the drug into the system.

Relief. Blessed, even. But short lived. Methadone was good, but not as good as the real thing which Nevison knew he would need very soon, otherwise he would really crack up.

'Hell's teeth, is that the time already?' Roscoe jumped to her feet. 'Got to get down to the murder scene, then go with the body to the mortuary.'

Henry rose rather more sedately. 'So you come to me, saying you haven't got a clue and then you reveal that you're only just going to the murder scene?'

'What are you saying – that I should've
266

gone straight away? I had a DS controlling it and I didn't want to get in the way of SOCO or forensics.'

'Exactly. Most DIs I know could not have resisted going down to the scene and tramping their size tens all over it. What you've done is spot on.'

'Thanks – more by luck than judgement.'

'There is one thing, though. Take your time when you get there. Don't let anyone rush you. You only get one chance at a crime scene and once something's lost, it's lost forever.'

'I'll bear that in mind. Can't say I'm enthralled by the prospect of the post-mortem.'

'Lots of valuable evidence to pick up there. Plus all the insights the pathologist might offer. Anyway,' Henry joked, 'the PM might not take too long. He's already been prepared, hasn't he?' Roscoe went pale at the thought. 'Who is the pathologist?'

'Baines – he's down at the scene now.'

'Oh, he's good. Give him my regards, we go way back.'

'Is there anyone you don't know?'

Henry winked enigmatically.

'Anyway, must go.' Roscoe brushed her skirt down and walked towards the living-room door. 'So you reckon the Khans aren't suspects?'

'Suspects, yes. They definitely need to be questioned. But offenders? I doubt it. They're pretty handy with knives and if I'd found Joey with his throat cut from ear to ear, I'd go straight for them. But the way he was left ...

you'll see for yourself.' He shrugged. 'The Khans do business first, then they might be killers, but to butcher someone like that takes a certain deranged mindset. But I could be wrong although it's never happened before, though.'

They both laughed. Henry went down the back steps behind Roscoe into the hall. Roscoe put her hand round the door knob.

'Thanks for your time.'

'Pleasure. I'm sorry I was such a fool earlier. Just me getting in touch with my feminine side, I guess.'

Roscoe smiled tenderly. She hesitated, then reached out to touch his cheek with her fingertip.

'I wanted to dislike you so much,' she said softly.

'Ditto,' Henry responded, almost choking on the word. In a flash of memory he was taken back in time to a different hallway, a different doorway, where he had once stood with a different woman in a similar situation. One which had led ultimately to his affair with Danny, a plethora of lies and deceit to his then wife and a very complex life which he had hated. Now he was a free agent, able to do whatever he pleased, but he was wary, though excited, by Roscoe's touch. This time it was the woman who was married, but the issues would be the same: lies, deceit, deception, betrayal. He did not want it to happen again.

They gazed at each other, suspended in

time, her warm fingers on his face. Neither really wanted to break the moment.

'Go back to bed,' she whispered. 'I'll see you later.'

Neither moved until Roscoe very slowly and deliberately leaned forward, went up onto her toes and brushed her lips against his cheek, sending the equivalent of a thousand volts searing through him. At the same time she was thinking what a God-awful mess she might be getting into.

Before they could pull away from each other with any degree of conviction, the back door opened.

'It's OK,' a voice was saying, 'I'll let you in to see him – Oh!'

Roscoe jumped away from Henry as though she had been stung by a bee.

'Well,' said Fiona. Behind her in the back yard stood Karl Donaldson. Fiona's face was set as though in concrete. Donaldson was expressionless.

'I'll see you later, Henry. Excuse me.' Roscoe ducked out between the door and Fiona and threaded her way past Donaldson.

Fiona remained rigid. 'This man wants to see you,' she said coldly. 'I'll speak to you after I've castrated a bulldog.' She pushed Henry out of the way and walked regally into the back of the surgery.

Donaldson contemplated his friend.

'Got a problem, Yank?'

'Nope.'

'You'd better come in.' Henry went back up

269

the stairs, the word, 'Fuck' stuck silently on his lips.

Henry and Donaldson had met several years earlier when both found themselves on the trail of a psychotic Mafia hit man operating in the north of England. Subsequently they had become close personal friends and ever since the two had snaked in and out of each other's personal and professional lives. Donaldson had non-judgementally supported Henry throughout the trauma of divorce without actually taking sides and alienating Kate, who was also a good friend. This was the first time they had spoken on a one-to-one basis for a while.

'How's it going?' The big American gazed around the huge living room.

'Oh – bouncing back, I think. Probably at a quicker pace than I'd intended, but that's down to our mutual chum, FB, putting me into uniform.'

'Yeah, I was surprised to see you dressed like that. It kinda suits you. I didn't know about the transfer from the detective branch.' Donaldson's last sentence was slightly accusatory.

'Nor did I until last Thursday.'

'So fast?'

'Yeah – this organisation can pin its ears back and make things happen when it wants to.'

'And what's the position romantically speaking? Is that homely DI Roscoe next in line for the famous Henry Christie chopper?'

Henry giggled. He was glad the slight air of tension had gone out of their conversation and pleased that his friend lacked so much subtlety that he could broach such a potentially delicate subject head on.

'No,' Henry replied firmly. 'She's got my sodding job so how could I possibly want to screw her, unless it puts her on maternity leave? I'd more likely be plotting a nasty death for her. I despise her, obviously.'

'Yeah, obviously. Goes without saying.' Donaldson smirked.

'Actually she is quite nice in a sisterly sort of way, but that's as far as it goes,' Henry said, trying to convince himself. 'As you probably gathered, I'm seeing Fiona, the vet from downstairs, but after that little bout of foot stomping we could be on shaky ground. Not that I'd be too concerned if it fizzled out ... I don't feel comfortable with her, she's far too intellectual for me.' He shrugged. 'We'll see.'

'And Kate?' Donaldson asked delicately.

The question stopped Henry dead, as it was designed to do. He inspected the carpet, scuffed it with his slippers. 'Mmm, Kate,' he said thoughtfully, sadly. A heavy silence descended like a shroud. 'Dunno,' he admitted. 'Haven't seen or spoken to her or the girls for almost two months.'

'Miss her?'

Henry cringed and nodded. Like he'd had his heart cut out.

'Still love her?'

'Fuck! You don't half ask some tough

271

questions.'

'Part of my job. I suppose you know she speaks regularly to Karen?' Karen was Donaldson's wife, an ex-Lancashire police-woman, now a chief superintendent with the Metropolitan Police.

'I didn't, but I'm not surprised.'

'I pick up that she still loves you, y'know. Despite you being the biggest jerk this side of Birmingham. I think she regrets the hastiness of the divorce.'

'Who doesn't?' Henry sighed, a melancholy mist beginning to envelop him. 'But it's over now. Separate lives and all that. She has a new boyfriend.' The last word was said with a sneer of contempt.

'Had a new boyfriend,' Donaldson corrected him. 'Ditched him.'

Henry digested this titbit.

'Look, H, I gotta lay it on the line and hope you won't be offended by this.' Donaldson cleared his throat. 'I'm here to see you for two reasons: one is professional and I'll come to that soon; the other is personal. When Kate learned I was coming north she specifically asked for me to deliver a message to you, one for you to think about.'

Henry's throat constricted and went very dry. His stomach churned, and it wasn't with wind.

'She wants you to ring her, see her, contact her somehow – but make contact.'

'To what end?'

'She wants to talk things through, sort

things out,' Donaldson said quietly. 'She misses you, the girls miss you. Their lives are all upside down without you ... maybe there's a way ahead.'

Henry swallowed the lump in his throat. 'I've given her too much to forgive.'

'Speak to her, Henry,' the American urged, 'can you say you're happy here?' Donaldson flashed his hands around the room. 'I mean it's–' He struggled to find adequate words. 'OK but not exactly home from home.'

'Yeah, I get the picture.' Henry stopped him.

'And if you still have any feelings left for Kate, if there's any chink of light there for her, you owe it to yourself and her to talk. Just talk – you never know what might come of it.' Donaldson slapped his thighs and sat upright. 'Here endeth the lesson. I now wish to turn to more pressing, professional matters.'

The heavy key clunked in the lock on the cell door and turned the bolt back.

Kit Nevison, laid out on the plastic mattress on the bench-bed, opened his eyes and sat up, wiping his face on the rough blanket.

'OK, Kit, how're you feeling?' PC Standring asked.

Nevison had been asleep. It had been short, deep and untroubled, made all the better by the methadone which was now well into his blood stream. He was dithery, and feeling weak, but otherwise on a fairly even keel. He twitched his shoulders in response to the

273

officer's question, unable to get his brain to engage his mouth to speak.

'Time for court.'

Nevison grunted something and swung his legs off the bed.

'Can you fold the blanket, please?'

Nevison complied. As he carried out the instruction he was able to utter a sentence, 'What d'you think'll happen to me?'

Standring grinned wickedly. 'Put it this way, Kit – you assaulted some poor guy in a club with a broken glass, you slashed open a cop's face and you held a solicitor hostage. You are obviously a danger to society, so what d'you think'll happen?'

" 'Aven't got much chance, have I?'

'No, probably not,' said Standring. 'Still, stranger things have happened.'

The conversation had moved on, but what Donaldson had said to Henry about Kate lingered in his mind. He had to concentrate hard on what the American was saying to keep his thoughts from drifting back to her.

'I didn't get a chance to talk to you in as much detail as I would have liked,' Donaldson explained to Henry. He laid a briefcase on his lap, clicked open the catches but did not lift the lid. 'I told you about the bomber operating across the States, if you recall.'

'New Offender Model Terrorist,' Henry nodded.

'You were listening,' Donaldson said, impressed.

'I've read about him in the papers – big spread in the *Sunday Times* recently. I've got my plans to distribute photos and some warning posters to the gay bars tonight.'

'Yeah – that's good. One of the things I wanted to share with you was the up-to-date intelligence on this guy, but I was told not to by FB in case of panic – but I'm gonna tell you anyway because I think you should know. I trust you not to blab.'

Henry sat up. 'Sounds interesting.'

'It is,' Donaldson said wearily, 'and you'll probably understand why we really want people to be on their guard this week. One thing the newspapers haven't yet picked up is that the bombs used for the four bombings in Europe in the last two months were all built by the same person. It's pretty hot news and we've only just put it together.

'All the bombings are claimed by right-wing groups. Two in Germany, one in France and one in Spain. All were targeted at minority communities and all took place either immediately before or during major political conferences. It's only now that the scientific side of things has been linked together that it shows that the bomb-maker is the guy from the States.'

'You're saying your man has gone international? He's offering or selling his services to right-wing organisations across the world?'

'That's exactly what I'm saying, though he's probably doing it for free or at cost price. These organisations don't have a lot of money to spend on freelance assassins.' Donaldson opened his briefcase and removed a large envelope. 'Here are some photos of the damage and injury he's caused.' Granite-faced he handed the package across to Henry who shuffled the photographs out onto the coffee table. They were vivid images of bomb scenes across America. Full-colour death and destruction.

The devastation was incredible. As ever, Henry was astounded by the extent of damage that such small amounts of explosive could bring about. Whole building fronts had been blown out and destroyed, the insides of buildings ripped out. The horror was un-thinkable. Henry shook his head in disbelief.

One series of photographs showed CCTV footage of an explosion. First there was a still of the street in question going about its normal, day-to-day business. The time in one corner of the frame showed 18.03.30. Next there was a massive fireball bursting out of a bar frontage. Time: 18.03.30. Then a raging fire and dense smoke filling the street: 18.03.31. Then just black smoke and devasta-tion: 18.03.32.

'Two people died in that one,' Donaldson pointed out. 'Eight injured.'

Two deaths, two seconds, Henry thought.

The next pictures were of bomb victims. Henry did not want to see these because they chilled his blood, yet at the same time he found them fascinating and revolting. He sifted slowly through them, a testament to a calculating murderer. The devastation that could be caused to a human body was awful in the extreme.

'Not nice,' he said in understatement. 'Who's claimed responsibility?'

'No one, which is where the lone terrorist theory comes in. However, all the right-wing terrorist groups thoroughly approve.'

Henry gave him the photographs back. 'You think this guy might be in town?'

'There's no firm intelligence,' Donaldson admitted, 'but if you look at the MO of the last four bombings in Europe – high-level government conferences and an attack on a minority group – it's a worrying possibility. If nothing happens, great. Let's all breathe a sigh of relief.'

'Well, thanks for that...' Henry stretched. He needed to get back into his pit. 'It has been good to see you, pal.'

Donaldson hesitated. 'There is one more thing.' He slid the photographs back into his briefcase and took another envelope out. 'If this guy is in the country and he does hit us, I want to catch the bastard if I can.' There was venom in his voice. He tapped another set of photos out of the envelope and offered them to Henry.

Henry looked at the top one, then quickly up at Donaldson.

'I want him bad, because he killed an old friend of mine.'

Another blood-soaked Technicolor photograph of two bodies. Both male, lying side by side in a pool of deep, almost black, blood. Both had massive gunshot wounds. Henry was transfixed by the image.

Donaldson went on, 'For this one he had a major change of MO. He hit a gay bar in downtown Miami, usual style. Then he exploded a bomb underneath the FBI RV point, killing three agents. Next he kills the two agents who found him on a nearby roof-top.'

'Why the change of tactics?'

Donaldson shrugged. 'Anybody's guess. Maybe to show us who's boss ... I just don't know. How do these guys' minds operate?'

'How did he manage to plant a bomb at the RV point?' Henry asked curiously, trying to get his head round the scenario. 'Surely the RV point would have been established after the bomb had gone off in the gay bar?'

'It was planted in a drain before the RV point was set up.'

Henry scratched his head. 'He definitely didn't have the opportunity to sneak it in?'

'Nope.'

'How did he know where the RV point would be set up?' Henry's tired mind cleared of its fuzziness as he worked through this one, the photo of the two dead law enforcement officers and the RV point bomb being the catalysts.

'Good question: knowledge of FBI tactics at the scene of such devices, plus a thorough recce of the area which would have given him a good idea where we would be likely to set up. It's possible he planted bombs at other possible RV points, we don't know.'

'Maybe he's trying to send you a message.' Donaldson looked quizzically at Henry as he twisted the photograph round in his fingers, tilting his head sideways.

'The one on the left is my pal, Col Briscoe. We were partners for a while when I worked the Miami Field Office. He was a close personal friend and a damned good agent. I'm still shocked how he got caught like that. He left a wife, two kids, one grandchild. Fucking tragedy. Amazingly he was still alive when our guys got to him. Died minutes later in the ambulance, but couldn't talk or communicate anything before he died.'

'I'm sorry,' Henry mumbled. His attention was fixed firmly on the photograph. 'I hate to suggest this, but have you and your colleagues considered that the perpetrator, as you call 'em, could be a rogue agent? Or an ex-agent, fired, maybe with a grudge.'

'Considered: dismissed,' Donaldson said crisply.

'Really?' Henry sounded surprised. 'Not some disaffected ex-agent, or serving agent with a downer on the organisation and minorities; someone recently fired or under investigation or disciplined?'

Donaldson said no. He sounded a little annoyed at Henry's persistence.

'Stick with me here, Karl. Have you ever seen a word puzzle which, when you first see the word, looks just like a few disjointed blocks, shaded grey. Then someone says to you what the word is and you go, "Hell, yes, I see it now!" '

'Can't say I have.' Donaldson's brow creased.

'The one I've seen is where the word is "TIE", written in capital letters. All you see at first on the paper are a few square, grey shaded blocks, then when your mind fills in the lines for you, the word becomes obvious. It's all about perception and some people will never be able to see the word, even when it's blindingly obvious to other folk. You'll definitely have seen that famous one that looks like a Grecian urn one minute, then two faces staring at each other the next. Or the old woman/young woman one – yeah? It's a matter of a bit of mind adjustment.'

'I know 'em. They're very well-known ones, always cropping up in training – but haven't you lost the plot here, pal?'

'Possibly.' Henry gave the photo back. 'Have a look at the blood next to your friend's body, hold the photo the right way up to start with.'

Donaldson peered closely, then held it further away from his face. 'Looks like he slipped and slid in it, tried to stand up, maybe.'

'Could well be,' Henry admitted. 'Now start to turn it round very slowly – you said this guy was a good agent?'

'One of the best.' Donaldson rotated the photograph as instructed, tilting his head too.

'Keep your head still.'

'Naw ... nothing.'

'Well, maybe it is nothing, perhaps my exhausted brain going into overload, y'know, the one with three hours sleep, now a blubbering jelly. Give it here,' Henry took the photograph back and laid it on the coffee table. 'But, I'll lay a pound to a pinch of shit – an old, northern saying,' he said in answer to Donaldson's expression of incomprehension, 'meaning I'll give you good odds, that no one has looked with a really critical eye at the pattern of the blood, but if you look at it and tell yourself it's not blood you're looking at, it's ink, what do you see?'

'I think I'm being dim here.'

'No, you just need to open your mind a bit.' Henry placed his fingertip on the photograph. 'I know it's rough and I could be wrong, but I'd say your old pal wasn't a good agent – he was an exceptional one right up to the end.'

Henry traced a shape in the blood with his finger. Then another.

'Anything yet?'

Suddenly Donaldson gasped and sat bolt upright. 'Jesus – unbelievable.'

'The very last efforts of a dying man to identify his killer, maybe,' Henry finished cautiously.

'Once you see it, it's so obvious!'

'He probably couldn't finish it off – fatally injured, shot in the head, that's not a surprise.'

Donaldson could not stop shaking his head in disbelief. Now he could clearly see the letters 'F' and 'B' written in blood next to Col Briscoe's body.

'Unless he's saying that ACC Fanshaw-Bayley is the killer – which would be fantastic because I'd love to lock the twat up – could he have been trying to write FBI? And if so, why?'

Kit Nevison stood in the dock of court number one at Blackpool Magistrates Court, hardly even listening to the heated exchange between prosecution and defence. It meant nothing to him. Words. Garbage. Either he'd get bail or he wouldn't. Eventually the magistrates retired to have a private conflab, returning about fifteen minutes later.

'Stand in court,' the cloaked usher said loudly.

Everyone rose, including Nevison. He was flanked on both sides by security guards from Group 4.

'Mr Nevison,' the chief magistrate addressed him. 'We have reached a decision concerning the matter of your bail.' Nevison swayed slightly. 'You will be released on bail on the condition that you report daily to Blackpool Police Station at 10 a.m. and 7 p.m. prior to the next hearing on the fourth of next month.'

'Eh?' Nevison replied dumbly, scratching his head.

'In other words, once you have signed the

bail forms, Mr Nevison,' the magistrate said testily, 'you are free to go.'

Two minutes later, Nevison staggered unsteadily from the court having had his property returned to him. He stood at the top of the flight of steps outside the court building and with dithering fingers rolled himself a ciggie. He lit it and sucked deeply. He patted his pockets in the forlorn hope of finding something. They were empty. Shit. He needed to score. But without money and feeling incapable of even robbing a granny, things were pretty desperate. Then he had an idea: he would go and see his friend. Yeah, that was it. Davey was always a soft touch. 'And,' Nevison thought, 'I have a key to his flat somewhere – where the fuck did I put it?' His eyes narrowed. If he could find it, he could let himself into his friend's flat and help himself. Davey was always leaving shit lying around.

Thirteen

David Gill was shivering. He was becoming colder, the more he held himself back from walking out of his little flat onto the streets, picking up the first dark-skinned person he saw and butchering them. He was desperate to kill, but knew that if he did so, everything would be put in jeopardy because it would be unplanned, careless and he would probably make a mistake. A thoughtless kill could ruin years of meticulously planned work; but he had spilled so much blood over the last two days that he had become addicted to it and longed for more. He had to pull himself away from it, but he knew he could not do it alone. He needed help. There was only one person capable of giving it.

Gill picked up his mobile phone and keyed in the letters V I N. The phone at the other end rang and was answered.

'It's David.'

There was no response.

'Vince, it's David,' Gill whispered desperately. 'I've done it, done what you asked—'

'You should not call me,' Vince Bellamy said. He had picked up the inflection in Gill's voice. He had heard it before and knew what

284

it meant.

'I need help.'

'Not here, not now – it's too dangerous for us all,' Bellamy said worriedly. 'I can't see you this week for both our sakes.'

'You must. I've done what you asked, extra. Now I need to see you.'

'No.' It was short, sharp. Bellamy hung up.

Gill closed his eyes. He began to rock back and forth, trying to catch his breath. Then his eyes clicked open. He knew what he had to do.

He changed quickly into his bicycle leathers, revelling in the sensation of the animal skin against his own. One day, he thought, I'll kill and skin a cow and wrap myself up in its hide. One day. Promise. He pulled the full-face helmet on and clamped down the black visor, ensuring no one could see his face.

Outside the flat, the walkway was deserted, as was the narrow stairwell leading down to the lock-up garages at the back. He saw no one, no one saw him.

His motorbike was inside the garage, just as he had left it: fuelled up, ready to go. He pushed the bike out of the garage and stood it on its stand while he went back inside where, despite himself, he unlocked the big chest freezer which was pushed along the back wall. The cold, escaping air misted his visor for a few moments, then it cleared.

Gill smiled grimly at the contents of the freezer, then slammed the lid shut and re-locked it. He secured the garage door and mounted his bike which fired up first time. He throttled back gently.

Time to get some counselling, he thought.

The Berlin Hotel was on Bairstow Street, running at right angles off the promenade, south of Central Pier. As had many establishments in the town, the Berlin had been through many incarnations, name changes and hands, finally being bought for a knockdown price five years earlier by its present owners after eighteen months on the market. They were a man and wife with extreme right-wing leanings. Both had been minor political activists in their younger days, and also Hell's Angels. They had bought the Berlin (as they named it) intending to make a living by providing an environment which pandered to that particular right-wing niche in the market. Being fanatical Nazis, they had spent money decorating the hotel accordingly, even down to the carpet which had been specially made, with a swastika pattern repeated throughout. They also opened a sleazy beer cellar, claiming that it was authentic German – and it did sell real German lagers. The boisterous evenings attracted the leather-clad biking fraternity as well as right-wing activists; closed political meetings became common and an affiliation to the 'Right Wingers' grew up and, through Vince Bellamy, the splinter group Hellfire Dawn. During this particular week of the conference, Hellfire Dawn used the Berlin as their own conference headquarters.

Extra decorations had been put up. Banners displaying huge swastikas and various provocative slogans were draped along the facade of the hotel. Immense photographs of the glorious leader, Adolf Hitler, accompanied these, his steely, slightly mad gaze watching passers-by.

David Gill knew it was a risk, but one he had to take. He had to see Vince. There was every chance the Berlin was under some sort of police surveillance, particularly this week, and there was the possibility he might be recognised. He found a parking spot for his bike on Caroline Street and walked the hundred or so metres down to the Berlin Hotel, wearing his helmet all the way.

At the foot of the steps leading up to the front door of the Berlin Hotel, Gill stopped and gazed upwards. Inside the all glass front doors, two tough-looking men lounged indolently. They glowered down at him. He nodded imperceptibly at the most prominent photograph of Hitler and trotted up the steps.

The two bouncers opened the door for him, but would not let him go through the next set of doors.

'Who are you?' one of the bouncers asked, stopping him from entering the hotel by putting a hand on his chest.

'I've come to see Bellamy.'

'I don't think so.'

'Yes,' said Gill. 'Let me through.'

'I think not.' The other bouncer moved towards him with menace.

Gill reacted swiftly, catching them unawares. He kicked the one in front of him swiftly in the testicles, hard and accurately. He went down like a lead balloon. Gill turned to the second one who, before he could punch Gill in the guts, received the full weight of the crash helmet on his nose which splashed open instantly. He staggered back holding it, unable to stem the gush of blood.

'Jesus Christ, David, you didn't have to do that.'

Gill turned quickly to the voice. It was Vince Bellamy. 'I needed to see you, Vince. No one should try to stop me.'

'And why the fuck do I employ you idiots?' Bellamy said to the groaning bouncers. 'Go and get yourself cleaned up f'Christ's sake. You couldn't protect a damn thing.' To Gill he said, 'Come on.'

He led him through the hotel. They went past the reception desk and down a short corridor. On the right was a large bar area with a fair-sized dance floor and stage. Dozens of rows of chairs had been arranged to face the stage and the walls had been festooned with Nazi-related literature and photographs of the German 'top team', circa 1939-45. They passed a large dining room to the left and went through a door at the end of the corridor marked 'Private – staff only'. This opened out into a further, shorter corridor with three doors off it.

288

The first door was open. Two men sat at a table with a Citizens' Band radio console on it and a transmission microphone. This was the radio room: Hellfire Dawn operatives were positioned at strategic points throughout Blackpool, equipped with radios, relaying information back to the Berlin Hotel about the movement of police and politicians. They were well organised. Last night the co-ordination of the rioting in Shoreside had been done from the Berlin.

Bellamy led Gill to the third door along and ushered him in ahead of him. He closed the door and locked it.

Vince Bellamy regarded Gill with a fatherly smile.

The two men had first encountered each other while students at university. Bellamy, the older of the two, had been a post-graduate and very politically active in a brand of extreme politics which had appealed to, and sucked in, the younger man. Bellamy, even at that age, his early twenties, had been able to exert great influence over others, particularly the weak. He and Gill had spent many hours together discussing the right-wing movement into the early mornings; Gill, who went by his real name then, listened attentively, rather than spoke, nodding in firm agreement about the way things should be, how Britain even then was losing its way, and how action had to be taken to make changes.

It had been during the course of these conversations that Bellamy had fuelled Gill's hatred of minorities, feeding his mind with twisted logic and suspect political argument. One night, after a long session, Gill had expressed his loathing of an Asian girl student in his year. She seemed to be given opportunities denied to white students, seemed to be getting favouritism, despite the fact she was coloured.

Under the influence of alcohol, Gill had revealed he would like to kill her.

In response Bellamy had said simply, 'Why not?'

At first Gill had hesitated. However, over a period of weeks the idea grew in his mind. It became an obsession which Bellamy nurtured until one night Gill said he was ready to do it.

Undetected, both young men entered the student accommodation in which the girl lived. They found her in her tiny bedsit, sleeping. Bellamy watched with excitement as Gill strangled her with her pyjama cord. Gill himself got a brutal pleasure from the taking of life and Bellamy got another idea for his political strategy: pick off individuals who somehow played a part in the decline of the country either by their presence or their actions. Like a sniper.

The police investigation did not come anywhere near the two men.

Before leaving university – to a job suggested by Bellamy – Gill murdered once more: a high-flying female student who was also suspected of being a lesbian. He murdered her with a knife and relished every single slice he took off her.

Since then, on Bellamy's instructions, Gill had murdered fifteen other people, all in some way connected to the 'corrupt system' that Bellamy wanted to make right. The methods of his killings varied and the police never really made any connections, which Bellamy found ironic and amusing, and fitted in nicely with his strategy.

There were occasions, though, when Gill needed to be cooled down for his own good – usually when he had carried out murders close together. Then the urge to kill was very strong in him and he needed to be talked down to some kind of normality, though Bellamy could only guess at the normality which existed in Gill's mind.

'David, you have done well this week. It has been hectic for us all. We all have had to go the extra mile. Things are coming together nicely. The end result is close. I'm sorry I had to ask you to kill the girl, but she knew too much about me.'

'You petrol-bombed the detective, didn't you?'

Bellamy nodded. 'It was an opportunity not to be missed, it increased the pressure. But Geri knew and I could not take the risk of her talking to the police to save herself. That was why I asked you to kill her, even though I know it was a difficult thing for you to pull off. But you did it and I thank you.'

Bellamy patted Gill's arm. 'Now you need

291

to step back, David. David – hah! David. I can't get used to calling you David. Here, come here.' Bellamy beckoned Gill into his arms. Gill fell into the embrace and held onto his mentor. 'That's good, that's good. You've done well. Other things are starting to happen on other fronts now. The American is here,' Bellamy whispered.

Gill drew back, wide eyed. 'That's fantastic! Can I meet him?'

Bellamy shook his head. 'No one meets him, not even me. That is how he wants it. I don't even know where he's staying. I just know he's here and he'll be producing a bomb for us. I'll keep you informed of where it will be placed, for your safety. In the meantime, though, David, keep a low profile. Your next job is the most important you will have ever done. Your crowning achievement.'

Once more he and Bellamy embraced.

Bellamy could do this to Gill. Twist him, manipulate him, make him realise he was wrong, take him in any direction he wished. Gill nodded, once again awed by Bellamy, the man he most respected in the world. He reckoned Bellamy was the one who had made him what he was, who had shown him the way. Bellamy had been the one with the big ideas and the way to achieve them. Gill knew he was simply a cog in the bigger machine of right-wing extremism. A miner beavering away at the coalface, doing the dirty but vital work.

★ ★ ★

The bomber breathed in the fresh sea air deeply. He looked out across Morecambe Bay from where he stood on the promenade in Fleetwood, to the north of Blackpool. In the distance, rising up from the swirling mists like two medieval castles were the twin nuclear power plants at Heysham. He wondered what the hell it would look like if they blew up. Pretty spectacular, he thought. From a purely professional point of view it was something he would have liked to witness. On a personal note, he hoped he would be in another continent if it happened.

He put his binoculars to his eyes and focused on the twin reactors, then swept across the bay, holding for a moment on the Isle of Man ferry which had just departed Fleetwood docks. Then he moved to a point on the shoreline, some fifty metres in front of him where several hundred oyster catchers had gathered to feast on the harvest uncovered by the receding tide. He watched them with some pleasure for a few minutes before strolling on.

Eventually he found a seat in a large shelter near the miniature golf course. Both shelter and course were devoid of people. He slid the rucksack off his back and fished out a small flask from which he poured himself a very welcome cup of coffee. It tasted wonderful against the chill of the fast disappearing afternoon.

Few people were about the place. One or two old folk with dogs, that was all.

The bomber sighed contentedly. Life had been good for the past couple of months on tour, as he thought of it, in Europe. His offer to several organisations had been snapped up on the back of his lone success in America and he had fulfilled his promises to them, and more.

Germany had been fantastic.

He had combined his visit there with a sight-seeing tour of the remains of the concentration camps and of Berlin. He had felt an emotional rush to be so close to what had been a wonderful campaign and those who had led it. He had been more than happy to provide two bombs which helped keep the movement alive and in the public eye and in which two Jews had died.

Then there had been France and Spain. One bomb in each. These countries did not have the buzz of Germany, but they had been pleasant nonetheless. Now he was in England which he was also enjoying. After this he would head home to resume business there.

He placed the rucksack between his feet and unzipped the hood. He eased a pair of latex gloves onto his hands before sliding his fingers into the rucksack and removing a plastic sandwich box. There was a timer strapped to the outside of the box and inside was a lovely nail bomb. Instead of big fat nails, the bomber had packed over a thousand steel panel pins into the plastic explosive. These would have their own particularly devastating effect. He had used a similar one in Chicago and had taken out forty eyes, totally blinding eight people and killing two blacks. That had been a good one. A delicate bomb, he had called it. Refined. It was also equipped with a beautiful trembler device just in case someone moved it either by accident or design once the timer had been set. He put the bomb into a plastic Asda shopping bag and wrapped it tightly with elastic bands.

He pushed the deadly package down behind the bench in the shelter, wedging it out of sight of the casual observer.

Now he could relax. Delivery made. He finished his coffee and walked back along the promenade, making a quick call on his mobile phone.

'Well?'

It was a demanding word, requiring explanation.

For a moment, Henry thought it was part of a dream.

'Well?' The word came again, probing, piercing.

Henry moaned, feeling very ill because the word had pulled him back up from the depths of a deep, black sleep. He wanted to ignore it, roll over, burrow into the bed, wrap the pillows tightly round his head and just bloody ignore it.

'I want to know who she was, what she was doing here and what the hell has been going on!'

Henry's eyes flickered open. Difficult, as they were caked in sleep. He was on his back, staring at the cracked ceiling.

'Who – what?' he said, mouth dry.

'That woman – that woman!'

He moved his head and blinked at Fiona. She was in her veterinary gear, green overalls and wellington boots, her hair tucked inside an elasticated cap on her head. Her arms were folded across her chest. She meant business, but was on the edge of tears.

'What woman?' he asked dumbly. His brain had not clicked into gear and he was beginning to resent being woken up again.

'The one who was kissing you – that woman,' Fiona explained.

'Oh ... right,' it dawned on him. 'You mean Jane?' He shook his head. This was the confrontation he had been dreading.

'I don't know who I mean because I don't know who she is, do I? All I know is that when I opened the back door I saw you and her kissing ... and God knows what else had gone on before that.'

'Right, right, I'm with you now,' Henry said, trying to pacify her and slow it down so he could get his own head round this and manage the situation. 'Here, Fi, come on, sit here.' He patted the edge of the bed. 'Come on,' he coaxed. She was resolute, unwilling to move. Her face and jaw were set hard, eyes glistening with anger. 'Look, come down to this level, I'm getting a crick in my neck.' He smiled boyishly.

Despite herself, she weakened and sat down, clenching her fists. Henry propped himself on one elbow and tried to touch her face gently.

She shied away, not wanting the intimacy of the gesture. Henry thought she looked beautiful, even in her working clothes with her hair pulled tightly away from her face and neck, tied into a school-marm bun under the cap. It accentuated her fine bone structure. From a looks point of view, Henry knew how lucky he was. When she was 'done up to the nines' she was absolutely stunning. Unfortunately, Henry had started to find her personality somewhat grating. While admitting his own was probably not much better, he was struggling to feel close to her emotionally and intellectually.

He glanced at the clock. 3.30 p.m. Only an hour since Karl had left. He had planned to have another three-quarters of an hour sleep, which now seemed unlikely. Henry – being a sensitive soul – sensed that tears were not far away and he wanted to avoid a blubbering scene at all costs.

So he lied.

'Jane Roscoe is a DI dealing with a murder that happened on South Shore last night. I had some information she needed as a matter of urgency, that's all.'

'So you pass information in the police mouth to mouth, do you? Kissing? Did you have a secret message in your spit?'

'No, no, no, no,' he cooed, holding up a

hand. Here was the lie, 'She also happens to be a very old friend. I know her and her husband very well. He and I used to play rugby together. It was a friendly kiss, nothing more. Certainly nothing sexual.' God forgive me, he thought, but needs must.

'Is that the honest truth?' Fiona snuffled.

Henry nodded sombrely.

'Oh, thank God,' Fiona gasped in relief. 'I thought you were going off me.'

'Never,' he said softly. Crisis diverted. He lay back. 'I could do with a bit more kip before I go back to work, sweetheart,' he suggested.

She seemed not to hear. She pulled off the hair net, shook her gorgeous locks free and kicked her mini-wellington boots off, then slid in next to him. He was very hot and naked.

'I was worried,' she admitted, hugging him.

'No need.' He yawned, hoping she would take the hint.

Next thing he knew, Fiona had disappeared under the duvet and his limp cock was in her warm mouth. He groaned, but not with ecstasy. Although he was unable to prevent an immediate erection, he would rather have slept than had a blow job. Which in itself said something about the relationship, he thought.

Gill was changing out of his motorcycle leathers, back into his casual gear. He had a quick glance round the flat to satisfy himself that everything was hunky-dory. He slid his denim jacket on, ready to leave and head to his real home.

When the 'rat-at-at' spanked on the door, Gill's bowels almost opened. He did not move. He closed his eyes. Maybe they would go away, whoever it was. More knocking. They were persistent. The sound of the letter-box flap opening.

'Hello,' someone called, 'could you come to the door, please?'

David Gill's legs turned to a sort of mush.

'I know someone's in,' the voice called. 'I heard you moving about, so please come to the door. This is the police.'

Fourteen

Jane Roscoe decided that any time spent at the scene of Joey Costain's murder was well spent. There was no point in rushing anything and thereby losing evidence. Once the forensic and SOCO people had done their initial work and withdrawn, Roscoe, kitted out in the latest high-fashion overalls and overshoes, together with the pathologist, Dr Baines, reassessed everything.

Baines was useful to have around. He had been to hundreds of murder scenes and had carried out the subsequent post mortems, so his experience was vast. He wasn't very old, either, Roscoe noted. Not like most of the pathologists she had come across before who were usually of or approaching pensionable age. Baines was in his mid-forties at most. He was also modest and helpful which endeared him to her. He recognised she was the senior investigator and that he was there to support her, and seemed to have no problems with that state of affairs.

She bled him dry with her constant questions. Patiently he answered them all, even when they had been repeated several times or were silly. An hour and a half of minutely working through the scene saw both of them parched. A break and a drink was needed. They peeled off their protective outer garments and left the flat, body and entrails still in situ.

Outside there was a good deal of uniformed police activity. The front of the house was cordoned off and uniformed officers guarded the scene closely. Roscoe and Baines ducked under the crime-scene tapes and strolled to a nearby café. Roscoe bought the brews and an Eccles cake each.

'What do you think then?' she asked Baines. She had a lot of her own ideas but wanted to see if his matched hers.

He chewed pleasurably on a mouthful of currants, swallowed and had a swig of tea from a cracked mug. 'He was murdered by a maniac – sorry I don't have the correct psychological terminology to go with that rather obvious conclusion.'

'That's OK – nor do I.'

'A maniac, but someone who is cold, calculating and very prepared. I think this attack was pre-planned. I'd also hazard a guess that the victim knew his attacker well or at the least trusted the attacker.'

'What makes you say that?' Roscoe's mug stopped halfway twixt table and lip.

'Unless I'm mistaken, there is no sign of forced entry to the flat, no sign of any defensive wounds on the victim's hands or forearms, although when I get the poor sod on a slab, such wounds might become apparent, though I doubt it. My cursory examination of the skull shows a massive concave dip around the crown, consistent with something like a ball hammer. Joey had been comfortable enough to have turned his back on his killer, so he wasn't expecting trouble.'

'Unlikely to be a member of the Khan family then.'

'Sorry?'

'Nothing, just musing out loud. Go on, please.'

'Little more to add at this stage. I think he knew his killer and I also think this killer has killed before.'

'Two issues there,' Roscoe picked up quickly. 'Him? How do you know it's a him?'

'A man or a very strong woman. I think the victim had been dragged and placed where he was. I don't think most women could have achieved that. It's not a sexist remark, it's factual.'

'I'll go with that. Now why do you think he might've killed before?'

'I've been to a lot of murder scenes. Murders committed by first timers are always rushed and messy. This one was done by someone who took his time, was supremely confident, who knew what he was doing. Probably one of a series, I'd guess.'

'I'll look into that, thanks, Dr Baines.' Roscoe picked up her Eccles cake and bit into it, experiencing a moment of pure, unadulterated joy as the sugar and fruit burst onto her tongue. How could anything that tastes so good be so bad for you, she thought – 'a moment on the lips, a lifetime on the hips'. Sod it! She took another bite.

'I believe you know Henry Christie quite well,' she said through the mouthful.

Baines perked up visibly at the mention of the name. 'Henry? Yes – we go back a long way. Haven't seen the old libertine for some time. How is he? I'm surprised not to see him, actually. This kind of thing is right up his street.'

'He's OK. Sends his regards. He's been transferred into uniform.'

Baines almost choked on his cake. 'Uniform? Well I never.'

'I came here directly from seeing him. We'd been discussing the murder. He has some views on it. He was the first officer on the scene.'

Baines looked languidly at Roscoe, a hint of knowledge in them.

302

She thought abruptly, He thinks Henry is shagging me. She could tell from the look on the good doctor's face. Something inside her said she should be angry, but she wasn't. Instead she wished it were true and, fleetingly, she imagined making love with Henry.

'You OK?' Baines asked with a slight smile.

'Yes, yes,' she murmured, trying to disguise the flush up her neck.

They chatted further about the murder, finished their food and drinks and decided to get back.

Next thing on the agenda was how best to transport Costain's body to the mortuary while disturbing as little evidence as possible. Roscoe was also starting to think about the Costain family who had to be informed of Joey's demise. There would need to be a formal identification before the post-mortem could start. It would be an uncomfortable time. She was not looking forward to it. Not just because of the unpleasantness of having to deal with the family, a responsibility which rested firmly on her shoulders as senior investigating officer, but also because of the knock-on effect as far as the streets of Blackpool were concerned.

There would be a war unless she could convince the Costains that the Khan family had not killed little Joey.

Evening was fast approaching as Baines and Roscoe walked back to the murder scene; with it came a very Blackpool chill tasting of salt, directly from the Irish Sea. They were about to cross the road when there was an 'Excuse me, excuse me' from behind. They turned.

An elderly gentleman, waving a walking stick at them, shuffled towards them at a fair pace. 'I take it you are in charge of the investigation?' he said to Baines. His accent, though northern, did have a trace of plum-military to it. He sounded like someone used to getting their own way.

'No, I...' stammered Baines, but was chopped off mid-sentence.

'I,' said the man huffily, 'have been sitting and waiting for someone, preferably a detective superintendent, to come and speak to me. I was expecting house-to-house enquiries would be commenced. That is usually what happens when a murder occurs – am I correct, officer?'

'Er – yes,' said Baines unsurely, eyeing Roscoe for some support.

She stayed quiet, smirking. It was often the case that members of the public assume that a man would take charge of any investigation, even in this day and age.

'So why haven't they begun yet?' the old man demanded. 'I've been sitting at my front window waiting. It's no dashed wonder the police can't solve anything these days when they don't even ask the questions.'

'Yes, sir, you're absolutely correct,' Roscoe said assertively, stepping forward. 'May I introduce myself?' She offered her right hand. 'Detective Inspector Roscoe. I'm the senior investigating officer. This is Dr Baines, the Home Office Pathologist – and you are?'

The man shook Roscoe's hand formally and almost clicked his heels. 'Please excuse my faux pas – understandable error, wouldn't you say? It's a man's job, after all.'

Roscoe stared coldly at him. 'Is it?'

'I'll get back up there,' Baines said to Roscoe and moved away.

The old man cleared his throat. 'Ah hem ... anyway, I am John Blackthorn, Captain John Blackthorn, Durham Light Infantry, and I am the neighbourhood watch co-ordinator for this area and let me tell you – there's not much goes on around here without me knowing about it.'

'Resources, you see,' Roscoe said, tutting apologetically and explaining at the same time, 'or lack of them. House to house would have come sooner rather than later, I can assure you, Captain Blackthorn, but we are very stretched at the moment, with the party conference and all.'

'Yes, resources and money are always a problem these days,' Captain Blackthorn said. 'But it astounds me that two million can be spent protecting politicians, yet hardly anything is spent protecting the public who put them in power.'

'Quite,' said Roscoe.

They were sitting in the lounge of his well-appointed flat on Withnell Road. The wide bay window overlooked the street and was about fifty metres away from the entrance to the converted terraced house in which Joey Costain's flat was situated on the opposite side of the road. There was a good view across to it.

Roscoe tried to stay cool, but inside she was shimmering with excitement at what Blackthorn might be able to tell her because it was the early leads which often led to solving a case. If things dragged beyond seventy-two hours, the likelihood of a result lessened dramatically.

From the look of things, Captain Blackthorn was a widower. Photos of a dignified old lady were all around the room on windowsills and on the raised hearth where a solid brass companion set with brush, tongs, shovel and poker stood ornately by the gas fire. He probably spent a lot of time at his front window, secreted behind thick lace curtains watching life go by. There was a high-backed reclining chair in the bay which looked extremely comfortable, next to this was a small coffee table on which was a monocular, telephone, note pad and pen. Underneath the table was a stack of quality daily newspapers. In all, the perfect nosy-parker outfit.

People like this could be gold to the police. People who sat, observed and made notes. Roscoe was the first to admit that they were not used effectively enough. She nibbled her fruit cake. Slightly damp and musty, but OK. She sipped tea from a delicate translucent

China cup with a large black crack in it.

'You have some information, then?'

Blackthorn got up from the settee and hobbled across the room, using his walking stick for support. 'Bad hips,' he explained, 'soon to be plastic ones.'

He picked up his note pad, returned to the settee next to Roscoe and handed it to her.

'Yesterday afternoon, pretty early, one p.m.,' he said in a clipped tone, 'that little good for nothing Costain arrived on foot.'

Roscoe read his notes. ' "Mon. 1. Cost app." What does this mean?'

'Monday, 1 p.m., Costain arrives.'

'And "Cost ent"?'

'Costain enters the building,' he said proudly. 'Here,' he indicated he wanted the book. She handed it back. 'Blah, blah, blah ... right, he goes inside. Two minutes later another chappie arrives in a van and goes into the building, though I'm not saying this is connected with Costain's death, you understand? Obviously he should be questioned. He was carrying what looks like a tool box.'

'How do you know Joey Costain?' Roscoe asked, just holding Blackthorn back a touch.

'Ever since he moved in a couple of weeks ago he's been round to people in the area offering insurance – if you know what I mean?' Blackthorn winked. 'Bloody protection racket in other words. Got short shrift from me. Sorry to say he won't be missed in the neighbourhood.'

'Can you describe the man who entered the

307

building after Costain?'

'Well, I didn't get that close a look at him.' Roscoe tried to hide her disappointment.

'But to be honest, seeing the van the man came in was enough for me.'

'Why?'

'As I said, there's not much I don't know around here. I always keep my eyes open for anything suspicious or any toerag good for nothings. I make it my business to know them and their vehicles.' He sat back, smiling.

Roscoe felt something shoot down her body, a living thing inside her. She stopped herself from screaming, Well fucking tell me who it is, you stupid old bastard! Don't keep me in suspense. I'm nearly wetting myself here. Instead, she kept her cool and smiled sweetly.

'Another scumbag lives at 33c Larkside, Boscome Avenue, the flats. He's called David Gill.'

Hallelujah! Just around the corner.

'Come on please, we know there's someone in there. Just come to the door. We'd like to ask one or two questions.'

The first voice had been a woman's, the second a man's calling through the letterbox.

Is there just the two of them, Gill wondered. Or were they backed up by a bunch of big, hairy-arsed coppers looking for a rumble? It was a calculated gamble, but that was what Gill was about. He reckoned just the two, otherwise why hadn't they kicked

308

down the door? He picked up his bike helmet and pulled it on. He had one chance and one chance only. The cops continued to bang on the door. It was about time to answer it.

Fifteen

Henry Christie was not a political animal. He did not give two stuffs about councillors and politicians and their sad, power-hungry egos. This was probably why he had not progressed any further than the rank of inspector – as well as being unable to pass the promotion-assessment centres, which was in itself a bit of a stumbling block. He thought it was ludicrous that the police service kow-towed to politicians and found it a huge joke for the claim to be made that the police service was apolitical. Of course it was political.

The truth was that ever since the miners' strike of 1984 and probably before that, the police had been used as blunt instruments by whatever party happened to be in power to do their dirty work. And to align policing divisions with local political boundaries seemed to Henry to be the ultimate act of self-sacrifice. He waited for the day when there would be an office in each police station for councillors to use.

But that was the way things had progressed

and though he hated it with a vengeance, Henry accepted the harsh realities. The government set the policing agenda, chief constables were mere puppets with no real clout whatsoever, and police forces had to remain placid and compliant to keep White-hall happy. If they were foolish enough to upset the home secretary they went right to the bottom of the queue when the yearly budget begging bowl was rattled under his nose.

So he hated all politicians and resented their continual intrusion into everyone's private lives as well as the constant nosying into operational policing. All he wanted to do was solve crime, put offenders before courts and hope they got their just desserts – then lock up some more. An old-fashioned concept, he knew, but it was why he joined the police in the first place but somewhere down the line the idea of catching criminals seemed to have been forgotten by high-ranking officers who simply wanted to further their careers by simpering up to politicians.

As in the case of FB.

Henry was extremely displeased to see Basil Kramer in the former officers' mess where he had been told to report to FB at 5 p.m.

Kramer and FB were deep in conversation, FB nodding furiously, agreeing with every-thing, eager to please, feathering his nest. Henry hoped it contained vipers.

Also in the room were Karl Donaldson and Andrea Makin. They were drinking coffee, idly chatting, both dressed in casual gear.

The Kramer-FB conflab broke up with a raucous laugh and a pat on the shoulder. They looked round guiltily as Henry came in.

'Come on, take a pew.' FB waggled his fingers, beckoning him like he was a servant. 'Managed to get some sleep?'

'Oh aye,' said Henry stonily. He felt like a sloth. No energy. No commitment. Not happy. His eyes sported luggage like saddle bags. He flicked his thumb behind him. 'I've brought Sergeant Byrne in. He's night-patrol supervision. I thought he should be here.' He was going to add, 'Hope that's OK,' but refrained. He wanted to remain assertive.

'Sure,' FB said.

'Hello, Inspector,' Basil Kramer said. 'Nice to see you again.' He nodded to Byrne. 'Sarge.'

Henry and Byrne sat down.

FB glanced at Kramer, who took the lead and spoke. 'Just to put you in the picture, Inspector, the PM is in town, staying at the Imperial Hotel tonight.'

Henry nodded, repressing the urge to say, 'Woopee doo! Bully for him.'

'And I think he would like to sleep soundly,' Kramer added, smiling thinly.

'Which is where you come in.' FB emphasised the word 'you'. 'So what are your plans to keep the peace tonight?'

Twenty minutes later, Henry and Byrne were walking towards the parade room on the ground floor.

311

'I think we got through that OK-ish,' Byrne commented.

'Surprisingly,' Henry said. 'The problem we now have is making our promises come true with the small number of staff we have available. Not easy, Dermot.'

'We'll have to be creative, won't we?'

'And pray we don't have another riot to deal with. God give us rain – lots of it.'

Their radios blasted out. 'Blackpool to DI Roscoe or DS Evans receiving – DI Roscoe or DS Evans.'

Both Henry and Byrne twisted the volume down on their sets.

Dermot Byrne paraded the twelve-hour night shift, due on just before 6 p.m. Henry stayed for the briefing which was short and precise. The team looked haggard from the previous night's fun, but they seemed raring to go. A riot gave them something to do. Henry was surprised to see PC John Taylor in the line-up, he had expected him to be off sick. He looked as though he had not slept all day and had watery eyes and a sniffy nose. Henry admired him for coming in.

To keep Taylor out of mischief for a couple of hours, Byrne gave him the relatively painless task of visiting all the licensed premises in town known to attract gays. He was to speak to the licensees about suspicious parcels and stick up one or two warning posters which Henry and Byrne had quickly run off the computer before the parade.

After the briefing Henry walked back to the inspectors' office. He needed to catch up with some paperwork, then find out how Dave Seymour was progressing and about the two murder inquiries. After that he intended to hit the bricks with Byrne. He was keenly anticipating the night ahead now that he was at work.

'Blackpool to patrols,' communications shouted over the radio again. 'Does anyone know the present location of DI Roscoe or DS Evans?'

No one replied.

'Inspector to Blackpool,' Henry called up. 'Is there a problem?'

'No, I don't think so,' the operator said hesitantly. 'The DI should be at the mortuary for a post-mortem. The pathologist is waiting for her to turn up, but she hasn't shown. He's been on the phone.'

'Roger.'

Odd, thought Henry. He turned into the inspectors' office and bumped into Burt Norman who was on his way out, his motorcycle helmet in his hand.

'Burt,' Henry said pleasantly.

'Bye,' Norman said, brushing past and was gone. 'Oh, by the way,' he said, suddenly putting his head back round the door. 'Tea fund – need to speak to you – tomorrow, maybe – bye.' Then he was really gone.

Henry smiled to himself. He kitted himself up with all his equipment and picked up a set of car keys. He decided to visit a friend.

Henry had spent many a gruesome hour at the public mortuary, presiding over post-mortems carried out on murder victims. There had been times when the place had been like a second office to him, but instead of being surrounded by stationery and in-trays, he had been surrounded by hearts, livers, dissected brains, entrails and stiffs. He had become so immune to the process that these days he even failed to recoil at the smell of death, that peculiar, all-clinging odour which escapes from the dissected human body. But he could recognise it immediately.

Joey Costain's cadaver was on a steel trolley. He was covered by a white plastic sheet. He had not been hoisted across to the slab because the formal identification still had to be carried out before the post-mortem began. It would not have been appropriate to wheel the family in to do the distressing task if he was already on the slab. It was bad enough as it was.

Dr Baines, the pathologist, was sitting chatting to Jan, the mortuary technician. She was a pretty woman in her late twenties, a prettiness totally at odds with her profession. Many police officers were driven wild by their morbid sexual fantasies about her. Obviously not Henry Christie. He was far too clean living and moralistic to harbour any such dreams. Besides which, she scared him slightly with the air of Morticia Addams she had about her.

314

Baines clambered to his feet when he saw Henry approaching.

'Henry old boy.' He beamed and looked down at the uniform. 'You don't half look strange,' he commented.

Henry did a fashion-model twirl in his size ten Doc Martens. 'Like it?'

Jan, the technician, had a twinkle in her eyes.

'Naah,' said Baines, 'doesn't suit you at all.'

'Actually I like it,' Jan said in a rather unsettling way. 'Makes you look sexy. I like a man in uniform,' she admitted.

Henry swallowed nervously. 'Thanks, Jan.'

She licked her lips provocatively and Henry shuddered inwardly. He knew she was single after a short, disastrous marriage and she was on the look-out, rather like a black widow. Henry got quickly back on track.

'Doc, I think you're waiting for Jane Roscoe to land?'

'I am. Been waiting ages.' He glanced at the wall clock. 'Well over an hour now. She said she had a quick enquiry to make and would be along asap. Bad form if you ask me. Time is money, as they say.'

Henry knew just how much Baines claimed for call-outs. A small fortune.

'I agree,' he said, 'but from what I know of her, she's the sort who wouldn't let you down without a very sound reason.'

'Cause for concern, uh?' Baines said quickly.

Henry shrugged. 'Unusual, that's all at the

moment. We can't make contact with her or the DS she's with.' He crossed to a desk in the corner of the room and picked up the phone. He dialled the station, feeling very uneasy. He ascertained that communications had tried to call both Roscoe and Evans on their mobile phones without success, paging them had got no response either. What made Henry's flesh creep even more was that their cars had now been found parked up near to Joey Costain's flat. Henry thanked the operator and hung up slowly.

Baines and Jan watched him carefully with concerned looks.

'The family need to be informed of this death,' Baines said, sliding in some extra information. 'Perhaps she's with them. I believe they can be a handful when riled.'

'You could be right, although her and DS Evans' cars are still parked near to Joey's flat in South Shore. I can't see them having walked two miles up to Shoreside. The whole thing seems out of character. I know Mark Evans well. He's dead reliable.' That unwelcome feeling in the pit of his guts was starting. 'What did Jane say when she last saw you?' he asked Baines.

'That she was following something up. She'd been approached by an oldish, military-looking man in the street and been to see him. Seems he gave her some useful information. She didn't share it with me, but she looked pretty excited by whatever it was.'

'Who was the old guy?'

'I'm sorry, Henry, I don't know.' Baines looked wounded. 'He was seventy-odd, maybe, military bearing as I said, well dressed, walked with the aid of a stick.'

'Right,' said Henry, 'do you mind hanging on here for a while longer? We'll try to get hold of Jane and Mark and I'll go to see the Costain family and do the dirty deed. I'll get one of them down here to ID Joey, then you can get on with the PM. I'll also ensure a detective comes and stays for the PM, and I'll get scenes of crime.' Henry nodded sharply to them both.

'Be as quick as you can. I've already done one murder victim for you today.'

'Oh, the girl, Geri Porter? Suffocated?'

Baines nodded. 'She also had an interesting bump on her head, caused some time before death, which I don't know what to make of.'

And for the first time Henry thought, Now what a coincidence. Two people closely linked to a right-wing extremist organisation murdered within a short time of each other. Some coincidence, even though on the face of it their deaths seemed unrelated. Geri Porter could have been killed because she knew too much. She was expendable. But what about Joey Costain? Was he expendable too? Joey the gypsy. What was a gypsy doing being a member of Hellfire Dawn?

'Henry! You went blank for a moment,' Baines observed.

'Far from it, far from it,' he said. 'See you soon.' He hurried out of the mortuary,

317

already transmitting instructions down his radio.

'Get in,' Henry shouted to Byrne through the driver's door window as he screeched the patrol car to a halt on Richardson Street at the back of the police station. Byrne almost slid across the bonnet of the Astra, jumped in and sank down into the tired seat springs. Henry executed a wild three-point turn as quickly as he could, wrestling with the power-less steering. He gunned the clapped-out motor back down the street.

'Where are we going?'

'The humble Costain household.'

'Nice.'

At the Berlin Hotel, Vince Bellamy was talk-ing to one of the Hellfire Dawn committee members, a man called Martin Franklands. He had been a steady member of the organisation for about two years. He helped sort out the money side of things and dealt with day-to-day administration matters for them. The two men were standing in the foyer of the hotel. Bellamy handed Franklands a mobile phone.

'Sorry to ask you to do this. I know it's a bit of a pisser, but can you get this phone to Don Longton out by North Pier. He's near the War Memorial. He's just phoned in from a public call box to say his own phone's battery is dead. He needs a charged phone.'

'Sure, anything to help,' Franklands said,

318

slipping the phone into a back pocket. He grabbed his donkey jacket from a coat stand. He knew Don Longton was one of the many observers round the town, reporting on police movements and anything else of interest to the hotel control room. Batteries were always crashing, needing to be replaced.

'Thanks, Martin, see you soon.'

Franklands trotted out and down the hotel steps, glad of the break and the opportunity to get some fresh air. He turned out of sight of the hotel, onto the promenade.

Bellamy watched him go. He unhitched his own mobile phone from his belt and called one of the listed numbers.

'Don?'

'Yep.'

'He's on his way.'

'Thanks.'

Bellamy went back to his office.

'Anything from Jane Roscoe?' Henry asked Byrne, just in case he had missed something.

Byrne shook his head.

Henry hit the steering wheel with frustration. 'I suppose she could be up at the Costains, but to remain out of contact for so long is worrying.'

'Just a bit,' Byrne agreed. 'Is that why we're going there?'

'One of the reasons, just to check they haven't beaten the crap out of her and Mark, but I don't think they would. The other reason is to tell them about Joey Costain, if

319

Jane hasn't told them already, and the next reason is to quell any possibility of a riot.'

'Oh?' Byrne twisted in his seat. 'And how do you propose to do that, boss?'

'Community policing at its best and most basic,' Henry said mysteriously.

The chill on the promenade was bitter and came through the fabric of Martin Franklands' donkey jacket. The wide paved area between road and sea was virtually deserted. A tram trundled past, lit up brightly, the people inside looking warm and protected.

To his left, Franklands could hear the sea, a sound drowned out as he walked past the entrance to north pier which was basically an amusement arcade. Loud music pumped out, but there were very few punters inside playing the machines. Franklands walked on to the war memorial, leaving the sound of the music behind, once more picking up that of the sea less than twenty metres away.

There was a dark figure lurking by the memorial where the promenade dropped into an incline behind the Metropole buildings, out of sight of the road. Even without seeing the man's face, Franklands knew the guy was Don Longton, a fellow with whom he had struck up a passably decent relationship over the past few months. Longton was standing in the shadow cast by the memorial, his face completely obscured.

'Don,' Franklands said in greeting. 'Got a charged-up phone for you.'

Longton did not say a word. Franklands knew he was being sussed up and down through the blackness. He could feel Longton's eyes on him.

There was actually nothing in that moment to give it away; even so, Frankland's instincts burst into life like a ruptured appendix. He knew there was big trouble afoot and that he had been lured to this spot for some reason.

'Everything OK, Don?' he asked the big, silent figure, almost unable to utter the words, he was so frightened.

It was not.

Franklands heard a shuffling noise behind him, turned quickly and found two men standing there, having stepped out from the other side of the monument. Franklands edged away a pace, recognising the two immediately. They were the men who had been acting as doormen for Vince Bellamy at the Berlin, the ones who had been done over earlier by some mad guy or other. Their names were Baxter and Higgins. Both were peas out of the same pod. Hard nuts, London upbringings, Nazi tattoos, brainless cunts. Baxter had a plaster over his nose where he had been head butted and a cottonwool bud screwed into each nostril. Both his eyes were black and swollen. He did not look well. He and Higgins – who had been kneed in the balls by the mad guy – looked like two pissed-off individuals who wanted to vent some spleen.

Franklands quaked in his boots.

'What's this?' he asked shakily, knowing his time had come, but not knowing why. His eyes flicked back and forth between all three men, weighing up the distance between them and him, calculating if he could make a break for it.

As if reading his thoughts, Longton stepped menacingly out of the shadows.

'Snitches need sorting,' Longton growled like a bear. 'Good style.'

All three towered as he cowered.

'Hey, this is shit,' Franklands pleaded. 'What's going on? I ain't no snitch to anyone. There is a fucking error here.' His hands rose defensively, palms out, trying to pacify them and make them keep their distance.

He decided to try and run for it. It was his only option. They had obviously been given their instructions and nothing he said would change that – rather like the Gestapo, he thought. He turned, about to leg it.

With no warning whatsoever, Longton turned towards the bouncer called Baxter, the one with the plastered nose. The other man, Higgins, grabbed Baxter, who was not expecting this, and gripped him in a vice-like bear hug.

'What the—?'

The word 'fuck' was cut off as Longton, who had eased a spiked knuckle duster onto his right fist, smashed Baxter heavily and accurately in the face. Baxter's face exploded. His already broken nose burst open. Blood sprayed everywhere. The next blow slammed into his left eye and cheekbone, the spikes of the knuckle duster piercing his eyeball, breaking his cheekbone. The third blow, in more or less the same place, tore the eye socket open and put Baxter into semi-consciousness.

Higgins opened his arms and let the limp body crumble to the ground.

Franklands, appalled, looked on, his hands covering his wide-open mouth. 'Jesus, Jesus,' he kept repeating, never having witnessed such dreadful, focused violence.

Longton and Higgins started kicking Baxter. Kick, after kick, after kick. Both were wearing steel toe-capped boots. After this they began jumping up and down on his head, smashing the soles of their shoes into his skull with as much power as they could muster. He was dead before the two of them dragged his body to the sea wall. Longton and Higgins rolled him to the edge and kicked him underneath the railings into the waves below. His body made a splash, then the waves tugged him away and pounded him back against the sea wall like flotsam.

Longton and Higgins stood there breathing heavily before turning to each other and exchanging a high-five of victory.

Franklands, silenced and terrified, watched them. His whole being shook. He felt physically sick.

Longton put an arm around Franklands' shoulder.

'Got that phone, pal?'

'Y-yeah,' he stuttered.

'Give it here.'

He handed it over. Longton punched in a number.

'Me,' he said. 'It's a done job.' He ended the call and gave Franklands a big hug and a pat. 'Well done, mate.'

Shoreside was still like a war zone. The council had been unable to start any repair work during the day, so the estate remained in absolute darkness.

'Spooky,' Henry observed, driving onto the estate, speculating whether it was really such a good idea to go to the Costains. Perhaps Jane and Mark had made the same mistake, had been ambushed and were lying injured in some dark alley – or worse. But that still did not explain their cars down on South Shore.

Gangs of kids roamed the streets, hanging out on corners like packs of wild dogs. They were dark shapes, evil and frightening, even though they were only kids. People were trapped in their houses again, afraid to step out. Henry could taste the fear and the tension in the air coming through the partly open car window. Fires burned on waste ground.

Henry drove slowly past a dozen youths gathered at the entrance to a ginnel. They jeered, spat and flashed V signs at the car, making his blood simmer. He did not react but drove on by, gritting his teeth, pulling on his shirt collar to let steam out.

There was a loud crack on the car roof: a half house brick lobbed by one of the gang. Henry and Byrne ducked instinctively. Henry's right foot slammed down on the gas pedal.

'Shit.'

'Yes – shit,' Byrne agreed, thankful they were quickly out of range.

Both men were tense.

Henry did not stop to check the damage. They could do that later, somewhere safe. Nor did he try to root out the offender. Both acts would have been foolish and potentially dangerous. The gang would have loved it and things could have got very nasty very quickly. It was always the wise cop who knew when to let things be, because every dog has its day.

There were no further incidents and they reached the Costain household unscathed. The house was lit up. Faces peered through the window at the car and its unwelcome occupants.

Henry sat pensively for a moment, elbows resting on the lower rim of the steering wheel.

'How are you going to handle this, boss? I'm intrigued.'

'Let me put it this way, Dermot, my plan is still in its infancy, but I think I have an ace up my sleeve. Let's just hope the cards get dealt my way. Come on.' He got out of the car and strode confidently up the path to the front door.

It opened before he even reached it.

Henry breathed a sigh of relief when he saw

who it was: Troy Costain, Joey's eldest brother. Named, Henry suspected, after the great Troy Tempest of *Stingray* fame. He was the first person Jane Roscoe's search team had encountered on their early morning raid, the one who had wanted a fight.

'What the fuck do you want?' Troy yelled.

Henry did not break his stride, but bore down on Troy and stuck his forefinger into his chest and said, 'You, Troy. I want you, now. I want you in your coat, out of this house and in the back of that cop car before I can say "Alakazoo" – get me?'

Troy swallowed. 'Why, what the fuck have I done?'

Henry poked his chest again. 'Fucking do it now,' he hissed and under his breath, so that only Troy could hear, he said, 'Do not piss me about, Troy. This is serious shit.'

Costain sneered, but wilted. He withdrew with a nod and closed the door behind him.

Henry glanced back at Byrne, some ten feet away at the garden gate. Henry smiled and tossed the car keys to his sergeant. 'Stand by the car and get ready for a quick getaway.' Henry looked past Byrne's shoulder. A bunch of youths were beginning to filter in and gather on the opposite side of the road, drawn by the police presence, looking for any excuse for trouble. If Troy did not co-operate with Henry as he hoped he would, it could be a signal for bother and the two cops could be in for some real grief. Henry licked his dry lips. He had policed the streets of Blackpool, on and off, for a lot of years. Never had he known such a feeling of hatred in the air, never before had he felt so vulnerable on Shoreside where he was very well known by the good guys and the bad guys alike. He'd had moments of anxiety, even been whacked a couple of times, but they had been run-of-the-mill things that every cop got at some time or another. This was different. Dave Seymour had made it different. Cops had become game animals. 'C' mon y'prick,' he whispered.

'Black bastard,' one of the gang across the street called – terminology often applied by scrotes to police officers, no matter what the colour of their skin.

Byrne walked to and stood by the car.

Henry was about to rap on the door again when it opened. A waft of shouts and abuse flowed out from the family inside as Troy came to the door. 'It'll be right,' he shouted back into the house, pulling on his denim jacket. 'This better be good,' he growled low to Henry. 'My folks are going ape-shit in there. I've had to really think on my toes to give 'em some bullshit.'

'What did you tell them?'

'I said you wanted me to identify some property.'

'Not far off the mark,' Henry muttered. 'Let's get out of here.'

Every shadow hid a potential petrol-bomber, every wall a rock-thrower. The two officers expected to be attacked at every turn but although the estate was buzzing, they drove off safely.

Byrne was at the wheel, Henry in the sagging passenger seat. He turned and looked at Troy, a less than debonair man of the Shoreside underworld where violence and intimidation were currency and drugs meant power. Henry knew the Costain family were driven by violence and held much of the estate in fear of them, hence few people ever willingly came forward as witnesses against them for fear of reprisal. The only challenge to their dominance had been the Khan family and now that challenge had erupted into violence and death.

'Where we going?' Costain demanded.

'Head out towards the hospital, but find somewhere to pull in on the way – somewhere intimate,' Henry instructed Byrne. He squinted nastily at Costain. 'Somewhere we can have a chat. Woodside Drive sounds nice.'

Byrne nodded.

Henry smiled at the back-seat passenger. Troy was very much like the rest of his family in many ways. He came across as a tough cookie, was respected by kids whose dads were never home. Troy liked beating people up who could not or would not fight back, but sometimes, unless backed up by other members of his family, he could not always pull it off. He often hid behind the reputation of the Costain clan because in truth, like so

328

many other bullies, he was a coward at heart, something which Henry had turned ruthlessly to his own advantage.

Although the use of police informants was tightly controlled due to past abuses, many detectives unofficially still ran informants, or 'sources' as they were correctly known. Strictly against force policy, but what the hell. Some jacks had sources going back twenty years who did not want their relationship 'formalised' and monitored. As was the case with Henry and Troy Costain.

Troy had been the ripe old age of fifteen when Henry had first arrested him on an allegation of assault. Once in custody, Troy had crumbled and offered the arresting officer information in return for leniency. Their relationship had blossomed into a financial footing and had lasted well over twelve years. Troy had served Henry well, giving him some good information leading to good arrests. He'd also given him some duff gen too.

Costain had become Henry's direct link to Shoreside – and Henry had kept it to himself.

Henry had decided that his contact with Troy would have to be stretched or even broken now because of the present circumstances. The greater good, corny as it might sound, was more important than information leading to an arrest.

'OK, what's this about?' Costain said.

'Let's just go somewhere where we can park and talk, eh? Be patient.'

329

Costain put on a sulky pout and watched the street lights spin by.

'Sorry you had to witness that,' Vince Bellamy said. He was speaking to Franklands who now had two large whiskies circulating in his stomach, though the alcohol content of them was not getting into his blood stream as quickly as he would have liked.

'What was it all about?' he spluttered.

'You don't need to know, other than the fact you have just helped rid our sweet organisation of a traitor who could possibly have destroyed us,' Bellamy explained. 'He had to be lured to a place and dealt with and the best way of doing it was to let him think he was going to help us sort you out. But as we know, you're not a traitor, are you, Martin?'

'No.' He helped himself to another shot of whisky. He was sitting on a chair in Bellamy's office at the Berlin.

Bellamy sat down in front of him. 'It was vital,' he said reassuringly, 'and you've proved your worth. We know we can trust you ultimately because,' and here he dropped the bombshell, 'that man was a cop.'

Franklands swallowed the vomit in his throat. He pictured images of the assault: the first blow, the kicking, the jumping on Baxter's head, crushing his skull like they were stamping on a beetle. Franklands could hear the noise. It was horrible and he shuddered. Oh God, a cop, he thought bleakly.

'You are truly one of us, Martin.' Bellamy's

voice became lilting and hypnotic. 'Sometimes these small things have to be done for the good of the movement – you know how true that is, don't you?'

'Yeah,' he croaked, his breath coming in judders.

'Will you do something else for us?'

Franklands looked up quickly into Bellamy's eyes. 'I ... I don't know ... I'm in shock, Vince.'

'I know, but again, it is only a small thing, another piece of the jigsaw which will eventually lead us to power.' Bellamy paused, smiled and reached across to put his fingertips on Franklands' jaw line, tilting his head up so their eyes were on a level. 'You are one of my boys, Martin, part of the top team now. Yes, I mean it – irreplaceable.'

'What do I have to do?' Franklands could not stop himself asking.

'Deliver a package.'

Woodside Drive was off the busy East Park Drive which leads up to Blackpool Zoo, now closed for the day. It was an unlit road, often used by courting couples at night. A perfect place for a conversation.

Byrne pulled the car into the kerb, switched off the engine, killed the lights. Henry laid a hand on his shoulder. 'Stay put. We won't be long.' He jerked his head at Costain, meaning 'out'.

Costain reluctantly complied and Henry ushered him away from the car.

331

'You could've fucking compromised me, you silly twat,' Costain hissed worriedly. 'If they find out I'm a grass, I'm dead. My family'll fucking do me, never mind any cunt else. What's happened to your fucking carefulness?'

'Just at this moment in time, Troy, I don't give a monkey's,' Henry said. A sentence which, even under the circumstances, made him smirk because on the word monkey's, a tribe of them started howling loudly in the nearby zoo, obviously offended by Henry's turn of phrase.

'Then it better be better 'n good,' Costain spat.

'Shut it and let me speak.' Henry's tone of voice, coupled with the forefinger poked threateningly an inch from Costain's face, made the young man clam up. 'Has DI Roscoe been round to see you and your family?'

'Yeah, bitch rousted us all early this morning, searching for Joey.'

'Has she been back since, this evening?'

He shook his head.

'You sure?'

'Course I'm fucking sure. Look, what's going on?'

'She's gone missing. Her and another detective.'

'Well at least that's two less of you fuckers.'

It was the wrong thing to say and Troy knew it immediately when a chill came over Henry's face. He snapped and his open-palmed right hand came out of nowhere and

332

whacked Costain across the face. The blow lifted him off his feet and sent him sprawling onto the ground. Henry stepped over the prostrate form with menace. Anger, like an internal demon, rushed through him.

'Not a good choice of words under the circumstances,' he said. 'I am not here to play silly fuckers with you, Troy, so I suggest you get up to your feet, keep a civil tongue in your head and answer my questions nicely and listen to what I have to say, because it's very important. Now get up.'

Henry hoisted him up, but Costain drew his arm away, frightened and cautious of a side of the policeman he'd never really seen before. He cradled his sore jaw which was starting to swell. Henry had hit him very hard.

'Right – has she been back to your house since the raid?'

Costain shook his head.

'When she raided your house, did you know where Joey was?'

'Might have,' he said sullenly.

'Did you, or not? Just fucking tell me.'

'Yeah. At his new flat.'

'Why didn't you tell DI Roscoe where he was?'

'Oh, get real, Henry. Like we would – no effin' way. We just wouldn't, would we? We tell the cops fuck all – well, y'know what I mean.'

'When did you last see Joey?'

'Dunno.'

'Think!'

'Er ... yesterday mornin' I think ... I really

333

don't know. He comes and goes – Look, Henry, what is this? Tell me what's going on.'

Henry knew that what he was about to say was probably untrue, but because he was feeling bad, he wanted Troy to feel even worse.

'If you had told her exactly where he was, Troy, you might – just might – have saved his life.'

She could have been dead and not known it. There had been blackness – nothing, just nothing. No dreams, nothing. It was only now she knew she was alive. The first thing she felt again was her heart beating. It was unpredictable, all over the place. Fast, slow, irregular. That was what had woken her, the beating of her heart.

Next some kind of consciousness seeped back into her brain, like water dribbling through stones. Drip. Trickle. Senses returned. She shivered and knew she was alive, knew she was naked, could feel goose bumps on her skin. Then pain returned.

And with pain, fear.

Sixteen

A grief-stricken Troy Costain paced up and down the road, displaying a mixture of extreme emotions which surged and surfaced while he ranted, raved and cried like a demon. He flapped his arms like a wounded gull, or wrung his hands like a motor mechanic using gunk. Anger, despair and pain all came and went, sometimes singly, sometimes in combination.

Henry let him have his head for a while, just to get this initial response out of his system.

'I want to see him, Henry. I want to see him now, my baby brother.'

'Good, that's good – we need someone to identify him formally.'

Costain stopped, head to head with Henry. There was a cold intensity in his voice as he said, 'I want to see what those bastards have done to him.'

'Which bastards are those?'

Suddenly Costain slumped to the side of the road and down onto his knees and was violently sick. He stood up, wiping his lips with his sleeve. He came back to Henry. His breathing was out of control and now smelled of vomit. His eyes were wide and staring like a mad man.

'You know which bastards – those fuckin' Khans. They've done this, haven't they? Don't tell me they haven't. They're all gonna die for this, they're gonna get torn to pieces and I don't give a toss what you say, Henry. I'm past caring now. My little brother is dead – and I loved him.' The last few words brought on a rainstorm of tears. He sank to the ground again, sat on the kerbside and buried his head in his hands.

'You think the Khans killed him?'

'Yeah,' snuffled Costain, snot dripping from his nose. 'Obvious, innit? Revenge for their father. They think Joey killed him, don't they?'

'You're saying he didn't?' Henry asked with surprise.

'No way, no fuckin' way. Joey gave him a bit of a kickin', that's all. He were well alive when Joey left him. That's what Joey said, anyway, and I've no need to disbelieve him, have I?'

'Joey would say that, wouldn't he? I thought Mo Khan was against Joey seeing his daughter. That's why Joey killed him, isn't it? Because he wouldn't let Joey see her.'

'No, no, no, you got it all wrong.' Costain, dribbling, spat something substantial into the gutter which landed with a heavy splat. 'It weren't serious. He were just shaggin' the black bint for fun, just to wind the whole family up, to get 'em riled. He didn't take it seriously. She's a slag, gaggin' for white man's dick and she got Joey's. He just wanted to stir

336

the twats up.'

Interesting, Henry thought, taking this twist of information on board. Did that fit in with the Hellfire Dawn strategy – to incite racial problems during the week the government came to town? Did Joey Costain really leave Mo Khan in a recoverable state? Henry knew that Mo's injuries had been brutal and horrific, coming from more than just a slapping, which Troy seemed to think was all that Joey had given Mo.

'What was Joey's involvement with Hellfire Dawn?' Henry slid in.

'Eh? Oh, that bunch of tossers? Just a bit of fun for him. He liked gettin' into fights with 'em.' Using the bottom edge of his shirt, Troy wiped his wet, slimy face thoroughly. 'Take me to see him, Henry. Yeah, I'll identify him – and I want to see exactly what they've done to him.'

'Not a good idea, Troy.'

'I want to see,' he insisted.

'Mind if I ask a question, boss?' Dermot Byrne asked Henry as they drove towards the hospital. 'How come you didn't let on about Troy being an informant?'

Henry shifted uncomfortably. The reason was because of sheer bloody-mindedness at the way FB had treated him and also because at the time it did not seem so important. 'Next question,' Henry said.

'OK, you're not really going to let him see Joey, are you?' Dermot Byrne said.

337

Henry's lips remained tight. 'If he insists.'

'Out of order and you know it,' Byrne said, not afraid to challenge a senior officer. 'It'll do his shed in.' Byrne jerked his head backwards, indicating Troy in the back seat, head lodged between his knees, mentally out of it, immersed in a myriad thoughts.

'It might knock some sense into the little shit,' Henry said, maintaining the hard line, but deep down knowing Byrne was right. For anyone to see the body of a relative in such a mess would blow their minds. He refused to relent. 'It might make him realise that the Khans didn't kill him and that might just stop any further rioting tonight.'

'Might, might, might,' Byrne mimicked him angrily. 'So this is your master plan, is it?' he added contemptuously. He screeched the car into the roadside and halted. He opened his door, got out, leaned back in and said to Henry, 'I need to speak, boss, urgently – out here.'

Henry looked blandly at him, his mouth slightly skewed. He considered advising the sergeant to fuck off, get back in the car and drive, follow orders and stop being such an insubordinate twat. Instead, groaning inwardly, he got out, slammed his door and stood on the pavement. On the rise above them, across the road, loomed Blackpool Victoria Hospital. Henry folded his arms defensively and waited for Byrne.

The sergeant got straight to the point. 'There is no way on God's earth that I will allow you to show him the body of his brother other than as much as is necessary to identify him – his face, in other words. I know he's a shit, but you can't do this, otherwise you're as bad as he is.'

Henry's lower jaw rolled left to right and back again. He stood firm, silent.

'I fuckin' mean it, Henry. I fuckin' mean it.' Byrne was resolute. And what was more, the angels were on his side. 'It's ethically and morally wrong, don't you see? And it won't solve a damned thing.'

Henry spun and glowered into the darkness behind which was Stanley Park. He swallowed and lifted his head skywards towards dark clouds spitting a light rain. He knew Byrne was exactly right and wondered what the hell he himself had been thinking of. He knew what was overriding his professionalism – the unknown whereabouts of two officers. He was desperate to solve one problem by whatever means possible so he could concentrate on the one he really wanted to get to grips with – Jane's disappearance, even though he knew other officers were already out searching for her. Logic told him that if the Costains were satisfied that the Khans had not killed Joey, then the problem on Shoreside could be reduced somewhat. It seemed that the best way to convince them was to show Troy Joey's mutilated body, because otherwise they would just think Henry was spinning them a line in order to quell a riot. And maybe, Henry admitted to himself, that was the logic of a man who was back at work too soon and not fully recovered from stress.

He would have to convince Troy by being the good cop he knew he was and not resorting to means which were well below the belt.

He sniffed. 'You're right, you're right,' he admitted.

Dermot Byrne watched and listened to Henry Christie in action and was impressed. Not only by his interpersonal skills, but because Henry, unlike most other officers of higher rank, was prepared to take on feedback and change his opinion.

The inspector sat next to Troy Costain in the mortuary waiting room. Both men were hunched forward, heads low, elbows on knees. Henry talked softly but firmly, empathetically and sympathetically. He was good.

Costain's emotions were still on a roller-coaster ride of extremes, but Henry hung in there like a cowpoke, staying with the young man all the way, coaxing, cajoling, resting a hand on Troy's shoulder or back when necessary.

Yes, Byrne thought: Henry Christie was very very good when he wanted to be. The organisation had shot itself in the foot by taking him off CID. The good side of it was that the uniform branch had gained. But, if Byrne was as good a judge of character as he believed himself to be, it would not be long before Henry was back where he truly belonged.

It took thirty concentrated, wearying minutes, before Henry felt he was in a position to signal to Byrne that things were ready to proceed to the formal ID. On the nod, Byrne slid quietly through to the mortuary viewing room where Joey's body had been wheeled in on a steel trolley and laid out next to the viewing window. He had been draped with a white sheet which was held off the body by a raised cage.

Byrne pressed a button on the wall. The whirring electric motor drew back the purple velvet curtains, revealing Henry and Troy Costain on the other side of the window, standing in half-light. Costain looked beleaguered.

Henry nodded. His arm was around Costain's shoulder.

Byrne took the edge of the sheet and folded it back to reveal Joey's head. It was not too bad, not disfigured by the attack at the front, but because it had not been cleaned up, was blood splattered.

'Is that your brother, Joey Costain?' Henry asked softly.

Troy stepped out of Henry's grasp, pressed his nose up to the glass, smearing it. His eyes were red raw from crying.

'Yes,' he said simply.

Henry nodded to Byrne. The sheet was drawn back over Joey's head.

Troy screamed, making both Henry and

Byrne jump. He twisted away and ran out of the viewing room before Henry could grab him. 'Liars!' he yelled. 'Fucking liars!' He ran like a rugby player, dodging out of the door, down the corridor, skidding through a door marked, 'Technicians Only'.

He surprised Dr Baines and Jan, the mortuary technician, both of whom were slurping a slice of rather sloppy pepperoni pizza, which resembled body parts, into their mouths. With wide eyes, and pizzas poised above their mouths, they watched Costain tear past. He ran to the viewing-room entrance where Byrne was waiting to receive and stop him. Costain's screams turned into an ear-piercing war cry. He swung his weight into Byrne and heaved him back against the wall, winding him, and burst through into the viewing room. He dragged the sheet off Joey's body.

And stopped dead. He did not move other than for the rise and fall of his heaving chest, transfixed by the horrifying sight of the gutted body which had once been his brother.

Henry came in behind, too late.

'Now do you believe me?' he said quietly. 'Not even the Khans are capable of doing this.'

Troy Costain nodded dumbly, then keeled over in a faint. Henry caught him before he hit the tiled floor.

Her eyes were open, but she could not see because the darkness was total, absolute. Not

342

a sliver of light. Not even enough to dimly make out anything.

She listened. Somewhere there was the hum of something. Indistinct, but constant. She was unable to tell what it was. An engine, perhaps.

She tried to move her hands, but they were bound tightly behind her, no play in the binding, whatever it was. Some sort of sticky tape. Same with her legs, bound together tightly by tape – thick, parcel tape.

Christ! Parcel tape! She started to sob. Parcel tape – just like the tape that had bound and gagged Joey Costain.

While ensconced in the rather cosseted world of the detective, Henry had forgotten just how much pressure the uniformed side of the constabulary was under. Not that there wasn't the pressure on the CID, it just seemed easier to manage and there seemed more time to get things done. The uniform side, and in particular those engaged in response duties, were being run ragged and had little quality time to devote to jobs.

That evening Henry was painfully very aware that, as he kept one ear attuned to the radio round his neck, the officers on his shift – scale D – were constantly busy, going from job to job relentlessly. Henry was finding it quite hard to keep abreast of what was going on because in the past he had always used the radio for his own selfish means, as and when needed. He had never been at its beck and

343

call as he was now. He just wanted to turn the sodding thing off, but could not.

'Let's get back in,' he said to Byrne as they pulled away from the Costain household. They had delivered Troy back into the bosom of the family, broken the news and then spent three-quarters of an hour dealing with the emotional fall-out. Henry was exhausted by it all. He had enough of his own baggage; dealing with other people's was draining. 'Head into the nick and we'll take stock of things.'

Byrne drove through Shoreside.

'What the hell's happened to Jane and Mark?' Henry mused out loud. It was bugging him.

The estate was alive with activity. Things seemed to be hotting up for another night of fun and games. This would be Henry's priority, keeping the peace on the streets. It frustrated him because he believed he should be searching for Jane and Mark. This was where his skills would be used to their best advantage – detecting. He was pragmatic enough to realise he would not be given a chance at it and would have to do what he could when he could.

'That support unit from Blackburn should have arrived by now,' Byrne said, and to confirm this, in one of those moments that never happen in real life, Blackpool communications called Henry.

'Go ahead,' he said.

'The Eastern Division PSU have just

arrived and they're awaiting deployment.'

'I'll be in shortly to brief them.'

'Roger. There's some other things you need to know about, too.'

Henry's heart sank.

'The custody sergeant wants to speak to you urgently about last night's attempted suicide.'

'Yep, got that.'

'And I've just deployed a patrol from the station to a report that someone thinks they saw three guys throw something into the sea that looked like a body.'

'Got that, too.'

'ACC Fanshaw-Bayley wants to speak to you as soon as possible. He's in the Gold Room.'

'Got that. Anything else?'

'Standby–' There was a pause. 'Inspector?'

'Receiving.'

'Blackburn have just been on – you're not going to like this much–' Henry did not say anything, but waited, 'and report that twenty-odd cars have just left the Whalley Range area of Blackburn, en route to Blackpool, all containing Asian youths. Intelligence is that they're out for trouble on Shoreside, led by Saeed Khan. They're going after the Costains.'

'That's all I need,' Henry said to Byrne. Into the radio, he said, 'Roger. There couldn't be anything else, could there?'

'Standby – treble-nine just come in,' the voice of the operator rose a couple of tones.

'From the Pink Ladies' Club on the promenade. The landlord thinks there's a suspect device in the premises. Repeat, a suspect device.'

'On my way,' Henry said crisply. 'Blue light,' he said to Byrne, who flipped the rocker switch and jammed his foot down hard on the gas pedal.

Seventeen

It was desperately cold on the promenade. An icy biting wind slashed in like a razor from the Irish Sea. It was certainly no weather to be dressed in a thin, white silk blouse, unbuttoned to below breast level, the lack of support for a very fine pair of breasts underneath the material very obvious from the outstanding (literally and aesthetically) nipples pushing up and out. A tight leather skirt cut off high above the knee, fishnet stockings and high-heeled shoes completed the outfit.

John Howard, known professionally as Pussy Beaver, flicked his bobbed silver hair, dusted with sparkling glitter, back off his face and inserted a cigarette, in a long, thin, penis-shaped holder between his high-glossed lips. His arms were folded under his splendid breasts and, as he shivered, they wobbled divinely.

346

As ever, he looked completely amazing – his long tapering legs coveted by many real women – very voluptuous and desirable.

He was standing outside the Pink Ladies' Club which he owned and ran with ruthless efficiency. The place had become one of the north of England's leading night spots. People from all over the country and abroad came in their thousands to experience the outrageous shows and behaviour on display every night of the week. It was a favourite venue for hen parties. It had made John Howard, who described himself as 'Head Pussy', a millionaire.

There was a long queue outside, several hundred people, mostly raucous groups of half-drunk females. By the time the night was over, two thousand people would have passed through the doors. At £12.50 a head and the cheapest drink at the bar £2.50, the Pink Ladies' Club turned over £40,000 a night, five nights a week.

'Oh, thank God you've arrived,' Pussy Beaver fawned and tottered unsteadily over to the police car which pulled into the side of the road.

Henry climbed out, a smirk on his face. Byrne was out less quickly.

Only when he was a few paces from him, did Pussy recognise Henry.

'My my! It's Henry Christie,' he chirped. 'It's you! In uniform too! My God, but you look totally fuckable in that outfit! Oh God, I could just lick your dick here and now, in the middle of the thoroughfare.'

'Jesus,' Henry heard Byrne remark with disgust behind him.

'And if you had a fanny,' Henry bantered, 'believe me, I'd let you.'

'That was always your sticking point, wasn't it?'

'I'm finnicky like that.'

They laughed and shook hands. Henry had known Howard for several years, first meeting him when the club had been petrol-bombed by some local youths who hated what people like Howard stood for. Henry had arrested two nineteen-year-olds who had been subsequently imprisoned and a friendship of sorts had sprung up between him and Howard.

'So what's the crack, John?' Henry asked. More police cars pulled up, one containing Karl Donaldson and Andrea Makin hotfoot from the police station.

'I think we might have found a bomb inside. It's a suspicious package at least.' John had dropped his high-pitched feminine tones and his voice had lowered an octave to become more masculine.

'What makes you think it's a bomb?'

'Lunchbox left under a table in a dark corner of the main bar. It doesn't seem right, if you know what I mean?'

'Anybody touch it?'

'No.'

'Anyone see who put it there?'

Howard shrugged his shoulders.

'How about your security cameras?'

'I'll get them checked.'

'Ah well, at least we've done some good tonight,' Henry said, thinking about the job PC Taylor had been doing, warning people about the possible danger.

'How have you done that?' Howard's face screwed up quizzically.

'Haven't you been visited by a PC this evening, dishing out leaflets asking you to be on your guard?'

'Nope.'

'Oh, never mind then. He can't have got round to you yet. Let's get on with this. How many people are inside?'

'Hundred and fifty, maybe a few more. I haven't let anyone else in since it was found.'

'Good.' Henry beckoned to Karl Donaldson. 'You want to come in, Karl, just in case?'

'Yes.'

'OK, John, lead the way.'

Pussy Beaver twirled on his stilettos, resumed the acting voice and led Henry, Byrne and Donaldson through the clearly irritated and impatient crowd, drawing jeers of contempt.

'C'mon, out of the way, luvvies – out of the way – can't you see the main act has arrived?'

Henry whispered to Byrne, 'He once let me feel his tits.' The inspector laughed, while the sergeant recoiled. 'Just like the real things,' he added.

With the efficiency Henry always associated with the man, Pussy Beaver had ensured that his bouncers (woman wrestlers capable of dismembering anyone foolish enough to have a go) had sealed off a good proportion of the bar area. They were standing guard, preventing any punters from entering the exclusion zone around the seat under which the package had been discovered.

As good as the cordon was, though, Henry knew that if it was a bomb under that seat and it did explode, everyone in the club would have a better than average chance of being blasted to pieces.

'It's under there.' With an expertly manicured finger, Pussy indicated the offending spot – a bench in an alcove, out of sight of the bar.

'Thanks. Now you go and stand well back and get everyone as far away as possible, too.' Henry touched his radio to ensure it was switched 'off' for definite. 'Is yours off?' he asked Byrne, who nodded. It was standard procedure to switch personal radios off because bombs had been known to be detonated by radio waves before now.

Henry took a deep breath and wondered if this was one of those times when the inspector should take a purely strategic view of events and order a lower-ranking officer to do the dirty work. Tempting – but he could just imagine the word that would circulate the station if he did. He would be branded a coward. Having said that, better a live strategist than a dead tactician, he thought. The idea went out of his head as quickly as it had come into it.

'I want to have a look, too.' Karl Donaldson stepped forward.

Henry saw the look of determination on the American's face. He knew it would be useless to object. Donaldson had a very personal interest.

'Suit yourself, but don't blame me if you get blown up.'

Donaldson placed a hand over his heart. 'Promise.'

At least Henry knew he would not die alone.

Henry told Byrne, Makin and everyone else to get well back and take some cover if possible. He and Donaldson then approached the alcove. Henry expected it to be a false alarm. Either a hoax or a mistake, or a piece of lost property. Nine hundred and ninety-nine times out of a thousand this was the case.

But as he walked towards the package, there was the niggle this could be that one time, the possibility it could be the real thing. The only consolation was that if it blew, there wouldn't be much to feel. A surge of heat, noise and then death.

Some consolation. Both men felt very vulnerable.

'You made a will?' Henry asked.

'Yep. You?'

'Yep.' As Henry answered a stab of thought cut through his mind of Kate and his two daughters. He saw all their faces. Then it was

351

gone. It was a short, painful thought.

'My throat's as dry as the bottom of my cockatoo's cage,' Donaldson admitted.

Henry stopped walking and laid a hand on his friend's bicep. 'You have a cockatoo?' Donaldson nodded. 'I never knew that, you sad person.'

'Thanks for that.'

They continued to walk.

'I'm actually feeling dead cool about this,' Henry boasted, paused and added, 'not.'

The short journey seemed endless. Then they were down on their knees on the carpet among the beer stains and fag ash, noses almost to the floor. Henry flashed his Maglite underneath the bench seat.

There it was. A lunchbox. Tucked behind a seat leg. Not in a place where it could have fallen or rolled accidentally. To get where it was it must have been placed there deliberately. Through the opaque plastic, indistinct shapes could be seen inside. Not sandwiches or Kit-Kats. Strapped to it by tape was a detonator.

'He's here,' Donaldson breathed.

Getting the general public to take any evacuation seriously was difficult. No one ever truly believed the danger, that it could be a real bomb, that they could get killed. It did not help when most of them that evening were half-cut.

Once, though, Blackpool had been the target for the IRA when incendiary devices

352

inside several shops had caused massive amounts of damage. So it could happen.

Henry ordered all available officers to attend the scene, including the recently arrived PSU and those officers recently deployed to investigate the possibility of a body in the sea. He began the tiresome job of emptying the club of people who did not want to leave, then trying to evacuate and close all the surrounding premises which consisted mainly of amusement arcades, another night club and several burger joints. Next, the promenade itself had to be closed two hundred metres in both directions. All traffic had to be diverted inland and the trams had to be stopped. Chaos reigned.

Then he needed to establish a rendezvous point.

The only easy thing was calling out the bomb disposal squad: they were already resident in the town because of the party conference.

Henry did a lot of shouting, ordering, threatening and cajoling, and found himself very much the centre of attention. In a perverted sort of way he enjoyed it all, even if at the back of his mind the worry remained about Jane Roscoe and Mark Evans.

'One thing, bud,' Karl Donaldson said in his ear. 'Don't put the RV point in the obvious place, just in case it is our man.' Henry gave him a blank look. 'Remember, he bombed the last RV point in Miami with a secondary device. I don't want that to happen here.'

'Good point, well made.'

With that in mind Henry decided to use Adelaide Street West, which, though a one-way street, could be used to allow access to emergency vehicles from both directions. It was out of a direct line of sight of the club, some hundred and fifty metres north of it. Henry got the traffic department to cordon off the street and park the big accident unit in it to be the centre of the RV point.

Amazingly this was all achieved within about fifteen minutes, adding fuel to Henry's belief that the police were a great 'doing' organisation. They liked being told to do things, just didn't like to think about anything else too deeply.

As everything fell into place, the bomb disposal squad arrived on scene.

Within minutes they were reversing the robot 'wheelbarrow' out of the back of their vehicle, intending to use it instead of a man. It was a safer option than sending a man in to fiddle about with what increasingly appeared to be a real bomb. The wheeled machine, which resembled a small tank, was equipped with a camera through which the operator – who never left the back of the equipment van – could see exactly where it was going. He could manoeuvre it down, up and around most obstacles using a remote-controlled joy-stick; the wheelbarrow was also fitted with a double-barrelled shotgun which, when loaded with the appropriate shot, could be

354

discharged into a suspect device to bring about a controlled explosion. The wheelbarrow was a common sight on the streets of Belfast. It was not so well known in Blackpool.

It set off on its journey.

Henry peered over the shoulder of the operator and watched the monitor which was showing the picture from the camera on the front of the contraption. The wheelbarrow trundled up the pavement rather like something out of *Star Wars*, a very hi-tech piece of machinery, developed over the years by the army to do a dangerous job. It had saved the lives of countless soldiers in the battle against the Provisional IRA.

The journey continued up the promenade to the front entrance of the club. The operator did a right turn and the machine lurched through the first door which Henry had left wedged open.

'Here we go,' the soldier said.

The wheelbarrow moved through the door into the entrance foyer, straight across the tiled floor to the stairs leading down to the main bar where the package was located. The steps were easy. Like a tank on Salisbury Plain tackling a steep hill, the wheelbarrow just took them in its stride, even the one-eighty degree turn halfway down was no problem. Henry was impressed. The skilled soldier at the remote control manoeuvred the wheelbarrow round and into the bar, where it stopped and had a look round.

'Mine's a pint,' the soldier said.

Henry looked closely at the image on the screen.

'Straight across, then bear slightly right,' he said helpfully.

The machine trundled on, slowly approaching the corner of the room. The soldier made minor adjustments to direction constantly.

'Under that bench, dead ahead,' Henry said.

'ACC to patrol inspector.' It was FB on Henry's radio.

'Shit,' Henry said. 'Go ahead.'

'Sit rep, please. I'm monitoring.'

'EOD in attendance, wheelbarrow deployed, should have a result soon.'

'Well that's nice to know,' FB whined sarcastically. 'I'd like to be kept informed.'

'Understood,' Henry said, wondering why FB had not just asked a communications operator because Henry had been relaying a blow by blow account for the log.

'I'll be in communications if you need me,' FB transmitted helpfully.

'Thanks for that,' Henry said. He shook his head despondently and turned his attention back to the monitor.

The wheelbarrow had moved forward and was now peering under the bench seat at the lunchbox, displaying a very clear image to the monitor.

Two army types were whispering to the operator. One nodded then turned and introduced himself and his handlebar moustache to Henry.

'Captain Renfrew.' The two men shook hands.

'Henry Christie.'

Renfrew did not beat about the bush. 'Taking all factors into consideration, I propose we blow it up in situ, cover the cost of damage as necessary. No point taking any chances.'

'I don't have a problem with that,' Henry agreed. 'In fact, I think—' But whatever Henry was about to say was lost forever when the wheelbarrow operator gasped, 'Oh, fuckin' Jesus!'

All heads spun to him, then the monitor.

'I thought the place had been evacuated,' he said.

On the screen was the face of a man staring directly into the lens of the camera fitted on the wheelbarrow. He was a big, happy, smiling man who was tapping the lens with his knuckles and saying something – more words lost forever. He looked excessively drunk.

Henry ground his teeth and the blood drained from his face. He had assured the army guys the place was empty because he had been so assured by a sergeant from the visiting PSU who had carried out the search and evacuation of the premises. Not well enough, it transpired.

The man on the screen put his tongue out, stuck his thumb in his ears and flapped his hands and blew raspberries. Then he looked

357

in the direction in which the camera was pointing. It was clear he had seen the lunchbox.

On his hands and knees he got down and reached for it.

'Oops,' the operator said.

All eyes turned to Henry as the officer in charge. It was as if the world was holding him in sharp focus. Everything else was blurred and only Henry stood out. He did not know what to do. His mind was a complete blank.

'If there's an anti-tamper on it and he moves it...' the operator said bleakly.

Then, for Henry, the world seemed to resume some of its normality. 'Move the wheelbarrow. Jab him with it. Do something. Try and distract him from touching the bomb – I'll go and get him out.'

'You must be barking,' Renfrew said. 'You can't go in there now.'

'I've been in once and it didn't explode. If he doesn't touch it, then it probably still won't explode.' Henry's eyes flashed back to the screen. The man was stretching out towards the lunchbox, could not quite reach it. 'And if it's on a timer only, it's more than likely to be set for a busy period. I'm going,' he said. 'Distract him if you can.'

The operator thumbed the joystick. The wheelbarrow arm extended and pushed the drunken man in the ribcage and knocked him over. He rolled and recovered. The extending arm went out towards him again, attempting to push him over again. The drunk struggled to his feet and lumbered towards the wheel-barrow. The screen got a close-up shot of his fat legs and then the sole of his boot as he tried to stamp on the nasty, horrible thing that had attacked him.

Henry moved like lightning.

He ran up the promenade and skidded through the door of the club, hurtling across the foyer and down the steps into the bar. If it hadn't been so serious, it would have been ridiculous. The fat drunk was laying into the wheelbarrow as though it was an adversary in a street fight. He rained kicks on it, which must have hurt him, because they were having no effect on the wheelbarrow which just stood there placidly absorbing the on-slaught without complaint.

Henry hurried across, shouting, 'You need to get out of here now, that could be a bomb under there.'

'Eh, what? Fuck off, copper.'

That was all the negotiation Henry was prepared to do. With strength induced by fear, anger and danger, Henry looped an arm around the man's neck, grabbed his shirt and started to drag him across the bar using the momentum of the man off balance. He managed to get him as far as the foot of the steps which led up to the foyer. He dropped the gasping man, who landed on the small of his back, legs akimbo. It was only past bad experience that prevented Henry from boot-ing him in the testicles. Last time he'd done that, the recipient of the kick had lost a ball and caused Henry no end of grief.

Such had been the speed and power of Henry's attack, there was still a look of utter surprise in the drunk's face – which Henry tried to use to best advantage.

He said menacingly, 'You get the fuck up them steps, or I'll beat the living shit out of you here and now. There's a bomb in here.'

It was as if the man had not heard.

'Fuck you,' he shouted and dived for Henry's feet. He got them before Henry could move out of the way. Henry cursed as he fell onto his hands. He kicked back at the man's chest and extricated himself from the grip.

Large and drunk though the man was – and the stench of booze on his breath was overpowering – he was moving pretty quickly now that Henry had lost the element of surprise. He threw himself onto Henry's back and flattened him on the floor. It was like being crushed by a bed and doing a belly-flop at the same time. All the air whooshed out of him, winding him. The man pummelled him, though the punches were not well placed or particularly effective. Henry rolled away, jerking his elbow into the man's face, satisfyingly connecting with a hard bone somewhere. The man emitted a scream of anguish, but only got madder. He came after Henry with his feet, starting to boot him before he could stand up properly.

'You idiot,' Henry yelled to no effect.

He took a kick in the lower stomach and

recoiled against a pair of double doors marked 'Store Room – Private'. The doors did not give even when the back of Henry's head whacked hard against them.

The drunk bore down on him, a snarl on his lips. 'I've always wanted to do a cop.'

Henry's mind clicked into clarity. He ducked and side-stepped, spun on his heels and drove his fist into the side of the man's head, hard, right on the ear. The blow had no effect, except to make the guy even angrier. Henry hit him again, hurting his knuckles on the man's cranium. Still no effect. The man turned like a Challenger tank, roared and grabbed Henry. He wrapped both arms around him, pinning Henry's arms to his side and squeezing tight. The men were stomach to stomach, chest to chest, both now with red faces: the drunk's from exertion, Henry's from his chest being constricted. The man swore at Henry, who felt his feet leave the ground. The drunk started to move in a circular motion, round and round, still trying to squeeze the life out of Henry, to crush him, while bouncing up and down.

He began to laugh. 'I'm gonna kill you, cocksucker.'

Which was OK, but why? Drunks do not reason well and Henry did not want to die by being squeezed to death by a bloated, admittedly strong, inebriate, nor by getting blown to bits by a bomb. This thought gave him a surge of self-survival.

He braced his arms and, using all his

361

strength, pushed them outwards and up-wards and broke the man's vice-like grip. Henry's hands went to either side of the man's head, each grabbing an ear, holding the head steady as he head-butted the bridge of the man's nose with his forehead. The nose did not burst as expected, nor did the man seem to have an adverse reaction to the blow. He just laughed and tried to grab Henry again. Henry pushed against the man and they crashed back against the double doors. This time, they flew open with a clatter. The men reeled through into a room full of collected rubbish onto which they tumbled. They continued their struggle amongst black bin liners crammed with all sorts of debris which burst open, spilling everywhere as they fought.

Henry was hitting hard now. Punching, kicking, kneeing, gouging. The rules of restraint deserted him because he was fighting for his life – and the life of an idiot he was duty bound to try and save.

The fat man was running out of steam. Huffing, puffing. The fight was deserting him. His flab, which had been a weapon in its own right in the first few moments of a con-frontation, was now draining him of energy and becoming a useless burden. Henry found himself standing over the man, breathing heavily, knowing he had won.

'You arsehole, have you had enough?'

Blood dribbled out of the fat man's nose and bubbled with his breath.

'Yeah, yeah ... no need for that.'

'There – is – a – bomb in there,' Henry panted. 'How the hell did you get in?'

'Whaddya mean? I was havin' a shit.'

So the toilets hadn't been properly search-ed. 'Right, we need to get out now, do you understand me? This whole place has been evacuated. Didn't you think something odd was going on?'

'Yeah, but...' he said inadequately.

'Up, now. Let's get going.'

Henry offered his hand. The man reached up and, rather like the Michelangelo painting on the roof of the Sistine Chapel, their fingers never actually came into contact because the bomb exploded.

It was as though someone had opened a furnace door and at the same time whacked Henry on the shoulder blades with a shovel. He was lifted off his feet by the blast and thrown down into the fat drunk's arms. For the second time in a matter of seconds, every drop of oxygen was forced out of his lungs and out of his bloodstream.

Fortunately for Henry and the fat man they were not in the direct line of the blast and it was this that saved them. Before the blast reached them, it had to do a right turn into the store room, thereby losing some of its hurricane-like force. It was fortunate their conflict had rumbled into the rubbish room. Had they been standing at the foot of the stairwell, they would have been hit by a flying wheelbarrow which had been blown right across the bar, through the doors and halfway back up the stairs, accompanied by pieces of chairs and tables, reduced to matchsticks by the explosion and even more insidiously, the thousands of panel pins which the bomb maker had packed into the device.

The sound of the explosion had been stunning. The loudest bang Henry had ever heard. His brain rang, his ears buzzed and echoed.

He opened his eyes slowly. Swirling smoke filled the room. Several fires had started in the rubbish.

Henry was on top of the fat man, lying between his open legs, holding him in an embrace as though they had just made love. He lifted his head and looked down at the face of the man underneath, which was blank with horror.

'Well, no thanks to you, we're still alive,' Henry said. He clambered off him, stood up, testing each limb, finding they all worked. He poked his head around the door, wafting the dense smoke away, trying to see into the bar. The smoke was too intense. Flames licked out of it, telling Henry that the next threat was being burned to death. 'Now can we get out of here without fighting?'

'Ugh, right.' The man was totally dazed and confused. His drunken state did not assist in his understanding of the situation. Gallantly Henry heaved him to his feet. Not an easy task. 'What happened?' the man asked.

'You've just survived a bomb blast,' Henry

informed him. 'Something you'll be able to tell your kids.'

'I doubt that, unless they start letting gay couples adopt.'

'At least you'll have something to talk about at dinner parties, then.'

'Eh? So, what's happened?' he asked, losing the thread again.

'I'll tell you later, now let's just get out of here.'

The shock hit him about twenty minutes later, sending him into a convulsive, retching fit. It took a large coffee laced with brandy before he returned to anything like normal.

He relinquished control of the scene to a chief inspector on conference duty because the shakes were approaching fast. He thought it would have been unwise to be a blithering wreck while running the next stage of the response to the bomb. Dermot Byrne had driven him back to the station, deposited him in the inspectors' office and somehow tracked down the coffee addition from somewhere.

When Henry picked up the mug, his hand was trembling so much that there was a mini-storm on the surface of the beverage. He had to put the mug back down on his desk, lower his head to it and take the first sip out of it from the desk top.

Deep breathing and some mental-relaxation techniques he had acquired for his stress, helped calm him down. This tranquil state did not last long. His stress levels rose, pulse quickened, when the office door opened without a knock and FB came in, all of a bluster.

'Hero or fuckin' arsehole, can't quite work out which,' he said.

By which time Henry had gone well past the caring and sharing stage.

'I'm the hero, you're the arsehole – I find that quite easy to work out,' Henry said.

That stopped FB dead, then a smile flickered onto his lips and grew into a good-natured laugh. 'Good one, Henry ... I like it.' Then his face became deadpan. 'Hey, you just called an ACC an arsehole.'

Henry wasn't for relenting. 'If the cap fits.'

'Twat,' FB uttered, but, again, without malice. 'Right. Actually, well done, Henry. I mean the fat guy should not have been left in there in the first place, obviously, but even so, well done. A bit drastic, a bit foolhardy – but well done.'

Praise indeed from FB.

'Thanks.'

'Yeah, well, don't get too cocky. You've still got a hundred Asian youths about to land in town intent on causing problems – so don't even think about going off sick again.'

'What about heading them off at the pass – turning them back onto the motorway at Marton Circle.'

'Under what power, may I ask?'

Henry had to think. 'Breach of the Peace. To prevent a breach of the peace – like we did in the miners' strike.'

FB thought for a moment. 'Go for it. You'd better get moving, then come and see me later. We need to discuss the night ahead again.'

'Anything new on Jane Roscoe and Mark Evans?'

'No.'

Henry slurped his coffee and with mug in hand headed to the communications room for an update on the whereabouts of the Asian youths, wondering if his proposed tactics were actually lawful. Under the circumstances it was arguable, but then again, when had that ever stopped the police from doing something which might just prevent any aggro. Once the Asians got onto Shoreside, there would be real problems.

His head was spinning by the time he got to communications. He knew he needed time out from all this, but was unlikely to get it.

At least there was one thing settled for him when he got there: the Asians were almost in town and he was too late to get enough staff together to turn them round and send them home.

The board displaying the number of officers actually on duty was not much help. Almost everyone was deployed at the scene of the bomb blast, dealing with keeping the scene secure, ensuring emergency vehicles could get to and from it, and also dealing with the growing traffic chaos in town.

Which gave Henry an idea.

'Where is the convoy now?' he asked a radio operator.

'On the M55 at Wesham, heading towards Blackpool. They'll be coming off at Marton in less than 5 minutes.'

'How many patrols are with them?'

'Two motorway, two traffic and a couple of motorcyclists.'

Henry picked up the radio set and called up one of the patrols. He asked, 'Do you think you could actually keep the convoy on the motorway, stop them coming off at Marton and get them onto Yeadon Way – without putting anyone in danger?'

'We can try and block the exit.'

'Do it – try and keep them coming into town. Shepherd them down Yeadon Way onto Spine Road and onto the main town centre car park at the end.'

'Roger – we'll try,' the patrol said.

Henry smiled at the radio operator, who looked puzzled. 'You want them to come into town?' she asked.

'No, I don't. I'd like them to go home, but I don't want them to get onto Shoreside, so if they can get snarled up in the town-centre traffic, maybe that will split them up – divide and conquer.'

'Oh. Good idea.'

Now, he thought, there's something else I have to do. It came to him. 'If you need me, I'll be in the custody office.'

The custody sergeant was looking tattered

and harassed as he booked two prisoners in who were being particularly obnoxious. He acknowledged Henry with a curt nod. At least, Henry thought it was an acknowledgement, it could have been a nervous tick, often found in stressed-out custody officers.

As the man was busy, Henry did a quick review of what was happening. Only three prisoners in, none requiring his attention. He took out the binder containing completed custody records to see what had happened to Kit Nevison at court earlier that day. The record was marked off as, 'Released on bail with reporting conditions.'

Henry could not help but chuckle at the outrageousness of it all. Sometimes magistrates seemed to live in a different world to normal people. There was no profit in getting sore about it, it was just a fact of life. A dangerous man was back on the streets.

He replaced the records as the custody sergeant finished off the booking-in process and sent the two prisoners to the comfort of their en-suite accommodation.

'Sorry I couldn't make it earlier, Bob,' Henry apologised. 'Got a bit tied up with one or two things.'

'Believe so.'

'You wanted to talk about the suicide attempt last night?'

The sergeant looked deadly serious and worried. 'Have you got a few minutes? I want to show you something.'

Henry followed him to the female cell wing.

It was all quiet, none of the cells were in use.

'There's something troubling you, I can tell.'

'You're not kidding.'

The cell in which Geri Peters had been incarcerated was locked, unlike the others where the doors were wide open, ready for the next incumbent. The sergeant opened the cell door and at the same time took something out of his pocket which he held up, dangling. It was a bootlace.

'This is the same length and thickness as the one she tried to hang herself with. The original is bagged up.'

'OK.' Henry was intrigued.

The sergeant took a breath. 'It's been on my mind ever since she tried to top herself, so much so I couldn't sleep. I was back in here at ten o'clock this morning. The first thing is that I'm a hundred per cent certain the prisoner was thoroughly searched. You were there, boss. Two WPCs searched her, found some drugs and a hidden knife. She was strip searched and given a zoot suit, so how she got the bootlace worries me.'

'Maybe it was in the cell already.'

'When I come on duty, I make a point of searching all the cells in the complex. I did that last night and this cell did not have a bootlace left in it. I had a prisoner kill himself on me once using a razor that'd been left lying about. I'm very touchy about things like that.'

'So you searched this cell when you came

370

on duty last night?'

'I did. But OK,' he said slowly, 'it is possible I could have missed the lace. I admit it,' he said honestly, 'but I don't think I did. I am as certain as I can be that she was put into a clean cell, which had been searched properly. Of course, she could have had it stuffed up her vagina or anus – but the lace was dry and it didn't smell, so I don't think she did.'

Henry waited uncomfortably. The sergeant was obviously a professional who cared deeply about the job he did. Henry was impressed.

'So that's one part. The next part is this.' He dangled the bootlace. 'I know full well that it's possible to loop ligatures around the door hatch plates and it causes us major problems. Hatches come loose with use, the metal warps and prisoners who are intent on taking their own lives will do it. Having said that–' He went to the door and closed the cell hatch. From inside the door he pushed the hatch and was able to feed the bootlace through the gap between the bottom of the hatch and the door where the metal had twisted slightly. 'I can do this, but I can't manage to loop the lace around the hatch handle like the girl did.' To prove his point, he made a loop in the lace and tried to manoeuvre it around the handle without success. 'I spent an hour trying to do it this morning. I tried it on other cell doors and I could do it on some of them, so it's not as though it's impossible. But I cannot do it on this cell

371

door,' he said firmly.

'Let's have a go.' Henry took the lace off the sergeant. He held both ends of it and fed the loop through the gap, letting it hang down. He tried to swing it up over the catch. Missed. Tried again. No joy. After five minutes he gave up.

The sergeant stood and watched patiently. Henry handed the lace back to him. A horrible feeling was in the pit of his stomach.

'You believe there is no way she could have got into the cell with that bootlace in her possession, unless it was maybe inside her, and you don't think that was the case?'

'No.'

'And even if she had somehow smuggled it in, she could not have used it to hang herself in the way she did?'

'Correct.'

'What are you saying?'

The sergeant inhaled a deep breath and shook his head despondently. 'I don't know, I just don't know.' He looked to Henry for assistance.

Henry stalked up and down the corridor, kicking an imaginary stone, reviewing what had just been revealed. He stopped walking abruptly.

'She must have had help to hang herself, or she must have been hung by someone else. Either way, another person is involved,' Henry stated. Then what had been a vague memory came back into his mind: the comment the pathologist had made about a

372

bump on the dead girl's head sometime prior to her death. Henry was certain she did not go into the cell with any injuries, even after the tussle he'd had with her when he made the arrest. Perhaps this explained the bump – being overpowered in a cell, maybe knocked senseless while the bootlace was wrapped round her throat then attached to the door. Henry felt slightly queasy. He said nothing to the custody officer.

The sergeant looked down at the tiled floor.

'I do not like what I've just said.'

'Nor do I,' replied the sergeant.

'Right, keep this cell out of use. Get scenes of crime to come and take some photos of the door, the hatch and everything – just keep it a matter of course for now. No scaremongering, OK? Find out, if you can, the name of everybody who came into the custody office last night from when I brought her in to when she was found and obviously anybody who you saw going up to the female cells – not easy, but do your best. And let me have a think about how to take this forward. Bob, I don't like what you've turned up here, but well done.'

The relief of unburdening himself was very visible on the sergeant's face. 'I'll let you have a list of everybody I remember within the hour.'

'Right.' Henry nodded. 'Let's just keep it low key for the moment, between you and me. If what you're suggesting is right, we don't want to spook whoever might have

done this. In fact, we don't really want anyone to know that we might have an attempted
murder in our own cells, possibly committed
by one of our own people.'

Henry did not have any time to consider
what course of action he might take in the
matter as once again, his accursed personal
radio squawked up and asked him to make
his way to see ACC Fanshaw-Bayley urgently.

Eighteen

David Gill had some time to play with. Not
much, because he had things to do, appear-
ances to keep up, but he could not resist
visiting his prisoner. He had to see her, talk to
her, just for a little while, because he thought
she was wonderful. Delivered into his hands
by divine intervention. Turning up on the
doorstep like an offering from the gods.

He made his way to where he was keeping
her. A safe place, entirely appropriate for the
occasion. He made his way to the locked
room underneath ground level, a room no
other person in the whole world knew
existed. His own private room which he
entered torch in hand, the beam shining into
his captive's eyes.

'Hello,' he said. 'Thought I'd pop in and see
you.'

Jane Roscoe did not respond, or move. She was stricken with terror.

'What's up, cat got your tongue?'

Roscoe tried to see beyond the torch light to see his face. It was impossible. She was having trouble focusing with the beam burning into her pupils after having been in the dark for so long.

'No point being difficult,' Gill said, 'that won't get you anywhere.'

'You won't get away with this,' she croaked dryly.

'Oooh, she speaks,' he applauded. 'Get away with it? Course I will, you silly girl. I always do.'

'Always?' Roscoe said, picking up on the implication of the word.

'Always,' he confirmed.

'You've done this before?'

'What, is this an interview, Jane?'

She fell silent. The light was in her face. 'Where's DS Evans, the officer I was with?' She had been trying hard to remember what had happened when the door to Gill's flat had opened, but could not. It had been a blur.

'Dead, I'm afraid,' he said in a matter-of-fact way.

Roscoe gasped then screamed, long, loud and piercingly. She could not help herself, it had welled up inside her uncontrollably, something she did not wish to do, but was unable to stop.

'Oh now shut up,' Gill said impatiently.

'Come on, shut up.'

Still she screamed.

'It'll do you no good,' he said, becoming angry. 'No one will hear you. You are in a sealed tomb.' Roscoe continued to scream. 'Right, if that's the way you want it, you can suffer.'

'This is the voice of the military wing of Hellfire Dawn...'

Henry's eyes flickered around the room at the same people who had been here to brief him before: FB, Andrea Makin, Karl Donaldson and Basil Kramer. All their eyes were riveted on the tape player on the table around which they were gathered. Only Kramer looked up and made eye contact with him.

'I repeat,' the gravelly voice on the tape stated, 'this is the voice of the military wing of Hellfire Dawn. Now you can see it, now you can feel it. The backlash has already started. Our mission is to take the struggle to the streets, to bring about an uprising and in so doing exert the moral rights of the white majority. Your town was chosen as the one in which our fight to victory will commence. Last night we drove a family of black bastards from an estate where they were known to be drug dealers, corrupting our children. To-night you have felt the power of the Hellfire Dawn movement through the force of the bomb. Be warned – this is only the beginning. This week Blackpool will burn and the

376

government – that weak-willed bunch of queers and coons – will start to topple as the force of the true people of this once proud nation drives them from power – there will be no prisoners taken. Turncoats and informers will be weeded out and destroyed. Bombs are everywhere in the places you think are safe and secure. This is the voice of the military wing of Hellfire Dawn.'

The tape ended. No one in the room spoke.

Henry sat back thoughtfully.

One by one the others did the same with the exception of FB who remained on the edge of his chair, hands clasped, elbows on knees, knuckles white.

'They've finally come out,' Andrea Makin said.

'Not the turn of phrase I'd use under the circumstances,' Henry said. His remark brought a smirk to the faces of Makin and Donaldson. Basil Kramer gave him a hard stare. FB looked as though the words had not registered with him.

'How did we get the tape?' Henry asked.

'A young lad dropped it off at the front desk,' Makin said. 'He's on video handing it over, but at the moment we don't know who or where he is.'

'He'll've been paid to deliver it,' Henry said. 'I can't see one of the major players doing such a menial, but potentially danger-ous job – dangerous in that there was the possibility of being recognised. I know I shouldn't need to ask this – but has the tape

377

and whatever it arrived in been properly preserved for evidence?'

'Once it was established what it was – yes,' said Makin.

Silence fell on the room. Henry decided to keep quiet now. He wasn't exactly sure why he had been made privy to this.

'Lady and gentlemen,' Basil Kramer announced, 'we have a very big problem on our hands. What are we going to do about it?' He looked expectantly at FB, whose eyes remained evasive.

For the first time since he had returned to work, Henry was glad that all he had to do was keep the peace on the streets of Blackpool. It seemed like the easy option.

'I shall rephrase that,' Basil Kramer said coldly. 'The question, ACC Fanshaw-Bayley, is what are you going to do about it?'

For the first time ever Henry saw FB at a loss. His spirit and drive seemed to have deserted him and maybe the true man was now apparent. Conceivably underneath all that bluff and bluster lurked an inadequate personality which was hidden by being overbearing and sometimes outrageous. Henry thought that he should have felt for him but, wicked as it seemed, he rather enjoyed the moment. Revelled in it, actually.

Donaldson and Makin shifted uncomfortably. Henry folded his arms.

Basil Kramer was remorseless, giving a glimpse of the ruthless streak in him which had enabled him to become such a massive business tycoon and an MP at such a relatively young age. 'What are you going to do about the fact that last night riots tore apart your town on the eve of the party conference? That an Asian family were driven out of their home? That one of your officers is critically ill suffering from severe burns? That an Asian man has been murdered and another young man murdered? Two of your officers are missing under mysterious circumstances and a bomb has gone off destroying a club frequented by gay people. Just what are you going to do, ACC? You have simply lost control. The press are having a field day, and tomorrow – God, I hate to think what tomorrow will bring – and tomorrow is the day when the PM delivers his law and order speech. This police force and the government will look like fools. So I say again, ACC, what are you going to do about it?'

Henry exhaled, unaware he had been holding his breath. The public drubbing he had received from FB was nowhere near as bad as this.

FB took the tirade and reeled with the verbal assault. Henry wondered if he was seeing his hopes and dreams of advancement into the HMIC disappearing before him. If so, it must be a devastating sight. Black rings circled the senior officer's eyes. He did not respond for a few moments. The room was deathly silent.

Slowly FB raised his head, his eyes fixed firmly on Henry Christie, making Henry's heart sink down to his boots. Then he looked at Basil Kramer. 'I can assure you,' he said, 'that I have lost control of nothing.'

Twenty minutes later, FB came back to Gold Command from an office on the floor below where, apparently, he and Kramer had exchanged views with a certain frankness.

Henry, Donaldson and Makin were helping themselves to coffee, chatting and wondering what the hell was going on.

They all looked at him as he entered. FB seemed to have returned to normal. Henry had liked the battered version better, but realised that all good things come to an end.

'OK, this is the plan of action,' the ACC said smartly. 'It may well seem that everything is going to rat shit for us this week – and that may be a correct assumption – but let me assure you I haven't completely lost sight of the squirrel yet. To say the least, resources are stretched. Everybody and his dog is now going to be dragged in to police the conference following the bomb and the disturbances – hardly a riot, in my book, still–' he shrugged. 'So the streets of the rest of Lancashire are going to be devoid of cops, pretty much, for the next seventy-two hours, but that's the way it goes. What the government wants, the government gets,' he said expansively. 'As far as the bomb goes, I've got a team on it, scraped up from the bottom of the barrel, but what concerns me more than any of this is the disappearance of Jane

380

Roscoe and Mark Evans. I'd like to think they've eloped. I could handle that – and sack the bastards – but I seriously doubt that is the case. I just have the vaguest feeling that their disappearance has something to do with the bigger picture – just a hunch from a man who used to be a real detective.' He sighed. 'Only problem is that I haven't got anyone to put on to it.' He paused and pursed his lips. 'Except you three.'

Without exception, their chins dropped.

FB held up a hand. 'I know, I know. Andrea, you are a Met officer and you are here to assist us in other ways and I can't order you to do anything; Mr Donaldson' – Henry noted FB's retention of formality to Karl – 'you are an employee of the US government and have no powers in this country, but I do appreciate you have highly developed investigative skills and I can only plead for your assistance. You don't have to give it and I won't blame you if you don't. But I also know that you've worked very successfully with Henry in the past. Your choice. The only one I can order about, and it gives me great pleasure to do so, because I saw your expression of happiness when Kramer was bollocking me, is you, Henry.'

'And I'm the recently transferred reactive inspector and I've got Blackpool to look after,' he pointed out, hiding a gush of inner excitement.

'Well tough shit. I want you on Roscoe's case. I'll get Dermot Byrne to act up. I want

381

you to pick up where she left off and find her.'
FB's eyes roved across all three of them.
'We've got seventy-two hours before the
conference ends. I'm asking you all to give
that time to see if you can find Roscoe and
Evans, alive or dead. What do you say?'

'I say yes,' said Makin.

Karl Donaldson nodded.

'I don't have a choice,' Henry said. He
checked his watch. It was one minute before
midnight.

WEDNESDAY

Nineteen

The slow, almost sensual removal of his epaulettes was something that gave Henry Christie a great deal of pleasure. Opening a drawer in the desk in the inspectors' office and letting them drop from between his finger and thumb, closely followed by his black, clip-on tie, was a wonderful feeling. As was the unbuttoning of his shirt collar. Not that he was under the impression that his days as a uniformed inspector were over, far from it, this was just a blip.

He looked at Dermot Byrne, who was watching this little ritual, feeling that Henry would have burned the items on a bonfire if he could have. 'Congratulations,' Henry said. 'Bit like a field promotion for you.'

Byrne smirked. 'A necessity for the organisation, nothing more. There isn't even time to get me a white shirt and one pip,' he said, talking about his temporary promotion to the heady rank of acting inspector. 'Having said that, I won't say no to it. I'm not stupid enough to believe that I wouldn't get a black mark against my name if I did – so, anyway, it's been a pleasure to work with you, Henry, even for such a short space of time. It's been interesting to say the least.'

'You talk like I'm gone for good. I'll be back with you on Saturday night.'

Byrne had a sceptical expression on his face. 'Don't kid yourself, boss. That uniform won't have you in it again.'

'Wishful thinking,' Henry said.

He did not feel he had time to go to the flat and change into civvies. He wanted to get straight on with the job, despite the time of day. There was an argument, he supposed, that there would be very little that could be done, but he would have felt incredibly guilty getting some sleep and starting again at eight in the morning without having at first thought about the job. Jane Roscoe and Mark Evans were just as missing at midnight as they would be then. He had decided that at the very least he would do what he could now, then maybe get some rest.

At 12.30 a.m. he – in his white shirt and black uniform trousers – together with Donaldson and Makin convened in FB's Gold Command room. Henry had pinched a freestanding flip chart from somebody's office on the floor below, together with some felt-tipped pens, and set it up at the front of the room.

Makin had filtered some fresh coffee. She passed a steaming mug of it to Henry. 'We'll be operating on this for a while,' she said.

Donaldson sat down and looked expectantly at Henry. Makin sat down next to the

American, but seemed a little distracted, constantly checking her pager as if she had missed a message.

Henry was not feeling confident, but he was comforted by the two people sitting in front of him. Donaldson was an outstanding detective. His successes as an FBI field agent had been tremendous and his time as the FBI legal attaché in London had resulted in some major-league international criminals being snaffled in Europe. Henry did not know Makin, but he had every reason to believe that at the very least she would be a competent detective.

'I don't have a good sense about this one,' Henry said, curling the fingers of his hands as though trying to grasp thin air. 'The whole set of circumstances is odd and unsettling. I believe that if we don't act quickly and push–' he accentuated the word with a jab of his fist – 'there will be tears shed.' He saw Makin check her pager again. 'So let's have a quick look at what we've got, then take it from there.'

He was interrupted by a knock on the door, and Basil Kramer came in.

'Hope I'm not interrupting anything,' he said.

'Actually you are,' Henry said. 'Police work, actually.' He hoped Kramer would get the message. Obviously the ruse did not work.

'Won't keep you long.' He pointed at Makin and beckoned her. 'Andrea, can I have a quick word out here, please?'

A hard-edged expression came over her face. Reluctantly and very annoyed, she slowly left the room, closing the door behind her.

'Does that wanker have carte blanche to go wandering around the police station un-checked?' Henry demanded of Donaldson. 'Gets on my tits, it does.'

'So it would seem,' Donaldson said mildly. 'What does "wanker" mean? Another quaint olde English expression for loathing, I guess?'

'It means,' Henry said, leaning forwards – but his vivid explanation did not get off the ground. The door opened and a flushed Makin came back in and sat down. She looked vexed.

'Everything OK?' Donaldson asked.

She nodded. 'Yeah, let's get on with it.' She smiled warmly at Henry. 'Over to you, Inspector.'

'OK, so what have we got?' He picked up the felt-tipped pen. 'Let's have a bit of a brainstorm – or do they call it a board-blast, in these days of political correctness? I under-stand brainstorm is offensive to lunatics.'

'I suggest you stick to brainstorm, then,' Donaldson said.

Henry chuckled. A few minutes later the flip chart was full. There was enough things on it for a full team to get their teeth into. For three people there was far too much.

'Who's going to do what?'

Makin jumped in. 'I'll start looking at the MO aspects of the crime itself. I'll send a message to all forces asking if they've had similar crimes committed, say, in the last year – undetected, that is. That could give us a start.' She peered at the chart for something else, struggling to read Henry's spidery scrawl. 'I think the key to this is finding out who Jane talked to before she disappeared–' she held up her hands defensively – 'I know it's obvious, but I think that's where you two should be looking. Y'know, trying to track down this "military type".'

The men nodded agreement. 'We should start in the street Joey Costain lived in,' Donaldson said. 'See if any lights are on, then maybe knock a few people up. He sounds like he could be a well-known sorta guy.'

'I wonder if there's a neighbourhood watch in that area? Maybe a word with the co-ordinator wouldn't go amiss. I'm sure he or she wouldn't mind a phone call under the circumstances. Could save us some leg work. I'll check with communications,' Henry said.

A silence descended. Triple brain power in action. Lots of heat being generated by grey matter, but little else.

'The husband aspect needs to be checked out,' Donaldson pointed out. 'You said Jane Roscoe told you she had an argument with her husband in the morning – could her disappearance be connected?'

'Anything's possible,' Henry conceded. His mouth turned down. 'Doesn't explain Mark Evans' disappearance.'

'Unless they were having an affair and the

husband has killed 'em both, or Mark Evans' wife has killed them or they've eloped together,' Makin said. 'Most murders have a domestic connection and we shouldn't overlook that side of it, even though we're pretty sure it's not the case here.'

'True,' said Henry. 'And at the very least, Jane's husband and Mark's wife need to know what's going on and be asked a few searching questions. I'll fix up for some personal visits.'

'Yeah,' Donaldson said speculatively, 'this could just be a very tacky domestic situation, nothing whatsoever to do with Joey Costain.'

'Well, let's keep an open mind,' Henry said. But he did not believe that the home life of either of the missing officers had anything at all to do with the present circumstance. He was drawn back to the two words on the flip chart at the bottom of all the others which he believed reflected the true situation. The words were: 'abducted' and 'murdered'.

Donaldson excused himself and announced he needed to pay an urgent visit to the loo. The excess of coffee, he said, was playing havoc with his bladder and bowels. Henry and Makin were left alone. Makin held her pager in the palm of her hand, checking it, tapping the display with a fingernail.

Henry sat down next to her. 'Problem?' he asked.

She bit her bottom lip thoughtfully, came to a decision and said, 'Yes – actually there are several things not quite right.'

Henry waited.

'The first thing is that I want to clear the air between you and me. I made a bit of a fool of myself the other night. I mean, all that "come on" I was giving you was just – naff.'

'I was flattered.'

She snorted a short laugh. 'Horrified, more like, I shouldn't wonder. I don't think Jane Roscoe was very impressed with me, either.'

'How do you mean?'

'The look in her eyes?' Makin's voice rose at the end of the statement, turning it into a rhetorical question.

Henry opened his palms, not getting it.

'You dummy: the green-eyed monster. She's got the hots for you, Henry, and I was muscling in on her patch. I'm surprised we didn't end up fighting over you.'

'But I've only just met her and I know she doesn't like me very much,' he protested feebly, knowing the statement was not really true.

'You'd only just met me,' Makin pointed out, 'and I would've jumped into bed with you.' She flashed her eyes.

'And she's married.'

Makin leaned towards him. 'That doesn't stop her being head over heels, so let's just hope we find her in one piece and if we do, you'll see I'm right. Anyway, please don't get the wrong impression of me. I don't just jump into bed at the drop of a hat with every gorgeous guy I meet – some I do, but not everyone. The thought of us was quite nice, but it's a non-starter.'

'Oh, I don't know,' said Henry, unwilling to let the embers completely burn out. He always liked to keep a welcome in the hillside.

'It was just that getting together with you might have helped me solve the problem of Basil "the bastard" Kramer.'

'How so?' he asked, intrigued.

Makin's face dropped. 'He's been harassing me for sex ever since I met him last week. Despite his money and position and power – and his looks – he gives me the creeps.' She shivered as though a snake had slithered down her backbone. The thought of the man was upsetting her. 'He uses his power to get what he wants. He's the most unethical git I've come across in a long time. Promised me all sorts for a fuck and blow job.' She folded her arms defensively.

'Is he bumming FB, then?'

The thought brought a smile to Makin's face. 'It would not surprise me.'

'What a fantastic picture,' Henry said, imagining the scene. He became serious again. 'If you want me to speak to him, I will,' he offered.

'No.' She put a hand on Henry's forearm and squeezed gently. 'I'll try and sort him myself – oops!' Quickly she removed her hand as though struck by electricity. 'There I go again. You must be irresistible.'

Donaldson came back into the room, singing some obscure country music song.

'Anyway,' Makin said, 'that's the personal dross over with, the real big problem is that,

392

as you know, I have an officer working under-cover with Hellfire Dawn. He should have made contact and hasn't done. I'm worried. It's not like him. He's missed his second fallback call, too.'

'That is a problem,' Henry sympathised. 'But going under cover is not rocket science,' he said reassuringly. 'Been there, got the T-shirt.'

'I know, I know,' she said, her face anxious. 'There is another fallback at noon. If he doesn't call by then, I'll really need to look at it.'

The three of them were about to leave the room and start their enquiries when FB and Basil Kramer entered the room rather like the Blues Brothers, though without the style or the sunglasses.

'Bloody hell, I'm glad we caught you,' FB breathed. 'Come with us now.'

'Why? Where? We were just about to get cracking,' Henry complained.

'Have to wait, have to wait,' FB blithered, his underpants apparently twisted around his testicles.

'Why?' Henry's question this time was more forceful. He did not want to get sidetracked by any more garbage.

Basil Kramer cut in with a 'Tch!' at FB. 'Because the prime minister wants to see you all now.'

'Well why didn't you say so?' Henry asked.

They all bundled into FB's police BMW.

Donaldson ended up in the front passenger seat where Henry would have expected Kramer to sit. The MP hovered and held back, jockeying subtly for position, and Henry realised what he was doing when he slid in next to Makin on the back seat. Henry sat on the other side of her, boxing her in between them.

Makin crushed herself up against Henry in an effort to keep away from Kramer. It was tight and uncomfortable for Henry, but not altogether unpleasant as he found that Makin had all the right bulges in all the right places.

FB gunned the car out of the police car park, ensuring the people in the rear were continually thrown against each other.

'What does he want?' Henry asked casually – as though the prime minister often asked to see him.

'To see us all,' said FB unhelpfully.

The car veered round a corner, tyres squealing. Makin got tighter into Henry. She was very warm, he noted. Her mouth turned to his ear, less than an inch away. Her hot breath blew against his ear lobe and he quivered. 'He's got his hand on my leg,' she hissed.

Henry looked down. There it was. Like a nasty, albino spider, right at the top of her thigh, his little finger lost in one of the folds of her jeans by her crotch. The hands squeezed, the little finger moved against the denim above her vagina.

'Do something.' She sounded afraid.

Henry leaned across. He lifted Kramer's fingers up and bent them backwards. Kramer gasped and tried to wriggle free. Henry's eyes looked into his astonished face. He did not release his grip. Between the two men, Makin tried to push herself out of the way, deep into the seat cushion. Suddenly Henry yanked at Kramer's hand, pulling the man down so they were face to face, their noses inches apart in front of Makin. Henry said one word, 'Don't.' He let go.

Kramer sat back quickly, anger contorting his features. He rubbed the joints in his fingers and glared at Henry who deliberately held the look with an impassivity designed to inflame Kramer's temper. Henry did not wilt under an expression which uttered a thousand silent warnings.

Kramer was first to give in. With a sneer of contempt, he looked away.

Henry relaxed. Makin's lips voiced a silent, 'Thanks.' Henry thought bleakly that it did not seem to matter what rank or how high up women go, it seemed they are always liable to be the targets of the power of men.

FB drove into the car park of the Imperial Hotel on North Shore, home of the British Prime Minister for the week.

He had the best suite in the hotel, of course, overlooking the promenade with distant views across the Irish Sea. The plush curtains were drawn at this time of night, blocking a view which was actually slightly distorted anyway. Three-inch-thick toughened glass, capable of withstanding a small rocket, does have a tendency to bend the light somewhat, as well as protecting the prime minister.

Only after two Metropolitan diplomatic protection officers had searched all three of them for a second time (the first being when they entered the hotel and had to submit to an electronic and manual search) were they admitted into the room.

The prime minister was sitting on a large sofa, legs outstretched across a coffee table. He was wearing a short sleeved-shirt, open at the neck, jeans and sloppy slippers. He looked casual and relaxed. He was leafing through a stack of official-looking papers. On the floor next to him was a tatty-looking red leather briefcase.

'Ahh, people,' he said. He tapped his papers straight and dropped them into the briefcase. He jumped up, smiling broadly. 'Basil.' He beamed at Kramer. They shook hands and patted each other's shoulders like old buddies.

'Prime Minister,' Kramer said, turning to face the four people he had brought with him, all standing there rather sheepishly. 'You already know ACC Fanshaw-Bayley from our host force, who is in charge of the conference operation.'

'Ah yes, we have met from time to time.' He shook FB's hand. 'How is your son, by the way. He was going to university last time we met, if I recall.'

'Oh, he's fine, fine,' babbled FB, thrown. 'In his last year now, doing well.'

'Good,' the PM said benignly.

Kramer continued with the introductions. 'This is Detective Superintendent Makin from the Met.' Handshake, more smiling. 'Karl Donaldson from the FBI legal attaché in London.' Handshake. 'And last,' Kramer said, missing out the 'but not least', 'Inspector Christie, Lancashire Police.'

Henry and the PM shook hands. Henry had only ever once been this close to a prime minister before. That had been in the early 1980s when Margaret Thatcher had visited Rawtenstall and Henry had accompanied her, with other officers, during a walkabout through the shopping centre in the days when a terrorist attack on the mainland was unthinkable. His lasting memory of her was that she was very hairy.

The first impression he got of the present PM was that he looked about twenty years too young to be doing the job. Like coppers get younger and younger, maybe the same applied to politicians.

'Please,' the PM swept a hand round, 'everyone take a seat.'

As bums touched seats the prime minister's wife, Diane, came out of the bedroom wrapped in a fluffy dressing gown and big bunny slippers. This was the PM's second wife, his first having died of cancer five years before. There had been uproar when he remarried not just because she was nearly ten years younger than him, or because she had been married before and was divorced, or because she owned a media-related business, or because she was very beautiful, or because it did not seem that enough time had passed between the PM's first wife dying, but mainly because she was black. And was now pregnant with the PM's baby.

Henry was agog at just how attractive she was in the flesh.

She smiled at everyone. 'Should I arrange tea, Richard?' she asked her husband.

'That would be lovely,' he said. She nodded and returned to the bedroom, closing the door behind her, presumably about to use room service.

The smile dropped from the PM's face and he became all business.

'Now, people, Mr Kramer informs me that we have some problems out there. I would like to be briefed from the horse's mouth, so to speak.'

Kramer eyed FB.

FB spluttered at being put on the spot, overawed by the company. 'Er ... yes ... erm ... I actually think that the appropriate person to explain is Inspector Christie. He has hands-on control of the situation. Inspector?' FB faced Henry, turning right away from the PM, giving Henry a nod and a look which said, 'Let me down at your peril.'

The uniformed inspector had a bit of a problem in stopping his bottom lip from dropping. He did a double-take on his boss, then looked at the PM who was already pissed off with the farce taking place in front of him.

More rapidly than he would have liked in normal circumstances, he got his thoughts together and spoke. 'Several things have happened this week. Firstly there was a large disturbance on a council estate in which one of our officers was badly injured. Three murders have been committed and now two of our officers have disappeared while investigating one of these, and a bomb has also exploded in a gay bar, but thankfully no one was injured.'

The suite door opened. A waiter and trolley came in, bearing tea, coffee and biscuits. Henry paused until the waiter left.

The PM asked, 'Are you saying that all these things are connected?'

Henry shrugged inadequately. 'There does seem to be a common factor, although it is just as possible that all these things could have taken place in isolation of each other. The common factor is the right-wing group Hellfire Dawn, in particular their paramilitary wing which has claimed responsibility for the bomb and the riot. They are a nasty thread running through all the incidents.'

'So what are you doing about it?'

'As much as we can. The media will get blitzed tomorrow, the already massive police presence is being increased—'

Henry was cut off by FB saying forcefully, 'We'll be coming down hard on law breakers and ensuring that Blackpool remains as peaceful as possible.'

'But my priority,' Henry said, stepping in with equal assertiveness, because he wanted to get things into perspective and it was not often that you have the ear of the prime minister, 'is that we have two officers missing.'

'Ahh,' the PM said, astutely, 'meaning that you actually don't give a toss if the government is made to look stupid in a week when law and order is high on the agenda.' He said it lightly, but seriously.

All eyes fell on Henry. 'I want to find out where these officers are. My main concern is for their safety and, if I'm allowed to be honest–?'

The PM nodded. Kramer squinted angrily at Henry. FB looked down at the carpet, wishing he hadn't brought him along.

'Sitting here talking to you, as big a deal as it is for me, is actually wasting my time, sir.'

FB groaned. His face had become almost without colour. Tension hung in the air.

The PM regarded Henry Christie icily. 'I think you are right. I am preventing you from doing your job. I admire your honesty. I promise you I won't keep you much longer.'

Henry nodded. Words would no longer come from his dried-up mouth.

The prime minister's attention moved to Karl Donaldson. 'I have heard there may be an American angle to the bomb?'

400

Donaldson, who tended to slouch while sitting, pulled himself up. 'You hear things fast, sir.'

'I know the right people. Forgive me.' The PM reached for a feature phone on the coffee table, pressed a button to select the conference facility. The dial tone sounded. He pressed a button which started an automatic dial. A long number. As it dialled, the PM said to Donaldson, 'Someone wants to have a word with you.'

The ringing started. On the third ring it was answered.

'Bob, is that you?' the PM asked.

'Yeah, pal,' drawled a male American voice. Karl Donaldson shot upright immediately, recognising the owner of the voice straight-away.

'Bob, I won't keep you long. I've got Karl Donaldson from the FBI legal attaché in London here with me – can I put him on?'

'Sure.'

The PM indicated the phone and that Donaldson should move closer to it. 'It's the President of the United States for you,' he said casually.

Everyone in the room became rigid.

'Mister President, this is Karl Donaldson speaking.'

'Hi, Karl, how the hell are ya?' he asked like he was an old buddy.

'Better for hearin' y'all, sir,' Donaldson said, drawing a short laugh from the most powerful man in the world.

'Good. Karl, to business. The bomber, this terrorist.'

'Yes, sir.'

'I won't beat about the bush. I am very concerned that one of our citizens is causing havoc across the pond. I want him stopped. I want him caught. Do I make myself clear?'

'Yes, sir,' Donaldson said.

'I am authorising you to work alongside the British authorities and bring this bastard to justice. I've already spoken to your boss in London and this has been cleared. Give it a hundred and ten per cent, Karl. Go for it. I don't want to put you under any pressure, but this guy needs stopping and if anybody can do it, you can.'

'Yes, sir,' the American snapped smartly. Henry thought Donaldson was about to jump up and salute.

'Richard?' the President asked.

'Yes, Bob?' the PM responded.

'Speak to you soon.'

'Bye.'

The call ended. The PM pressed a button on his phone and sat back.

'Thank you, people – that is all. My bed is calling, because even a prime minister has to sleep.'

Dismissed, they shuffled out of the suite, dumbstruck and more than amazed that they had had an audience with the British Prime Minister and been patched through to the President of the United States all in one go.

'Shit – pinch me,' Donaldson breathed once they had cleared the room. 'He doesn't want to put me under pressure? Is the man mad? Jeez, I did not say that. The President of the United States is not mad, understand, not mad. Guys, did that really just happen?'

They stopped at the top of a flight of stairs.

'Yes it did,' Kramer said cruelly. His veneer of pleasantness so beloved by the public and the media had vanished. Underneath was the harsh, ruthless man with massive ambition. 'And, let me make this clear on behalf of the prime minister that just because he did not come out and state that the pressure is on all of you, it is. ACC, I expect to be kept fully informed of all developments as I will be briefing the PM regularly.'

FB nodded unhappily. He did not seem to like Kramer as much as he had done forty-eight hours earlier. FB led them down the steps, Henry being the last in line. Before he could step down, Kramer took hold of his arm. 'Chat, please, inspector, if you don't mind.' Kramer's eyes were grey, tinged with steel, laced with snake venom.

'Do I have a choice?'

'We all have choices.' He steered Henry across the corridor and drew him into a room, very similar to the prime minister's.

'What's this? The big warning?'

'You could say that.' Kramer's voice reflected the message in his eyes. 'I hope you have no ambition left in your job, Inspector. Because if you do, you've just fucked it up by

403

laying your hand on me. Nobody denies me, Inspector, not in any aspect of my life, least of all a low-ranking dickhead like you – no one.'

'Your ambitions must be rather warped then, if you can only achieve them by intimidation.' Henry sniffed.

Kramer raised a hand to strike Henry in a flash of violent temper. Henry did not flinch. The hand remained raised, ready to strike.

'If you hit me,' Henry said, 'I promise your reputation will never recover.'

'It would be my word against the word of a police officer who had a past which, to say the least, is littered with complaints, violence and mental instability – who do you think would be believed?'

'It seems I have nothing to worry about, then, does it? As I have no job prospects, which is what you intimate.' Henry smiled dangerously. 'But I'll leave it at this: if you lay one uninvited finger on Andrea Makin again, I'll have you. Above board and bang to rights – promise.'

'What's this then?' FB said scornfully, a trace of jealousy as Henry joined them in the hotel foyer. 'Hob-nobbing with government spin doctors?'

'That's me, sir, a real high-flyer, but now I'm back to earth with a bump and I'd like to get on with the job I get paid for.' Henry's tone brokered no argument, even from FB, who sensed something not quite right.

404

'Good,' said FB. 'And remember,' he looked around at all three with a wicked grin, 'no pressure, absolutely no pressure.'

Twenty

Henry and Donaldson drove in a CID car to South Shore and onto Winston Road where Joey's flat was situated. They prowled slowly up the street looking out for signs of life in houses or flats with the intention of disturbing the occupants to ascertain if anyone knew of a 'military type' in the area.

Unusually for Blackpool, a town close to operating twenty-four hours a day, there was only one light to be seen in the whole street and no one responded to the knocking of the two law enforcement officers.

'Damn,' Donaldson said.

They were standing on the front steps of the house with the light on. Their breath steamed in the cold night air and they rubbed their hands to keep warm while they chatted.

'Already this is beginning to frustrate the hell out of me,' Donaldson complained. 'Everything is, like, coming into it so halfway.' He turned to Henry and with a pleading tone said, 'How do I catch a bomber who has evaded the FBI for the last six years, despite all those resources being thrown at him?

Who's to say he's still here anyway? He might have done his job and gone by now. I have absolutely no leads to go on here.'

'We could start with lodgings, rented property, I suppose,' Henry thought out loud. 'Where would a guy like that stay?'

Donaldson pondered. 'Somewhere quiet where he could work, assemble his devices, somewhere he's unlikely to be disturbed. So, not a hotel – maybe a rented cottage in the sticks?'

'We can get that rolling in the morning, get someone to contact all local letting companies to start with, then expand it as necessary.'

Just for the hell of it, Henry whacked the door once more. As he turned he saw a Neighbourhood Watch sticker in the corner of the window. That reminded him of something he had not done. He still got no answer at the door, though.

'But you're right, pal,' he said to Donaldson. They trotted back towards the CID car. 'We've come into this whole thing part way. We need a good new starting point.'

Henry opened the driver's door, dropped in and started the engine, flicking the heater on to full. A frustrated Donaldson plonked miserably down next to him and turned the heater down. 'I can't believe it. Just my luck, the president telling me to get a result on a job I don't have an earthly chance of solving, as much as I personally want to nail the bastard.'

They sat in the car. Above them, the sky was

406

beginning to lighten, becoming less black as the first hint of dawn crept in. Each man was deep in thought at how best to unravel the whole mess.

Simultaneously, their heads swivelled. They looked at each other jubilantly.

'We need to go right back to the beginning of all this,' Henry said.

'Yeah.'

'We need to go and rattle a cage or two, poke some sticks at the wild animals therein. We need to get to grips with Hellfire Dawn, for cryin' out loud. I even said it to the PM, maybe not in so many words, but that's it – we get into their ribs, find their weak link and snap it.' Henry tried to twist the steering wheel as he spoke.

'Great minds think alike.'

'Let's do it, then,' Henry said enthusiastically.

Henry held out his hand. Donaldson shook it.

Moments later they were en route back to the police station having been called back urgently by Andrea Makin.

Makin was at the door of the communications room, a message pad in her hand. She had circulated details of Joey's murder to all forces, asking if anyone had anything similar on their patch recently. Because of the time of day she had not realistically expected anything back before mid-morning.

Two forces had surprised her. Surrey had

407

responded that they had something similar about six months before but would be unable to give further details until later in the day. Cheshire police gave an even better response. A sleepy control room inspector at their Chester headquarters, on reading the message had immediately recognised the similarity with a double murder in Wilmslow which his son, a thirty-year-old detective inspector, was investigating.

'This is a possibility,' Makin said, handing the message to Henry. 'Three weeks ago in Cheshire.' Henry read it, absorbed it, passed it on to Donaldson.

'Let's call the DI now,' Henry said, noting the time with a wry smile. It was one of the drawbacks of being a detective inspector – telephone calls at unsociable hours. Tough, he thought, picking up a telephone and dialling the number on the message switch. 'Heard from your undercover man yet?' he asked Makin. She shook her head. The phone started to ring and was answered almost immediately and brightly despite the time of day. Once the apologies and introductions had been made the business began. Henry stuck a hand over his ear to cut out the background noise of the communications room and also because there was still a ringing noise in his head from the bomb blast earlier. He cradled the phone between shoulder and jaw and scribbled notes as he talked.

'Double murder, husband and wife,' the roused DI, by the name of Harrison, said.

408

'Hubby stabbed to death in the kitchen, wife murdered in the bathroom. They had marks on their chests indicating they could have been subdued by a stun gun, or similar. We think she was the target and husband got in the way because the killer had spent time with her. Wrapped her in parcel tape and gutted her, bit like a ripper murder. Forensically the place was as clean as a whistle.'

'Who were the victims, what did they do?' Henry asked.

Pause. 'She was a solicitor specialising in discrimination cases and she was black, husband was white. He was an accountant. They were pretty loaded. Lots of avenues we're following up.'

'Anything stolen? Anything written on the walls?'

'Nothing stolen, nothing written on the walls. They'd spent the day with friends up to about three-ish, then spent the afternoon alone, bumming around the house we reckon. We think the killer came into the house about eight o'clock and they died sometime between then and midnight.'

'Anything unusual at the scene?'

'A butchered body *is* pretty unusual – what do you mean?'

'Who found the bodies?' Henry said, still fishing.

'The cleaner – she found them just after nine in the morning.'

'Did she mention anything unusual?'

'Um – yeah, she found two dead people,'

Harrison said gruffly. He was beginning to feel tired again. 'Just tell me what you mean, will you?'

'Sorry, yeah. Was there any music playing?'

'She didn't mention anything. I've read her statement dozens of times, so I should know.'

'OK. It sounds similar to ours in some respects. Have you found any more around the country?'

'One in Surrey, two in the Met, one in West Midlands, but they're not a hundred per cent tied in yet, you understand.'

'And do you have any strong leads?'

'Nothing much. One witness saw a motor-cyclist in the area, but it's not tied in for definite, nothing more than that. It's maddening. I think it was a planned, organised job, not a spur of the moment thing. We have some observations from a psychological profiler.'

Henry stifled a yawn. Profilers, in his experience, while of some use, tended to generalise so much that half the population became suspects. He thought they were a bit like mediums, conning the shit out of people, ripping them off. 'Go on,' he said.

'White male, twenty-five to forty-five years old. Bears a grudge against women and black people.' Henry could almost hear the DI's brain ticking over. 'University educated—'

'Where did that come from?'

'Search me. Look, mate, I'm falling asleep here. I'll send you everything I have so you can review it. I'm not precious. I just want to catch a killer. I'll send a motorcyclist up with it first thing – nine at the latest, promise.'

The phone call ended. Henry hung up thoughtfully. All eyes were on him. 'It's a beginning.'

The communications room was buzzing with activity. Phone calls were coming in constantly even though it was the early hours of the morning. Officers were being deployed. Nothing ever changed in Blackpool: the tide came in and out twice a day; eighteen million people visited every year; and the cops did their best.

Dermot Byrne and PC John Taylor came in and headed towards Henry.

'How's it going, Dermot?' Henry asked. He had forgotten that other things were happening – such as twenty-odd car loads of Asian youths heading into town to cause ructions. 'How did my little plan pan out?'

'Pretty good. They all got snarled up in the traffic chaos from the bomb which took about three hours to clear. They got split up and didn't have any plans for regrouping, so they all seem to have sloped off home. Shoreside has been boxed up and it's all quiet up there, more or less. Some bits of trouble, but nothing we couldn't nip in the bud. So it worked.'

'Good – and how are you feeling, John?' Henry asked Taylor who was as pale and insipid as Henry had ever seen him.

'I'm all right, sir.'

'Any news on Jane or Mark?' Byrne inquired.

Henry shook his head.

'Not looking good, is it?'

'Keep a positive attitude. Which reminds me – neighbourhood watch co-ordinators, where do we keep a list of them? I want to know who the co-ordinator is for the area where Joey's flat is situated. Just before Jane and Mark went AWOL she spoke to some military-type old man. I thought that if we got hold of the co-ordinator for that area, he or she might know who the guy is.'

'Could I look into that, sir?' Taylor volunteered, perking up a little. 'I know where the list is kept.'

'Thanks.'

Taylor scuttled away.

'Is he really OK?' Henry asked Byrne about Taylor.

'I think so. He's keen to make amends. He'll be fine.'

Byrne gave a quick wave and said he had to go to the custody office.

It was 3 a.m.

'Well, team,' Henry said in a less than motivational tone, eyes moving from Makin to Donaldson, 'I want to be able to say, "do this" or "do that", but at the moment I'm not sure there's anywhere to go. Perhaps we should get some sleep, then reconvene in Gold at eight and give ourselves a full day. Observations?'

'I think you're right – we can't do anything

now,' Donaldson conceded.

Makin nodded her acquiescence.

'Right – back here at eight, bright-eyed and bushy-tailed.'

Even though he was shattered, the idea of taking some sleep did not appeal to Henry, but he had to admit that realistically there was nothing that could be done until morning. It would be far better to rest for the next five hours instead of sitting around doing nothing, only to find that when he needed a brain later in the day it was just cottonwool. It was imperative that he should be able to think straight because he had a feeling there would be a breakthrough some time during the day. There had to be, he thought desperately. If there wasn't, then statistically speaking, the chances of finding Jane Roscoe and Mark Evans alive were nil.

He shrugged his leather jacket on and made his way out past the custody office into the car park.

'Sir, sir,' came a voice behind him. It was PC Taylor, holding an index file card. 'I've found the name of the neighbourhood watch co-ordinator,' he panted.

'Well done.'

'It's a Captain Blackthorn, lives more or less opposite Joey Costain's flat. It could even be the person DI Roscoe spoke to. Sounds like a military type.'

'Yeah, it's a possibility.'

'Anyway, whatever,' said Taylor, eager to

please, 'I'll go round now and speak to him, rather than phone. It'd be better, wouldn't you think? If he's in and has any useful information, should I contact you?'

'Yeah. I'm going home now. My number's on the board in communications. If you think there is anything, give me a call.'

'OK, sir – if you don't hear from me, it's a dead end.'

Taylor sauntered smugly back into the building and went up to the CID office, humming to himself. The office was empty and he helped himself to a set of car keys on the rack by the door. He thought it would be more discreet to go and see Captain whatever-his-name-was in a plain car. It would draw less attention than a bright marked one. PC Taylor did not really like drawing attention to himself.

No one saw him take the keys or leave the station.

Five minutes later, in South Shore, he pulled up away from a street light, got out of the car and left his hat inside it.

The house in which Captain Blackthorn lived was divided into a number of good-quality flats, unlike most of the others in the area which were nothing more then glorified bedsits. Taylor pressed the door bell and kept his thumb on it.

'Who's that for goodness sake?' a sleepy voice said groggily.

'Sorry to bother you, sir,' Taylor said into the intercom. 'I'm PC Taylor from Blackpool police station. Can I speak to you on an urgent matter, please? I really do apologise, but it is extremely urgent.'

'Yes, yes, suppose so.'

The buzzer release sounded. Taylor stepped into the building.

Captain Blackthorn was dressed in a thick, mustard-coloured dressing gown over a pair of flannelette pyjamas. His feet were slotted into a pair of zip-up slippers. He came out of the small kitchen bearing two mugs of tea, one of which he handed to PC Taylor, whose leather-gloved hand received it and aligned it on the exact edge of the coffee table.

'As I say, I don't mind being disturbed at all. Gives one's life a sort of purpose. All part of the responsibility, eh what?' He snorted and sipped his tea. 'Ahh, that's good. You not drinking?'

'I'll just let it cool.'

The captain cradled his mug between the palms of his hands. 'Anyway, yes, it was me who spoke to your detective inspector – nice woman. Is there some kind of problem?'

'There is, actually,' Taylor said. 'She's gone missing and we're very worried about her. Obviously we're trying to trace her movements. It's possible you were one of the last persons to speak to her.'

'Oh, I say, you don't think that I...?'

'No, no, nothing like that.'

'Thank goodness for that.'

415

'Could you tell me what exactly you said to her?'

The captain accompanied Taylor to the door of the flat and let him out.

'You've been very, very helpful, sir.'

'I do hope she is all right.' The captain was very concerned.

'I'm sure she'll be fine,' Taylor reassured him. 'Sorry to have disturbed you.'

'Not a problem, not a problem.'

'Good night.'

The captain closed his flat door. Taylor walked down the dark hallway to the front door of the building.

David Gill emerged from the shadows.

He had been curious as to how Roscoe had found him. He had not asked her yet, had not had the time for a long, loving chat. That would come. But now he knew. A nosy neighbour. A man with nothing better to do with his life except sit by a window, watching, making notes on other people's comings and goings. Prying into the private lives of others. The sad fucking bastard. Gill approached the front door of the captain's flat and tapped on it. As expected, he opened up immediately.

'Sorry about this,' Gill said. His left hand shot out and grabbed the captain by the throat. He barged in, forcing the old man down the short hallway, kicking the flat door closed behind him.

The knife in his right hand curved upwards,

416

plunging deep into the captain's chest, under the ribcage and up into the old man's already weak heart. He drove the blade in harder, hard, hard, twisted, pushed more, twisted, withdrew and let the captain fall. He was already dead. The frail body crimped to the floor.

Even though Gill knew he was dead, this did not prevent him kneeling down next to him and repeatedly stabbing and slashing the body in a frenzy of anger.

'No one,' slash, stab, 'no one – tells on me,' stab, 'no one gets away with it you silly – fucking – idiot – mad, old cunt!' Stab, stab, stab. 'Now you try to finger me.'

Jane Roscoe thought she was going to suffocate. Gill had wrapped the parcel tape tightly around her head and face in his anger at her screaming. It had gone round and round, covering her nose and mouth, leaving the smallest of slits through which she could breathe.

She lay there. In his lair. That was how she had come to know it. What, in her mind, she called this living tomb in which he kept her. A lair.

She lay there, trying to control her breathing, to keep her heart rate down, to stay in control. She knew that inner control was the only way in which this ordeal could be survived. She had to control herself and then she had to control him, even if it meant subjugating herself to his will. If he wanted to rape her, fine, let him do it. Anything to survive. Unfortunately she didn't think he wanted sexual domination.

Her mind wandered uncontrollably. She thought of her husband and her failing marriage and wanted to cry. She had been so unfair to the man. Was there anything that could be salvaged? Lying in this cold place she realised she'd had plenty of opportunity to put things right, to make an effort, and had never done a thing. She had allowed them to drift apart. He had a responsibility too, but the biggest part of the blame was on her shoulders. Why had she let it go? Maybe love had fizzled out. Passion certainly had. No fire any more, but wasn't that the way of marriage?

And Henry Christie? What of him? The first man in years who had got under her skin. One whom she had wanted to hate but who, instead, had made her feel something she hadn't felt for years. The only man who could send a shiver down to her sex ... she had to force herself to stop thinking like this and start thinking about how to get out of here alive. Then you can start making life choices.

She listened to her surroundings for some clue. Nothing seemed to make sense. Was it day or night? If she could only remember what had happened, but all she could bring to mind was knocking on David Gill's door, it being opened by a guy in a motorcycle helmet then – zap! – a huge jolt of something against her chest, the blackness of unconsciousness then awakening here, wherever here was.

Footsteps. A door opened.

He was back. Gill had returned to his lair.

Twenty-One

The detective inspector from Cheshire was better than his word. A police motorcyclist dropped a thick file off at the front office at Blackpool police station with Henry Christie's name on it at 7 a.m. It was in Henry's hands five minutes later because, try as he might, he hadn't been able to sleep. He had dropped off for about an hour at 5 a.m., but awoken with a start at 6.15 when one of Fiona's patients started howling down below.

The police station was hectic. Seven was the turn-around time for officers working on the conference.

Henry collected the package from the front desk and gravitated to Jane Roscoe's office which, not long ago, had been his own. Not much had changed in it. His own personal belongings and mementoes had been replaced by Roscoe's. Everything else was as it had been. He eased himself behind the familiar desk – under which he had found Jane Roscoe searching the other night with her bottom swaying provocatively in the air,

419

trying to reach a piece of paper. Briefly, the memory made him smile.

He ripped open the package from Cheshire, while thinking that the DI down there must have been another early riser. He shuffled the contents out.

'Graveson: Lucinda and Thomas. Murder' the file was headed.

Inside were several bound books of crime-scene photographs which Henry flicked through, then put to one side. He picked up the written materials and started to scan them. He had read many murder files. On some murders he had worked specifically in the capacity of statement reader, dedicated solely to reading and rereading statements for clues, connections, leads and discrepancies. He could read a murder file quickly and be certain at the end of it he knew as much about it as anybody.

There were many statements to go through here.

With a note pad by his side, pencil in hand, he started.

Three-quarters of an hour later he picked up the crime-scene photos again. Shots of the Graveson house in Wilmslow, Cheshire, a very different part of the world than South Shore, Blackpool. This time he looked closely at every picture. When he had finished he knew he had something, but did not know what. It was something from the photos. Something that did not quite gel properly.

At 8 a.m. he did not have the answer. He

got on the phone to Cheshire and spoke to the DI again.

As soon as Donaldson and Makin arrived, Henry hustled them down to the garage without any explanation and hurried them into a plain, traffic enforcement car. It was a Vauxhall Omega, the fastest and best car he could blag at short notice with the promise to the traffic sergeant that, honestly, he would bring it back in one piece.

He almost had his first accident speeding out of the garage doors, but managed to avoid the bread delivery van.

'Oops,' he said, giving the white-faced van driver an apologetic wave.

'Oops, my ass,' Donaldson growled, taking his hands slowly away from his face. 'Is it safe to look now, you reckless son of a bitch?'

'Sorry,' Henry said, jamming the brakes on at the first junction, then accelerating left to put the car into a slot in the early morning traffic which did not look wide enough for a mini. 'Here, have a look at this.' He picked up the envelope from his lap and tossed it across to Donaldson. 'The murder of Louise Graveson and her husband.'

Donaldson picked it out of the footwell and extracted the contents. As he read each statement he passed it over his shoulder to Makin in the back seat.

Henry pushed the car hard and unlike most police cars it revelled in it. He enjoyed the experience, whizzing past every other car on the motorway and not caring whether or not he was caught on a speed camera. This was a business trip. The firm would have to write off any fixed penalties that came his way. He motored along the M55, then south on the M6, through Lancashire and down into Cheshire.

His two partners were silent as they ingested details of the double murder, each giving the occasional exclamation of horror, particularly when they got to the crime-scene photos, which were appalling in their depiction of the violence suffered by the victims.

'Poor people,' Makin said sympathetically. 'What a way to die.'

She handed the file back to Donaldson who repackaged it neatly into the envelope.

'Well?' Henry said. He had stayed quiet while they had read the file. He glanced at Donaldson, then quickly over his shoulder at Makin.

'Well what?' she asked. 'Looks like it could be the same offender.'

'Anything else strike you?'

'She could've been a target for right-wing extremists,' Donaldson suggested. 'Looking at her line of work – bit OTT, though.'

'But a possibility,' Henry said. 'Anything else?'

They each put forward several thoughts, none of which seemed to satisfy Henry. Eventually Donaldson became irritated. 'Look, buddy. I think you'd better tell us what

422

you're thinking, because it's darned obvious something has hit a note with you and neither of us two idiots seem capable of seeing it.' He leaned across to Henry. 'So tell us, put us out of our misery, or I'll smash your face in, one hundred miles an hour or not.'

Henry deflated visibly.

'I'm not sure,' he said hesitantly. 'There's something there, but I can't quite see what it is – sorry,' his voice was pathetic. 'That's why we're going to visit the scene, see if I – we – can pull that "something" out of the ether.'

With the parcel tape over her eyes Roscoe could not see him, but she knew he was there. Nor could she speak to him, the tape having been wrapped under her jaw and over her head as well as across her mouth, sealing her lips, making her jaw immovable.

He had said nothing. He'd come into the room and remained silent.

Roscoe's whole body was rigid with terror and she began to feel the loss of control again, this time down in her bladder and bowels. She had managed to hold on for all this time – somehow – but it would be impossible to do so for much longer.

She tried to speak. The sound was trapped at the back of her throat.

'Are you trying to make contact?' Gill asked brightly.

She nodded.

'If I take the tape off your mouth, you will not scream, do you understand?'

She nodded again.

'If you do, I'll just kill you, OK?'

She could sense him moving nearer. She could smell him and then she felt him touching her face, trying to find an end of the tape.

'I've wrapped you up too well.' He laughed. 'I'm going to have to cut a hole where your mouth is. At least where I think your mouth is. If I get it wrong, you'll have two mouths. Then I'd have a real problem shutting you up, wouldn't I?'

She felt a sharp point press onto her face. The tip of a knife. He jabbed it deliberately into her cheek.

'Is your mouth here?'

She flinched.

'Or is it here?' He prodded her forehead with the instrument. 'Or here?' The knife jabbed the top of her head. 'Or here?' She sensed Gill moving, but this time he did not press the blade into her for a few moments. She waited, trying to anticipate whereabouts on her head it would be pressed next. Then jumped when she felt a sharp jab on her inner thigh and he dragged the knife upwards towards her vagina. Just then it did not matter any more because the abject fear she was experiencing made inner control impossible.

'Oh, you fuckin' bitch,' Gill cried. 'You did that on purpose, didn't you?' Fuckin' women! Fuckin' bitches. I hate you all.'

This was it. Roscoe knew she was going to die. She waited for the blade to pierce her. Where would it enter her body? What would

424

it feel like?

Gill placed the tip of the blade under her chin and pressed.

'We appreciate this,' Henry Christie said to DI Harrison who was waiting outside the Graveson house where the double murder had taken place.

'Not a problem. We need to work together on this one,' the DI said.

Henry introduced Donaldson and Makin, then they all turned and walked up the driveway to the house.

'As a murder scene, we've finished with it, handed it back to the family and everything, but I know they haven't been able to touch the place. Nothing's been moved since we withdrew, I know that for a fact. The family are devastated and can't bring themselves to do anything with the house,' Harrison explained.

'Understandable,' Makin said.

'And fortunate,' Henry said, 'for us, that is.'

At the front door the DI asked Henry, 'What do you expect to find here, if you don't mind me asking?'

Henry shrugged. 'Dunno.'

No house which had been the scene of such tragedy could ever be the same again. The nature of what had taken place had seeped into the very fabric of the building and destroyed what was once a happy and loving environment. Now ghosts drifted around, demanding justice. Not revenge, but justice.

And until it was achieved there could be no rest for them.

Henry walked around the house alone. From the kitchen where the husband had been murdered, into the lounge, then up the stairs to the bathroom where Louise Graveson had been butchered. Dried blood was everywhere. It was a mess.

He closed his eyes and wished both dead people peace, and made a vow to them, there and then, that he would do his best to find that justice for them. When he opened his eyes, DI Harrison came into the bathroom.

'Not pretty,' he commented. 'We've offered to get cleaners in for them, but the family have refused.'

Henry thought he understood why. 'As gruesome as it is, it gives them some sort of lifeline to their loved ones. To get it cleaned up, wash the blood away, would be like washing their memories away.'

'I suppose so.' The DI shrugged. 'So – found what you're looking for?'

C' mon Henry, time to get operating, he told himself. 'Let's go back downstairs,' he said, 'I think it's there, but I'm not sure.'

Makin and Donaldson were in the living room.

Henry stood by the hi-fi, a modern Bang and Olufsen contraption which would have looked more at home in an operating theatre. 'The cleaning lady found the bodies, yeah?' Nods all round. 'She doesn't mention any music playing in her statement. I think she

426

needs asking if there was any.' Henry was musing out loud. 'She came in the front door and though her statement doesn't say it, I'll bet she came into the lounge before she found the husband in the kitchen.' He looked at Harrison. 'You say this crime scene hasn't been touched, nothing been moved?'

'Nothing,' he confirmed.

Henry switched on the hi-fi and pressed 'play' on the CD. Immediately and automatically the haunting opening chords of 'Midnight Rambler' began. He bent down and inspected the controls. It was on repeat play.

'This is a connection with our job. I'll bet the cleaner came in, switched this off and then found the husband. She probably totally forgot about the music with the shock of finding him, and who could blame her?'

'Well done, H,' Donaldson said.

He took a small bow. 'But that's not all.' He looked round the room, with the exception of some newspapers spread around, it was all very neat and tidy.

'Have you taken eliminatory prints off everybody? Family, friends?'

Harrison feigned offence.

Yet, still, Henry did not know what it was that had drawn him to the scene of this murder. 'C' mon, it's staring us in the face,' he mumbled. His eyes roved around the room as he mused out loud. 'They spent the morning with friends, dossing around, having brunch, whatever.'

One Sunday newspaper, the *Mail*, was on

the floor by the sofa, its separate sections spread around. Another, the *Telegraph*, was on a chair, having obviously been opened and read. Then it hit him, yet it seemed so pathetic and minor that it did not seem enough but, he tried to assure himself, it was the little, inconsequential things that often solved murders. He pointed at the newspaper on the coffee table. The *Sunday Times*. 'That's it,' he declared. 'I think.'

'Better explain yourself,' Donaldson cut in.

'OK. The Gravesons have two friends round on a Sunday morning, yeah?' Nods. 'They doss about. Chat. Have brunch. Read the newspapers?' Nods again. Henry jabbed his finger towards the newspapers in disarray. 'These ones look like they've been read,' he said, trying to work out what message he was trying to get across. 'Yet the *Sunday Times* here looks almost pristine. Why?'

'Tidy people?' suggested Makin.

'Who only tidy up one out of three newspapers?' Henry was as frustrated with the process as anyone else in the room. 'It just doesn't sit right with me. Why do two newspapers look as though they've been read and one doesn't?' He addressed Harrison. 'Is it possible for you, or me, to talk to those friends now? See if they recall reading the *Sunday Times*, see if they remember anything at all, what they did with it. Did they refold it?'

'I'll do it now.' The DI pulled his mobile phone out from his jacket and went out of the

428

house to get a good signal.

Henry sat on the sofa and looked down at the newspaper which had attracted his attention. He did not touch it. Then he smiled at Makin and Donaldson. 'Nice here, innit?'

Makin shivered. 'Gives me the creeps.'

'It's spooky,' Donaldson agreed. 'Feels like walking through spiders' webs or ectoplasm.'

'I think the bastard sat here and read the newspaper then folded it up nice and neat. Because he's a pretty neat operator. The bodies he leaves are a mess, but everything else is neatly tidied up. No loose ends. He's very in control of everything.'

'And if he did read a newspaper, so what?' Makin asked.

'Then the fingerprint people go through every single page and pick off any fingerprints and smudges they find, because maybe the guy made a mistake here.'

Makin hid a look of disappointment. 'Bit thin, isn't it?'

Henry smiled. 'Wedges have thin ends.'

Harrison returned. 'Just spoke to one of the Gravesons' friends. They read all the newspapers and when they left they were pretty much scattered around.'

'I won't say "bingo" yet,' Henry said, 'because he probably wore gloves, but can you get your SOCO people down here now, please?'

Through the slit Gill had kindly cut in the

429

tape covering her mouth, Roscoe said, 'I'm sorry.'

Gill had calmed down. Roscoe wanted to keep him sweet. Did not want to do anything further to upset him. Wetting and soiling herself had been bad enough. The smell was atrocious, the discomfort unpleasant, but she was past caring. That was unimportant. Staying alive and breaking free by whatever means were what mattered now.

'What was that?' he teased.

'Sorry – so sorry.'

'You messy bitch.' Gill shook his head sadly. 'You're the second one who's done that to me. I mean, really, it just confirms everything about females, doesn't it?'

As he talked he moved around the room. Through a minute break in the tape over her eyes, Roscoe could see a chink of light, nothing more.

'I mean, what the fuck, eh? What the fuck, for example, are you doing pretending to be a detective inspector? That is a man's job. It's not something a woman should even be contemplating. Being a cop is man's work. White man's work, at that. I mean, what member of the public would want a woman or a blackie turning up at their door? No one in their right minds. They want to see healthy, fit, big white guys. Not Pakis or split-arses.'

Roscoe listened to his ravings. The final phrase he used sent a message to her. 'Split-arses' was a derogatory phrase, used very little now, to describe policewomen. She

430

wasn't aware of any other profession which used the term.

'Are you a policeman?' she asked.

Gill stopped. He did not respond for a few moments. 'Why ask that?' he said suspiciously.

'Because of what you just said – split-arses.'

'Hm. No. Good try, detective.'

Something in the way he had responded made Roscoe wonder if she had hit a nerve.

'So why me? Where do I fit in?'

'You don't fit in. You just came along and I reacted. Otherwise I'd now be sitting in a cell, contemplating suicide.'

'Where do the other people you've murdered fit in?'

'Good question – and it sounds grand, this, but it's all part of the master plan. It's like a big chessboard, except it's for real. I'm with white, of course. And there are little battles going on all over the field. Pawn takes pawn. In this real world, pawn kills pawn. I kill people, the black team. Part of a strategy. Guerrilla warfare. A strike here, a strike there, then withdraw. But this is the week when it all changes. Up to now I've been picking them off one by one. The ones who have played their part in the downfall of the fabric of British society. Yes, I'm doing this for the sake of the country, Britain, the heritage.'

'For Britain? You're murdering people for Britain?' Roscoe was losing it again as she had to listen to the ranting of a mad man.

'Yes,' he said in total belief. 'I'm a patriot.

431

I'm going to be part of a movement that saves this country from itself and restores its pride.'

The sea can never be trusted. Sometimes it will keep its victims to itself and they will never be found, sometimes it will return them immediately and other times it will play with them like a cat with its prey, tossing them up, reclaiming them, having fun.

In the case of the body which had been bundled dead over the sea wall, for reasons known only to itself the sea decided to deposit him in almost the exact same spot from which it had taken him when offered. The body was found by a man walking his dog along central beach. The body was wrapped around the foot of one of the stanchions of Central Pier.

There was nothing that could be done to speed up the process. A scenes-of-crime officer was at the house within fifteen minutes, ready to roll. With gloved hands she began to leaf through the newspaper but found nothing to excite or interest. No smudges, nothing. The *Sunday Times* magazine was more interesting and when she held the back page up to the light there were some clear prints in the black ink of an advertisement for an Alfa Romeo car. She found other prints throughout the magazine on its shiny surface and carefully lifted and transferred them onto glass plates, logging each one carefully.

Henry watched, desperate for her to get a move on. He also knew that if he pushed her she would either do a poor job or would fall out with him. He wanted neither to happen. Outwardly, therefore, he remained patient. Inwardly he was paddling like a demented duck.

After finishing with the magazine, she bagged it up, logged it and placed it with the prints inside her bag of tricks.

'I'll take them straight to fingerprints,' she said. 'They'll be expecting me.'

'And you might as well head off back to sunny Blackpool,' Harrison said. 'I'd love to offer you my hospitality but I do have a murder inquiry to run.'

'Understood. Thanks for everything,' Henry said dully, wondering if this had all been a waste of time and effort. Do killers sit down and read newspapers? He kept on the positive side by telling himself that if someone can kill another person, in itself a very weird thing, they are capable of doing anything. 'We'll tootle back.' He looked at Donaldson. 'And to kill a bit of time, maybe we can start rattling those cages we were talking about.'

'Yeah – I need some action,' the American responded.

Gill was sitting next to Roscoe, knees drawn up, arms folded round them. He had become quiet, reflective. 'You see, essentially, this country is white through and through.

433

Dominated by white men with their women tagging along, supporting them.'

Had Roscoe been able, she would have bitten her lip.

'Just think what we have achieved as a nation. The empire. Subjugating India, almost ruling Africa – and where are we now? The standard of living is shite, we hardly produce any goods and blacks and women are taking over. What's happened?' His voice rose, quivering with hysteria. 'Everything has been turned on its head, but now it's time to make a stand. Look at you, as a case in point, how the hell did you get to be a detective? And look what they did to the guy who got shoved out for you.'

'How do you know about that?' Roscoe mumbled. 'How do you know this?'

That stopped Gill again. 'Because I do,' he said inadequately.

The journey back was less hectic than the one south. It lacked the imperative. Henry stuck to the speed limits, lost in his thoughts. Once on the M55, heading west, he switched on his radio to hear anything of interest that might be going on in Blackpool. This was how they managed to come into a conversation halfway through between a patrol and communications.

The patrol was saying: '...white male, mid-thirties. Could have been in since last night. Looks as though he's been beaten up before hitting the water. I'll need CID here, please.'

434

'Any ID?'

'Standby.'

'It might be the guy who went in last night,' Henry said to his travelling companions. 'Someone reported seeing three men dumping what could have been a body into the pond, but when the patrol arrived there was no trace of the informant or a body.'

The patrol in Blackpool transmitted again. 'Found a wallet. Money still in it – driving licence in the name of Terry Baxter.'

In the back of the car Andrea Makin emitted a squeak. She had not been listening to the radio, particularly, but the name made her sit upright.

'What was that name?' she asked.

'Baxter – Terry Baxter,' Donaldson said.

Makin slumped back with a groan. 'Oh my God.'

'What's wrong?' Donaldson asked.

'Terry Baxter was the undercover identity of Jack Laws, my DC who was undercover with Hellfire Dawn.'

The body was still on the beach when they arrived in Blackpool, so Henry drove straight to Central Pier and parked on the inner promenade alongside other police cars.

Makin did not hesitate about going down onto the beach. She was a hardened detective and the sight of a body was nothing new, even if it was a colleague. With Henry and Donaldson at her heels she pushed her way through the onlookers, flashing her badge to make

435

them get out of the way. She knelt at the head of the body, curled down and looked at the face of a man who had been seriously batter-ed. It was her officer. She stood slowly, head shaking, then elbowed her way through the crowd and stamped away down the beach, terribly upset. She had no specific destination in mind and found herself walking towards the water's edge, several hundred metres out. Here she stopped, head hung low.

She thought she was alone, but Henry had trailed her at a discreet distance, then come up behind her.

'Stupid question, I guess, but I take it that's him?'

'Yeah, stupid question.' She did not look at Henry, not wanting him to see the tears in her eyes.

'Who knew about him?'

She gulped. 'Me, you, Karl, FB – God, how the hell did they find out, Henry? Who told them? He was a bloody good operative. If he knew he'd been compromised, or suspected it, he would've pulled out pdq. He can't have been expecting it – so it must have happened quickly, without warning. Somebody must have blabbed.' She spun defiantly on Henry. 'So who was it?'

David Gill paced the room. Roscoe could hear his footsteps circling her. Around and around. Making her head spin.

'It's a statement of intent that I'll be mak-ing,' he said, very matter of fact. 'From the

436

people to the government. To the prime minister. He must be made to see the error of his ways. But he is a weak man, it must be said. Swayed left and right, depending on who shouts the loudest. Misguided idiot. I'll be taking the game right to his bedroom door, literally.'

'Are you going to kill him?'

Gill snorted. 'I wish. It'd save the country some bloody grief. No, it's much better than that, Janie, I'm going to hit him where it really hurts.'

'Where's that?'

Gill stopped moving. Suddenly Roscoe could no longer hear him, place him. Had he gone?

Then she felt his hot breath over her nose as he kneeled over her and held his face over hers. His breath smelled awful. There was garlic in it. There was also the odour of his stomach contents.

'I'll tell you where,' he whispered. Roscoe twitched as he pushed the point of his knife into her chest. 'And when I've done it, I'll come back and share the victory with you, and then I'll kill you, ever so slowly and delicately.'

Roscoe held her nerve. 'Where are you going to hurt him?' she asked again.

'Why, Jane,' he said, pressing the point of the knife into her chest, 'in his heart, of course – I'm going to kill his wife and unborn child.'

Twenty-Two

At 3 p.m. on Wednesday there were perhaps two hundred and fifty people gathered outside the Berlin Hotel. To Henry, who hated stereotyping, they all looked much like peas from the same pod. Mainly males, aged between sixteen and twenty-five, heads shaven, wearing denims, T-shirts and Doc Marten boots with their jeans tucked in the tops. Their T-shirts bore logos promoting hatred and racism. Their tattoos – and there were many – spread the same message. They were the epitome of the right-wing movement in Britain. Henry hated the sight of them. They made his face curl with distaste, but more sadly, he wanted to punch them.

The street was sealed to traffic while these people were allowed the privilege of getting themselves ready to march up to the Winter Gardens to coincide with a march coming in from the opposite direction led by gay-rights activists.

Despite pleas from many quarters, both marches would be allowed to proceed. Such was the nature of a democratic society.

'I feel the same,' Donaldson said, seeing Henry's expression.

'They make me feel physically sick,' Henry said. 'Come on, let's do it.'

They pushed their way through the gathering protesters who were just starting to clear their throats and practise their chants, winding themselves up in the process. By the time the two officers were in the middle of the crowd, their ears were ringing with, 'Kill the gay twats! Kill the gay twats!'

Martin Franklands was sitting in the front window of the hotel, looking out onto the street from the dining room. This gave him an elevated view of proceedings. In spite of reassurances not to worry, his insides were constantly gurgling and churning over. He knew he was out of his depth and was struggling to handle the emotional backlash of the two things in which he had been involved over the last day.

Although he supported the ideals of the movement, he was not a true man of action. He was a thinker and a writer. His job was to prepare pamphlets and newsletters, to help in the back room with the admin, to look after the accounts, to be a gofer. He was quite happy to lend his voice to demonstrations, such as this afternoon's show of solidarity (although, he had to admit, the two hundred or so people who had shown up was a pretty poor turn-out). But that was all. He was the one who did a runner if things turned nasty. He was quite happy to tell Paki bastards to get back home and screw his face up into that peculiarly nasty trademark thuggish look of the right wing, but if challenged, he would run a mile.

He had been suckered in by Vince Bellamy, the manipulative tyrant.

Franklands had seen Bellamy do this to other people: set them up and then use them. He had vowed not to get caught like that, but had failed. So now here he was, shitting himself every time a new face showed up, expecting to be locked up at any moment, watching, always watching – and now seeing. He saw them coming. Two biggish guys, easing their way through the crowd with no great problem. No way intimidated by the crush of people surrounding them, yet obviously not a part of the protest.

Franklands made them immediately: cops.

Suddenly everything inside him turned to jelly: flesh, bones, blood. It was inevitable this would happen, that the cops would come knocking. One of their undercover guys had been battered to death, of course the cops would come. They had to. And if they smelled a rat, they would be relentless: they would come back again and again. Bellamy had said to keep cool if it happened – say nothing, give nothing, deny, deny, deny. Let him handle them. Do not worry. Easier said than done, especially now that they had shouldered their way through the crowd and were walking purposefully up the front steps of the hotel. Two mean-looking bastards.

The remaining bouncer, Higgins, stepped

440

in front of them, stopping them from entering the hotel. Higgins had been the one who held the undercover man while Longton first set about him and here he was, chatting casually with two other policemen. Franklands despised Higgins, hated his bullying ways, but also envied his poise under the circumstances because, surely, he must now be kacking bricks talking to the cops, no matter how laid back he appeared to be.

Franklands had been right. They were definitely police. One of them, the thinner one, flashed his badge and warrant card. At first Higgins remained firm until the cop stood nose to nose with him and demanded to come in then he backed down.

The cop looked tired, mean and irritable, itching to punch someone in the jaw. Though he was of a smaller build than Higgins, who was a towering shit-house of a bloke, he came over as being harder and tougher and, backed up by the beefier, more filled-out guy with a crew-cut, they made a formidable pair. People would only mess with them at their peril.

They brushed cockily past Higgins, who eyed them dangerously, and entered the hotel through the glass doors.

Franklands was on the verge of wetting himself.

'I don't know what this will achieve,' Donaldson whispered to Henry as they approached the reception desk.

441

'Nor do I, but it'll be fun while it lasts.'

'Female' was not a completely apt description of the woman behind reception. She looked more like a man on a building site only with breasts and the irony was not lost on Henry. He knew right-wingers hated men who dressed up like women, but, almost by default, they had got one living among them.

She was as big as Higgins, and not much better looking. Her blonde head was shaved (another irony, Henry thought, these people seemed to mirror the ones they despised) and each ear had a cluster of gold and silver studs fixed to its outer perimeter. She wore a low-cut T-shirt, tight fitting so her bulges were not disguised. Her tattoos were numerous, with the obligatory 'CUT HERE' on a blue dotted line across her throat (I wish, Henry thought), down to the 'love' and 'hate' across her knuckles. The best visible tattoo, though, was Adolf Hitler's face on the downward slope of her huge left breast, and a woman's face on the other. Henry assumed it was supposed to be Eva Braun but did not know enough about German history to recognise her.

Trying to prevent himself from cracking into laughter, the first chuckle he would have had in a while, Henry dug out his badge and warrant card again, both housed in a natty leather wallet, and said, 'DI Christie, Blackpool Central.' He thumbed to his companion. 'This is my colleague, Karl Donaldson.'

'And to what do I owe the pleasure?' she

asked, voice as smooth as gravel being flung off a shovel.

'Vince Bellamy, please.'

'Dunno where he is.' She shrugged her big shoulders unhelpfully and Hitler and his lover seemed to chat to each other with the wobble of her breasts, something Henry found to be vaguely obscene. 'Like what you see, luvvie?' she asked Henry, who for a moment had seemed transfixed by the sight.

'It has merit,' he grinned, 'but I'd rather be looking at Vince Bellamy.'

'As I said, sweetie, don't know where he is, but I know a man who might–' She pointed across the foyer to the double-doored entrance to the dining room where a man was sitting by the window, watching them.

Franklands gave a silent scream as the two cops turned to look in the direction in which the receptionist's finger was pointing. The silly, stupid bitch. She was telling them where he was.

The smaller of the two detectives, smaller being six foot two as opposed to six foot four, thanked her with a nod. They started to walk towards the dining room.

It was only the timely appearance of Adolf Hitler that gave Franklands the break he needed.

Hitler strutted from the rear of the hotel into the foyer, surrounded by a team of four leather-jacketed bodyguards with jeans and laced-up Doc Martens, stopping Henry and Donaldson dead. He was a perfect replica, from the grey uniform, the swastikas on his arms, the belt and shoulder strap with the Luger pistol in a holster at his hip, hat tucked under his left arm, down to the shiny black jackboots, the shock of black hair down his forehead and the comical moustache under his nose. He went past them, raising his right arm in a lazy Nazi salute and a 'Heil'. It was all they could do not to respond.

He went through the front door of the hotel and appeared on the top step as though at the Munich Olympic games, flanked either side by the bouncers. He raised his right arm and extended it. A roar of approval emanated from the crowd.

Henry and Donaldson, fascinated, moved to the door for a better view. Both were shocked and sickened to witness a sea of extended hands raised towards Hitler and a chant starting of 'Heil Hitler'.

It would have been a farcical spectacle had it not been so utterly abhorrent and nauseating.

'I see he's still got his pulling power,' Donaldson commented.

'I wonder if it's Bellamy. Andrea said he did quite a good Hitler.'

One of the bouncers handed the Hitler lookalike a loud hailer. He began to address his glorious followers.

'Shit,' said Henry despondently.

'There'll be tears at bedtime,' Donaldson predicted.

With overwhelming sadness, Henry turned

444

away. 'Let's have a word with this guy anyway—' He did not manage to complete the sentence because the man they had been directed to see was legging it down the corridor towards the rear of the hotel.

Contrary to what most police officers would like to believe, running away from a cop is not an offence, unless the person already happens to have been arrested. But doing so, whether guilty, innocent or plain stupid, is like a red rag to a bull. Very few cops are able to resist the challenge of the chase because as soon as someone is on their toes, a police officer's body gets an input of energy and the pursuit is on.

It was a conditioned response in Henry. Almost before he knew what he was doing, or why he was doing it, he was after Franklands. American cops are no different: Karl Donaldson was with him all the way.

Franklands hared down the corridor and burst through the double swing doors into the kitchen. A couple of female cooks and two young girls skivvying looked up from their tasks with disinterest as he ran past them, nippily side-stepping all objects in his way, heading for the exit door at the far end.

'Oi,' another woman cook yelled. 'Fuckin' watch it.' She manoeuvred a huge pan of cabbage in water towards the gas stove.

The doors crashed open again. Henry and Donaldson burst through as Franklands reached the exit.

The cook – a big woman – with the cabbage

pan in her hands immediately put two and two together. She knew Franklands was a hotel guest, but had never seen either of the two men who were chasing him. Without a second thought she heaved the pan up and hurled the contents at the chasers, then swung the pan at Donaldson's head because he was the nearer of the two. He ducked the intended panning, but neither he nor Henry could avoid the dousing in water and un-cooked cabbage.

Henry ran on, undeterred. Donaldson took a quick moment to jam the palm of his hand into the woman's large round face and send her sprawling backwards against a rack of pans. Then he was past her.

The exit door led into a storeroom with an emergency fire door at the far end of it. Franklands threw himself at this door, slamming down the locking mechanism. He swung outside onto a metallic landing at the top of a set of fire stairs which dropped down into the back yard of the hotel. He flew down the steps, clattering into the yard which was full of junk.

Henry and Donaldson hit the metallic landing as Franklands got to the yard door and spun into the alleyway.

'Fuck, he's fast,' Henry panted, grabbing the fire-escape rail and sailing down about a dozen steps, touching down and then taking off again for the next ten, hitting the ground running. As he turned into the alley, Franklands, as ever it seemed, was about to go out of sight, running towards the promenade.

Now that the two officers had a clear run, Donaldson, fitter and faster than Henry, powered into the lead, stretching out, totally confident of catching the man.

Franklands, without looking and without any thought for his own safety, or any tactics for avoiding his pursuers, ran straight across the road onto the inner promenade. Miraculously, not a single car came close to whacking him. It was only when he realised where he had run to did it dawn on him that he had made a bad tactical error. He was out in the open expanse of the promenade and it felt as big and wide and exposed as the Serengeti because it gave him nowhere to hide.

When the two cops emerged from the alleyway on the opposite side of the road, Franklands knew he was beaten. There was a hundred metres between himself and them but it was no advantage out here. He was trapped in the open and he knew it.

But there was a way out. It was trundling towards him at an aristocratic 10 mph from the north. Franklands headed towards the tram. This was his only means of escape and all his focus was on its approach.

If the cops caught him he was as good as dead anyway. He did not have the experience or resolve to hold out under questioning, he would blab everything because he was weak and pathetic. And if he did, Bellamy would ensure that somewhere along the line, he died. He had that power. Geri Peters was a case in point. She had been in police custody, yet Bellamy had been able to get to her. Not personally, but her death had been his doing.

The tram loomed larger. It was slow-moving but would provide a quick death, crushing his head with exceptional efficiency.

Franklands judged how best to do it. It would have to be a last-second thing. Make certain the driver did not suspect it was about to happen. He looked at the front of the tram. It was only ten metres away. Franklands gritted his teeth and did not think of the pain. His focus was now intense, like looking down a telescope backwards. A pulsing, throbbing noise seemed to surround him. Five metres. The metallic sound of the tram on its tracks grew louder.

Now! Throw yourself under, just behind the safety guard. Do it, you soft bastard, he yelled to himself.

The tram, only inches away, passed in front of him.

Franklands stood there, head bowed, crying.

Donaldson grabbed him and yanked him away from the track and shook him. 'You idiot, you could'a killed yourself.'

'That was the idea.' Franklands sobbed. He rubbed his eyes. The tram had gone. The sound surrounding him receded and became background noise. 'I wish I'd had the courage.'

'Jesus, you scared the hell outta me,'

Donaldson confessed.

Franklands raised his chin. Henry came onto the scene, breathing heavily.

'I'm sorry,' Franklands bleated, 'I'm sorry, but I didn't kill him. I was there when it happened, but I didn't kill him.'

Henry stood back an inch, not quite knowing what or who Franklands meant. However, he was canny enough not to ask which would have shown ignorance and given Franklands a get-out clause. 'Who did kill him?' Henry asked.

'Higgins and Longton. Longton was the one who really kicked him, stomped on his head.'

'Where exactly did it happen?'

'There, down there.' Franklands pointed along the promenade to beyond Central Pier. Now Henry knew. He gently placed a hand on Franklands' drooping shoulders and said, 'You're under arrest on suspicion of murder.' He cautioned him to the letter, then called up for some transport. While they waited for the van to come, they quickly searched Franklands – regular police procedure. While doing this, Henry said to Donaldson, 'Wedge of thin end the – please arrange those words into a well-known phrase or saying.'

Andrea Makin hung up the phone as Henry and Donaldson entered the CID office. Henry had booked Franklands into the custody system and done all the necessary evidence gathering, such as seizing clothing

449

and taking fingerprints before slamming him into his en-suite accommodation, leaving a constable on suicide watch outside the cell as per force instructions for persons arrested on murder raps.

Makin was red-eyed. She smiled sadly at the two men. 'That was Jack's wife – she lives in London. I've arranged transport for her to come up here as soon as possible to identify him, but with two kids to sort, and the time of day–' she checked her watch: 5 p.m. – 'she won't be up here before morning.'

'How did she take it?' Donaldson asked.

'With resignation, almost as though she was expecting it.' Makin rubbed her eyes, took a deep breath. 'Like all families of undercover cops. Anyway,' she tried to brighten up, 'how has your afternoon been, guys?'

She noted their reaction to this question.

Henry gave a modest shrug. 'I think we're well on the way to catching Jack's killers.'

'Really?'

'Yep.' But now it was Henry's turn to look depressed. 'Having said that, I don't know if we're any closer to Jane Roscoe or Mark Evans.'

He sat down heavily on a spare chair. Donaldson perched on the corner of the desk. At the far end of the room a phone rang, picked up by one of the detectives on duty.

'Or my bomber,' Donaldson said despondently. 'The president will not be pleased.'

'Henry? What extension is that?' the

detective across the room called. Henry peered at the phone on the desk and gave him the number. 'It's for you,' the DC said, transferring it across.

'Henry Christie.'

'DI Harrison from Cheshire.'

'Oh, hi,' Henry said, expecting nothing.

'Got to hand it to you, Henry, I think you got the bastard!'

'Sounds like you are in deep pooh-pooh,' PC Standring, the constable on suicide watch, said to Franklands conversationally. Standring, the officer who had dealt with Kit Nevison, had now been given the task of babysitting the alleged murderer and was actually getting a little brassed off with getting the shitty jobs. However, this was a fairly interesting one and he had been listening to Franklands' stream of consciousness ramblings, trying to pick out any useful gems for the investigating officers to use in interview. Franklands had moved on to wittering about the murder on the promenade, making Standring prick up his ears. Theoretically there should be no conversation between them, but it was a difficult situation to be in and not say something.

'You can say that again,' Franklands came back, 'and the rest.'

'Why, what else have you done?' Standring could not resist posing the question, but he did it almost with feigned disinterest.

Franklands had been sitting on the edge of

the cell bed. He stood up abruptly, knowing he had already said too much, but now that he had started to blab, he could not stop himself. It made him feel light headed, light chested and the feeling was just so fantastic.

'What else?' he said. 'I planted that bomb.'

Shit, thought Standring.

'I think I want to talk to the detectives now – and I want a solicitor.' His face cracked. He started to cry.

It was all Henry Christie could do to stop himself leaping up and down, punching the air, planting kisses on everybody in sight.

He had nailed the bastard. Christ, he had done it – or at least a partial fingerprint found at the scene of a murder which should not have been there had done it. And it belonged to one of the inhabitants of Blackpool. It was not enough to be used in a court of law, but it was enough to go and effect an arrest.

David Brian Gill. Born 21/4/58 in Blackpool. The man had come to the attention of the police only once before at the beginning of the year when he had been arrested and cautioned for a minor public-order offence committed outside a pub in the resort. Despite the fact that there had been no prosecution because it was a first offence and not particularly serious, Gill's fingerprints had been taken as a matter of course and then gone into the system, together with descriptive forms.

That was how he had been caught, from the

only set of fingerprints taken.

Henry had a copy of the custody record in front of him relating to the time Gill had been locked up. There was a copy of the caution form with it. The descriptive forms which had been submitted to HQ were being searched for. With some pleasure Henry saw that the custody officer on the night in question was the inscrutable Dermot Byrne. PC John Taylor had been the arresting officer. Members of his new shift who had done a good job several months before, who had made sure everything was done and dusted for a minor offence, had played some part, subsequently, in the identification of a serial murderer. So simple. Yet it was the simple things that caught people.

Henry ran a hand over his face.

Outside on the streets Henry knew that the Hitler-led right-wing demonstration had come to nothing and everyone had dispersed. The conference had ended for the day, the PM having made his law and order speech to great acclaim and the home secretary his speech on immigration.

Henry thought about David Gill. Where the hell did he fit into this picture? Had he abducted Jane Roscoe and Mark Evans? Henry struggled to get his head round it all. Had they stumbled onto him from evidence provided by this 'military type' and therefore been unprepared for an encounter with a seriously dangerous man?

Gill's address was not far away from Joey

453

Costain's. Roscoe and Evans could easily have walked to it, leaving their cars parked near to Costain's flat.

Henry was eager to get going, to pull the guy in, but he wanted to do it properly and if possible involve Byrne and Taylor. It would be a nice thank-you for having done a run-of-the-mill job so well and could go some way to reviving Taylor's spirits following his horrendous night when he'd let Geri Peters get murdered and been there when Joey's body had been found. Poor lamb. Henry decided to wait until they came on duty at six.

Henry wanted to do it right. This included having a fingerprint expert on call as well as scientific teams on standby.

There was also the other issue of Franklands. He was Henry's prisoner and he had a responsibility to deal with him as expeditiously as possible. If Henry went out on what could be a completely unrelated matter while his murder suspect lounged in a cell, very serious questions would be asked when the case got to court. Henry had an idea how this could be addressed.

He was sitting in Roscoe's office again.

'Well?'

Henry looked up sharply at the figure by the door. FB.

'I hear things are moving.'

'Yeah – but whether we'll find Jane or Mark is something else.'

FB looked seriously exhausted. 'Do your

best, Henry,' he said without energy. 'Find them, please.'

'I will.'

FB disappeared down the corridor.

Henry immediately went back to the papers on his desk. These now included the responses from all the police forces who had had similar murders to Joey Costain's on their patches: Surrey, the Metropolitan and the West Midlands. He had not had the time to look at these yet and he thought this might be an opportunity to do it now. He took each one and read them carefully.

At first he saw nothing to link the crimes beyond the obvious similarity of the way in which the victims had been murdered. Beyond that there seemed to be no connection, but Henry instinctively believed there must be something. He wrote out the names of the victims on a blank piece of A4, listing them down the left side of the paper. Two victims were black. Their occupations did not seem to have any similarity. It was frustrating. Henry read the files again, concentrating on the background and interests of the victims.

Twenty minutes of hard reading and analysis gave him the answer.

Gill's flat was on a small, dilapidated council estate where the number of vacant and derelict properties outnumbered the ones which were inhabited. It was in a small block of flats about six storeys high at one end of the estate with a complex of garages at the

455

back. The flat was on a corner, reached by a concrete stairwell leading onto a walkway which ran along the front of the flats, past the front doors. A quick enquiry with the council had revealed Gill's name on the rent book and that the rent was paid up to date, something which surprised Henry. Council records also showed that Gill rented one of the garages at the back.

Henry and Karl Donaldson sat in a beat-up unmarked Astra about a quarter of a mile away awaiting the arrival of back-up before they hit the flat.

'If we get this guy,' said Donaldson, who was there only as an observer, 'then tomorrow I'd like to try and catch my bomb-maker, pretty please. My president said I should.'

'You and your president.' Henry laughed. 'But of course we can. Serial killer today, serial bomber tomorrow. Piece of piss.'

'Ahh, such a quaint term – "piece of piss",' Donaldson remarked. 'Called your ex-wife, yet?' he asked, filling a gap.

'Nope.'

'Going to?'

'Yep.' Henry nodded. He checked his watch. 'I wonder how Andrea's getting on with Franklands.' She had jumped at the opportunity to interview someone who might have been present at the murder of one of her officers; it gave Henry the space he wanted to go for Gill and hopefully get a lead on Evans and Roscoe.

'They're here,' Henry said, glancing into

456

the rear-view mirror. Dermot Byrne and John Taylor pulled in behind them in a plain car, civvy jackets over their uniforms. He gave a wave over his shoulder and moved off slowly. There was going to be nothing loud and flashy here. No blue lights, two-tones or screeching tyres. Just a slow approach, park quietly and trot slowly to the front door of the flat (there was no back door or exit, other than windows) then bust the door down, pile in and disable the suspect.

'I don't want you to get involved, Karl,' he reiterated to Donaldson firmly. 'You're just here to watch the finest of the British police in action, OK?'

'Gotcha.' Donaldson smiled grimly. He picked up the sledgehammer which was wedged between his knees in the footwell. Henry laughed.

They parked a hundred metres away from the target premises, out of sight of it, and alighted. Donaldson, Byrne and Taylor slotted in behind Henry as he strode swiftly towards the flat. A minute later they were up the steps, and at the door.

Henry went to one side. Byrne the other. Donaldson and Taylor hung back. Henry tried the door handle which opened and they were inside.

On silent feet all four moved into the short hallway towards the living room. Henry gently opened the door. The back of the tatty settee was facing them and on the settee was a dark figure, totally engrossed in a game

457

show on TV and also cranking up. A belt was wrapped round his left arm, tightened by pulling the end of it with his teeth and he was injecting the bulging vein on the inner elbow with a blood-filled hypodermic.

On a signal, Henry, Byrne and Taylor leapt on the guy. Henry focused on the needle, ensuring it presented no danger. It was over in a few seconds, the man did not have a clue what was happening and within moments he was cuffed, face down, arms up behind his back.

'Turn him over,' Henry said excitedly, wanting to see the man he believed had murdered so many people.

They did.

'What the fuck's going on here?' the man demanded to know.

It was Kit Nevison.

Henry was reluctant to take the cuffs off him. By negotiation and threat, Nevison's hands were re-cuffed across his stomach for more comfort and he was allowed to sit back on the settee on pain of death if he caused trouble. The towering figure of Donaldson brandishing the sledgehammer just in the periphery of Nevison's vision was sobering enough to keep him sitting there.

'What are you doing here?' Henry demanded.

'I've come to see me mate, Davey. I haven't seen him for months.'

'David Gill?'

'Yeah.'

458

'And you let yourself in?'

'Yeah, got a key. Couldn't find it for ages, then I found it today, so I thought I'd come an' see 'im.'

'Where is he, then?'

'I don't know. Told ya, haven't sin him for months. I just woke up an' thought I'd bob round and see if he'd let me in. He's always bin good for a bit o' junk.' He nodded to the needle out of reach on the top of the TV.

'What d'you mean, you thought you'd see if he'd let you in?' Henry asked.

'Er ... well ... I bin round once or twice recently an' he told me to fuck off through the letterbox. I thought he were ill, like.' Nevison looked confused. 'What's this all about, anyway?'

'Do you know where he is?'

'No, I fucking don't,' Nevison said crossly. 'Now unless you're gonna lock me up for somethin' I haven't done, tek these fuckin' things offa me.' He held out his manacled hands.

'I want David Gill for murder,' Henry said, bending close to Nevison's face. Nevison blinked and thought about the words. Then he was engulfed by racking laughter.

'What's so funny?'

'Davey? Murder? He wouldn't hurt a fly. Soft bugger, soft as shite.' Nevison roared. 'He's a fuckin' namby-pamby veggie.'

His laughter continued unabated.

Henry stood up straight. He looked at Byrne who, together with Taylor, had done a

459

quick visual search of the flat and found nothing. They shrugged.

'Shit,' he breathed. Then he had a thought. 'Let's check the garage.'

Kit Nevison was having a whale of a time now. Still laughing fit to burst, he followed the officers out to the garage. His handcuffs had been removed on the understanding that if he tried anything, or did a runner, he would be arrested on suspicion of burglary and possession of controlled drugs and that Donaldson would whack him across the back of his head with the sledgehammer.

The garage was in the middle of a row of about a dozen. Most of them were unused with broken and twisted doors or none at all. Only a couple, including Gill's, had locked up-and-over doors on them. It was very well secured with padlocks on either side of the door. Without the necessary keys, the officers resorted to force. Donaldson, who was itching to get swinging with the sledgehammer, smashed the padlocks off with perfectly aimed blows.

'Very good,' Henry congratulated him. He pushed the top of the door and up it went. There was no electric light inside, so four torch beams criss-crossed the interior. Not much inside. A powerful motorbike with a helmet on the seat and a large chest freezer along the back wall.

'Is the bike Gill's?' Henry asked Nevison.

'Never sin it before.'

460

'Don't touch it,' Henry instructed everyone. He recalled that around the time of
Louise Graveson's murder in Cheshire, a
motorcyclist had been seen in the area.
Henry walked round the bike and went to the
freezer. Although Henry, in his married days,
had had a chest freezer in the garage, it
seemed odd to have one in this garage. It
wasn't as though it was an easy trip to get
frozen food back up to the flat, especially in
wet weather.

'Is this his?' Henry asked Nevison, pointing
at the freezer.

'Yeah – he, uh, sometimes does a bit of rustling.'

'Rustling?'

'Uh – yeah, gets lamb and stuff sometimes
from a mate he has in Rossendale who works
at an abattoir.'

'Right,' said Henry, unimpressed. 'What
about this motorbike?'

Nevison looked doubtfully at it. 'No, his
was a knackered thing. This is too new. That's
his van, though.' Nevison pointed to a Transit
van parked behind the flats.

'OK,' said Henry. He went to the freezer,
tried to pull the lid up. It was locked and he
could not budge it.

'Sledgehammer,' he called.

Donaldson responded. He lined himself up
in front of the freezer, worked out the necessary upwards trajectory he would need and
swung the sledgehammer, catching the
freezer lock perfectly, springing it and making

461

the lid fly open to reveal the contents inside, illuminated by a light in the lid.

Henry stared, horrified. The others crowded in behind him and looked over his shoulder.

There were several frozen legs of lamb and beef joints, obviously David Gill's rustling booty – and there was also Mark Evans' body, folded at the knees, lying on top of another body. The detective's throat had been sliced open and copious amounts of blood had run and frozen over the body below. At first Henry thought it was Jane Roscoe, but on closer inspection he saw it was the body of a man.

'Come and have a look in here,' Henry said to Nevison.

Warily, the big man approached the freezer. Henry shone his torch onto the horror-frozen face of the man at the bottom of the chest.

'Wauh – fuck,' Nevison said, appalled and recoiling.

'Who's that?'

'It's Davey – Davey Gill, me mate.'

'Anybody got a hairdryer? I'll never be able to get this guy's prints while his hands are frozen solid like this,' the scenes-of-crime officer shouted, leaning over the edge of the chest freezer. 'Need to get a bit of thawing done.'

Police activity was intense in and around David Gill's flat and garage. Lights had been erected to illuminate the garage. The macabre task of lifting Mark Evans' frozen body out of the freezer had been carried out. He was now zipped up in a bodybag waiting for the hearse to turn up and take him to the mortuary.

Four hours since the discovery of the crime scene, Henry was still pacing up and down, directing operations. He stopped and watched as Evans' body was carried out past him, the bag, literally, containing a stiff. Byrne and Taylor had looked at the other rigid body and neither had been able to identify it positively as David Gill, the man whom Taylor had arrested all those months before. Taylor said the corpse looked 'familiar', but seeing him frozen solid it was difficult to say yeah or nay. Cops at Blackpool dealt with thousands of lock-ups like Gill, and PC Taylor said he could hardly even recall arresting him. Byrne remembered cautioning him, but again, he was one of dozens he had dealt with that night in the custody office. Henry was waiting for a photograph to turn up but it could be a long wait. Photographs tend to enter the system with less precision than fingerprints, and it was not unknown for them to get lost or mislaid.

It seemed logical, therefore, to take the dead guy's fingerprints and get the on-call expert to do some cross-checking. The first thing Henry wanted to discover was if the fingerprint found at the scene of the murder in Cheshire belonged to the dead man. If it did match, then it raised a whole bunch of questions. If it didn't, then it raised a whole bunch more questions.

Henry decided to take it one step at a time. Make no assumptions, jump to no conclusions, just deal with facts.

'Hair drier?' a uniformed constable called out.

'Over hair.' The SOCO laughed.

The constable, who had scrounged the drier from a woman living nearby, handed it over. She would never have offered it had she known it was going to be used to defrost a dead man's fingers.

Henry offered the fingerprint expert a seat in Roscoe's office. The guy was called Lane and he was one of the constabulary's top experts, twenty-two years of cross-matching loops and whorls and providing the evidence that had sent thousands of baddies to prison.

'Tell me,' Henry prompted.

On Lane's lap were two sets of prints. One from the dead man in the freezer, one from the man arrested six months earlier, giving the name of David Gill.

'They don't match,' he said flatly.

'Is that your final answer, or do you want to phone a friend?' Henry said.

'The prints of the dead man in the freezer are not the same as the prints taken from the man who was arrested six months ago for a public-order offence. However, the partial print recovered from the scene at Cheshire matches the forefinger of the prisoner who gave his name as David Gill.'

'So if the dead guy in the freezer really is

David Gill, then who the hell do the prints belong to which were taken by PC Taylor?' Henry pointed to the offending set. 'Because they are the prints of a serial killer who, it would seem, has taken on David Gill's identity after killing him – or something,' he finished unsurely.

Henry was suddenly depressed. He felt nowhere further forward and believed that every minute now was wasted time and made it even more unlikely that Jane Roscoe would be found alive, particularly if the abductor knew that the police had found Gill's and Mark Evans' bodies.

Roscoe was dead. Henry was certain of it. But why wasn't she in the freezer too?

Lane, the fingerprint officer, left.

'It's doing my head in, this,' Henry said when he was joined by Donaldson and Makin. 'How is it going with Franklands?'

'Better than good. I'm going to arrange protected status for him. He was there when the two guys kicked Jack to death, but maintains he took no part in it, and I believe him. And he planted the bomb in the club. Both things were done on Vince Bellamy's instructions. So Franklands is going to be a witness for us and one way or another, the demise of Hellfire Dawn is on the cards.'

'Excellent.'

'He also told me something else, which is very very interesting.' Makin went on to tell this to Henry. It was fascinating stuff, but did not help Henry with his task.

When she had finished Henry asked her how she intended to take it forward and she said she had an idea, but added nothing more.

Which left Henry holding two sets of fingerprints which did not match and a puzzle that was beginning to stress him out.

He watched with distress as the clock ticked up to midnight.

THURSDAY

Twenty-Three

There could be no post-mortems carried out until both bodies had defrosted sufficiently for the pathologist to stick his knife in. Mark Evans' body was less frozen and Dr Baines reckoned he would be ready to start on it in about eight hours; David Gill, literally a solid block of ice, could take up to thirty-six hours before he had thawed enough to be autopsied. Which meant nothing could move forward on the pathology front other than some general observations by the pathologist which boiled down to: it looks like their throats have been cut.

Gill's flat and garage were being top-to-bottomed by all manner of experts, forensic, scientific and search. Henry had decided that this might as well happen. He had thought about withdrawing everybody and mounting an observation on the place on the off-chance that Gill – or whoever the hell it was – would turn up and the police could nab him. He had decided against that because there had been so much police activity anyway that there was a good possibility that whoever was using Gill's ID and home had already been alerted and would not be coming back.

469

It was half-past midnight. Henry was alone in Roscoe's office, thinking about her.

The office door opened, FB came in. He drew up one of the chairs and plonked himself heavily down on it, throwing his heels up onto the edge of the desk.

'Y'know what's really shitty?' he asked.

Henry said no.

'Special Branch have just told me that the Irish cops have uncovered a plot to assassinate the prime minister at the conference this week.' FB laughed, cackled really, as though he was on the verge of going under. Henry had never seen him like this. Normally supremely confident and brash, the stress of the week, the lack of sleep, the pressure of ambition were pulling him down. 'And you know what? There's absolutely fuck-all I can do about it, and what's more I don't care. I've had one officer seriously injured this week who is still on life support, another has turned up dead in a fridge and a third is missing, probably dead too, and I've just spent two hours with Mark Evans' widow–' he shook his head. 'She's devastated.' His head continued to shake. 'And on the back of that the government is in town demanding to be protected. Every available cop I've got is here, looking after the namby-pamby idiots, and I can't even pull a full murder squad together to dedicate to the death of one of my officers and the possible death of another. It's absolute shite. I need a drink.'

Henry remained silent, watching FB open

470

up. It was an amazing sight.

'It's all power games to them, one big fucking ego trip – then they'll be gone on Friday afternoon and won't even give us a second thought as we clean up all the dross left behind them.'

'I thought you liked politicians.'

FB gave Henry a hard stare. 'I was angling for a job, I admit it. Still am. Doesn't mean to say I like 'em.'

'We need more people on Jane Roscoe,' Henry said. 'Sooner rather than later. We can't afford to wait till weekend. The trail will be well cold by then.'

FB sighed. 'If I could give you more, I'd give you more, but I can't and I don't feel good about it because, and you probably won't believe this, I do care. I even care about you, which is why I pulled you off CID. It wasn't a decision I took lightly, Henry. I thought I was acting in your best interests.'

Henry shuffled the papers in front of him and sniffed. 'Yeah, well, it would have been nice to be consulted about that. Anyway, that's by the by now. Catching the bastard who killed Mark is all I want to think about now, that and finding Jane dead or alive. I hope you won't take me off this.'

FB shook his head. 'I won't.'

The man who had used the name and taken the identity of David Gill was sitting and thinking about the events of the last few hours.

The police had finally rumbled his address. Mentally he worked through the flat inch by inch, visualising what was there, what he had left behind, what might be used to incriminate him or reveal his true identity. He was pretty certain there was nothing.

The relationship with Gill had been good while it lasted. Gill had been just the sort of low-life thicko he had been searching for. A man of low intelligence, who had few friends, and lived alone with no family who gave a shit about him. A bit of a druggie, a bit of a tealeaf, living for the most part on state handouts in a flat with no neighbours, whose only interest in life was his clapped-out motorbike. He had been perfect. The real David Gill had been the fourth such person he had used over the years to provide a cover for his murderous activities.

He had watched Gill for a while. Learned about him and his habits. Saw his occasional friend. Saw where he lived and had come to the conclusion that he could easily become David Gill whenever the situation required. He could pull Gill on like an overcoat and that would offer him a veneer of protection should he ever get caught – which was something he never intended to happen.

He had befriended Gill, something that had not taken long once Gill's natural reluctance had been broken down. And then he had killed him and frozen the body.

And from that day on he came to believe that it was David Gill who had committed all

472

the murders. It was Gill, not him, who came out of the dark and actually carried them out. But now Gill's body had been discovered. Unfortunate. He would have to find some other poor, sad soul who could be bought for the price of a pint and then disposed of.

But before any of that could happen, two things had to be sorted out.

He had decided Jane Roscoe had lived long enough. He was getting tired of her now. He would just kill her quickly, nothing flashy, just slash her to pieces in a frenzy and enjoy it for what it was. And secondly he had to do the thing that would show the world that the backlash had truly started: kill the wife of the prime minister.

'Sorry, boss, I was miles away,' PC John Taylor said. He was sitting in the report-writing room. He looked up at Henry Christie.

'I said, how are you feeling?'

'Oh, much better.'

Henry hovered by the doorway.

'Just redoing my statement from last night. Want to get it right,' Taylor explained.

'Good. I just wanted to ask you something.'

'Go ahead.'

Henry waved the note Taylor had left him about the neighbourhood watch co-ordinator. 'I know you got no reply from that neighbourhood watch co-ordinator. It says one of the neighbours told you he'd gone on holiday, didn't say where to.'

'That's right,' Taylor nodded.

'Did you find out when he was coming back?'

'Er ... next week sometime ... Tuesday, I think.' Taylor seemed flustered.

'Can you give me the name of the neighbour?'

Taylor thought for a moment. 'No, don't recall it,' he said worriedly.

'Where does he live?'

Taylor scratched his head. 'Next door but one – no, two.'

Henry sighed. 'Would you be able to take me there? One way or another I need to identify this military man who Jane spoke to. It's just possible the neighbourhood watch co-ordinator might know who he is if he's a local character, or it could even be the man himself – after all, the co-ordinator is called Captain Blackthorn. But, whoever it is, I need to get hold of him. He's the key to this and the sooner I see him the better.' Henry dangled a set of car keys between his fingers. 'I'll drive. You show me which house it is. If we can't bottom it tonight, we're going to have to go house to house in the morning, major style.'

Taylor looked rather peeved to be interrupted from his paper work.

They drove silently to South Shore. Taylor sat primly with his hands clasped between his thighs, slightly distracted.

'How's things?' Henry asked.

'OK.' Nothing more was forthcoming.

'What's your background?' Henry asked, more to keep the conversation going than anything. He found Taylor quite difficult to connect with. He had seen him around over the years but never really spoken to him at all because Henry had been so CID-focused and Taylor had been in uniform. It wasn't unusual not to know someone at Blackpool police station with it being so large.

'University of Salford 1980, then into the police. The rest is history.'

'What degree?'

'Psychology.'

'Interesting delving into people's minds. Never got any qualifications myself. Bone idle, that way. Too interested in girls and getting a job.'

Taylor smirked.

They reached Winston Road.

'The neighbourhood watch co-ordinator is that one,' Henry stated, peering at the numbers on the doors, shining his torch out of the car window at them. 'Which way did you go to see this neighbour, up or down?'

'Down, I think. That one there I think.'

Henry stopped. 'Can you just hand me my radio?' He had tossed it into the passenger footwell at the start of the journey. Taylor reached down and fumbled in the dark, dropping it once, then handing it to Henry who got out of the car saying, 'This one, you reckon?' pointing to the house.

Taylor nodded.

'Come on then.' Henry walked across the pavement to the front gate of the house, went through and up the steps to the door. It was a house divided into flats with six doorbells in the wall next to the front door. 'Who did you speak to?' Henry asked. There was no reply from Taylor, who he expected would be right behind him. Instead the officer was standing by the gate, looking sheepish. 'Which one did you speak to?' Henry raised his voice, shining his torch on the cluster of doorbells.

'I'm trying to remember,' he said feebly.

Henry felt a gush of impatience and anger well up. He came back down the steps, face to face with the PC, who was actually as tall as him and quite a bit broader. 'This is a murder inquiry and I'm just about getting pig sick with you, PC Taylor. You volunteered to do this job for me, to come and see the co-ordinator, and as far as I can see you've made a complete balls of it.'

'Sorry, sir,' he gulped.

Henry grabbed his shoulder and propelled him up the stairs to look at the names on the doorbells. 'Which one was it?' Henry demanded.

'I can't remember,' he wailed.

'Right, in that case I'm going to have to apply a process of elimination here and ring every one of the fuckers, aren't I?'

Taylor's shoulders drooped. He looked ready to cry.

'You did actually go and knock on the co-ordinator's door?' Henry asked suspiciously.

476

'Yes I did,' Taylor came back defiantly. 'And he wasn't in.'

'And you did visit a neighbour?'

Taylor's mouth pursed. He looked down at his feet. 'No,' he mumbled.

'Fuck-shit!' Henry shouted, turning on him. He grabbed hold of his blouson and slammed him up against the front door of the house. 'How dare you?' Henry said through gritted teeth. 'How dare you fuck-up and tell me a lie? One of our officers has been murdered by a fucking maniac and another is missing, probably dead too – and you tell a fucking lie!' Henry let go of him like he was flicking shit off his fingers. 'I don't know what your game is, pal,' he growled, 'but when this is over I'm gonna pin your hide to Blackpool Tower, and now, just for my own piece of mind, I'm going to knock on the door of the neighbourhood watch guy because I'm not sure I believe you even did that!'

He trotted down the steps and marched down the street to the relevant address, absolutely boiling over with rage, vowing that Taylor would lose his job if it was the last thing he did.

Up the steps, putting his thumb on all the doorbells until some irritated resident buzzed open the front door. That the door opened did not surprise Henry, it was a tactic police officers often used to gain entry to multi-occupancy premises. He stepped into the hallway.

He knew Captain Blackthorn's flat was

number one, the first one on the right on the ground floor. He knocked hard on the door. Knocked and knocked. There was no reply. Maybe Taylor had been telling the truth. He swivelled away in frustration, his hand going for the door knob in a gesture of despair, not expecting it to open, but it did. The door swung open – creepily – with a long moan of the hinges.

PC Taylor came through the front door of the building and Henry looked at him before pushing the flat door open fully. The short hallway was unlit. Henry called out, 'Captain Blackthorn. It's the police. May we come in, sir?'

Henry's voice carried and reverberated around the hallway. He repeated his words. Again, no reply. The hairs on the back of his neck tingled. To find the door unlocked at this time of day, no security chain across, no sign of an alarm having been set, was disconcerting. He imagined the captain would be one of the most security conscious people on the planet, especially in his volunteer role. There would be no way he would leave his home unlocked.

Henry walked down the hallway of the flat, his radio in his right hand.

The smell of death hit him.

'Damn,' he whispered under his breath, jumping to the conclusion that he was about to discover that a natural sudden death had occurred, that the old guy had popped his clogs which had been the reason why Taylor

478

had been unable to rouse him. Already he was angry at the temerity of the man to die without a thought for the murder investigation.

Where would he be, Henry wondered. In bed? On the bog? Many elderly people died while straining on the loo.

He opened the living room door and fumbled for the light switch. Then froze. This was no natural sudden death.

Blackthorn's body was on the hearthrug in the middle of the room, in the space between the settee and the fireplace.

Like Joey Costain he had been gutted like a fish. His insides were flipped out, wrapped around his head and neck. Henry squatted down next to the body and inspected it without touching. His eyes roved round the blood-splattered room and spotted a walking stick resting against the settee. In blood, the word 'grass' had been scrawled.

'Gill must have been here,' Henry hissed, remaining down on his haunches. His thought processes whirred and clicked, going back to only moments before when he had reflected on the likely security consciousness of Captain Blackthorn. There was no sign of forced entry on the door, although it was possible an intruder could have entered by other means, such as a kitchen window. Failing that, someone had been invited into the house, someone Blackthorn knew and/or trusted. As was the case for Joey Costain who had turned his back on someone he knew or trusted or thought he could trust. And to confirm it, Henry saw two mugs of tea on the coffee table. Two mugs.

Henry was aware of movement behind him: PC Taylor.

Henry stayed where he was down by the body and hoped that his thoughts had not transferred themselves to his body language as his skin chilled. God, he hoped he was wrong, but he was sure he was not.

Taylor was behind him still. Not good. Henry sensed him to be by the living-room door about six feet away, a little bit of distance.

'Where's Jane Roscoe?' Henry asked quietly. He stood up slowly, his knees cracking, betraying his approach to middle age. Taylor was immobile by the door. Henry had it in his mind that if he was wrong, he could just say he asked the question rhetorically, out of frustration, but when he looked at Taylor, he knew he was right, so he said it again. 'Where is Jane Roscoe?'

Taylor smiled confidently. A transformation from the 'big softie' he had been described as. His face had a dark shadow over it. He was not the person Henry had come to know recently.

'I made two mistakes,' Taylor said quietly. 'One, reading the *Sunday Times*. Two, leaving you that note and pretending to be the keen constable. Very foolish of me. I should have known you'd not accept it at face value. I was hoping it would put you off for a few days, give me time to do what I have to do, then disappear. As it is, you've given me even more things to do now. I need to kill you, Henry.'

Taylor's right hand appeared from around his back, holding a baton. He did not say anything, just maintained that enigmatic smile.

Henry brought his radio up to his mouth and pressed the transmit button. Nothing happened.

'Don't bother,' Taylor said. 'I've changed the channels. By the time you tune it back to Blackpool, you'll be dead.' He raised the baton. For the first time Henry saw it was an electronic-shock baton. 'High voltage, low amperage, non-lethal shock,' Taylor explained. 'Just enough to put you down long enough for me to slit you open like all the rest.'

'Like Mark Evans? Louise Graveson?'

Taylor shrugged. 'Something like that.'

Henry's mind spun. He tested the water: 'What about Mo Khan?'

Taylor smirked. 'I finished off what Joey started. He left Khan bleeding, but I whacked him to death, very satisfying,' he said with pride. 'Then I killed Joey before I came into work that evening. I phoned in about his death from the hospital; remember when I was supposedly vomiting at the thought of letting the prisoner in my charge die? I was telling communications all about Joey being a mess. And that nice Sergeant Byrne was being so caring. You weren't, though, were you? Nasty man!' He smirked cockily. Henry's hands bunched into tight fists which

481

he wanted to smash into Taylor's face. 'Joey was an imbecile and we used him.'

'We?'

'Hellfire Dawn – the saviours of this second-rate country.'

'And Jane Roscoe? Where the hell is she, PC Taylor?'

'I'm not PC Taylor at the moment,' he came back stiffly. 'My name is David Gill.'

'Really?' Henry guffawed, picking up on the brittleness in Taylor's voice. 'My understanding is that David Gill is lying in the mortuary defrosting like a frozen lamb.'

Taylor pointed the baton at Henry. 'Wrong. He is who I have become. He is me, when I need him. He is my raincoat, my comfy pair of slippers. He was just a shell waiting to be inhabited, a good for nothing loser, better off with his throat cut. At least he now has a purpose in life.'

'Well that's fine and dandy for the judge and jury: I become someone else so I am therefore not responsible for my actions – fuck that,' Henry spat. 'You can convince them that you're Jekyll and Hyde for all I care, but I guarantee you're still going down for a long time. You can take my regards to Ian Brady.'

'I don't think so. You see, no one knows I'm here with you, do they? So once you're dead, I'll go and do the business with Janey, then my pièce de résistance, then I'll be gone. I'll find some other shell to inhabit, rather like that nice, but sensitive policeman PC Taylor,

482

so deeply affected by the sight of blood and death and a little bit soft – PC Taylor – who the hell was he but a shell?'

'There's a slight hitch in your plan,' Henry said. His voice held, but he was starting to feel it going, starting to quake as, with his right hand, he fumbled with the channel selector on the radio. 'I'm not dead – and I don't intend to be.'

Taylor moved into the room proper and closed the door behind him.

Henry stepped back over the captain's dead body, his feet slipping in the blood, which had a crusty top on it, but a slimy underbelly. He wanted to keep his distance from Taylor and the shock baton.

'There's quite a bit of a difference here,' Henry pointed out, 'between you and me.'

'Oh? You victim, me killer,' Taylor said. 'Where's the difference?'

'Difference is that I'm expecting you. None of your previous victims were ready for you, were they, PC Taylor? You either surprised them or got them to trust you, then you whacked 'em. I'm not surprised and I don't trust you, PC Taylor.'

'Gill, David Gill,' Taylor corrected him sternly. 'Call me David.'

'Bonkers, more like,' Henry said. 'So come on then, let's have a bit of action here. You don't like this, do you? Face to face, level terms, with someone who's going to disarm you and beat you. How does that feel, John?' He emphasised the name blatantly. 'Gonna

483

wrap me up like a parcel?' Henry taunted. 'Just put the baton down and any other weapon. Make this easy on yourself.'

Taylor hesitated. Henry stood there giving the impression of composure, which underneath he did not feel.

'Fuck you!' Taylor screamed. He shook the baton angrily and stepped towards Henry.

Henry moved back to keep out of range.

'You're the one who's fucked – make it easy on yourself: give up now,' Henry said, soothingly. 'Life won't be bad for you, cosseted in a padded cell. It'll probably be quite nice. You can be who you want to be all the time.'

'Oh, I don't think so. You see, it's not my time yet. I have things to do, wrongs to put right. I mean, take this job, for instance. I came into it in the first place because it was the last bastion of the white man. Now look at it. A shambles. Promoting Pakis and women, leaving us behind. I mean,' he babbled, 'you should be pleased by what I've done for you, Henry.'

'Why?' Henry said, eager to keep the talking going.

'You're back on the investigation, aren't you? I got the lovely Jane Roscoe out of the way. You should be thankful, but you're not, are you? You just don't see it, do you?'

'All I see is a person who needs help.'

'Fuck you!' Taylor shouted again, losing it. He went for Henry.

The baton sliced through the air. Henry

484

ducked and lost his footing in Blackthorn's blood, his ankle twisted under him and he fell awkwardly, knee-down onto the dead body. Automatically his hands went out, palms down, to break his fall, but they went straight into Blackthorn's gaping stomach. Henry twisted away from the intestines, repelled and horrified, but also aware that Taylor's baton was swinging towards him again. He bobbed his head and launched himself away from Blackthorn's body, rolling across the room, aware his hands were covered in blood and body slime. He scrambled towards the fireplace where he could see a poker.

Taylor moved quickly. He whammed the baton into Henry's side. The pain was incredible, but it was only from the strike of the baton, not an electric discharge. Henry rolled with the blow, reaching desperately for the poker with his fingertips. Missing it.

Taylor bore down on him, raising the baton, a scream on his lips. Henry covered his head and kicked out wildly, catching the back of Taylor's knees, forcing him to stumble backwards. Henry drove himself at Taylor, going for a bearhug. Both men, entwined, struggling for advantage, rolled across the floor and over Captain Blackthorn's body, which suddenly seemed to come to life as they fought over it, his legs and arms twitching madly, head turning, and noises being driven out of the windpipe.

With a roar, Taylor broke free, still keeping hold of the baton which he tried to bring back into play, to get it onto Henry's chest to deliver the stun.

Henry pulled away and punched Taylor as they rolled back over the body, its arms flailing. The two men battled amongst entrails and loops of rubbery intestines. At the back of his mind, Henry was utterly repulsed by this, but could not afford to give a shit. He might well be sloshing about in the organs and innards of a dead man, but he was fighting for his own life too. The two men split apart.

Henry tried to come in with a head butt. It did not connect. Taylor managed to swing the baton across Henry's lower back with a stinging blow.

They were face to face, still on the floor, pawing at each other, each trying to get into a position of power. They slid towards the hearth. Henry kicked and punched, while Taylor tried to use the shock baton. Henry found himself underneath Taylor, trying to grab the wrist of the hand holding the baton – then, bang! Henry's head smacked against the edge of the raised hearth with such force that his brain jarred for a precious moment. A split second was long enough for Taylor to rear up on his knees and press the end of the baton onto Henry's chest, above his heart. Taylor laughed victoriously. Henry waited for the punch of the shock. He knew that all Taylor had to do was lightly pull the trigger in the baton handle and 150,000 volts would shoot through him and then Taylor would butcher him. Henry braced himself.

Click. Nothing.

Taylor pressed the baton harder into Henry's chest. Click, click. Still nothing.

The realisation suddenly passed between both men: for whatever reason the baton was not working correctly.

Henry was first to react. He grabbed the baton and tore it out of Taylor's grip. Taylor lost his nerve. He ran. Henry went after him, leaping across the gutted corpse and out of the flat, spinning into the hallway to see Taylor disappear out of the front door, which he slammed behind him. Henry slowed slightly, thinking that Taylor might just be on the other side, waiting to pounce.

He opened it gingerly but the man had gone down the front steps and was running towards the promenade. A car was coming slowly up the street which Taylor flagged down, having no trouble in so doing because he was in uniform. Henry shouted a warning, which was lost in the night. Taylor opened the driver's door and heaved the poor unsuspecting driver across the bonnet of a parked car. Taylor dropped into the seat and accelerated towards Henry who was now in the middle of the street.

Henry was no fool. He jumped smartly out of the way of the approaching car and ran to the CID car, scrambled into it and had started it as Taylor veered left out of the street towards the town centre. Henry crunched into first and stepped on the gas.

Christ, he had been good. Taylor's histrionics at the scenes of the murders of Geri Peters and Joey Costain had taken everyone in. But it had all been a tissue of lies: he had not chased anyone through the hospital at all; he had raced along the corridors himself, forcing people out of the way, chasing a shadow that existed only in his mind. Henry realised why he had been so unsettled at the scene of Geri Peters' murder: there had been no coffee cup. Taylor had said he had been out to get coffee when Geri Peters was being murdered but, of course, he had himself been smothering her. No doubt he had tried to hang Geri earlier in her cell and attempted to make it look like suicide. Taylor's name had been on the list of people the custody officer remembered seeing in the office that night. Taylor hadn't had any prisoners in the cells, so why had he been there? Henry remembered Geri Peters' words before she had been put into the ambulance: 'One of yours.' At the time they had meant nothing to him. Now they meant everything. 'One of yours' meant PC Taylor.

Taylor drove onto the promenade. It was virtually deserted at this time of night. He wasn't going too fast and Henry was about a hundred metres behind him.

Henry had the list of similar killings, all linked by MO, but not by motive – until he had worked it out. Louise Graveson was a lawyer specialising in equal opportunity and racial cases. She had just won a quarter of a million pounds for a black female police officer at an employment tribunal where the allegation had been of sexual and racial abuse by a white male sergeant. Another victim, a black woman councillor from north London, had been a witness at another employment tribunal where a black man had won damages for unfair dismissal on racial grounds. Then there was the police support staff worker, again in London, who had ended the career of a white police inspector who had harassed a black PC. A journalist in the West Midlands who was constantly rubbishing the way in which minority groups were treated by large organisations.

Taylor had been waging an insidious guerrilla-like murder campaign against anyone with the temerity to stand up for the rights of the minority on behalf of Hellfire Dawn.

Taylor speeded up. So did Henry who was desperate to stay with him.

Henry picked up his radio; glancing down at the display he fiddled with the channel button and glancing up, he drove. He locked back onto Blackpool's radio frequency. 'Thank God for that,' he breathed.

'Inspector Christie to Blackpool. Urgent. In pursuit of a silver Honda Accord being driven by PC John Taylor, who is a murder suspect. No time to explain. Suspect is armed and dangerous. We're on the prom, north towards Talbot Square. Assistance to stop him please.'

The communications operator was cool despite the shock of hearing what he had just heard. He began to deploy patrols, then stopped and said, 'PC Taylor, go ahead.'

As the radio was not on talk-thru, Henry could not hear Taylor's transmission.

'Inspector Christie,' communications called.

'Yes.'

'Message from PC Taylor. If you do not withdraw, the little package will not be found. Understood?'

'Received.' Shit, the bastard was making demands now.

'PC Taylor also requests talk-thru be put on.'

'Denied – we keep with him. Keep deploying patrols. I want him stopped and arrested.'

Henry was now right up behind Taylor in his hijacked car, leaving just enough room between the two cars to brake if necessary. Taylor's car surged ahead.

'Change of plan,' Henry said, 'put talk-thru on.'

'Talk-thru on.'

'Inspector to PC Taylor. Come on, pull in, it's over, John, there's nothing more for you to achieve.'

No reply.

'Talk-thru off,' Henry ordered again, and when it was off he almost shouted, 'Where is my assistance? I haven't seen another cop car yet. Just passing the junction with Chapel Street – he's just run a red light, I'm going through too.' Henry shot through, unscathed.

The Tower rose above them on the right. At

the next junction was another set of lights, again on red. Henry watched as Taylor's car hurtled towards the lights, accelerating all the time, obviously with no intention of stopping. He must have been approaching 60 mph as he crossed the junction. Suddenly a police transit van shot out in front of him, blue lights flashing, and skidded into the path of Taylor's car.

Instinctively Henry braked.

Taylor's stolen car broadsided the police van, driving into it like a piston. The Transit van was hit right on the seam in the centre of the side panel, the impact bursting it open. The van flipped over onto the tram tracks and Taylor's vehicle skidded off at right angles from its original south–north path, slithering out of control, brake lights flashing, towards the sea-wall railings. It crunched into them probably still doing in excess of 40 mph, with a shredding, tearing of metal.

Henry skidded to a halt. He leapt out, shouting the situation down into his radio, requesting an ambulance, and ran towards the smashed police van which had rolled to a halt on its roof. The back wheels were still spinning, the engine roaring. Henry was terrified of what he might find.

As he got there, the driver was extricating himself out of the shattered driver's door window, unscathed. He stood up shakily. It was Dermot Byrne. He smiled coolly, if a little wonkily, then leaned on the van for support as his legs buckled under him.

'I'm OK ... I think ... go get him.'

Other police cars were now turning up. Henry moved away reluctantly and trotted to the mangled wreck of Taylor's car. The owner would not be well pleased to be told that a car commandeered by a cop – who had assaulted him in the process – was now a write-off.

Steam hissed out of the engine block. Henry could smell petrol. Taylor was slumped over the wheel. There was a head-shaped indentation in the windscreen. Henry shone his torch in and could see that Taylor's body was contorted under the steering column and dashboard which had crumpled with the impact. There was a lot of blood about, a lot coming out of Taylor's right ear. Not a good sign.

'Don't be fucking dead,' Henry said.

He pulled at the door. It would not budge. He used his feet for purchase and wrenched at it as hard as he could. It opened, twisting on broken hinges, but only about eighteen inches. Just wide enough for him to shoulder in and lean towards Taylor's mangled body.

He reached for Taylor's blood-soaked head and lifted his face away from the rim of the steering wheel, turning it towards him. It had been smashed beyond recognition into a bloody pulp. The eyes were closed, there was no sign of life. Repulsed, Henry was about to lay Taylor's head down when suddenly his eyes flicked open, startling him. It was like something out of a horror movie. He almost dropped the head in shock. One eye socket was just a black hole and Henry could not work out where the actual eyeball was. It had either been pushed into his head, or was in the car somewhere.

Taylor's breath blew bloody bubbles from his lips as his mouth worked. He was speaking. There were words there. Henry put his ear close to the lips.

'Vince, is that you?'

'Yeah,' Henry said immediately.

'I did it ... I did everything you said, didn't I?' He coughed, spraying Henry's face with blood and spittle.

'Yeah,' said Henry, keeping in there, trying to ignore the blood, 'but you have to tell me where Roscoe is.'

'I did them all for you ... is it done?'

'Yeah, it's done. Where have you put Jane Roscoe?'

'Have we won?'

'Yes, we have.' Henry knew that in a matter of seconds Taylor would be dead. He asked again. 'Where is Roscoe?'

'In the garden, buried,' he gasped and died. Henry dropped the head back onto the steering wheel. With his handkerchief he wiped the blood and saliva from his face.

'Shit,' he said, drawing out of the vehicle. He sank to his knees and in despair, held his head in his hands. He was overwhelmed with horror that he had been unable to prevent the death of another woman. He rocked, choking back the sobs.

A hand touched his shoulder. Through his

fingers Henry looked up at Byrne who had staggered from the Transit. Other cops were behind him.

'I've lost her,' Henry wailed. 'I've lost her.'

'Who – lost who? What's going on, Henry?' he demanded.

'Jane – it was him. He did it. Killed Mark Evans, too. Took Jane and now I've fucked it up and we'll never find her. She could be alive, he talked about her still being alive. She won't be for much longer.'

Byrne was still dazed from the accident. He slumped down by Henry and placed an arm across his shoulders. 'Did he say anything?'

'In the garden – buried in the garden – that was all. Christ, she must be in a tomb somewhere.'

'No, no, wait,' Byrne's mind cleared quickly. 'Taylor was on the pre-conference search team. He searched and sealed the Winter Gardens. He called them the garden.'

The words permeated only slowly into Henry's brain. 'How many search teams are on nights?'

'Two, I think. One at the Winter Gardens, one at the Imperial.'

'Let's get moving then.'

FRIDAY

FRIDAY

Twenty-Four

He watched all the faces around the table very carefully, judging their reactions as the voices on the tape recorder spoke. Only he and Andrea Makin had heard the tape fully before and knew what to expect. Makin was sitting impassively, deep dark rings around her eyes, probably wishing she had never ventured north of Watford. Karl Donaldson was another at the table. He had a good idea of what the tape contained, so was not surprised.

The other two men had not heard the tape and it would be a shock to them. They were ACC Fanshaw-Bayley and the British Prime Minister.

They were in the main restaurant of the Imperial Hotel. The only other people in the room were the PM's two protection officers lounging by the doors, out of earshot, preventing any unauthorised entry.

The first tape they listened to was an edited version of the interview between Makin and Martin Franklands. It began with criminal matters concerning the murder of an undercover police officer on Blackpool promenade. Franklands named the two men who had beaten the cop to death. The interview progressed to the planting of a bomb in the Pink Ladies' Club, a bomb which had been sourced from an American terrorist whom Franklands claimed he could not identify. Franklands went on to freely implicate Vincent Bellamy, leader of the right-wing organisation called Hellfire Dawn, in the murder and the planting of the bomb, saying that both had been carried out on his instructions.

Makin stopped the tape. 'He's singing like a demented budgie,' she said, 'telling us everything about Hellfire Dawn. Bombs in Soho, Birmingham and Brighton, not American sourced, but all planted and planned by Bellamy. Also the murder of two Pakistani youths in Tooting and the firebombing of a Jewish family in York, which killed two little kids. All Bellamy's work.'

The prime minister fidgeted. 'All very interesting, but purely police matters as far as I can tell. Where is this leading?' he asked frostily. 'I deliver my end of conference speech in under an hour.' He looked pointedly at his Rolex.

Andrea Makin was unfazed. Having managed to pull this meeting together by getting the Chief Constable of Lancashire to intervene directly with the prime minister and request it as a matter of urgency, she was not going to be hurried. 'Please bear with me, sir,' she said, equally frostily.

The timbre of her voice made him sit back.

'I'll fast forward it a little.' She pressed the button, watching the counter click by, stopped it and pressed 'play'.

Franklands was speaking again. He was in full flow and had a lot to get off his chest. This time the PM leaned forwards, elbows on the table, listening hard. His face dropped in shock.

FB's face changed dramatically, too.

After ten minutes more, Makin stopped the tape, ejected the cassette and slotted it into its plastic box.

'These are very serious allegations,' the prime minister said gravely.

'Which is why I wanted you to hear them, and no one else, for obvious reasons,' Makin said.

'Can they be substantiated in any way?'

Makin nodded. 'As a result of what Franklands said to me, I arrested Vincent Bellamy and the other two implicated in the murder early this morning.'

Makin had taken a well-tooled-up arrest squad and raided the Berlin Hotel just after six that morning. Using a diagram of the hotel provided by Franklands, she and her teams quickly found the rooms of the suspects. She had gone for Bellamy. There had been no knocking – they had burst in unannounced, finding Bellamy, dressed as Adolf Hitler still, being fellated by the hotel receptionist with the tattoos on her breasts. Makin found that there were swastikas tattooed on her buttocks, too. The whole thing had been a sight to behold ...

She rid her mind of the montage and continued, 'Once Bellamy realised he was being dropped in it big style, it didn't take long for him to start running scared at first, and then to start boasting about his achievements for the people of Britain.'

'And this is leading where?' the PM cut in again.

Makin apologised. She was tired and rambling a bit. 'I put to him the facts that Franklands had told me about Hellfire Dawn and its backers.' She paused. 'Incidentally there are two financial analysts already beginning to unravel accounts ... however, this is what Bellamy said.' She dropped a new tape into the machine and pressed 'play'.

'We have been bank-rolled one hundred percent.' Bellamy cackled on the tape. 'A government minister has provided us with funds to finance our activities from his own resources – he is a multi-millionaire in his own right and believes in the work of Hellfire Dawn. He intends to change the face of British politics in response to the backlash across the country against the favouritism shown to blacks and ethnics. He intends to stamp out immigration and the ridiculous employment practices which ensure niggers and Pakis get jobs which rightfully belong to white folk. Where necessary we will drive them out of their homes, destroy their businesses. We will be his army. Hellfire Dawn will rule the streets–'

500

Bellamy started ranting. Makin fast-forwarded the tape, commenting, 'The guy is barking mad, of course, but very believable.' She pressed play again. Bellamy now sounded proud. He was boasting.

'Mastermind? Yes, I suppose so. I see the big picture. It was necessary to start a war of subtle attrition to support the overt war on the streets.'

'Is that where David Gill came in?' Makin asked on the tape.

'A one-man killing machine, wound up, pointed in the right direction and set off. I gave him the targets and he struck – people who are part of the corrupt system which supports the injustice, people who had to be picked off one by one, anyone who helped the blacks, the women, whoever, anyone who had a hand in taking away the God-given rights of white men–'

'At which point my blood was boiling,' Makin said

'The pièce de résistance was to dispose of the black wife of the prime minister, but Gill obviously got careless, got caught, killed himself – a pity.'

'How did he intend to kill her?'

'He had access to the Imperial Hotel. He was going to enter their bedroom suite and kill her – simple as that.'

'And did this politician of yours know about this?'

'And approved. Saw it as a way to step into the breach.'

'Shit,' said the prime minister.

Everyone looked quickly at him.

'What is the name of this man again?' Makin asked on tape.

There was a pause on tape long enough for Henry to zoom in on the prime minister's reaction.

Vincent Bellamy named a name.

'And this man,' Makin cut in quickly, switching the tape off, 'was one of the few who knew that there was an undercover police officer working in Hellfire Dawn. He knew because of his position in government, because he's informed of all undercover police operations in the country. He must have passed that information on to Bellamy.'

The PM rose from the table. 'It is apparent that I have been betrayed. Excuse me,' he said. He ran across the restaurant, pushing his security men out of the way and dashed into the nearest male toilet where he was violently sick. He returned a few minutes later, after washing his face, and said to one of his guards, 'I want to see Basil Kramer now.'

Epilogue

'Hold my hand.'

Henry took the small, weak hand, squeezed it gently.

'Now kiss me again ... but nothing sexual, you understand – I'm not up to that.'

He laid a soft kiss on her fragile lips.

Roscoe sat back. She tucked the blanket in under her knees. She and Henry were in the conservatory built onto the back of her house in Fulwood, near Preston. It was a week after the end of the conference. Roscoe had spent a couple of days in hospital after she had been found, now she was recuperating at home with the assistance of all the welfare support systems Lancashire Constabulary could offer, plus her husband who had stopped work indefinitely to care for her. She was being well looked after.

It had taken a full day for the search teams to find her in the Winter Gardens. The two night teams who had started the search had refused to go home and had continued searching when their day-shift colleagues came on.

It takes many weeks to search the Winter Gardens prior to a conference, so it was never going to be a doddle finding her, especially when every seal on every door, hatch, window, cupboard – whatever – had to be broken and everything searched again. To find her quickly would have been a matter of luck.

The Winter Gardens is an immense complex, much larger than most people imagine. It consists of theatres, ballrooms, play rooms, amusement arcades, bars, shop, plus an under-complex which the public never see which itself is a maze of corridors, passages and heating systems big enough for a grown man to walk through – the place was a nightmare.

As the teams got on with their job, Henry was baffled as to how Taylor had actually been able to get Roscoe smuggled into the place. Taylor himself could come and go at any time he got the opportunity, whether on or off duty, because he had kept hold of his official pass which he should have handed in after he had finished his pre-conference search duties. He could enter through the security checks with impunity, but how he had got Roscoe in was a puzzle which made Henry's mind whirr and click.

But as Henry followed and chided the search teams – after he had showered and cleaned himself of the blood and gore from Captain Blackthorn's eviscerated body – he thought he might have found the answer.

Eventually they found her.

Taylor's arrogance astounded Henry. He had been holding her in a storeroom underneath the main stage in the main Winter Gardens theatre in which the conference had taken place. She had been wrapped up twenty feet away from the prime minister's seat on the stage in a room no bigger than a police cell.

She had been in a bad way, but Henry admired her spirit when the first thing that she said when the parcel tape was pulled gently off her mouth was, 'Stop him, he's going to kill the PM's wife.' After that effort she lapsed into a semi-comatose state.

Henry regarded her now, a week later. Frail was too strong a word to describe her: her ordeal had totally sapped her of her energy; her skin was almost transparent.

'A sick, sick man,' she said vehemently.

'Certainly. We're still delving into his history. It's a confusing picture. He was controlled by Vince Bellamy, and Bellamy's claim to be a mastermind was pretty accurate. They met at university and Bellamy steered him into the police, where he was almost like a sleeping agent. He'd been a cop for nearly twenty years and wheedled his way from his original posting at Preston to serve at Blackpool and therefore be at the hub of the party conference, getting access to many aspects of it. Very clever stuff. I think Bellamy recognised both his potential as a killer and his mental sickness, filled his then juvenile mind with right-wing clap-trap, brainwashed him almost, and used him. Taylor was very malleable.'

'Where does poor David Gill come into the picture?'

'He wanted Gill's personality. Again, arrogance combined with sickness. Gill was an ideal candidate for him. Taylor got to know him, arrested him, substituted his own finger-prints so if he ever made the mistake of leaving one at the scene of a crime, the police would target David Gill and give Taylor a chance to cover his tracks. And, of course, he knew that the fingerprints of police officers – which he obviously had to give when he joined the job – are not checked as a matter of course, only in very exceptional circum-stances. The ones he submitted as David Gill's have since been checked against his own and they match. In a way it was a bit like an undercover cop taking on an identity to cover his tracks – with the exception that undercover cops don't kill people to steal their IDs.'

'And he made the mistake of leaving a dab at the scene of a murder.'

'And the mistake of using Gill's Transit, which Captain Blackthorn recognised and told you about. If he hadn't done that, we probably would never have caught him and bad things wouldn't have happened to you and Mark.'

Roscoe's chest rose and fell. 'And he killed the old man.'

'He killed people who wronged him. If he'd managed to kill me – and if that shock baton he used hadn't had an intermittent fault, I would be well dead now – then you, then the PM's wife, he would have disappeared, I think. He would never have been caught.'

'And Mo Khan's death was the start of it all?'

'Yeah, as a cop Taylor knew the situation between the Khans and the Costains. According to Bellamy, Hellfire Dawn used Joey to inflame the situation by going out with Naseema Khan, the daughter. Taylor finished off Mo after Joey had beaten him up to provoke further trouble during conference week. Nothing works better to inflame a situation than a death, does it? But we don't know that for sure. It was to be the start of the big push on the streets. The only good thing about him was his taste in music which I never got round to discussing with him, unfortunately.'

Roscoe looked puzzled by the remark but was unable to ask the question as, behind them, there was the rattle of teacups. Roscoe's husband came in with a tray and deposited it on the glass-top table and left, smiling at Henry, who did the honours.

'I don't think I'll be coming back to work,' Roscoe said.

Henry must have looked startled.

'Jamie and I have had some long talks. What's happened has made us both realise we don't want to lose what we have. We want to spend some time together. I might take a career break, and try for a baby before it's too late.'

'Good luck to you.' Henry raised his cup.

'Thank you.' She sipped her tea. 'How's Dave Seymour?'

'Getting better, but not out of the woods yet. His biggest problem is that he was saved by a woman – yuk! – and an Asian, Rafiq Khan who extinguished the flames – even yukker! – two types of people he can't cope with. He won't come back to work either, but he'll live. And his long-lost daughter has made contact, so that's good news.'

'Good. Andrea Makin? Did she get into your pants?'

'Sadly, no.' Henry smiled sheepishly. 'She's back down at the Met, sorting out Hellfire Dawn.'

'And hunky Karl, the all-American boy?'

'Interestingly he has been recalled to the States to spearhead the FBI investigation into the bomber who we singularly failed to catch. Recalled at the behest of the president, no less.'

'Oooo,' Roscoe said, impressed. 'That won't please his wife.'

'They'll survive. They have an airtight marriage.'

'Lucky sods ... and what about you, Henry?' She tilted her head and smiled affectionately.

He shrugged. 'Well, FB's got his much sought-after HMIC job and he'll be going soon, which will be nice. His leaving present to me is to get me on the senior investigating officer team at headquarters which suits me very nicely.'

508

'And in your private life?'

'Who knows.' He finished his drink, checked his watch. 'Time to hit the road – it's all paperwork now.'

Roscoe insisted on accompanying him to the door. In the hallway she said, 'You still haven't told me how Taylor got me into the Winter Gardens. I don't recall anything about getting there. I have no memory of it at all.'

'He dealt with a date-rape case about twelve months ago and the offender got off in court – a white guy on an Asian girl, so no surprise there – and the offender used scopolamine, which makes people very compliant and leaves them with no memory of what they've done. I checked the property store for the drug, but it wasn't there. I think he used it on you and simply walked you into the Winter Gardens and through security at a time when no other bobbies were around who could identify you. The security people wouldn't have known you from Adam – or Eve. Once inside, he just steered you down into the basement to that room which he'd discovered during the pre-conference search. He could come and go pretty much as he pleased, without anybody questioning him. We found your warrant card cut up in his flat and he'd stuck your photo on a conference pass he'd stolen and Bob's your uncle.'

'Ahh, I see.' She looked up at Henry. Once again, he was in a hallway, face to face with a woman. She reached up, kissed him, then they embraced and said goodbye.

Henry drove away, glancing quickly over his shoulder to see Roscoe and her husband watching from the front door.

Back in the conservatory, Roscoe settled down on the pine settee and picked up the newspaper. The headlines told her of the shock resignation of the home secretary for 'personal reasons and political differences' and the intimation that the police were investigating his right-wing connections. It looked like a story with much more to come. There was also the parallel story of the fast-track appointment of Basil Kramer into the vacant position. There was a photograph of Kramer shaking hands with the PM and a few quotes from Kramer about what he would be doing in the future, in particular with regard to law and order, pledging more money to forces and promises to put more cops on the streets, where they should be.

Before Henry reached the motorway, he pulled into the side of the road and picked up his mobile phone, thinking, 'Sod the paper work.' He knocked a number into it. It was answered quickly.

'Kate? It's me, Henry...'

Boston, six months later

Another rooftop, this time in Boston, looking down towards a gay bar, his next target. The bomber sat on his favourite fishing stool,

510

remote control in hand, waiting for the most appropriate moment to blow the shit out of the bastards.

He felt good. He had done his bit for society by providing tools of terror for right-wing groups across Europe, and now he was back on home ground, about to take up the mantle again in his home country. Maybe next year he would do another tour of Europe.

He checked his watch. Through his binoculars he watched the sickening activity spilling out of the bar onto the sidewalk. The perverts in their tight white vests, leather trousers, their bulging muscles and ridiculous moustaches. Did they not know how obscene they were to decent, right-minded folks? Disgusting.

He picked up the remote control. Time to kill.

Then he felt something cold, hard and round being pushed into his neck. The muzzle of a pistol. The bomber swallowed, his thumb hovered over the red button. A voice whispered in his ear.

'My name is Karl Donaldson and I am an FBI agent, just like yourself. You have a choice. Place the remote down slowly and live; press the button and you die – make me even think you're gonna press the button and you die. Which d'you fancy?'

Over the past six painstaking months, while heading the investigation to bring him to justice, Karl Donaldson had got to know this man intimately. He knew what drove him, what motivated him, what his beliefs were and what he would die for. The only thing he had not known about him was his identity, but now he even knew that. He also knew that the bomber would feel he had no choice. He would believe he had to carry on destroying people to the end.

The thumb twitched.

Karl Donaldson did not have a choice either.